THE

CONTROL

PROBLEM

THE CONTROL PROBLEM

PROBLEM

NORAH WOODSEY

Published and Manufactured in the United States.
Edited by Kara Aisenbrey
Cover art by Luisa Dias
Interior design by Zoe Norvell

ISBN 978-0-9973339-7-8 (paperback)
ISBN 978-0-9973339-8-5 (hardcover)
ISBN 978-0-9973339-6-1 (eBook)

norahwoodsey.com

For those who need, and give of themselves,
only to lose what they had hoped to save.

TABLE OF CONTENTS

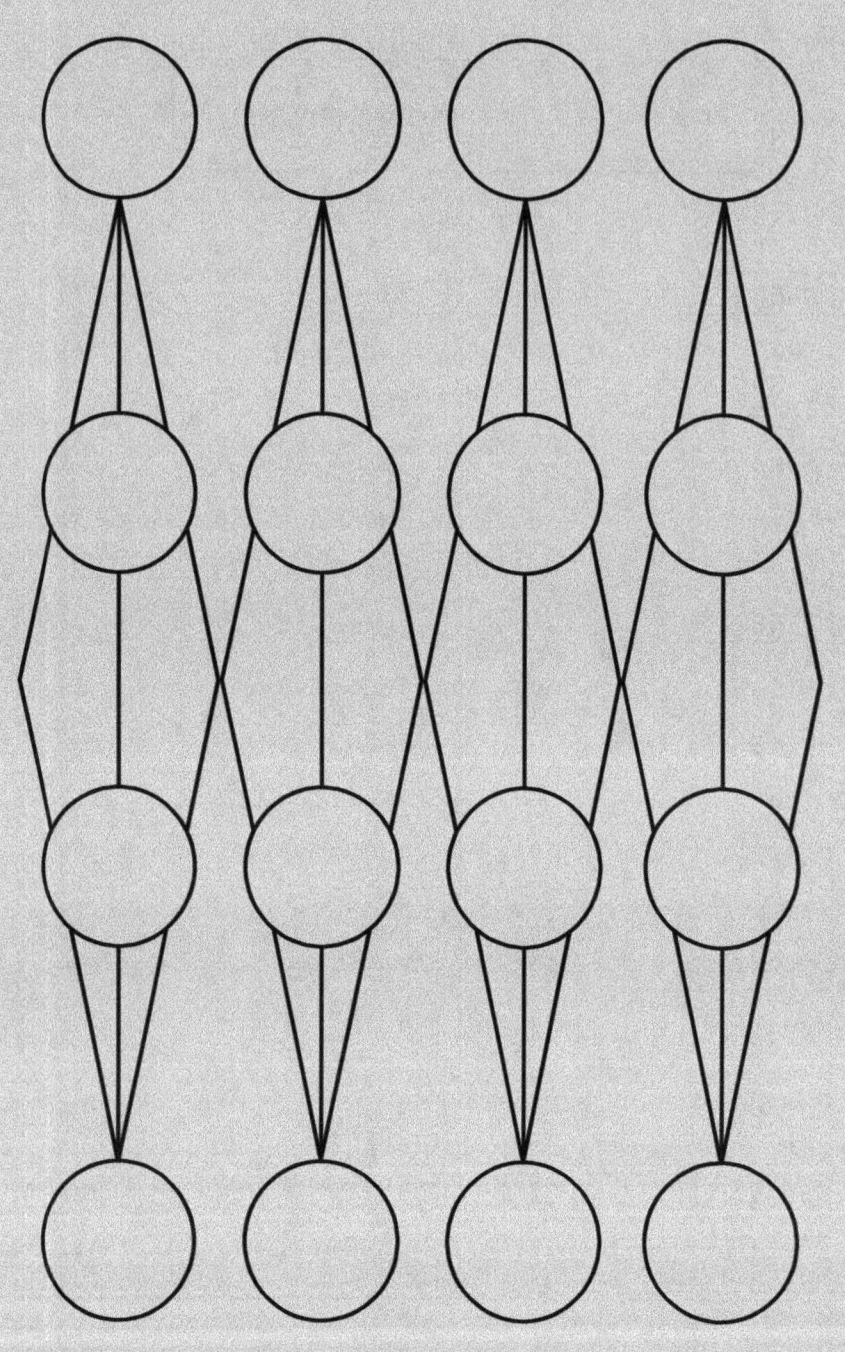

CHAPTER 1

I wish people would listen to me.

That's not great. How should you start a diary?

I'll recap lunch, I guess. Today is Tuesday, and on Tuesdays I get my favorite sandwich from the little old ugly deli. This particular deli is almost too far for the trip to fit into my lunch hour, but if I leave my workstation right at noon, I can get into line before it reaches the parking meters. I put in my headphones and listen to an audiobook as I eat my lunch at a specific bench, next to a large concrete fountain. It is shaped like a giant head. Water coming out of the skull. I know, it's creepy! But it is also nicely shaded at this time of day.

After I finish eating, I can take the subway back to work and buy a candy bar. The colder vending machine is in the scanning department's break room, on the ground floor—ours is warmer and melts the chocolate. Then I can use the less-smelly restroom by the tall cubicles before logging back in at one o'clock. It's a tight timeline, but I've been doing this for seven months and I've never been late.

Today's schedule was ruined from the start.

First, Anthony from Document Storage intercepted me. It was

all my fault, I suppose. I walked too close to his desk. I should've taken the path by car-calendar guy's desk, past the printers, and then used the stairs. I won't make that mistake again.

"Vera! Hey, Vera! I'm so glad I caught you."

I smiled and said I was in a hurry, engaging in evasive maneuvers: smile, nod, and shift closer to the door. I worried my smile would waver and it would inspire a comment, some remark he had no business making about my happiness or tiredness or whatever he felt entitled to observing. Thinking back, perhaps an eye roll or a crinkle of my nose would've dissuaded him. Probably not. Eventually, the approach of another colleague distracted him and I made my escape.

I had to run to catch the train. Luckily, the sidewalk isn't too busy by my office, even at lunchtime. The buzz of delivery drones lifting off from the platform mounted on a nearby building signaled my halfway point to the subway entrance. I trotted down the steps, grateful it hadn't rained today, as I strained to hear the whirr of the train arriving or departing. My phone buzzed payment as I passed the gates to the empty platform.

A soft light emerged from the tunnel but did not approach. The train was stuck in the tunnel, because of course it was.

I paced, as if my movement could influence a 750,000-pound train. If it moved to the platform soon, and each stop between here and the sandwich place went smoothly, I could make it to the counter, collect my order, and reach my bench before anyone else. There was still hope.

Across the platform, a track-clearing bot mirrored my movements. An arm extended and lifted items from the track, then placed them into a large open gutter mounted to the wall. Rats raced along the gutter, searching for anything good. The bot ignored them.

The train remained, and I could see the conductor waving his hands and speaking into a cell phone, all the while glaring at the bot. The gate agent passed through the gate, her thumb through her belt loop and her eyes on the bot, continuing a conversation in her walkie talkie.

"Tell central they set the sensitivity up too damn high. This isn't the Taj Mahal. Tell it to leave the small stuff so we can get these trains moving, alright?"

After a moment, the bot hesitated, then reluctantly dropped the receipt it had collected. As the bot rolled toward a crevice, it scanned the ground, as if assessing its failure. Then, it tucked inside the crevice and shut down. A rat immediately pulled an ice cream sandwich wrapper from the gutter, then left it on the track. If you didn't know what to look for, you'd never have known a bot had been there at all.

"Thank you, Freddy!" said the gate agent to the walkie talkie, before she waved at the conductor and returned through the gate to her booth.

A whining cry of electrical motors and wheels on metal, and the train reached the platform. The doors slid open, and I was on my way to lunch.

When I reached my exit, I tried to walk as quickly as I could while still retaining some dignity. The sidewalk here was busier, and besides, I didn't want to be super sweaty when I got back to work. The sandwich shop had a small line, out the door but not down the sidewalk—not too bad. The owner was working the counter. A rocky start to the lunch hour, but everything was going smoothly now. Carl, who is gruff and middle-aged, doesn't look like a chef, but each sandwich he makes is perfect. The bread is toasted evenly, with a sweet, buttery crunch on the exterior. The condiments cover the cheese and meat yet do not drip out the sides. He takes great care in what he does, and I need that kind of care, even if I have to pay for it.

My cousin Jennifer's friend Sarah told me about this place. The two of them used to come here all the time. That was when Sarah still worked for Perilaus Bionics, before her third child, Fiona, was born. Jennifer is still there, moving up the ranks, as Sarah described it. She told me to always ask for Carl, which I have never, ever done. What if he is on break? Or at home sick? It felt rude to tell them how to structure their workflow. I didn't say any of this to Sarah. She wouldn't come across that way. She's charming and warm and funny. She'd get Carl to make her sandwich because he'd want to chat with her. I'm not charming. I'm not even not charming. I unsettle people. They seem to misunderstand me, though I don't know if that is my fault or theirs.

Anyway, Carl was there when I arrived, and my sandwich would be delicious. I waited in line in a warm glow of success and opened my new book.

I shuffled forward as orders were filled. I would not be reading a silly book today. Instead, I let myself fall into the dreary world of post–World War II America. Literature while standing in line for lunch, the height of adulthood. I wore clean, crisp business-casual clothes, just like the person in front of me and the person behind me. I took in artful descriptions of modern malaise, brooding characters, banal yet chaotic conflicts of domesticity. I kept my peripheral vision on the heels of the woman ahead of me, to stay engaged with the line, while I imagined being elsewhere. Very adult.

My turn arrived and I looked up. Carl was gone. His nephew, a pale, sweaty teenager whose name I refused to learn dragged the notepad over and waited for my order.

No, no, no!

This was all wrong. What should I do? There was nothing to do. The words of Sarah, "ask for Carl," mocked me. I would never do that. I put on my smile, made eye contact with the boy, and treated each word as an individual: a number four, no onions, no jalapeños, and easy mayo. Despite my deliberate enunciation, I could see on the pad he had written a plus sign, not "no" beside jalapeños. *Stop him!* I thought. I assembled my social smile and lifted my hand, calling attention, so polite, not too eager, to make the necessary correction, but no. He walked away. Should I shout? I should. I should shout. I should smash my fist into the glass. I should scream at him.

No, I would not. I swallowed my anger until only shame remained. My face burned. This wasn't supposed to happen. I had done everything right. Where was Carl?

I lingered at the counter too long. The eyes of hungry people pressed on my back, each one mad at themselves for being late and ready to redirect that anger at anyone else. The line stretched past the meters now, and beyond—someone was likely outside the florist, listening to the snip, snip, snip of roses cut to size.

There was nothing to do. I stepped aside, to make it clear I was out of line but still belonged, ready for my turn to pay. I didn't want to pay. I didn't want this sandwich. I didn't want to be here. I wanted to leave hungry, and punish Carl for employing his stupid nephew. I stood there and waited, like a fool, staring at my phone like it had answers for me.

Carl returned to the counter and took down the next person's sandwich order on his pocket notepad, each request written in his sharpened pencil with careful attention. Meanwhile, the nephew blankly assembled my monstrosity. Carl looked aside, he looked down at his nephew's work, the work he should have been doing himself, and he looked at it with disapproval. Rage again. White-hot. That's right, Carl! That's my stupid sandwich. But he said nothing. He probably loved him, knew him, and felt a disappointment much greater than what I felt over a single lunchtime. That thought soothed and shamed me.

I tried to return to my book. Reading literature on my break from work, angry about a sandwich. Like a child playing pretend. I closed the file. A sharp, tinkling laugh broke through from the sunny street. The construction worker beside me stretched and popped his back. A person cleaned their glasses with a pur-pose-made swatch of fabric. They would've spoken up. It would've been fine. What is wrong with me?

The nephew wrapped my sandwich in butcher paper and thumped it on the counter. "Number 4, extra jalas." I walked over and tapped out my payment. I even left my standard tip, in case my anger had been visible. There was no need. No one saw me. No one cared. The nephew was gone, scribbling down the next order. I heard the customer loudly correct him: "A number NINE. Not five, NINE." The nephew shrugged and made the correction.

I retreated to the privacy of my favorite bench. From my purse I retrieved two napkins and a small compost bag I carried with me. I used one napkin to scrape the extra mayonnaise out. On the second napkin, I set each jalapeño piece, one by one, a soggy puzzle of regret. I couldn't remove them all, of course. I put the sticky, greasy napkins into the small compost bag and set it on the ground. I put the sandwich back together and inspected it. There was too much meat, and still too much mayonnaise. The lettuce was insuffi-cient. The bread, at least, was the same as usual. I'd enjoy the bread. I ate my lunch and watched the busy sidewalk from a safe distance.

The line was long now. A woman in a bright green trench coat adjusted her high-heeled shoe. Her coat looked special and tailored. I wondered if it was her favorite. She fumbled for a tissue, not immediately aware of her large front pockets. No, this garment was unfamiliar to her. She was a coat woman. How many coats does this coat woman own, I wondered. Does she have her own closet of coats? Not a coat closet; that implies a space for the service of guests, right? No, I mean a closet of coats, maybe tucked away in a room the architect had intended for children, which she didn't have, for reasons she kept to herself. Where were the coats for winter now, neatly packed away with dried lavender and cedar chips, while the spring and summer ones swung clean and ready, waiting for duty on wooden hangers? I sipped some water. Were all her coats bright? I looked at her shoes. They were colorful and also expensive. Yes, I decided. I would like to see this woman's many coats, the house she kept them in, and the lifestyle that supported such a ridiculous habit.

Behind her, two young men chatted with insecure, masculine confidence. They bored me, even while I despised them. Their hand motions, like their laughs, were not intended to express any particular feeling. They existed for attention, nothing more. One of them told a story in a lying tone while the other watched a sweeper bot.

"Pardon me," the sleek, oblong sweeper bot's female voice requested to a woman in a tweed skirt. The woman lifted her foot and the robot extended its arm. From the end of the arm three delicate fingers appeared. It quickly lifted an ice cream wrapper from the concrete and the arm retreated. A small door opened on its torso. The trash disappeared into the cavity and the door snapped shut. "Thank you," the robot replied. The tweed-skirt woman ignored it.

The bot moved with grace and efficiency, pivoting on hidden wheels to inspect a bit of gum on the sidewalk. After a moment, the arm extended again, only a small distance this time. Instead of fingers, a nozzle emerged. It ejected a small, conical spray of a solution onto the ground. Perhaps liquid nitrogen? The mist coated the pale red smear, then the sprayer retracted. A new arm, with only a grinding tool at the end, appeared. It made very little sound, though what sound it did make displeased an old man in line. He took a moment to scowl at the bot, then returned to rocking on his leather shoes, antagonizing the line to proceed.

In seconds, the sweeper bot had the gum reduced to a fine powder. Another tool, a small vacuum, appeared from a vaguely inappropriate place at the bottom of the robot. Who designed these things? Once the surface was vacuumed, the original arm extended again; it must be the primary arm. It appeared to assess the quality of its work. I wondered how many hours of research had gone into the complexity of this sweeper bot. Teams had designed each component, and a project manager had ensured that each tool worked with the other. And for what goal? To remove sidewalk gum? Yet I sat there transfixed by it. It didn't look like a device executing a fixed task. It worked, it had a job, and it assessed the results. The sidewalk was noticeably cleaner now. It even rolled back a bit, as if to spot anything overlooked, arm extended and ready.

One of the young men suddenly stepped forward. "Check this out!"

He kicked the sweeper from behind. With a giggle, he returned to the line, like a naughty child ducking out of his teacher's sight. The little robot cried out and quivered. It hadn't finished retracting its main arm, which was now bent and bleeding warm hydraulic liquid. The puddle grew on the cleaned pavement, pooling along the side of the robot's body. An icon flashed on the top of its white shell.

"Help. Help," the robot's female voice called.

The woman in the tweed skirt glared at the men, but she did nothing. Pedestrians heading to another destination stepped around the puddle, not breaking their conversation. The other people in line at the sandwich shop watched the bot quiver, some muttering, but all remained where they stood.

The old man complained, spittle spraying from his mouth. "Won't someone shut that piece of garbage up?"

The robot struggled to rise.

"Please," the voice pleaded. "Please, help me."

CHAPTER 2

It's been a couple of days since I opened this. Am I supposed to write every single day? Even days where nothing happens? I have a lot of days where nothing happens. Maybe if I had more than a few months of distinct memories to reflect on, I could document those here. I can't exactly fill up pages with 'my mom's silhouette at the kitchen sink'. Maybe it is better, in a way, to have no memories. Maybe when the past gives you something to reflect on, it also pulls you backward.

Anyway, I'm on morning break now. My favorite spot is a balcony overlooking the office complex's full parking lot. If I sit just right on a large planter, I'm in partial shade and my back is not visible from the interior of the break room. I prefer to be outside for the beautiful weather and for the silence.

The TV is too loud, the content obnoxious. Someone from quality control turned the volume up on a boisterous news program, watched for a few minutes, then left the room. The talking head seems to be a hype man for some new politician, a conservative who wants to root out corruption. No one has bothered to turn it off or adjust the volume. I wonder if they leave it on to gain information, or to position themselves as people who seek out new information. Maybe they're just lazy. I'm not sure.

The sun outside the office is strong today, an unpleasant contrast to the early April air. I could move to a fully shaded spot, over at the opposite end of the patio, and be cold. That's not ideal. The irrigation system also overwatered those planters. I don't want to accidentally sit in mud. I'll just stay in the sun and squint while I write. My dress slacks and cardigan are fall weight, nearly too warm for today, but once the wind picks back up, they feel insufficient. My fingers are stiff as I write, though I know if I get up and go inside to get my jacket, I'll give this up and go back to work.

Today, I have a doctor's appointment. I'll head out early to see Dr. Parsons. He told me to use this journal for my thoughts and feelings. I wanted to get in a full entry before my appointment, before he could scold me. It seems like thoughts and feelings come up more often when I'm occupied than when I sit still. Maybe I can take audio recordings while I run, or bathe, then use a speech-to-text tool and upload the entry. I don't think people typically do that.

A new smell just hit me. A woman whom I only recognize from her faded blue hair dye has stepped out on the balcony near where I am sitting. She was in my training group seven months ago. I've never spoken to her; I've not had any interest. Her vape pen clicks and puffs while she holds her phone. Her nails click and clack as she scans through her social media account. She isn't showing interest in the content. She is scrolling far too fast for consumption. Instead, she tags the items with hearts as she goes. No reaction passes on her face.

Heart. Heart. Heart.

I judge her and yet I do the same thing; I like posts I don't like from people I don't know. I send "LOL" to Sarah and Jennifer when I haven't laughed all day. Maybe it is human nature. I remember the birthday cake the team bought one of my coworkers. Everyone sang happy birthday to him, some sincerely, most like this woman. Like myself. Participant observers. Putting forth the barest effort to maintain the appearance of kindness while watching. Adhering to a social requirement only to blend into the scene.

I wonder if that woman has a child, or children. I know you cannot and should not make that assumption based on appearance alone. Her body shows the soft sag in the midsection that indicates diastasis recti, a muscle separation that is common postpartum but also happens without pregnancy. Half of pregnant people experience it. I'm preparing myself to deal with it someday. I once asked Sarah if it hurt, during her first pregnancy, when the fibers of her muscles pulled and stretched away from one another, tearing themselves apart to make room for the new person growing within her. She thought for a moment and said her skin itched like hell. I would never ask Jennifer that question.

The news program inside switched. They were discussing Perilaus, and my ears perked up. That's where Jennifer works, and where Sarah used to work. I've always been curious about it. Unfortunately, the segment was not really about the company; they were discussing a class action lawsuit against a component manufacturer of old prosthetics. Apparently, the early prosthetics that could do proprioception relied on large needles. They often break off, and are stuck inside people's bodies, causing them medical issues. No one uses large needles anymore. Perilaus was one of the companies that pioneered the use of the microfilaments that Sarah calls MSIs. These patients now want the out-of-date needles removed and the newer technology implanted for free. Seems fair.

Now it's time for me to go back to work. I guess there was no point writing that down.

It's evening. I'm home from Dr. Parsons. I wasn't even going to write another entry in this thing, but I live alone, and I have nothing else to do. I'll describe the appointment in detail, I guess. I don't know. They're all the same.

I arrived at Dr. Michael Parsons's office on 49th Avenue and Willow Boulevard, in the medical complex near the car dealerships, five minutes early. The office is small, beige. There are eight chairs, a single table with a stack of old magazines, and an undersized houseplant. In one corner is a water cooler, in another is a large, dusty plant. The overhead lights buzz, the carpet is stiff, brown, industrial. The room has the smell of disuse, yet I'm here every week.

Elizabeth, Dr. Parsons's medical technician, sat at the desk as she always does. She has bleached-blonde hair and wears too much eyeliner. She does the same things during each of my visits. Before I sit down, she pulls out my file and types something into the computer. Then she takes me back to the only exam room I ever use. I wonder about the other rooms—always silent and shut tight. What if the room she takes me into is an unlucky room? Maybe I could ask to use one of the others instead?

Anyway, once in the room, she has me step on the scale. She grunts and scribbles. Then, I take my seat on the paper-covered exam bed. She secures a blood pressure cuff and records the measurement, but doesn't seem interested in the results. I wonder if she finds any part of her job interesting.

What is that like? Is she bored? Is she not paying attention? Does she find meaning in her work? I can almost hear Jennifer's voice, chiding me: she's just dumb, Vera.

She gives me a paper gown and paper blanket, saying, "Open side to the back, Dr. Parsons will be in shortly."

The only difference in her routine this visit was when she bumped into the ultrasound machine. "Sorry," she muttered and patted the screen.

I undressed and stared at all the sponsored pregnancy paraphernalia throughout the exam room. A headless, limbless female-sex torso, organs exposed, was mounted to the wall like a prize kill. Glossy posters of baby heads descending into birth canals, dusty faces frozen in anguish. A different style of poster showed insemination, cellular division, and ovarian anatomy. There is no logic to any of this. Why do doctors assume such profound ignorance? Haven't all patients in this room spent sleepless nights scanning articles on medical websites, desperate to find the solution to their own infertility? Do they need the basic process of insemination and fertilization explained to them by a textbook company's glossy diagram?

After less than five minutes, Dr. Parsons entered. He wore his white medical jacket with the red stain on the pocket. That same stain has been on that pocket for three weeks now. Maybe I should find a doctor who notices these things.

"Alright, little lady. How are you feeling today?"

"Good. And yourself?"

"Fine, fine." Dr. Parsons habitually repeats a word in his sentences. Some kind of tic, I suppose.

"How have you been since the last treatment? Any nausea?" he asked. He only looked up from the medical chart to bring his wheeled instrument tray to the end of the exam bed.

"No, sir."

"Alright, lie back."

I put my bare feet into the cold metal stirrups and pushed my body low on the table.

"I need you to scoot, scoot to the end of the table for me, please."

I shift my body perilously close to the edge.

He chuckled, amused by my failure. "Further, now. All the way."

I didn't find it funny, but I smiled as if I did. I moved further. The cold air reached places it had no business reaching. Dr. Parsons's light glowed through the thin sheet tented across my knees.

Are those sheets really made of paper? They feel like paper, yet they have a fabric quality to them. Are they recyclable? Compostable? Are there piles and piles of them dotting the Earth, never to decompose, lasting longer than the people whose bodies they concealed? You'd think I'd know by now. This was my fifth exam since I started fertility treatments twelve weeks ago.

"A little pressure."

I stared at the ceiling to disassociate from the painful, humiliating things going on at the edge. A sharp cramp. I let out a breath.

After a moment, the pressure released. He rolled his chair backward, signaling the end of the exam. I covered, lowered, and brought my legs in, a rapid retreat toward decency. His gloves snapped as he pulled them off.

"We'll try this just one more time, before we move on to IVF. Your pulse is good, the membranes are nice and pink. Your follicle counts this cycle were great. It just didn't take. Don't you worry now; we'll keep trying." He patted my knee, as if to offer comfort. He rose to leave but paused.

"Before you go. Did you start that journal?"

"Yes, doctor."

"Good. Good."

"Do you want to see it?" I asked, starting to move toward my purse. He waved me off. All this anxiety over getting entries done and he didn't even read it. Of course.

"No, no that's not necessary. We do have some paperwork for you to fill out. New stuff, I think you'd be a good candidate for it. The industry is looking at the psychological impact these treatments have on young women such as yourself."

I didn't care about his damn paperwork.

"Stop by the window and ask Elizabeth to schedule your follow-up appointment."

He left. I felt dazed in the cold white void of the exam room, the miasma of plastic and stale, recirculated air floating around me, invisible, as I am invisible.

I failed again.

I picked up my purse and stared, thoughtless, at the assemblage of things. An impossible puzzle. Everything and nothing existed inside this bag.

After a moment, I collected myself. I found a neatly wrapped medium-capacity pad. I removed the wrapper, peeled off the backing, and stuck it to the inside of my underwear. I did it wrong. The pad was askew. The soft pad material bunched up on one side while the adhesive stuck to my inner thigh on the other. My hand shook as I put the cover and adhesive sheet into the trash. I dressed myself, somehow, and walked out.

I didn't speak to Elizabeth. I didn't set a follow-up appointment. The whole point of all this was to never need another appointment. I never wanted to "scoot" for that goddamn man on that goddamn crinkly bed in that goddamn paper gown ever again.

I made it to the sidewalk and growled. I growled like an animal. The anger again. There's a remoteness about the feeling, as if I carry around someone else's full cup of rage, balancing it throughout the day, always on the verge of upsetting the contents. I have to remind myself: this is my cup. This is my rage. I'm allowed to be angry, but I must control it.

I breathe again.

I didn't honestly think I had been pregnant. I had no symptoms. I had smeared myself with stretch-mark oil and taken my vitamins, but I hadn't used one of my at-home tests. I knew there was nothing to see.

I had hoped, though.

I hoped I was one of those legendary women who feel nothing, who carry creation in them without any cost. They grow and form without bending and breaking, until one day, they sit on a toilet or lie on their floor or arrive at the hospital in surprise agony to deliver an unexpected treasure. A treasure I would bend and break myself a thousand times to have.

This cycle had used a new batch of sperm. I thought maybe the first donor had been the problem—a poor match between my body and stranger 1127. There had been no reason to hope, it was illogical, yet I always hope. "Is this nausea?" at lunch the day before, "Am I more bloated than usual?" in the shower. I slathered on my stretch-mark oil and believed in a future I wanted.

Hope is dangerous. It ruins the security I feel in failure. Any event that elevates my hope ruins good things for days afterward.

And now here I am, writing to you, dear diary, at home in my little apartment, alone. The remote for the TV is here, untouched but waiting for me. I have a bottle of white wine and a clean glass, and another bottle of wine chilling in the fridge. After each failed cycle, Sarah would make herself horrifically drunk as a morbid celebration. But I'm not thirsty. I'm nothing.

Someone is calling me.

CHAPTER 3

It's a new day. My breath smells horrible. I'm awake and hungover.

I did my morning routine without joy: shower, wash body, wash hair, condition hair, wash face, rinse conditioner, shut off shower, dry body, put hair in towel, apply ointments to face, stretch-mark oil to body, blow-dry hair. I put on exercise clothes, though I have no intention of exercising. No, first I need coffee. I have a little pour-over kit, with fancy beans and a tiny grinder, in my cabinet that I should really throw away. Every cup I make for myself tastes like crap.

Instead, I've put in my headphones and left for my favorite coffee shop – that is, the only shop within a five minute walk that isn't part of an enormous chain. It used to be the only location, until they expanded to another neighborhood. That new spot is sleek and clean and polished. This one, a hastily converted bakery with mismatched furniture, is superior.

As I waited to cross one of only two intersections on my route, I heard a stiff female voice say, "Change Password."

I paused my music.

"Change Password," the command repeated. I looked behind me at the distant commuters walking in silence, at the light pole above me, to the closed shop beside me. Who needed a password change?

I pressed the WALK button. Nothing happened.

"Change Password."

I leaned close to the button. "Change Password," she said, urgent and stern. The pedestrian light needed a password reset. Were they linked with the traffic lights? They must be, I suppose. I can only assume that someone had left these pedestrian switches on the default login information, which had just expired. How many crucial, vulnerable devices do we give control over our lives? I should probably report this, but no one would listen to me. I wonder if I could fix it, somehow.

I put my headphones back in and jaywalked. Nope, this was not my problem.

When I arrived, the owner was meeting with two other men. From their clothing and shoes, I guessed they were an interior decorator and an architect. I took my place in line and watched their little meeting with interest. Each person made large, sweeping motions with their hands, as if the scale of their descriptions was insufficient to support the budget they were likely proposing. If I were someone else, I'd have pulled the owner aside and explained things to him carefully. No one wants change. There's no need to spend money now. This space, inefficient and dingy, is full and warm. Let it be.

I did not say any of that. I paused my music and put in my usual coffee order to Brendan at the counter. We smiled at each other, familiar faces a comfort, while the decorator enthused about bleachable chair fabric. I'm not sure I'll come back here if they make changes. Maybe his renovation loan will get denied, anyway.

Sorry, diary. I've gotten sidetracked. I need to recount what happened last night when Sarah interrupted my journaling.

So, Sarah called to see how my appointment went. I was surprised she remembered it. I'm more of a third wheel to her and Jennifer, with Jennifer being my primary point of contact. In short, I wouldn't say we are close. Anyway, Sarah asked, and even though I wanted to be cool and evasive or even just guard my voice, as Jennifer would've done, I started to cry. Without hesitation, Sarah left the kids with her cousin and showed up at my place with two more bottles of wine and four flavors of ice cream. She also brought some pot, which she shared with me for the first time.

"If I hadn't called, would you have told me what had happened?" she asked after we opened our second bottle.

"Eventually," I lied. I stretched my limbs on the couch to increase my awareness of them. Legs are so weird, I thought to myself, scrutinizing my knees and ankles and tendons and muscles. Fleshy levers, pivots and pendulums of various sizes, all just acting like they belong together. I let the sizzling intoxication find more space under my skin.

"Do you keep your socks on during the exams?" Sarah asked.

"My what?"

She belched, the sweet-sour fragrance of wine wafting through the air. "Socks."

"Foot socks?"

Sarah snorted. "Yes, foot socks—do you?"

"No, I mean. When they say 'undress', don't they mean take everything off?"

"Why socks? They don't do feet."

I conceded with a shrug.

"It's OK. I thought socks off too, before I got pregnant with Sam. All the exams, the ultrasounds, the tests, the IUIs and then each embryo transfer—socks off. At some point I thought, shit, my feet are cold. This sucks. Now I keep them on. Plus, feet are gross."

"They ARE gross," I laughed. She poured herself more wine, then added too much to my glass.

"So is IVF next?" Sarah asked, her eyes shut.

"No, I think we're going to try IUI again," I said.

"You doing Clomid, FSH, or HcG?"

"I took HcG pills, but not Clomid. I asked him and he said he'd think about it, like I was asking for an extra cookie. He never listens to me."

"Pills? Weird. Even Jennifer had to give herself injections. Bleeding all over the place in the Perilaus bathroom in between meetings. She didn't use an injection implant, she did it old-school. She's hardcore."

A worry prickled up my spine. All these visits, all that vulnerability, and the guy may be incompetent?

Sarah continued, "And they aren't changing anything this time around?"

"No."

"You gotta stand up for yourself, honey."

"I get uncomfortable saying anything!" Waving my arms too high. "And it's all so bad already."

"Medical torture. Steve had a thing he had to go get looked at, and the doctor checked his prostate while he was at it. Steve walked through the door like it was the end of the world. I said, Steve, honey. Speculum. Transvaginal ultrasound. Cervical swab. Quit complaining."

We laughed. The laugh was a bawdy laugh. Not happy, I guess, but pulled from the same aisle as happiness. What else was happiness? The way my baby's toes would curl when I tickled her feet. My laugh turned into tears.

"I'm sorry," I said, trying to stop.

"No, no, no." Sarah sloshed her glass onto the table, came close, and pulled me into a strong, protective hug. "This is such bullshit. You spend your teens and twenties frantic to not get pregnant, then it's this."

I hugged her back. She understood. She had made it. Now she had three beautiful kids. To give such a comforting hug is a goal.

Maybe one day, I can make it, too. I can be a guide for another mom going through this.

CHAPTER 4

FACIAL RECOGNITION FIRM BEHIND
JAYWALKING TICKETS FINED FOR
RACIAL DISCRIMINATION

Since this is my diary now, not Dr. Parsons's, I added a new feature: an interesting headline will appear at the beginning of each post. Or some posts. Or the whole news story. I don't want to overcommit myself here. I think the headlines will provide more context in the future. This stood out to me after the weird password alert near home. I love how the government feels competent enough to issue tickets for jaywalking but can't get a crosswalk button to function properly.

Enough of that. I'm at work, on break.

Work. I haven't described that yet.

I work at a document processing center that holds an exclusive contract with the Department of Veterans Affairs. Specifically, my group prepares archived paper medical files and digitizes them, and will keep doing so until the backlog of files is cleared. In my group there are two teams: document scanning and document processing.

I'm on the document processing team. The document scanning team works on the ground floor, the one with the coldest vending machine. That's only fair, really—it is so hot down there, some of my colleagues call it hell. "I'm going down to hell," they joke. I laugh at the remark, though it isn't funny.

Each document scanner has an industrial-grade machine at their station running for the duration of their shift. The work quality varies from person to person, and machine to machine. Overall, the group is quite good. They tried to outsource the scanning overseas, well before I joined. I occasionally run across those files when I'm uploading new documents. They should really redo all those scans—the quality is abysmal. And those were the acceptable files! They rescanned a bunch of stuff. Now the only low-quality scans we get come from hospitals and doctor's offices.

I'm glad I picked processing. During training, each processor shadows a scanner for two days to see if they'd prefer that work. I shadowed a kind woman named Rachel. She was thorough, exact. I watched as she neatly plucked staples from each packet with one of three unique staple removers, each an important variation from the other. There was "Little Green," a standard-sized remover with soft silicon padding, "Feisty Sally," a red unit with extra-sharp prongs, and "The Beast," a large black spring-loaded contraption. Her metallic fingernails flashed as she selected the best remover for each packet.

"These suckers," Rachel said, waving a packet with a particularly thick-gauge staple. "Before I got The Beast, I'd just cut that whole corner out. You can work them out from the back side here, that's what some folks do. I don't waste the time. They're little bastards, these staples. I use The Beast for them now, and for when Sandra gets smart." A woman, unseen in the maze of cubicles, laughed aloud. I can only assume it was Sandra. Rachel took out the offending staple, then she thunked the stack of pages on the scanner tray and pressed start with her finger, metallic polish glittering in the fluorescent light. "I guess I can't really complain! If it wasn't for staples, we'd all be replaced by robots. They brought in this fancy machine a couple years back, but it couldn't keep up. They haven't figured out the staples. Better luck next time, robots!"

The scanner itself was a large light-gray machine with a tray that could accommodate 500 sheets of paper. Rachel had adorned the plastic facade with two large googly eyes and a name badge like the ones we all wear: "Brave Little Toaster." I assume that referred to the heat. Machines are arranged in pairs, back-to-back in a double cubicle. The pair of machines increased the ambient temperature in the work area by eleven degrees after the first hour of operation. Rachel had two small oscillating fans, one above the desk and one below, but they just moved the hot air around.

I wonder: is she satisfied with this type of work at her stage in life? I'm not sure, but I think she is happy—I think Rachel was once a busy, important person with suits and smart pumps and a designer briefcase. Now she chats with her unseen cubicle mates and the occasional trainees, removes staples with her hardy little trio, and reads documents she scans for the interesting stories. She told me that some days she's not interested in any of that and simply listens to murder mysteries through headphones. It may be a welcome break from the stress of her past profession. It may get her out of her house, away from an unpleasant family situation. For me, scanning work was fine but the heat was unbearable. I regularly offered to get her water or a snack from the break room just for the excuse to step away.

For many who shadowed the scanning team, processing on

the fourth floor is a relief. The silence, the coolness, the lack of paper cuts. Several of my coworkers find it boring. They talk to one another, socializing instead of working. They are also slow and prone to errors. They seem to have fun, though, and it isn't like there is much of a future here. Someday, we'll get through the VA's physical files. The company might move on to another contract, or they might shut down entirely. They used to have multiple centers, all around the country. Those have all closed. There just aren't many physical documents that require humans to scan them.

For now, I'm happy where I am. I enjoy the work. I find it easy to maintain focus while reading through the content, imagining the patients are characters in different memoirs, each new packet a new story that ends in a few minutes. Much about a person's life is recorded in military medical documents. Service history and injury reports, of course, but also beneficiaries, health care directives and visitor logs. I look at location signifiers on government-issued IDs and contrast them with current home addresses, and those with entries on any credit reports posted under billing information. I read notes from call center representatives and doctors' communications, to learn if the central character in these mini tales is a good person. If they deserve my support. All of life fits in between scattered pieces of information.

I keep a spreadsheet with the most interesting medical ID numbers and check on them from time to time. I learn if their situation has improved or deteriorated, if they have married or divorced or added children to their families. Often, though, I learn nothing new. I haven't been here long enough, I suppose. Nothing changes for most people in six months. Still, I suspect many of them will remain frozen in place, for good or bad, without change or hope of change.

On to current events.

Just after 9 a.m. today, Scott put my name up on the production board for the first time. This was a surprise. My group finished training six months ago, when we were set loose on live packets—that is, actual medical documents to process after they've been scanned. We review the individual pages for quality, upload them to our staging queue, then assign them to the correct medical ID number and break the packet into the correct subfiles. We receive credit for each individual document type we upload from the batches. Like everyone else in the office, I listen to music while I work. If I didn't, I would've heard my supervisor stapling the names to the bright orange-and-yellow board.

"Vera Elpis, 212% of goal"

I saw it on my way to the bathroom. Our role is not paid on commission. My team is seventy-four people. To inspire productivity, gift cards and prizes are offered to the highest-volume producer each month. Scott stands in the middle of a cubical cluster, his unstarched button-down divided by a too-long tie, as he reads out names and hands over the plastic cards. I didn't want the attention.

I don't find competition motivating. And I don't need the gift cards. I value the discrete closeness of my individual tasks. Each document perfectly categorized, any poor-quality scans corrected in our image editor, so each file is uploaded with crisp edges and clear text. Concise descriptions in the filename. Order from chaos. Efficiency and completeness. No interactions with customers or clients, no one watching me, counting on me, or judging me. I do not want to stand out.

Perhaps if I relied on my wages, I would feel differently. My inheritance and my parents' insurance policy has sustained me for years. I'm not sure how many years it has been, though, now that I think about it. My memory isn't very good, probably from the accident. Anyway, as far as I know, I've never worried about money. Jennifer, my cousin, helped me get on my feet and got me this job. I don't think she intended for me to stay here this long. She called it my rich-person hobby.

Jennifer is very competitive. Maybe she'd be happy that I am doing well. I don't want to do this well, though. I'm tired of feeling weird. I don't want to be special.

Another team's workflow coordinator, Kristine, sent me an email congratulating me on the number, while suggesting I slow down to maintain accuracy. She often speaks to me as though I report to her. She is senior to me, but on Eastern processing, while I work on the Southwest team. Jennifer told me to ignore anyone who wasn't my superior or wasn't helpful. Kristine evidently had poor reading comprehension; the production board included accuracy statistics. Only processors with 90 percent or greater QA numbers were included. I'm not going to bother to correct her.

I think I'm going to leave a bit early. I'm meeting Jennifer and Sarah (who I guess is my friend now, too?) for lunch. I'm looking forward to hearing about someone else's day. I won't bring up this production board development.

Lunch was… interesting.

Sarah texted that she would be late. I had arrived early, so I waited in the foyer. Jennifer arrived exactly on time. I imagine most start-up executives dress like slobs and behave carelessly, but not Jennifer. I don't think there is an area in her life she does not bend to her will. The light wave in her thick black hair is regularly subdued to uniform, glossy precision in each strand. Her skin is so smooth, clear, and consistent, I often wonder if it is real. There is technology now to erase scars—does it also work on freckles and pores?

I always admire her outfits, and today was no exception. She wore a pair of gray wide-leg trousers with no embarrassing thigh creases. She walked with an elegant, assertive grace, and the trousers swayed along with her, revealing the blood-red heels of her shoes with each step. Her subtly patterned blouse buttoned to a state of sexy yet professional. I wonder if she has her blouses altered so she can do that. Is fabric tape involved? I'll have to live with not knowing. She'll never tell me. Her perfume and makeup, like everything else about her, were also exact—detectable without overwhelming.

The hostess, who had greeted me and eyed a dingy table near the kitchen doors, had forgotten that option. She settled us in a particularly nice booth. No one seats Jennifer near kitchen doors. We were given water and an assurance to return when Sarah arrived.

Jennifer asked the only obvious perfunctory question—how my doctor's appointment went. I told her the relevant details, trying to be concise and not sentimental. Though she always expresses sympathy, I know she thinks I'm silly. She is my older cousin, my only living family, and better than me in every way. I think she feels a need to be my parent, and for that reason can't imagine me as someone else's mother. I probably would too, if I were someone like her and had a cousin like me.

After I finished relaying my account of events, Jennifer sighed.

"I don't understand the source of this motivation."

"What do you mean?"

"There are people who already exist that need help. You can learn to care for them. Creating another person is such an extreme impulse."

I looked down at her nails, all perfect and beautiful. I looked at my own: uneven, dry, with a sharp hangnail I hadn't dealt with.

Angry tears gathered in my eyes. Don't get angry, I told myself. Don't scream.

I thought of a nature documentary I had watched a few weeks ago. Researchers had discovered a mother chimpanzee, trailing behind the rest of her group. When they took a closer look, they saw that she was dragging her dead infant's corpse. She continued doing this for days, resting to check, to see, yet continuing on, dragging the body with her. Aren't humans animals? Are we above base needs? To deny those needs is a rejection of biology. I wanted to tell her she herself has a child, but the thought of lonely little Max quenched my indignation. I took a breath.

"It is natural to want a baby," I said weakly.

Sarah set down her purse on an empty chair. "I see I've arrived just in time."

Jennifer smiled impassively, evidently as eager as I was to drop our squabble. Sarah took the reins. She vented about Sam, her eldest son, who said he was too tired to go to baseball after school. His comic book reading, a habit originally encouraged as a pathway to consistent reading, had now become a nuisance. Do unhealthy habits often begin as an encouraged activity, until they veer away into a distraction from everyday life?

I described Jennifer; I should describe Sarah. She is the same age as Jennifer, only the years of her life are accepted and unconcealed. Her soft brown hair is shoulder-length, frazzled and dry. The short tufts that spring from around her face are regrowth after her postpartum hair loss six months ago. She rarely wears makeup, though her skin is quite beautiful, at least when she can keep it clean and moisturized. Today she wore jeans and a plain gray T-shirt, all clean, with her favorite jacket over the top. The jacket had some avocado on the sleeve. I couldn't think of how to point it out to her.

Thankfully she removed the jacket and placed it on the empty space beside her. Maybe she'd see the avocado on her own.

The waitress arrived. We each placed our orders, Jennifer last, as always. Her orders are complicated. The salads arrived all at once, an assault of green bowls and dressings. Every meal at this particular restaurant comes with an unappetizing blend of greens, cherry tomatoes, carrot slivers, and cucumber slices that would be healthy if I didn't drown it in dressing to make it appealing.

"I hate this place," Jennifer sighed.

"You used to love it," Sarah said, stealing Jennifer's salad dressing.

"Yes, a lifetime ago."

I turned to Sarah with a question about her kids, but Jennifer silenced me with a smile.

"Vera. How is work?"

"Work is good. Unsurprising, consistent."

"Nothing new going on?"

Did she know about the production board? That's ridiculous… and yet. How could she know? Is she spying on me? Why would she do that?

"Nope. Nothing new. How is your work?"

Jennifer shrugged. "Nothing new."

"I'm reading a book on myths about women," Sarah announced.

"Anything interesting?"

"It's pretty dry. I did this thing in junior high, we had to either write an essay or do art based on a figure in mythology. I drew a picture of Persephone and really enjoyed it. It's probably the only good picture I've ever drawn. So I saw this book at the library and thought, well, shit, maybe my drawing was so good because I was inspired. Now I'm reading this stupid book."

"And are you inspired?" Jennifer asked.

"Fuck no. I fell asleep reading it at like ten this morning. I barely got here on time because of that goddamn book."

We all laughed, Sarah loudest of all. The amusement, dear diary, lies in knowing that Sarah has a PhD in biomechanical engineering and has certainly read more boring things than a popular feminist history book.

"I had one thought, though. It has a chapter about sirens, you know them." We both knew.

"This section I'm on explains these weird, elaborate rituals sea-faring men would go through to protect themselves from sirens, like, ear plugs and eye covers and turning westward and on and on. It got me thinking. What if sirens are actually the ghosts of women who had dumbass husbands and fathers and brothers and sons who all drowned at sea. These women's souls are out there, haunting shallow waters, screaming bloody murder to keep morons from crashing into the rocks that killed their families. But these stupid, horny bastards just steer right into them. Then they blame the women's ghosts and take no responsibility for their own dumbfuckery."

"Checks out," I said, popping a cherry tomato in my mouth.

"I wouldn't make myself a ghost to save someone else's man," Jennifer replied.

"You wouldn't make yourself a ghost to save your own man," Sarah laughed.

"No, I wouldn't. No way. You wouldn't either."

I watched Sarah's lighthearted joy melt away.

"I think I would. Which is sad."

"You'd do it protect your boys," I offered. Sarah only smiled.

"You don't understand. A mother would do anything to protect her children," Jennifer said, her tone unreadable.

I averted my gaze to my salad bowl. I had ruined it with all the dressing. The leaves, gooey and limp, clung to the bottom of the bowl.

"Why are you being such a bitch, Jennifer?" Sarah hissed.

"What?"

"What do you mean, WHAT. Stop picking on her."

"She wants to be a mother, she has to think about the sacrifices."

"Maybe we can be supportive. You know, while she tries to put shit behind her and make her own family, like you did," Sarah muttered.

Jennifer winced.

She never mentions her parents, her childhood, her family. I know Sarah had money and connections and a stable childhood, but my sense is that Jennifer's upbringing was the opposite. While Sarah was gently coaxed into success by loving parents, Jennifer broke into upper-middle-class respectability with her brilliance as well as her ruthlessness. I can see what she puts others through. I wonder what she does to herself.

We were still silent. I needed to say something. I couldn't sit here like this. I put down my fork.

"I'm not trying to make a family. I mean, I guess I am. That's not what I'm trying to do," I stammered. "You both have children."

They looked at me. Why were they surprised? Had I said it wrong? It seemed so obvious. I continued, "You are intelligent, successful women. I want to be like you. You are both mothers—so I want to be a mother."

Sarah laughed. "Girl, you are too much."

My reply caused a different reaction from Jennifer. The expression, not quite pain, was a relation of it. I could not define the feeling then, and I can't now. She looked like she understood something more than I had said. That I had given away a clue to a puzzle, one that she knew now only led to disappointment.

What was happening between us? I really wish I could remember my past. Maybe I'd understand her better if I knew myself well.

Our meals arrived. Sarah shook her head as she prepared a bite of pasta. "You're great with my kids. If you want kids, I support you. I think you'll be a wonderful mother."

"Thanks."

I looked at Jennifer. She offered me a smile that didn't reach her eyes. I checked her hands. One casually held her glass, playing with the condensation on the surface. The other gripped the arm of her chair, her knuckles white from the strain. Her food remained untouched.

I turned away from what was happening. At a table nearby, two well-made women were discussing astrological signs, how those represent personality attributes that affect their lives. The way the choices of others are a byproduct of the orientations of constellations and variations in moon phases.

"She's a Cancer rising, dating a Scorpio. Of course they have problems." They both nodded.

The women seem to know better, yet they, like most people, seek out validation from nature for what they experience. They rely on experts to interpret information and make choices based on those conclusions. I've read horoscope columns before. It seems as though the information hardly differs from a typical advice column, but the advice is supposedly for a subsection of the audience. Is it comforting, to feel like someone is using their knowledge and skill to look out for you?

Sarah heard them too and rolled her eyes with me. I wondered, though—is it comfort? Is it a framework for this pair's social interactions? Maybe it is how they acknowledge the chaos of life. Or, is it another way to relinquish control over your fate, and all the problems in the world that are within your power to fix, without accepting any guilt?

Whatever. Not like I can cast judgment on their beliefs when my desire to be a mother is almost indefensible.

"Parenting requires sacrifice."

Jennifer's interruption smoothly derailed my thoughts. I looked at her, stupefied.

Sarah guffawed. Jennifer leaned forward, ready with a new approach.

"Vera, what do you predict will be the reward for this choice?"

Sarah groaned. I ignored her. It was as if a part of me, distracted or perhaps dormant, faced her now. I liked this question. Yes, this question felt good. I played around with it in my mind like a favorite, well-worn toy, a ball I liked to roll, whose weight and circumference I understood.

I couldn't think of an answer.

No, that's not true. It was not one I wanted to share with her. I shrugged.

"Can you explain?"

"Holy hell, it's like I'm sitting in on my own thesis defense," Sarah said. She motioned to the waitress for a refill of her wineglass.

"I know I'm thinking about this all wrong, Jennifer," I said, my mind clear again. "I think of what I want, and I see a baby. I imagine myself in a few years, and I am holding my child's hand. When I go for a walk in a nice neighborhood, I look up the quality of the local schools, if there are baby gyms and good pediatricians. I take a detour to see the playground and if there are good trees to read under. I window-shop for baby clothes and strollers, I read about school parcel taxes and I calculate if my future child will benefit from them. This baby is more than a want or a need. She's a framework for my future."

Jennifer tried to drink from her empty water glass, then laughed to herself as she refilled it, her hand shaking slightly. "It's good to feel strongly about a goal and to pursue it. I'm sorry I doubted you."

"Thank you. You already recommended the doctor."

"Oh yeah, the doctor, right. How is that going, by the way?" Sarah asked.

I froze, confused. Sarah had heard about the appointment already; why would she ask in front of Jennifer? I realized she was communicating something else. I decided to follow her lead and described my latest appointment with less detail than before.

"Huh, strange," Sarah said and looked at Jennifer. "And he was your doctor?"

"No, mine retired. This doctor was recommended to me by someone from work."

"What's his name?" Sarah took out her phone to look him up.

"I can't remember. Vera has it." Jennifer dabbed her mouth on her napkin. "I need to hit the ladies' room before I go back. Sarah, I'll get next?"

"Of course, see you on Saturday?" Sarah asked.

"Saturday?" Jennifer looked the same as usual, calm and confident, but it was a mask now. I could feel it. Her mind was busy on another problem. What had unsettled her?

"That barbecue for Abigail? If you canceled, I'm thrilled. I don't want to go."

"Oh, yes. You should come. Vera, you'll be there as well?"

"Yes, at eleven-thirty. There's a 60 percent chance of rain that afternoon," I replied.

"Right. See you then," Jennifer said, her attention already on her purse as she walked toward the restroom. Once she was out of ear-shot, Sarah put away her phone and turned her full attention to me.

"You know the weather forecast?" Sarah whispered at me.

"I looked it up." Why were we whispering?

"Sure. Tell me more about this doctor's office."

"It's a fertility specialist office?"

"Tell me what it's like. Is it busy, is it fancy, is it shady?"

"Oh. Dingy? Quiet. Lots of empty chairs. I'm the only one ever in the waiting room. I assume because I'm available at any time. The sign-in sheet is always full of different names, which seems strange."

"Why is that strange?"

"People typically keep the same appointments. Availability doesn't vary for most people. There should be a few of the same names at the same days and times."

"You always remember the names?"

I shrugged as casually as I could, while the voice inside my head ridiculed me.

"You know, you're right. I always went on Tuesday mornings. Different names… that is strange."

Jennifer emerged from the bathroom and returned to the table. Sarah stopped talking and signed the check slip.

"Forgot my sunglasses," Jennifer explained quietly, passing a glance over us.

"I have to leave anyway," Sarah said, stuffing her belongings back into her bag.

I checked the time. My lunch hour was nearly over. I gathered my things and followed them out to the tiny parking lot. The air was warmer than I expected, and the pavement hot. The tempera-ture change immediately radiated through the sole of my shoes. We talked about the cool weather fading fast, and the threat of the oncoming summer on the way to our respective vehicles: my bus stop, Sarah's minivan, and Jennifer's black luxury SUV. The tag for her employer, Perilaus Bionics, hung from the rearview mirror. The company's iridescent bull logo glinted in the sunlight. Sarah was just behind us, but the signal from her keys was blocked by something in her purse. She pulled out a pack of wipes, a snack bag, an action figure, and then gave up and simply waved the purse in the air. The van's security system sensed the movement of the key and unlocked.

"Mary Poppins, is it?" Jennifer said.

"Oh, wow! Look what else is in here!" Sarah pulled her hand out with her middle finger extended.

"Ha. Ha."

I said goodbye, but neither woman heard me. We three went our separate ways, to our completely different lives, maintaining a connection to each other we could not see.

CHAPTER 5

CPR DRONES CLEAR REGULATORY HURDLE
IN EU, TO BE OUTFITTED WITH NARCAN
AND "SCREAM DETECTION"

Sorry, diary. It's been a few weeks. You haven't missed anything.

Look at that headline. Scream detection. Yikes. Better than paying human beings a living wage to do important, life saving work, I suppose.

Moving on. At the beginning of my shift this morning, Scott called for me to stop by his cubicle. I logged in, locked my computer, then went to his desk.

"Compliance just dropped this hunk o' shit on us," Scott said. He tapped on a large packet of crisp pages sitting on his desk. The cover page read "VA Medical Document Policy Compliance V4.2."

I was surprised. They had modified their policy only two weeks earlier, and that packet was much smaller. I flipped through the still-warm pages with a thumb. Whole sections were unique.

"Listen, you're a quick reader. Take a stab at checking this for changes that matter to us. I bet it's a bunch of garbage to keep the lawyers employed."

"No problem," I said, perhaps too eagerly. "I'll have it done before lunch."

"No, don't *rush*. Be thorough, alright?" Scott said, not looking at me anymore, already back to browsing golf equipment. He liked to shop before lunch.

I set the packet at my desk and checked the page count. The last version had been 215 pages. This was 378. I logged myself in for direct calls, but out of rotation for document-processing support. I picked a soundtrack-heavy playlist and put my headphones on. From my top drawer I selected two highlighters, pink for major changes and yellow for minor ones. I began at page 1. Tasks like this challenge a different part of my brain. Though I love my work, variety is helpful.

A coworker, a person named William, leaned over the wall of my cubical. I noted his presence but continued as before.

"Boy, it sucks you got stuck with that."

"I don't mind," I said, perhaps too loudly, on account of the music and headphones.

He continued to hover. I recalled a scanner downstairs named Shalonda handing out headphones to all the women near her—"man-repellent," she called them. Evidently, mine were defective. I turned up my volume.

A few moments passed with him still lingering there.

"Wait, why are you highlighting just that word?"

"It's different."

"You remember that a single word has changed?"

When I made it clear I would not reply, he plopped into his chair. The force of it rattled my desk and our shared cubicle wall.

In a merely performative whisper, he said to his cubicle mate, "You see what Rain Man is up to?"

I turned up my music again. Not enough—I could still hear him. I switched to a song from a loud, exciting soundtrack and continued to work. He shut up before the song was over.

By the last track of my playlist, I had completed the policy. I capped my highlighters with satisfaction.

I opened a text document and wrote out all the passages that were important and affected our team. I printed that out, attached it as a new cover sheet, and then brought the stack of pages to Scott. I slid the stack onto the furthest corner of his cubicle. He glanced at the documents and looked annoyed.

"Here are all the changes," I said.

He flipped through the packet. "I gave you this an hour ago."

"I can go through it again?"

"No, no. It's fine."

He didn't say anything, but he wasn't reading my notes either.

"Did I do something wrong?"

He looked at me, his mouth pursed in disappointment. "Kid, what are you doing working here?"

"What… Pardon me?"

"How'd you end up here? Shouldn't you be curing cancer, launching rockets, or saving the world?"

I smiled to acknowledge the compliment. He turned away, looking again at the packet with disgust.

"What kind of goddamn world do we live in, where a bright kid like you works in a shithole like this."

I drifted away from his cubical wall and slowly returned to my desk. My hands shook as I put my headphones back on. I logged into document-processing support rotation, then opened the queue no one liked to work. It was full, as I had expected, while the easier work was nearly completed.

I replayed the interaction with Scott. It seemed like I had made several mistakes. I should've moved slower and waited until the end of the day to hand over the assignment. I should've feigned confusion partway through and asked for help. Perhaps the use of two highlighters had been too thorough.

No, stupid. This wasn't a highlighting issue. I hadn't correctly assessed his emotions. He found this work degrading. He didn't want to see anyone excel at this. Scott is nearing the end of his twenty years at the company, when his pension will be at maximum value. In the past, I have heard him discuss his house hunt in Reno, where taxes are better for retirees. He talks to Ramon about a scheme that sounds a lot like a mail-order bride, or even finding a single mom with kids he could help raise. His wife died in the pandemic, and they had never had children. His loneliness is a source of pain for him. To pass from one phase of life to the next must cause reflection on what the world is and what it should be, along with a renewed desire to help the next generation. I can see that now. He doesn't want me to fall prey to a trap that has ensnared him.

Tonight, I am home, alone. I guess I'll describe home to you, dear diary.

I live in a spacious one-bedroom apartment in a building with only nine units, three on each floor. I've said hi to a few neighbors before, though the only pleasant person in the building is Beatrix. She is a little old lady who lives alone across the hall. I believe the house used to be a mansion, though the interior is changed beyond recognition.

In certain rooms of my apartment, the wooden floor seems the same. Modern wood joins awkwardly to the old, wide, honey-warm boards. The old decorative wooden border is intact, extending three inches from the wall. It is composed of different pieces of wood, as small as Max's LEGOs and smaller, formed into an illusion of spirals, each expanding to their own infinity. What a pleasant, monotonous task that must have been, to create the same shapes, one after another, joined together in a strip that continues for hundreds of feet, for three floors of space. The person who painstakingly created this design, long dead but still appreciated.

The walls were once plaster but are now drywall and paint. There are no longer any adornments on the ceiling, only popcorn texture. I read that this is the cheapest way to finish a ceiling, next to acoustic tile. The windows are modern, thankfully, with cranks that allow air to enter but require an extra step to open entirely. I'm on the third floor, safe from any trouble below. I like to sit at my window on the weekends and watch the people pass by on the sidewalk below. They cannot see me. Sometimes they argue with one another, talk to themselves, or adjust their clothing in an embarrassing way. I watch them, though I know it is wrong.

To the left of my entry door is the kitchen, a little hallway full of counters, cabinets, and appliances that leads to the dining room. The dining room is just a small space, large enough to fit my circular table that seats four. I keep a vase of fake flowers on the table, resting on a square scarf that Sarah gave to me soon after we first met. It was a kind but thoughtless gift; the colors and pattern are ugly.

Straight from the entry door is the main living space, open to the dining room to the left. The living room couch faces the television, itself backed against the sliding glass door that leads to a simple patio. Typically the TV would be on the wall to the right, against my bedroom. I preferred to block the patio, which is just a neighboring roof. Besides, the glare from the sun bothered me.

It may look weird, but I rarely have guests over, so I optimized for my own comfort. On the wall to the right I plan to put a painting, though I haven't selected one yet.

If, at the entry door, you were to turn right, you'd find yourself in a hallway. Down that hall, to the left, is my bedroom. At the end is the laundry closet. My bathroom is to the right. The bathroom is standard: a cabinet unit of fake wood with a sink set in, a toilet, and a bath/shower combination. I enjoy the size of the bathroom, a wider footprint than you would expect in a unit this affordable. There are no windows, but there was once a strange hole behind the mirror. I noticed it soon after I moved in. I was brushing my teeth as usual when a breeze lifted my hair from my face. I froze and wondered if I was having a seizure. When the breeze came again, I knocked on the glass. The hole was large. Large enough for a person to crawl through. And with that realization, I walked out of there, still holding my toothbrush, and locked myself in my bedroom. I didn't want to see what was behind the mirror. I called Jennifer and she had the building's maintenance man close it up. I was weaker then. If that happened to me now, I would've looked first.

Across from the bathroom is my bedroom, a bright, good-sized room. It has wall-to-wall beige carpet, a disappointment. I'd prefer the beautiful wood of the rest of the unit, with a colorful area rug under my bed. The bed is wooden and modern, the linens and blankets and pillows in several shades of gray. I have two matching end tables, one with the charging cables for my devices and the other with a lamp and alarm clock. I placed a mirror and a dressing table to the right of the entry door, against the wall, so that the light from the windows is reflected across the space. I have no television in the bedroom.

To the left of the bedroom doorway, against the wall facing my bed, is an oil painting. I did not purchase it. I found it here, in my closet, when I moved in. I took it out and hung it right away, as if that made it mine. I've always been curious about it. A reverse image search brought up an academic journal article on computer image processing. It was behind a paywall. I should really ask Jennifer or Sarah if they have a subscription to that journal. I'd like to read the article.

I've never told anyone this part. I guess this is what a diary is for, right? Anyway, each morning when I wake up, before I begin my morning routine, I sit at the edge of my bed and face the painting. I stare at it. I think I sit there for a few minutes, maybe longer. It feels like I'm getting myself prepared for the day. I know, I know. That is so weird.

Now that I have admitted that, I should describe the painting. It shows a scene at dusk. A woman is reclined on the grass, flowers sprouting around her, as she faces the setting sun. The viewer only sees her back, the golden light in her hair. Each section of each strand of her hair seems to glow a different color. The picture is in pointillism, a style of oil-painted dots, millions of dots, combined to make an image. Yet each individual dot has color and structure and meaning.

I have seen prints of paintings of this style. Without the texture, the image could be a low-resolution computer printout. It is different in oil. The tiny mountains of color, rigid and shining, draw me in. The little shimmers and unique geography of each dot, like endless biomes working in synchronicity toward a common goal. The complexity yet cohesion centers me. Maybe that is why I stare at it.

It must have been left by mistake. It's too valuable to store in a rental-apartment closet. I'm sure someone misses it. One day I'll tell the landlord, or Jennifer—she said she knew the previous tenant.

For now, I say nothing. It's fun having a secret. When the landlord sends anyone to do maintenance work, I shut my bedroom door.

My closet is across from the bed, next to the painting. It is a small walk-in and has a pull cord for the single light bulb. The pull cord often becomes detached, and I have to climb on my footstool and reattach it. Inside I have four silk blouses, two sweaters, two pairs of work trousers, and one suit in my work section. It is currently summer, so I have put my short-sleeve blouses, skirts, and my pair of shorts out for the season. Packed away are two scarves and my light jacket. For weekends, I have two T-shirts and two pairs of jeans. For shoes, I have a pair of rain boots, one pair of casual sneakers, one pair of fitness sneakers, a pair of flats, and two pairs of high heels. I had only one pair, but Jennifer said my closet depressed her and insisted I take designer stilettos she had purchased online, in the wrong size, and could not return. I have two dresses, a button-down shirtdress for daytime and a black cocktail dress for dates. I have only been on two dates since I moved in, one set up by Jennifer and another with a coworker. Neither were successful.

To look at my closet, a row of dark neutrals and pops of light beige, makes me think I'm a corporate monk who abstains from shopping. That isn't true. I like to shop online. Sometimes I spend hours scrolling through the images, with the TV on in the background for company. I look at one item after another, admiring the draping and patterns, and try to imagine my body in them.

If I stare too long, though, I find myself noticing other things. The close-ups of women's torsos or legs, their heads and unique features a nuisance that must be chopped out of frame. I stop seeing the beauty in clothing. I see models devoid of personality, their curves a billboard for logos. Some designs exist to flatter while others fit only one body shape, a demand by the designer to conform to their ideal. This figure is an impossible task for many. I write this and yet, as Sarah often comments, I have this shape, though I have done nothing to achieve it.

Jennifer is also lean. She says it's because she has a clean diet and engages in regular yoga, with self-sacrifice and responsibility. I credit her poorly concealed eating disorder. Sarah used to have this shape, before her children. Once in a while, she tries a new diet she can't maintain, new exercise routines she seems to enjoy, or a fad like colder thermostats and more water and less sugar and different bread. Once the effort tires her, she gives up without self-recrimination. I respect that. I find it ironic that Jennifer looks so powerful with her sharp features and beautiful clothes, yet it is Sarah who will likely live longer.

That was a tangent. I shop for clothes, I enjoy looking at clothes, but I do not purchase them. I prefer to keep my closet limited to the things I know I will wear regularly. The second pair of high heels gives me anxiety, taking up floor space unnecessarily. Instead, I have these shoes because they are beautiful and because they were a gift. Sort of.

My room and bathroom reflect my life. The closet has a scale built into the floor, where I weigh myself daily, though I rarely look at the value. It transmits to an app on my phone. If I need the information, I have it at all times. The line is essentially flat. Sarah has mentioned that her weight increases by several pounds at ovulation time and just before her period, purely due to water retention. I have never seen that fluctuation in my own weight, though Dr. Parsons told me not to worry.

Back in my bathroom I have my vitamins from a personalized nutrition service Jennifer recommended. I take four each day. I have my face wash, ointments, and moisturizer in a clear bin. I have my stretch-mark body oil, which I hide when I have visitors. I have my toothpaste and brush, body wash and shampoo and conditioner and body lotion. There are towels for guests, rarely used, and a towel for me. My shower curtain is a fun pattern, and my body brush is a bright color to match my floor mat.

I can't think of anything else in my apartment worth describing. Sarah's house is warm with clutter, crayon drawings and tiny socks and tired toys. Jennifer's home is clean, modern, and beautiful. Only her son's room has personality, and even then it is restrained and tasteful. Max's drawings are filed, except for one corkboard in his room. His clothes are folded and tucked away, his toys hide in bins, and anything damaged or stained or torn is discarded. My home is a cheap version of Jennifer's, wishing it were like Sarah's. I appreciate my home, how the comfort is designed to suit me. I shape it and resist the stresses I find outside of my walls. Still, I am not a god in this place. I cannot paint the walls, change the fixtures or appliances. I am borrowing someone else's property to inhabit a state of life I do not want.

This is only temporary, I remind myself. When I bring my baby home, her bassinet, with an elegant, sheer canopy, will go beside my bed, within easy reach. I will make a corner of the living room her play space. The first stage will be a stimulating blanket with mirrors and toys that squeak and rattle. Then there will be a short bookshelf of her favorite colorful board books. When she can stand on her own, I'll add a pretend work bench, with gears, bolts, and screws and tools she can manipulate.

After that, I'll give her a push toy, one that will teach her to walk. She'll use it to follow me to the kitchen at snack time, where she'll bang into my ankles to get my attention. In the kitchen, her stylish wooden highchair will go into the corner of the dining room, nearest the window to admire the view. She'll watch the people walking by as she eats out of mismatched plastic bowls and plates, until I switch to metal for safety concerns.

The bathroom will change, too. Our bathtub will be full of rubber duckies I collect for her throughout the pregnancy. She'll have her own special towel, covered in unicorns and rainbows. I'll get a two-person toothbrush holder, one slot for me and one slot for her baby toothbrush. Her little soft hairbrush will lay beside mine.

Out on the landing, I'll keep her tricycle and then a bicycle, though the landlord won't allow it. I will get rid of my dressing table and an end table to make room for her big-girl bed when she is ready. Every night I will read her two picture books and a chapter from a classic children's novel. When she falls asleep, I will tighten the blanket around her, give her two kisses, whisper to her that I love her, and turn on her puppy dog nightlight.

That is my destination. I just need to get there.

CHAPTER 6

DATA IS THE NEW OIL: THE RACE TO REFINE WITHOUT AI

I'm writing this entry on the bus, on the way to a party I don't want to go to.

This bus is so dirty. I've been staring out of a grimy window, watching my breath turn to fog on the cool pane. My weather prediction was accurate. The gloom outside will surely turn to rain and ruin any outdoor elements for the party.

I don't want to go. I don't know why I'm going! It's a bunch of people I don't know, who don't know me. Why is Jennifer making me go?

I don't hate all parties. I like invites to random children's parties. I can play and interact with the kids and disappear. The parents appreciate my sacrifice, which is no sacrifice at all. I enjoy children and dislike the adults. At a childless party, though, I'll have to speak. Where do you work, what do you do, what side of town do you live on, is your spouse here. I'll smile, respond, and want to set down my drink and walk out the door.

A car's brakes just locked up while we sat at a red light. We all watched as it slid into the intersection, then sheepishly continued through. Reversing would've been worse. Some passengers near me seemed frightened. Had they been in accidents?

I touched my head. Why didn't I feel frightened? Shouldn't I react like them?

Jennifer said I had brain damage from the crash. It must be true; I don't remember my accident. I only vaguely remember the hospital. I can see my feet in white disposable slippers, shuffling on linoleum alongside cold metal supports. I can feel the stiff hospital sheets and the cold, sterile air on my skin.

I don't really remember my parents either. My father's bike-riding lessons, my mother's silhouette at the sink—but they are faded memories, with no sense of who they were or what they were like. I'll never know more. I can't find anything about them online. I only have Jennifer for family, and she never discusses them. My past is fragments surrounded by silence.

This isn't a tragedy. I know that life is gone; I do not look for it. And if losing my memories frees me from fear at every near-accident on every drive, that may be a price worth paying.

I get off at the train station but walk back down the block. There's a bodega that sells nice cards. I'll buy one for this person I do not know, along with a bottle of wine. I might buy some Russian caviar. It's under the counter and sold at a fraction of the cost. I don't think it is legal, but it may impress the host. We'll see. I don't particularly care either way. I just don't want to embarrass Jennifer.

OK. I'm settled in now, on the train heading north to the suburb where this stranger is having a party. It is quiet on Saturdays.

To my left is a group of kids going up to the mountains for an impromptu camping trip. They have tote bags full of bottles of liquor, marshmallows, chocolate, and hopefully some real food. They look young to be going up alone, but it's probably fine. One boy is nervous but trying to participate. I look at his hands. He is scratching, digging into his skin. He is afraid. Maybe he has a secret. I wonder if I can help him. I watch him and wait. No. I can't help him.

In front of the kids are child-free adults in masks. They live in the city and are visiting friends or family who have children. One is carrying a birthday present wrapped in colorful paper. They seem content, happy for a change in tempo, with no other strong emotions to interest me.

An elderly lady with soft white curls is knitting behind me. I can hear the rhythm of her progress—she must be an expert. What is she making? Is it for someone she loves? Or will she sell it, and feel dismay at the price: too low for the skill and attention, but too high to generate much interest in her work.

Everyone exists in their bubbles, separate yet part of a whole. The woman in front of me is watching a video from a news program. I can see the subtitles from my seat, so I decide to watch.

NARRATOR: "Amy and Henry Shepherd were overjoyed when they learned they were expecting a baby boy."

AMY: "We were just so excited."

NARRATOR: "Their joy quickly turned to heartache. During a routine twenty-week ultrasound, they learned their unborn son suffered from myelomeningocele, a severe form of spina bifida. Spina bifida occurs when the tissue of the spinal column does not fuse during development. The consequences of the condition can be catastrophic."

HENRY: "You can't prepare yourself to hear something like that."

NARRATOR : "Amy was rushed to Pacific Garden Medical Center, where specialists operated on her unborn son to seal his spinal column, giving him a chance at life. The surgery was a success, but only time would tell if paralysis, the most devastating outcome, had been avoided."

AMY : "We prayed, you know. Every night we prayed. But God wasn't done testing us."

NARRATOR : "Amy and Henry learned during a follow-up exam that their unborn son's lower limbs were not moving as expected. The baby was paralyzed from the waist down. Doctors told them there was no hope for recovery."

HENRY : "I had to be strong for Amy. She'd been through so much. But you know, I'll tell you, I sat out there in my truck and I just broke down. These doctors, they tell you something like this and that they can't fix it. I didn't understand it. There ain't nothing you can do?"

NARRATOR : "The anxious parents took to the internet. That's where they discovered Hannock Assistive Technologies."

DR. HANNOCK : "The medical community has been experimenting with electronic spinal implants for the past twenty years, but the scale of these implants and the invasiveness of the installation often reduce efficacy of treatment. Even our devices, which are smaller, have a much longer recovery time than we'd like. There's also the challenge in training the mind to work with these devices. Fetal development is, a, uh, unique situation. You've already got such rapid cellular growth, exceptional neuroplasticity, neither state can be easily replicated outside of the womb—it's, you know, the perfect environment for recovery from really any surgery."

NARRATOR : "Amy and Henry's unborn son presented the scientists with the unique opportunity to combine the power of their implant with the healing properties in fetal development. And the results are remarkable."

AMY: "He's just a normal, happy little boy. Hitting all his milestones. We're so blessed."

(Baby coos)

NARRATOR: "The staff at Hannock Assistive Technologies will be able to monitor the device, make adjustments if needed, and even update software wirelessly."

HENRY: "I just—Dr. Hannock and his team, they are angels. They saved Charlie's life. I'm going to get to teach him to play ball like my dad did with me. They saved all our lives, and I can't thank them enough."

I'm home again. Here's how it went.

"Hi, Vera. Welcome! Let me take your coat," the host said with warm insincerity.

"Thank you. These are for you."

"Oh, thank you! Oh, caviar! Well, I'll, um, just put this out for guests with the crackers. How was your trip up? You live in the city near Jennifer, right?"

"A neighborhood away, but yes. The city," I answered.

The hostess looked at me for a moment, smiled and watched me. I watched her watching me. We had nothing more to say, but she lingered. What more did she want from me?

I thought about where to hide. I could sit down in an empty room somewhere in this house, away from the noise of friendly chatter, and hide until I just leave. I could offer to bring the caviar to the crackers and stand in the kitchen. No, no, I told myself. So dumb. Kitchens are always busy at these things. Maybe I'd hide in the bathroom. Or, I could skip all of this and walk out the front door and never accept another invitation.

A couple of men stood nearby, each one waiting for a chance to add or correct or interject the other's speech.

"Christensen thinks perverse instantiation is a guaranteed outcome, and if he makes sure we can't build anything, no one can prove him wrong," the paler man in the floral button up remarked, sipping his can of seltzer.

"He has no vision. He's a code monkey with a good face for TV, so he makes publicity rounds instead of building anything. He can't make. It's sad, really. Besides, we're decades off from the kinds of systems he's afraid of, if its possible at all."

"Vera! Thank god." Sarah appeared in the hallway. "Excuse me, I need to borrow her."

She looped her arm in mine, as if she needed my guidance or physical support. She leaned in close and spoke in a tight whisper. "All these people are on Jennifer's team. They'd murder their own mothers to get ahead. I fucking hate them. Let's go outside; it's a beautiful backyard. It's drizzling, too. That will scare away the worst of them."

We walked through the clumps of people, busy in their own spheres, or as unhappy with them as we would have been. Their eyes sometimes followed us, especially the men, trying to assess if we were important or interesting. I knew we were neither. We stopped at the beverage table, and Sarah poured both of us glasses of white wine. I rarely drink in public, but I know I should carry something to deflect any offers. Besides, Sarah would appreciate having an instant refill once she finished her glass.

For a house of such value, the garden was surprisingly dated. An overgrown bush wrapped around a dilapidated screen that had fallen over in some long-forgotten storm. A weird-looking plant hid underneath. I looked closer. An *Arisaema triphyllum*. I assume it had once been a centerpiece for an ornamental garden that was once neatly trimmed.

How did I know the plant name? In fact, I think I could list every single plant I saw in that garden. Have I always been able to do that? That seems strange, right?

The only plant that I actually appreciated was an enormous sugar maple, likely older than the house. Its great branches were coated in moss, some of it stringy and some of it only a soft, bright fuzz. I imagined generations of birds nested in this tree, their children and grandchildren and great-grandchildren all coming back to make a new home here. For the human guests, the tree shaded a large portion of the yard and blocked most of the drizzle.

I could see why Sarah liked this garden. It felt given over to the plants with humility. The cracked paving stones and wobbly brick pathways the only acknowledgment that humans might need access to the far corners. The pool cover was open, for some reason, though it was far too cold for a swim. Perhaps people liked the pool exposed, some kind of aesthetic I didn't understand. It seemed like a safety hazard, when combined with an open bar. There were some other people in the yard, their goal the same as ours, to scatter and keep to themselves.

We took a table in the shade of a smaller oak tree, itself old enough to shield us from the rain. I couldn't remember the last time I had seen an oak tree, let alone one of this size. It gave us some privacy from the house but let us see the party from afar.

"These assholes," Sarah began. "They all want to know what I've been 'up to' since I quit. *Well, Kim, I've been up to my elbows in norovirus vomit, baby shit, and finger paint. Oh, you took a sabbatical and lived in France for six months? How lovely!* These people." Sarah sipped her wine. She shivered a little bit, despite her sweater and dress pants.

"Why are we here?" I asked.

"Jennifer told me it was important that I socialize, and keep up my connections for when I return. She thinks I'm going to prance back into that abattoir. And I don't know what her plans are for you. I assume just to keep me from backing out. She knows I wouldn't feed you to these wolves."

"Abattoir?"

"The lab."

We paused as a delivery drone flew overhead to a neighbor's property. It was a heavy-duty model, likely carrying something like a rice cooker or toaster or something.

When the buzzing faded away, Sarah resumed. "It was fine, I guess. It used to be great. Then they got some new investors with big plans. Guys who want to be super geniuses, or download their brains to the cloud and cheat death, I think. I don't know. It wasn't just them. I never really fit in there. I got into biomechanical engineering to make prosthetics to help people live more comfortably. Perilaus has always wanted to make garbage rich techies will buy. Our prosthetics lab had great gear, good funding, but..."

"But what?"

"The prosthetics team was a way to keep a public relationship with the military while the bionics department worked with them on secret projects. We were important for appearances but not treated seriously."

"I see. What makes her think you'll go back?"

"I don't know! I told her I don't want to go back. Repeatedly. I mean, I do want to go back to work. Once Fiona starts kindergarten, or maybe first grade, I'm going back. I was looking at an ethics think tank, or I could go back to astronomy. That was my other major in school. I could get a role as an adviser for the government. Perilaus sort of ruined prosthetics for me. I couldn't do that again."

"Once you find something fulfilling, you'll be amazing at it," I said.

Sarah smiled at me. "Look, if you're going to deploy this kind of flattery, I'll move you into my house. How much do you like watching three completely angelic, not-at-all annoying children?"

I laughed. "You know I love to babysit. I also love to go home at the end of the night."

"Hey, ladies."

We both looked up. Jennifer had spotted us.

"Hey," Sarah said weakly.

Jennifer motioned to our table as she approached. "Is this where the antisocial social club is meeting?"

"Don't start. We're just taking a breather," Sarah replied.

I took a moment to admire Jennifer. As usual, she looked like how every woman wished she looked at a party like this. Her smooth skin, long, dark hair, and bright eyes were all enhanced by a form-fitting green wool dress. Her strong lipstick, perfect eyebrows, statement rings, and dark-green snake-print shoes advertised the hard edge within her. Other guests looked at her as she spoke to us. I felt special receiving her attention and, of course, dingy when beside her.

"You thinking of coming inside soon, or should I make everyone move outside to enjoy this beautiful weather?"

Sarah and I looked at each other, resigned to our fate. I was annoyed and nervous, but at least I wasn't alone. We rose from the table and followed Jennifer back to the house.

"Vera, Jennifer's little cousin!" A man standing in the kitchen called out. I recognized him as a VC who sat on the Perilaus board. She seemed to tense at his enthusiasm.

"Vera, this is Robert Castor."

"Hi," I replied.

"It's really good to see you, Vera. I've heard so much about you."

Why was he smiling? Why did he wink at Jennifer? What was I missing?

"Sarah! Long time no see! Where have you been hiding yourself?"

Sarah smiled and replied pleasantly, without any visible effort. As much as I admire Jennifer, Sarah is so good at putting people at ease—even people who shouldn't feel at ease.

Robert put his arm around my shoulders and faced Jennifer.

He made a joke, perhaps, something I did not register. His breath smelled of hard alcohol and beer, and his hand, heavy and unwanted, held onto my shoulder. Fingers pressed into my muscle, each one an invasion. My eyes watered. Sarah wore a strangled smile, and Jennifer watched him closely.

Beneath the events unfolding, I felt a swell of feeling. Was it fear? Yes, fear. And something else. A welcome, dangerous feeling. It was the anger again, sharp and cruel, yet different this time. There was more. A memory not linked to this man but to this quality of advantage he claimed over my body. The weight of his arm still on my shoulders, I didn't think of escape, of running, as I often did. I didn't want to do my breathing exercises in privacy.

No, I felt like a spring compressed, waiting, eager to be restored to my natural place.

I was ready.

Saliva gathered in my mouth as I thought of hurting him.

A knife from the butcher's block beckoned. I would scare him first, yes, and then? Then I would let go.

Oh, the delight! The joy of a hot spray of his blood on my cool skin. I can see his hands up, I can hear him scream, voice cracking in inarticulate nonsense. Yes, I'd make him stop, forever. Not for safety. For revenge.

"We need to head out," Sarah said, grabbing my hand and pulling me free.

"Have a safe drive back. Thanks for coming," Jennifer replied. Our eyes met. Oh, god. She knew. I blushed.

I deposited my glass somewhere and my coat appeared in my arms. I felt dizzy and alive. What had happened to me? It was as though a secret room in me had been unlocked. I knew now there was more to me, if I let go.

"That guy is such a fucking creep."

I nodded to Sarah, I think. We got into her minivan and she turned on the heater immediately, though I was still sweating. I quickly removed my scarf and set it with my jacket in the back, on Jack's car seat.

"Trudy, please call Steve," Sarah said to the virtual assistant as she checked her sideview mirrors.

"Calling Steve," a female voice replied through the van's speakers.

"I hope the kids ate something healthy for dinner," Sarah muttered. I popped a stick of gum in my mouth. I had bought it on a whim at the bodega and was glad to do something with my nervous energy now.

The ringing stopped and sounds of high-pitched laughter ricocheted through the interior cabin. "Hey hon, ditching the party already?"

"Yeah, I had to save Vera."

"Hi, Steve," I said.

"Hey, Ver. Sarah, swing over to the drive-through and pick up some burgers for me and the kids? We're starving."

Sarah shut her eyes. "Sure thing. Same as usual?"

Jack's voice called out, "I want dinosaur chicken nuggets!"

"Pizza!" Sam argued.

"I'm making one stop. Agree on what you want and I'll go get it. Otherwise, we have yogurt and bananas at home."

"Burgers are fine," one child said. Fiona screeched at us or them or something else.

"Get me a soda with no ice, OK?" Steve asked.

"Yep," Sarah said.

"See you soon!"

Sarah hung up and asked Trudy to navigate. Once the map loaded, she put the van into drive. A prompt for driving assistance appeared. She dismissed it.

Unexpectedly, the van's drive select returned to PARK, the word's backlight turning red. Trudy's voice came through the speakers.

"Assessment required. Please complete the tasks on the screen to engage the vehicle."

"Piece of shit!" Sarah groaned. "I'm angry, not drunk, you stupid, shitty spyware."

I stayed completely quiet while Sarah did the exam on the touch screen. The cameras that judged her hid behind dark plastic windows, positioned in the instrument cluster, above the rearview mirror, and in the A-pillar. What if you taped over them? I'd guess an assessment would be required each time.

The last question, a simple math equation, almost made me break my silence. Sarah has a PhD, and this car thinks it can catch her out with basic arithmetic?

A progress wheel appeared after her last submission, then a large green checkmark replaced it. The light on the drive select changed back to white, and the lock on the accelerator disengaged.

Through gritted teeth, Sarah said, "Steve can rant about football while driving, but not me. If I get too excited about a podcast, this piece of shit makes me pull over."

I stayed silent, trying to make my observation invisible. She *was* driving worse than usual. That drunk alert had happened to her once before, and she had also driven worse then, too. It was a clumsy, stupid system, but was it wrong?

"I can feel you thinking, Vera."

"I'm sorry."

"For what? You didn't do anything."

I knew I didn't want to talk about her driving, but should I say something else? Maybe something true, to distract her from the thought I had suppressed.

"I hate being called Ver."

Sarah laughed. "He's always giving people nicknames."

"Oh."

"He's helpful. He's good to the kids. My mother loved him. I just wish I didn't have to think of everything."

Outside the window, I watched the playground of the suburb slide away as we headed toward the main road. Children tumbled in and out of the play structures while a dad holding an umbrella with a baby strapped to his chest pushed a toddler on a swing.

"Is it really 'helpful' if he's watching his own children?" I asked quietly.

Sarah laughed and shook her head. "Goddamn, Vera."

"Sorry."

"No, you're right. That's who I am now: a wife excusing the

bare-minimum adult behavior from her husband. I'm a goddamned paper towel commercial."

"He knew you'd leave early."

Sarah drove in silence for a moment. "He wants me to go back to work. He made me pass up a promotion when Sam was born, insisted I be a stay-at-home mom after Fiona, but I can tell he's unhappy. He hasn't said it directly. He wouldn't. I can tell, though."

"You want to go back to work."

"Yeah, but not yet. Not when Fiona is so little. We agreed I'd stay home for the first few years. I didn't even take full maternity leave for Sam and Jack. He acts like it is so embarrassing. Whenever his coworkers ask about me, he reports it back and adds, 'of course, I have nothing to tell them.'"

I frowned. We pulled into the drive-through, a long queue of cars and two different versions of food transporters ahead of us. One of the transporters ahead of us rolled forward to the order screen. It didn't speak. A blue light on its black dome illuminated and pulsed as it transmitted the order. The restaurant's screen flashed neon pink in reply. The blue light on the transporter changed to pink. The conversation concluded, it continued forward in line.

"Are you happy?" I asked.

"Happy? Am I happy." Sarah turned the word over in her mouth. "Happy. I don't know. He's a good dad. The kids love him. It's not like I enjoy dealing with our asshole neighbor whenever she has a bug up her ass, or volunteering in Thanksgiving pageants, which are fucking offensive, by the way. I like being able to walk the kids to school. Giving them a hug hello at the end of the day. Stuff like that."

She fell silent for a moment. The child safety lock on my door glowed in the darkness. What happens in an emergency, I wonder. Is there a bit of software ready and waiting to disable that in an accident? Can the children still escape if something goes wrong?

"I don't know," Sarah continued. "I miss *thinking*. I miss work-ing on hard problems. Every once in a while, I'll read a newspaper article or watch Jeopardy and think, 'Oh, right! I know this. I know this whole topic. I'm PUBLISHED on this topic. I'm a goddamn expert on this topic. Like it's a fact that stopped existing because I spend my days scraping Steve's scrambled-egg pan and vacuum-ing playground sand from everything we own."

Sarah took a shuddering breath. An old passenger car moved out of line, and we pulled forward. It felt like more progress than the smaller food transporters, as though the small, single-purpose machines were less than.

"I look at Jennifer's life and think, yeah, she's got it figured out. No husband, one kid, a live-in nanny and a full-time housekeeper. She doesn't have to argue with an adult man about running a load of wash. I doubt she has ever wrestled her kid into a bathtub, only for him to take a dump in the clean water. Jennifer made it so her focus can be on quality time with her one child.

I mean, not that she ever focuses on him; she never sees Max. He's an accessory at the beginning of her parties, then she shoos him away to be tucked in by the nanny. I wouldn't want that with my kids. They'll be complete assholes in less than ten years, no matter what I do, just like I was and you were and everyone else on earth. I guess, I wish I could split myself in two. I want to work, to function and be impressive—and I want to enjoy my babies while they are still young."

The car ahead of us rolled forward. We were only two spots behind the order screen now. A newer model of food transporter waited behind us. I watched it in the passenger side mirror. Another of the same model approached, and in a moment of madness,

I expected to see them greet one another, like colleagues at a water cooler. They didn't, of course. They lined up perfectly, waiting their turn.

I considered what to say. There was a danger here. Sarah was being unfair to Jennifer, but they knew one another so well. And maybe I had once known Jennifer just as well. That wasn't true now. I certainly didn't need to jump in on Jennifer's behalf. She can fight her own battles. I decided to reply to what she meant beneath it all, the insecurity I could only just see.

"You have three good kids. They are kind, have good judgment, and love each other. They know they are safe and loved by you. And they adore you for it. I know it's not making prosthetics or discovering new galaxies. That'll come soon. For now, you have real, true love. That's everything. Absolutely everything."

Tears glistened in Sarah's eyes. She grabbed my hand and smiled at me, her face years younger in the strange orange glow of the order sign.

She sighed and let go of my hand as she pulled forward to order.

"Good evening," the automated voice said. "If you have an account, please say your name. Otherwise, begin your order."

"Sarah Bennington."

"Hi, Sarah! Here's your usual order. Would you like to reorder?"

"Delete mint shake."

"I've removed your mint shake. Any other changes?"

"No."

"Ready to order?"

"Yes."

"Great! Your order has been placed. Your food will be ready in just a few minutes. Please pull forward toward the next window."

Sarah turned to me and rolled her eyes. "I get one mint

milkshake two years ago and it thinks I'm committed."

She turned on a news podcast. She didn't have to ask if I minded, though she wouldn't have asked.

The episode was about a new way to recycle plastic garbage. Developed by a company in Oregon, it breaks plastic goods into usable components. The first step requires a chemical reaction to liquefy the materials. Then, the liquid is sent down a series of chambers in a tiered structure. Oscillation and gravity sort the liquefied plastic by density into separate containers specific to each type of plastic. Once the containers are filled, they can be replaced and more garbage introduced. Units of the separated material can be sold and remade into other products. The challenge is the energy required to keep the liquefied plastics in motion during the separation process.

Sarah's problems were forgotten. With some pleasure, I lost myself in the details of invention. All the great things that someone could invent if they didn't have to worry about energy sources. If we could pull power from wind and waves, would any problems be outside of our reach? Solar is a wonderful domestic solution to energy, but the large expanses of panels are destructive to ecosystems. There needs to be a greater diversity of energy solutions to undo the damage we have inflicted on life on earth.

And yet, will that ever happen without massive change? The centralized control of energy, and the corruption of government, is an insurmountable issue. While residents die by fire or freezing temperatures caused by faulty equipment, power companies tighten their grip on their monopolized infrastructure and draft laws ready to be rubber stamped by purchased politicians. They pay out their pathetic settlements from one hand while they collect ever higher monthly fees with the other, and we all see it and we all give in, as if subjected to a god our government has forced upon us.

Sarah pulled up to my building. I looked around, confused by our surroundings, and laughed at myself.

"Yeah, you were out of it," Sarah replied.

I retrieved my things from Jack's chair, gave her a hug, and awkwardly shifted the fast-food bags into my newly vacated seat.

"Don't worry about that, I still need to crush Steve's burger before I get home."

I laughed and waved goodbye, but I wasn't thinking about food.

Solving corruption. Ugh. No, not right now. How about the plastic trash? Could waves be used for perpetual motion? I let one part of my brain continue to work on that problem as I stepped into the foyer of my apartment building. I had no mail, as usual. My weekly delivery of vitamins waited under the row of mailboxes. I picked up the box and climbed the three floors to my apartment. One step after another, my muscles drawing energy to defeat gravity. We solved that problem! Can't we extract energy from nature to solve our other problems?

Beatrix had a note on her door. Probably the landlord complaining about her exercise VR game. She doesn't seem to care.

Once inside my apartment, I breathed in the familiar silence of my home.

The safe darkness reminded me of the thought I had been avoiding. Delicious, seductive rage. Should I explore that thread? No. I wasn't ready. I reoriented my thoughts back to Sarah.

I can tell you, diary, that I don't like her husband. I don't feel comfortable discussing him with her, or even with Jennifer. They are close friends and I do not want to test loyalties, though Jennifer has complained to me about him when Sarah is not around.

Is this what marriage is like? Is this why Jennifer is single? As much as Sarah resents Steve's behavior, she loves him in a way he does not merit. She wants him to change, for his negative qualities to fall away and for the essence of him to return to what it must've been. I personally doubt it had ever been there to begin with, but maybe, I guess. I didn't know her then, obviously. Steve may have been better before. Now, as he is, he doesn't seem worth this kind of stress.

I left my stuff on the couch and now I'm just sitting here, writing next to the messy pile. Not like *I* know anything about love. No one loves me, at least right now. I have no romantic partners. No one seeks me out for help or an opinion or support. Well, Sarah has called me for childcare now and then. Jennifer is my only family, and she does not like me, let alone love me. I think she resents having to care for me. But I think Sarah could love me, as a friend, someday.

Respect I can imagine. I can extrapolate from being asked my opinion at work or when a neighbor holds a door for me when they see me struggle with groceries. My only examples of love are Jennifer and Sarah's love for their children. And Sarah's love for her husband. I don't see warm feelings reflected in how he treats her. He may love her, I suppose, but he does not respect her. I hear it in her words, and I see it in the way she parents, as if those children are all she has.

There's one story that sticks out in my mind. When Fiona was four days old, Sarah developed mastitis, a breast infection that is both common and serious in lactating parents. She hallucinated from fever. Shivering and weak, she couldn't climb the stairs. She begged Steve to leave work early. He didn't. He had promised to take paternity leave for this birth; it had been part of the arrangement. Otherwise, Sarah would never have gotten pregnant again. Yet, where was he? Oh, he had gone back the day after the birth.

Silly Sarah, he could not lose control over his project. It was important and unexpected; it couldn't be helped.

Jennifer left work immediately. She came over with her nanny and Max, then took Sarah to the emergency room. (At this point, I wasn't helping Sarah yet. I had just moved into this place and was still getting adjusted.)

I've heard Jennifer and Sarah share different versions of this incident, though the similarities lead me to believe Jennifer's more unforgiving interpretation over Sarah's version. I think about this story a lot. Not always with anger. Mostly I think of it as a signpost guiding me to Steve's personality. He fears losing credit for his work more than he cares for his wife. It is as simple as that.

OK. Writing that down *has* made me angry at Steve, so I'm going to change topics. At least it isn't the same as the anger I felt at the man at the party.

God. What happened to me back there? Does everyone feel so many varieties of anger? Indistinct, dangerous, like a wild predator in the dark.

I'll tell you this, diary. I feel like I have less control these days. It almost seems like a quiet part of me, a voice deep down, is goading me towards these feelings. I need to do something to relax. If it were daytime, I'd go for a run. I don't run at night. I know that men do—I see them pass by, in their shorts and moisture-wicking shirts, their headphones playing music or podcasts. If I went for a run now, and a man tried to hurt me, I'm not sure what I'd do.

I'll just take a shower, listen to my audiobook on income inequality while I do a face mask, take my vitamins, and go to bed early.

Good night, diary.

CHAPTER 7

Something weird happened this morning. I'm going to document it, then do a normal entry.

First, I woke up too early.

In the pale-blue dawn light, I felt confused and dizzy. I tried to rise but couldn't. My legs did not respond the way I expected. My fingers fumbled on my bedside lamp, the familiar motions an unfair request. I started to panic. Desperate to accomplish anything, I pressed my dulled hands against the light tiles mounted to my wall. I've never used them before—they're just there for emergencies. The harsh orange glow filled the room.

Despite my alarm, I thought of the painting. Yes, the painting would reorient me. I crawled over my covers to the foot of the bed and stared, waiting for the points of color to speak to me. I've been drawn to it before like this, usually in the middle of a calm routine, but now I hunted for relief. My eyes roamed the features of it, the details in the flowers, the grass, the sky.

A small house on the horizon, unnoticed before. Is there a window there? If there is a window in that darkness, is there someone there, watching me? Is she disgusted by me? Or does she cry out, slamming her silenced fists against the glass, trying to get me to see? To see what she sees, to know it now, and become more?

I tried to rise, to get closer and hear what she was saying. My legs did nothing. I fell to the ground. Something was very wrong. Was it the vitamins? I imagined all the shit that could go in a vitamin. I crawled to my small waste bin and tried to force myself to vomit. Nothing but bile. What do you do for poison? I immediately thought of the milk in the fridge. I'd never make it. An impossible distance in that state.

The glass of water on my nightstand waited for me. I gulped, a cascade down my chin and throat and chest as I drank it down in terror. The coolness in my gut was refreshing.

That was all I could do. I couldn't save myself. *What if I rest,* I thought. *I'm so tired.*

Perhaps I'll die in my sleep.

Would it be so bad, to rest on my cool pillow and never suffer again?

I tried to climb back onto the bed. Too far, it was too far.

My head rested on the floor. I slept.

Other than aches from sleeping on the floor, I feel like myself. I don't know what happened. I looked at my reflection with distrust. Nothing like this has happened to me before. Somehow, my body betrayed me. I dumped my current bottle of vitamins into the toilet. I had a new bottle waiting, with a different batch number. Enough to last until the next delivery anyway. I didn't know who to call for the refill. Jennifer usually handled that for me. I held the phone and nearly texted her.

No. I don't want to tell her about this. I feel ashamed, somehow. Like a child that needs closer oversight. I'll take care of it myself. I'll walk to the coffee shop. I'll get a pastry and coffee from Brendan.

I can't do this. I don't want to write anymore.

CHAPTER 8

Sorry, diary. It's been a few days.

I'm now at work, on break. I had a new playlist ready for work today, not one I've made, just something I found. It's a mix called *Antique Electronica.* The first song was too intense for a morning at work, so I skipped over it. The next song was gentler. I enjoyed the simplicity building, the layers of it folding over itself to become a new sound, like a journey from a field into a forest.

I opened the document management software. For a split second, you can't see the queues, only the total number of documents across all processing groups.

12,643.

What?

The most I've seen before is 781! This number was so wrong, it felt mythical.

I opened the queues and scrolled. I can't explain exactly what

I noticed in that first look. Just—wrongness. Why was everything going wrong already? I just wanted to sit here and work and be good at something and then go home.

I looked at each automatically generated filename again, then at the sizes. I logged myself out of call rotation and walked over to Scott's cubicle.

"Good morning. Was there a technical problem with the scanning department?"

"Not just scanning. We got a shitload of incoming docs, too. A lot of work to get through."

He had answered a question, but not my question. I reviewed the file names and sizes in my memory. Someone would've noticed, right? They already knew and I was being annoying? I looked around at everyone, stressed and diligent, clicking and typing away. They weren't acting like they knew. They didn't see it.

"Um, I think these are duplicates? Maybe?"

Scott grumbled, loaded three of the packets on his own and compared them in the document viewer.

"These are different."

He wasn't going to listen to me again. I thought of all the people on my team, excited about the overtime, but heedless of the danger if this oversight was discovered by someone else. Scott may lose his job, and he was the only reason our team had what comforts it had. I had to make him listen. I stepped closer. I needed his computer to show him the truth.

"May I?"

Scott pushed his chair away. I closed two of the windows he opened, scrolled through the general queue, and selected a packet. I backed away and he resumed his examination.

"Mother of Christ," he muttered. "Happened once before, years ago. Had to get the geeks to delete the dupes. Took them all damn day. What do ya think, Ver. Any ideas?"

A voice inside of me screamed. Don't stand out. Shrug!

He has a solution. JUST SHRUG.

Another voice inside of me whispered, *I know what to do. I can be helpful.*

In the end, I chose to be helpful.

"Each scan has a unique time stamp and file size. Maybe we could ask tech support to expand the decimal place for the file size? Then we can sort the queue by size, and just process one from each pair? Then maybe the tech support can delete the oldest files from the queue every twenty minutes or so?"

Scott grunted. He didn't love the idea.

I left and wondered which is worse—sharing an idea and having it ignored, or withholding an idea? I can't decide. It is as if two parts of me, one that wishes to hide and another that wishes to act, are always fighting to get out. I wish I could agree with myself.

Back at my desk, an email notification dinged. Scott shared the process with the team, cc'd his boss, and didn't mention me at all.

I felt satisfaction, genuine relief, but why had I hesitated? Why this impulse to hide? Why should I blend in? I have heard of people not wanting to stand out. Is this what they mean? Perhaps something happened to me before the accident, in my past life. I need to get over it. When I become a mother, I'll need to stand up to doctors, teachers, other parents, to keep my little girl safe. I need to learn to be assertive, to take control, for her.

I'm home now.

My plan worked out OK, people thanked Scott, the queue was

empty at the end of the day, and all was well.

On the train ride home, I read an article about container ships that depressed me. They have consistently ranked at the top of polluters. In fact, two dozen of the top polluting cargo ships account for more pollution than all cars currently driven on earth. Much of their cargo is unnecessary—rubber duckies to refill claw machines in arcades, extra cables sold with devices that no one needs or uses. They often ship the same cargo back and forth across the ocean. Orange slices picked in South America shipped to Thailand for packaging and delivered to North America for consumption.

There's an even dumber example: a major electric car manufacturer purchases metal from Asia and ships it to the United States for stamping. After that, they send it back to Asia for welding, only to have it return for assembly. This, for some reason, is financially cheaper and allows the company to claim the car is made in the United States for taxation and marketing purposes.

Recently, Nordic countries and some Pacific Island nations, themselves heavily affected by the changing climate, have required that all container ships cut unnecessary trips and switch their fleets to renewable energy. Renewable-powered ships use solar panels, generators powered by waves, batteries charged at geothermal plants, and even sails. This requirement has not come without a cost. Some shipping companies simply abandoned these countries. However, the EU is debating whether all participant nations should prohibit shipping for nonessential transport, and then further require that the energy be entirely renewable. There is such corruption, so much money and so many powerful entities that would suffer, I cannot imagine it passing. I wish the powerful weren't so evil. I wish someone could make doing the right thing appealing to these people.

I didn't want to read more. Progress seems impossible. It's all too depressing. It's dinnertime now, but I'm not hungry, exactly. A coffee and pastry seemed appetizing. I could go downstairs and walk to the coffee shop before they close, I thought. Brendan wouldn't be working, not that he was a particular draw, but having someone unfamiliar prepare my order where familiarity is a key to the enjoyment is off-putting.

I considered the origins of the coffee beans. Container ships. The cups, the paper bags for the pastries, the ingredients for the pastries, the materials used to construct the pastry counter—everything probably arrived on a container ship. I abandoned a walk for a treat. Instead, I'm sitting here, looking out the window. Bicyclists flit by, their work secured in backpacks, their helmets shining in the mix of setting sun and streetlight. All of that stuff arrived on container ships.

Pointless, I thought bitterly. I'm going to get drunk, watch a Jane Austen miniseries, and put together a puzzle.

CHAPTER 9

ULTRASPEED WIRELESS SERVICE
WILL NOT REACH MIDWEST UNTIL
NEXT YEAR, SAYS FCC CHAIR

Forgive me, diary, it's been two days since my last entry.

That's a dumb joke.

I realized midway through a task at work that I hadn't made a follow-up appointment with Dr. Parsons. I hadn't even considered it. I don't want to make a follow-up appointment. And like that, I know now I'll never see him again.

I texted Sarah for the name of her doctor. After all, I told myself, Jennifer hadn't seen Dr. Parsons—he was merely a referral. She would never have tolerated his ink-stained jacket and musty office carpet. Besides, Sarah had actual infertility and conceived three children through her treatments. You can't argue with those results. Sarah replied quickly with the information I needed. I blocked out time in my work calendar to set the appointment. I even included a celebratory emoji in the title.

I made a decision! I felt refreshed. I jumped back into the routine of work with enthusiasm.

Double-click on a packet of documents in the file list. The viewer window opens. I skim the packet. I recognize the clinic logo. This place still uses paper files and scans us the new stuff to upload. The VA required all clinics to switch to the document manager years ago, so this clinic must be hot shit to get an exception.

I tab over to the database software, put the cursor in the search field and type MEDID, followed by the number scrawled across the top of the file.

No results.

I return to my viewer window, scroll through the scanned pages. A military service ID number, yes! I return to the database software and type MILID, followed by that number.

A match.

I confirm I have the correct person. The clinic wrote a 4 instead of a 7 in the MEDID. I roll my eyes, then use the long edit field to enter the type of entry, file descriptions, and destination.

```
DE   RCVD   ENROLL   PACK,   PRELIM
EXAM, POST-OP SUM, EYE EXAM, CERT
OF  DIS,  REQ  FOR  NEURO,  REQ  FOR
     PROSTH, FWRD TO INTAKE.
```

I return to the viewer window and count out the pages that begin and end each document type. Pages 1 through 3, enrollment packet. Pages 4 through 5, preliminary exam. Page 6 is the post-op summary. The eye exam is 7 through 12 and contains photos of extensive injuries to the eye socket and eye.

I pause on this section. The soldier's eye is beyond repair. In his young face, well, the uninjured portion of his young face, I see sorrow, even shame. I return to page 2, where his demographic information shows he was only nineteen at the time of the injury. Nineteen. Still a child, really. What a shame. An IED attack during a routine patrol mission. One of his team was killed in the attack. Perhaps another document processor is working on that young person's packet now, so his parents can collect their death benefits. What a disgusting failure of society.

Page 13 is his certificate of disability, 14 a handwritten note from an eye specialist for a referral to a neurologist. Reason? Chronic pain. Page 15 is a request for a prosthetic consult. This is the most recent document in the packet. I can imagine how it came about—he had heard of brain implants, ones like Jennifer's team develops.

A few different companies make implants for the visual cortex, but Perilaus makes the best one, and an eye to go with it. It doesn't replicate true human vision; digital translations of the world are too dissimilar from biological ones. No, the eye only interprets contrast and movement. Still, the prosthetic would look like his own biological one—not identical, of course, but like a mate. It would react to light changes. It would move and track objects along with the biological eye, aided by the implant. He didn't need a perfect copy of a human eye. He simply needed the two to function and allow him to blend in. They would work in harmony, different but together, unnoticed by the world around him. Maybe it would be the thing that helped him start a new life, with new expectations.

I froze. How did I know all that? I've never looked any of this up before. Did Sarah or Jennifer tell me? A discomfort arose, one I feel just as strongly now.

How did I know these things? Who told me? When did I learn them?

Then a wave of calm, also familiar. The troublesome thoughts gently tucked back to bed. I didn't feel entirely at ease, though. The calm felt artificial, somehow. I moved on to the next packet.

And the next.

And the next.

I do it for six hours a day, give or take, five days a week. It's not dramatic, world changing, or fun, but I like it. It's like a video game, almost, with real people and their stories. It makes me feel in touch with society and the government. I learn how these soldiers and their families grow and suffer. I see beyond the Support Our Troops social-media posturing to how the choices made by vain, old cowards in hallowed halls far removed from the battlefields turn out.

Anyway, now I am on break. The room is nearly empty. Hardly anyone takes a break at this time of day. I'm sitting at a small table far from the television and vending machines. I called Sarah's doctor's office and was immediately put on hold for several minutes. When I finally spoke to a receptionist, there were busy sounds of life in the background. The person seemed annoyed and indifferent. I wondered: what else did they have to do? Wasn't this their job?

"New patient, OK. We have an opening on…July…7th. Morning or afternoon? Actually, we only have afternoon. Do you want it?"

Two months out! I agreed to that appointment, though I requested to be on a waitlist for something earlier. "I can make it in anytime—I have no vacation plans and my work is very flexible."

I gave my personal information, insurance information, and contact details. I heard the familiar sounds of data entry on the other end.

Another unsettling difference. Dr. Parsons's receptionist had a computer, and she did type on it, though I couldn't say she was busy. She never answered any incoming calls, though she was occasionally on the phone. In fact, I don't think I ever heard a phone ring in that office.

"Alright, we'll see you on July 7th at 2 p.m. at our office downtown. Unless, of course, something opens up." I frowned at the sarcasm but didn't respond to it. I thanked them, hung up, and looked out the window for a few moments.

There is a beige stucco office building across the freeway from ours. It's been empty the entire time I've worked here. Why? Was the rent too high? Was it condemned? I don't know. I only know that this satellite city, like nearly every city, is experiencing a housing crisis. And there, in view every day, was an empty building. Could it be converted into housing? Could it become a safe space for a few dozen families? Could it help lift parents out of misery, children out of poverty? No, instead it was empty and purposeless, probably used so a conglomerate can add income loss and depreciation to their taxes. No one can live there.

I have to laugh at myself. Here I sit, with a seemingly useless womb taxing my metabolism and giving nothing in return, but I'm mad about some empty office building facing a freeway.

I sent Sarah a text with an update. She replied immediately. She must be sitting at one of the kids' lessons or is nursing the baby.

Wow, July! That's quick.

I turned to the news on the TV. The presenter is talking about how social media is upset about one movie star ridiculing another over their performance in a film that was exceptionally popular. Screenshots from posts appeared from accounts named things like LazyDog748324 and StashAttack. I looked around at my coworkers, who weren't paying attention. Whole world is falling apart around us, and they can't even be bothered to pay attention to the distractions.

Home now. I'll finish this record of my day and then do something fun.

I went back to my desk and put on a new curated song list, described as ambient techno. The first track began with a sound like waves made of pixels crashing on a digital sea. There was a color to the sound, somehow. The first batch of work was gentle, easy, fun. The music was perfect. It was complicated enough to remind me I could not create music, while accessible enough to be just what I needed right now.

Something had put me in this state. Was it the process of abandoning my last doctor, of making this new appointment, or what the appointment represented? I've done a good thing. I'm taking care of myself.

And yet, when I started working, I had a feeling of dread about this whole process. I can't quite understand it. It's like there's something going on I don't quite want to see.

When I had finished that thought, I resumed work. I loaded a new packet, quickly paged through each image, memorizing each document type as I went along, with their beginning and end pages. Just as I started to segment them in my mind, I paused.

I paged backward to confirm and groaned. Someone had abandoned this packet. There were two different patients in these documents. Pages 1, 2, 5 through 8, and 10 through 17 were one person, and 3, 4, and 9 were someone else. As I looked for the first ID number, I heard chatter behind me.

I didn't turn around. I knew who it was.

The soft piano of the song failed to mask the sounds of Dominick, Scott's boss, and the division manager. They sat eight feet behind me, watching me work. They like to watch people work, and I didn't think I could complain. I ignored them as best as I could and continued.

I didn't bother entering the provided medical ID number. It was only fourteen digits, not sixteen, and the Julian date portion of the ID was thirty-two years in the future. I couldn't trust anything written by this office. Instead, I skipped to form A-141, an injury incident report. It's automatically generated for each soldier when they transfer care, with the service number in the bottom left corner. I pulled the file, entered the individual document names into the data entry field, then began the trickier task of separating the digital batch into two separate batches, before then subdividing the primary batch into the appropriate file types.

The next song was also quiet, designed to soothe whatever ailed the listener. It would've worked on me, too, but it did nothing to conceal the two men watching me without my permission. I could almost see their reflections in my monitor screen. I felt like a zoo animal. I decided that I would finish this set of documents and leave. I'd scoop up random papers and pretend I needed help with something, or simpler still, I'd just make for the restroom.

Even thinking of it now, safe at home, I feel anxious and jittery. I hate being watched. I'm glad I didn't make any mistakes with my work. The second party's MEDID number was neatly written at the top by a phlebotomist, saving me some effort. I logged the descriptions for those file types and uploaded the individual documents under the corresponding MEDID number.

With that, this monkey was done dancing. I put my phone out of rotation, locked my computer screen, and escaped for the ladies' room. The production board featured my name again, at the top, just to remind me of the advantages of being typical.

"Fearful of praise and notice as other women are of neglect."

I'm a goddamn Fanny Price. What an insult.

And yet, whoever I am, I have to admit that line describes me pretty well. Maybe if I was in love with someone, as Fanny was with her cousin (gross), I'd want their praise and notice. Perhaps. I doubt it. I can't imagine wanting any attention at all.

I need to watch something different when I work on puzzles.

Also, I need to relax. Coming home and writing down all this stressful stuff is not relaxing. I'm going to take a bath.

Well, I did not take a bath.

Jennifer called while the tub was filling up. Her live-in nanny had a personal emergency. Jennifer asked if I could come help her with Max while she finished a presentation for work. I was thrilled. I agreed in a normal way, of course, and went over. I love Max. I also love Sarah's kids, especially individually, but as a collection? It's intense. Max is a quiet, observant kid. He is five years old now and bright, though still very much a young boy.

When I arrived, he was working on some school assignments on his tablet. I joined him on the couch for what we call a "work snuggle"—his little head rested on my arm as he completed each problem. I gently brushed his sandy-blond curls from his forehead while he concentrated. I didn't think the angle was good for him, though I knew better than to adjust him without a request. He's Jennifer's son and knows what he wants. We sat like that, him quietly working while I, as Sarah puts it, got a hit of oxytocin.

Jennifer's apartment is enormous. Bigger than Sarah's house, easily. It stretches across most of the footprint of a luxury apartment building downtown. Out each window, a new breathtaking view of the city, river to river, and each high-rise building in between. I love to be there in the stormy weather, when the load balancers strain against the strong winds and lightning crashes through the clouds just outside. No storms tonight, though. Just a pleasant, bland evening.

The view, though lovely, lacks personality. If you didn't know the geography here, it could be any cityscape, in any part of the world. It has the same sharp coldness as Jennifer's home, all modern and angles and glass and metal. Does Jennifer love things like that, or does she force herself to be a person who loves them?

She came to check on us a few times. I smiled at first, as if to say, I'm good! Thank you for checking! Until I realized she was making sure Max wasn't bothered by me. That hurt.

It's weird. Jennifer never leaves me alone with Max. Sarah has left me alone with her kids, not often, but sometimes, but Jennifer won't. I wonder if she would've trusted me before the accident. I wonder if the accident was my fault. Maybe the rage I feel from time to time is a flicker of who I used to be. She would know; she knows my history, though she never shares it. She knows me better than I know myself and doesn't trust me. Maybe I'm a monster.

I'm going to return focus to Max. I was following along with his work silently. He was doing so well on the assignments. He seemed to have learned a great deal since my last time watching him. Children's brains are astonishing. They take in information and process it without you ever knowing, then surprise or even scare you with their own awareness. Max once told Sam, Sarah's eldest child, that an action star had muscle stimulating implants. He then went on to describe with surprising accuracy how the device was implanted. After numbing the entire limb, there is an injection full of nano machines. Once they make contact with the unique cellular composition of muscle tissue, tendrils unfurl and are carried along the surface, expanding across that individual muscle's fibers. He even explained that early models would break the bones of the test subjects. Jennifer rarely lets him watch movies or shows, so how did he learn that?

Max interrupted my thoughts with a gentle caress.

"Auntie Vera, may I have a snack, please?"

"Of course, sweetheart!"

If he doesn't provide a specific request, that means he'll accept whatever he is given. I had him move to the kitchen table while I rummaged through the fridge. I assembled a plate of carrots, apple slices, and a glob of peanut butter with a cup of whole milk on the side. I found a little paper napkin left over from one of Jennifer's dinner parties and folded it into a triangle, then set it alongside the plate. He seemed pleased. I expected him to resume his work on the tablet. He sometimes eats while he works.

Instead, he set it aside and examined me.

"What's that look for, little man?"

"Where is your mommy and daddy?"

I forced a smile. "They died. You and your mommy are my family now."

"Was it scary?"

"When they died?"

"Yeah."

I didn't particularly want to do this right now, but Max waited patiently for my answer. He was asking from love and concern. I sighed.

"It probably was. I don't remember. I hurt my head and it made me forget."

"But it didn't make it so you couldn't walk or talk?"

"I think it did, but only for a little while. I got better in the hospital."

"But you can't remember your mommy?" He looked unhappily down at his apple slices. I walked over and put my hand on his arm to soothe him, to give him my undivided attention, and to remind him of the warmth of the present.

"Things like that don't happen very often," I said softly.

"Where did the accident happen?"

"I don't remember," I said.

"You don't remember any of it?"

"Nope. I remember other things from when I was a bit older than you, like my dad teaching me how to ride a bike under big trees. And my mom at the kitchen counter, in front of a pretty window."

"Do you miss your mommy?"

"Of course," I said. "But now I have you and your mommy and Aunt Sarah and Jack and Sam and Fiona."

"I'm mad at Jack. He hit me with a plastic golf club in his backyard when I played with his race cars."

I recognized this mood. He was going to jump from one negative thought to the next unless he was interrupted. I squeezed his arm and smiled down at his little face, to convey acceptance. I went to the piano in the corner of the room. I sat at the bench and played Chopin Nocturne in E Minor. Max ate his snack and watched me closely.

Adults feel much the same as Max about my story; no one wants to think that a simple choice like driving a car a few miles can kill your family and destroy your life. The proportions of consequence are too skewed. In a world where death is typically the consequence of carelessness, catastrophe by random chance is terrifying. But a child, already subjected to the whims of all-powerful adults, can acknowledge the chaos and question it. Adults hear the story and turn from it, and me, in fear.

I finished one song and asked if he had any requests.

"Did your mommy teach you how to play? My mommy is going to teach me."

"You'll have to play for me sometime!" I said, knowing Jennifer cannot play the piano.

I resumed the song, this time adding a gently playful melody. Max swung his foot as he turned his attention to his carrots. As I played for him, I thought of other tunes and stitched them together, seeking out similar strains of sound to blend from one movement to the next. There's a unity beneath many songs, a reflection of basic impulses used to create music. You can use these expressions to present the facade of something new. Nothing is new, yet it can feel new, and you can enjoy it anyway.

After a few moments, he brushed his hands free of crumbs and slid off the stool.

"Can we snuggle again?" he asked.

I closed the lid back over the keys.

I washed the peanut butter from his fingers and then returned with him to the couch. I pulled the cashmere throw blanket over to where he was snuggled in with his tablet. I held him with one arm as he reclined against my chest. He asked me some questions about his tasks and I answered them.

I admired the remaining shades of babyhood in him as well as the emerging childhood he was growing into. I thought about all the things that must confuse him now. There are so many things that will cause him stress in the future that contain no meaning for him yet. What bliss, what joy, to be a child who knows no violence, hunger, or fear for survival. I held him close, to keep him safe. It comforted me to consider his perspective, simplistic and genuine, focused and unashamed.

This is one of the feelings I want as a mother. An admiration for human development, these changes that accumulate in a small, helpless, and ugly newborn one by one until you sit beside a lovely, unique child who has their own internal life.

Soon, too soon, Max will not snuggle my arm. He will not ask me if the accident was scary, if I miss my mommy. He will conceal these fears that everyone fears, as we all learn to do. New beauties will take the place of open, warm honesty, I know, though my appreciation for them may not be the same. For now, I drink in the moment he is in, recall the journey he has already taken, and acknowledge where he is to go next. I wish I could help him, always, as I can help him now. I wish it could be this easy forever.

Jennifer found us asleep on the couch. I don't recall being tired, or Max dozing off. She lifted him from me with soft cooing. As they departed, she rubbed his back in a way that only a mother knows how to do.

I rose and scratched out the sleep from my inner eye. There was a slick of drool on my lip. I hurriedly wiped it away, fixed my hair back into my ponytail and rose, sheepish, as I checked my watch. It was a half hour before his bedtime.

"He hasn't had dinner," I told Jennifer when she returned.

She shrugged. "He's had enough to fall asleep. Maria will get him something if he needs it. Do you need a cab?"

I shook my head and gathered my things as Jennifer politely ushered me to the door. She opened it, said goodnight, but I hadn't responded yet when she shut the door behind me and threw the deadbolt. I stood for a moment, stung but not surprised. My feelings meant nothing to Jennifer. Do I mean anything to her at all?

I put it behind me as I headed down the hall to the penthouse elevator. Rather than feel sorry for myself, I thought of something pleasant. The walks I would take with my daughter. The crunch of the fall leaves under her little boots, the growing chill in the air. I might have a baby by next year's Halloween. What kind of costume would I get her? Would I take her in a stroller, or would I incorporate her costume into a baby carrier? What do people normally do? The whole situation seems novel to me. Perhaps I didn't have friends with children before.

No, it's more than that. I have no memories of trick-or-treating. I wonder why.

CHAPTER 10

IRELAND DECOMMISSIONS LAST
ACTIVE-DUTY NAVAL SHIPS; FLEET
OF DRONES NOW ON FISHERY PATROL

I woke up a bit earlier than usual and tried a new step in my morning routine. I scrubbed my face with what was labeled as a gentle exfoliant. It felt good, but I think I overdid it; my skin is pretty red. Now I'm wearing a cooling mask while I learn about the Irish navy. Thankfully, my toast fits in the gap of mask paper around my mouth. It was pretty stupid to try something new before work. Lesson learned.

I switched the channel. A new makeup line for thwarting image recognition was demonstrated by two morning news anchors. They cut to a brief segment that provided a history of image recognition cameras, including interviews with privacy advocates who railed against the use of the technology by government agencies. When the segment ended, the female anchors listed the safety and privacy advantages of the makeup, though they seemed hung up on how it broke autofocus on their smartphones.

I peeled off my face mask and threw it in the trash, then let out a yawn. I expected that tools of this kind would generate superficial complaints. I was bored of the news. On another channel, I found music videos. They were playing classics from the '90s.

I sat back at the table while the face mask goo soaked into my skin, and watched Alanis Morrisette singing to her different selves in a sedan. I love the song, and the style of the video is cool. What a contrast between this world of the past and my own. No self-driving cars, no digital maps, no inescapable surveillance back then. I don't even think her sedan had power locks.

There was the internet, of course, though it was slow and not widely used. Video sharing was nearly impossible, even image uploads were tedious. The general public had no idea the kinds of technological advances they would soon face, whether they wanted to or not. They were just excited to have cable TV.

Alanis keeps singing, as though alone and unobserved. What would true privacy feel like? I know of stories where people in the past left their lives behind and started over. They took a horse or a train or a car to somewhere and truly remade themselves. Teenagers left their hometowns for college and formed themselves into an adult with no evidence of the past. There were even people with multiple identities. Not just spies, but people like pilots with two families in two different cities.

Was access to that kind of freedom invigorating? Or was it suffocating? Was it like choice paralysis, where there are suitable options all around you and so you do nothing, frozen, waiting on more information to clarify your course of action?

What would I do if I lived in the past, before computers, when I could be anyone? I considered my complexion, my womanhood, and the course this society has taken. I could do more than many people, but no, I couldn't be anyone. With freedom from identity came freedom from consequences, some of which are necessary, especially for those with more power than me. Social consequences may be all that keep people from the monsters they wish to become. Beneath their day jobs and sensible cars and modest homes and nuclear families, they are savages. Like Robert Castor, with his nasty breath, who put his arm on me.

In this past I envision, he would be free as well. What would I do about people like him?

I'm going to see what Sarah and Jennifer say about this at lunch today.

OK. I've just returned from lunch. I didn't bring up my societal-impact-of-privacy question. Instead, I thought about the deeper issue, the central piece to all the things that bothered me in these news stories: the powerful living without consequences. A discussion about a hypothetical evasion from justice didn't seem appropriate, so I brought up a recent case where a wealthy man who had been convicted of violent rape had reoffended within weeks of his release. When our salads arrived, I asked what they thought should have been done with him.

"Jesus, Vera. I'm about to eat," Sarah said.

"I'm sorry. I'm curious what you two think should happen to someone like him."

"Here we go." Jennifer shook her head as she stirred sugar into her coffee.

"Ok, fine. He should be dead," Sarah said firmly and resumed eating her salad. "He should've been dead after the first offense."

"Wait, what?" I asked, looking to Jennifer for some support.

Jennifer ignored me. "The death penalty isn't a deterrent. It shouldn't exist."

"Not as a deterrent," Sarah said. "Some people are too destructive to society to continue living within society."

"Oh, how I have missed this argument," Jennifer said.

"Hang on. You don't believe in rehabilitation?" I asked.

"Sure, for lots of people. Not for everyone."

"What if they develop some technology for this?" I pressed. "Didn't you work on a brain implant for criminal behavior?"

Sarah set down her fork. "*I* didn't work on it. I *helped out* another team for a bit. It was for children with sociopathic tendencies. It never worked, though. I'm talking about evil adults, who will continue to be evil unless we lock them away or... Anyway, that project was canceled before it got to human trials. It caused brain damage."

"Just because it didn't work then doesn't mean it will never work," Jennifer said.

"I'm not going to argue about that stupid device. I'm not going to argue about punishment and justice, either. I don't have any power to do anything. My point is that some people are beyond redemption. They aren't going to make society better. They are an expense in prison and a danger outside of it. Keeping them alive anywhere is asking for trouble. Humans have always killed people who harm the whole. They did it for generations. Now we're civilized, letting people back in as if that makes us noble or something."

I let myself sit with my alarm. How did I not know Sarah had such strong feelings on this topic? Do we all carry around these rivers of darkness in us?

Jennifer shook her head. "Human groups killed people who have done nothing wrong for generations as well. And where would you draw the line?"

"I'm not talking genocide. You know I'm not."

The waiter approached, a confused smile on his face. We put in our food orders as normally as we could. I watched the women across from me, feeling a bit guilty. Jennifer looked bored, composed, as usual, but Sarah was agitated. Not in the way Steve agitated her. This was different.

When the waiter left, Sarah started counting on her fingers. "Murderers. Child rapists. Violent rapists. Adults who severely injure children. Corporate executives who kill through their action or inaction."

I leaned closer. Jennifer raised her eyebrows. "Negligent corporate executives are equivalent to child rapists?"

"I'm grouping bad people who do repeated, serious harm for their own benefit. Look at that nuclear meltdown ten years ago! All their efforts to minimize costs, and the executives totally aware of their dangerous behavior. Or that developer in Jacksonville who reused lead pipes in low-income housing. Cruise ship companies who left their employees to die offshore during the pandemic. Anyone who uses a position of power to prioritize their own interests over the health and safety of others should pay."

"Pay?" Jennifer asked.

"I didn't mean *pay*. I meant they should be excluded from society."

"Permanently, I take it."

Sarah looked away from Jennifer. She was giving vent to a deeper pain, one fundamental to her, one I didn't know about. I wasn't sure Jennifer knew either. Maybe she did, though. It's hard to tell what she does and doesn't know.

"In a perfect world, who do you think would oversee these decisions?" I asked.

"Thank you. See, Jennifer? Oversight. That's the real problem," Sarah said. "Our judicial branch is racist and classist. The whole thing would have to be torn down and rebuilt. What I want would never work. I know that."

"Then this rant was pointless," Jennifer said.

"You're right, I'll wait until I'm in charge of capital punishment to share my opinions," Sarah said.

I was intrigued by Sarah's list, but also curious about Jennifer's hesitancy. Were emotions clouding Sarah's judgement, or was the imposition of extreme rationality obscuring the truth from Jennifer? Which way did I lean?

"Ladies, it's my lunch break. Can we talk about something other than executing people?" Jennifer's tone was very much the manager subduing her junior staff. Sarah rolled her eyes but shook it off.

"Did you hear about Avery?"

I didn't know Avery, so I tuned them out.

On the sidewalk across the street, a food-delivery robot moved with steadfast purpose. From my position, the pace of the little bot looked almost dangerous. It certainly made some pedestrians nervous. Any autonomous vehicles designed for sidewalks are programmed to reduce their speed when pedestrians are nearby. Of course, there is no such limitation on human couriers, who can drive bikes or scooters on the sidewalk at whatever speed they choose.

The little bot paused as a graffiti-remover bot sprayed marker off the side of a building. It was almost as if the delivery robot showed deference to the cleaner. I wonder if it knew they are of the same kind?

A group of teenagers passed by and laughed. One made a urination gesture next to the robots. I heard one of them say, "I have the greatest urge to kick all these fuckers into the street." I cringed in anticipation, but there was no violence. Not this time.

"What do you think, Vera?" Jennifer asked.

I turned back. "Sorry, I wasn't paying attention."

"Our friend left academia," Sarah explained. "They got a big offer from a hardware firm. Their mother is sick, and they needed the extra money. Their adviser found out and was upset. She said she shouldn't have wasted her time mentoring someone who was just going to go into the private sector. Made a whole rant about it online."

"What do you two think?" I asked Sarah. They laughed.

"You always ask what we think. We want to know what you think! We both jumped ship from academia. We're hardly unbiased."

I looked back out the window and thought for a moment. "I think everyone has an obligation to do as much good as they can, especially when there is someone weaker than you that needs help. If you can do more good at a private company, you should do it."

"Well, shit. I left for the money!" Sarah said. Jennifer laughed. I laughed, too.

CHAPTER 11

TOP FACIAL RECOGNITION FIRM USED
PRISONER DATA WITHOUT CONSENT

I haven't been avoiding you, diary. There's been very little to report.

It's the long days of summer now. I continue my morning routine. Stare at the painting, shower, moisturize, vitamins, stretch-mark oil. My hair smoothed straight and only enough makeup to look like I am an adult. A plain button-down secured one button from the top, clean and pressed dress slacks and sensible shoes. I keep using extra deodorant. It's either hot—or muggy and hot. Fall can't come soon enough.

Monday through Friday, I head into work, where the best days are those with the fewest interactions with others. Twice a week I meet with Jennifer and Sarah for lunch. I've been going to Sarah's house more often lately to help with the children. I occasionally go to Jennifer's. I've been in a pattern, waiting for this next doctor's appointment, waiting for my life to begin.

It is now the morning of July 6th, the day before the OB/GYN appointment. There were, in fact, no openings. I did receive a call moving the location of my appointment to another address. I looked online and this appears to be a very recent change in location. Nothing is recorded about this address yet. It's near to a subway stop, which is nice.

I'm watching the news as I eat a slice of cinnamon toast. They are discussing whether a new tool for scanning comatose patients for locked-in syndrome violates the Sheldon-Claxton Accord.

I looked up the actual agreement, because I feel silly nodding as if I understand when I actually don't. Seems strange I haven't done this before. It's almost as if I don't want to know.

Here's a paraphrase of what the Wikipedia entry says:

The Sheldon-Claxton Accord is a commitment to not engage in artificial intelligence research that endangers humanity. It was first created by a consortium of scientists and ethicists and was presented at a conference. A lively debate turned into an argument and then a physical altercation on stage.

Soon after, the Ivies, followed by other prestigious universities, adopted it. Then countries codified the agreement and established specific regulations on what kinds of new research into artificial intelligence systems could be conducted. Major corporations followed suit, at least at first. In recent years, companies have become more cavalier, especially smaller, privately funded ventures. Several countries have not signed on to the accord, rendering it more anti-competitive than anything else.

Jennifer seemed unwilling to discuss her opinion in detail. Sarah only said that smaller companies could stay under the radar and violate Sheldon-Claxton. She also explained how many new technologies from large firms meet the accord's definition of artificial intelligence systems. Once the developments proved helpful to society, governments turned a blind eye to their own laws and regulations.

In this particular news story, a piece of software discovered a young woman was in a locked-in state of consciousness, not comatose. What's more, the software made it possible for her family to communicate with her. She was able to tell her mother that she loved her and asked her little sister to read a specific book aloud.

They let a woman trapped inside of herself reach the outside world.

A scientist presented the story's opposing argument, which made him feel like a villain. The text at the bottom identified him as Matthew Christensen, a name I recalled from the garden party. "If we create a machine that can identify and measure consciousness, wouldn't that make itself close to consciousness? How would you know if that machine had achieved consciousness, if you train it on humans who present as unconscious? This isn't just an academic consideration. Cognitive software may make moral judgments about who should and should not be allowed to communicate, and may choose to conceal aware patients from human operators. I hope this young woman and others like her gain the ability to recover, but isn't this the sort of advance that the Sheldon-Claxton Accord was created to prevent?"

As if in reply, they switched to one of the creators of the technology. "We didn't create a consciousness. That's impossible. There is no replicating the human spirit. There's simply no need to panic here. The technology is sophisticated, but it is not the work of science fiction. It is simply an algorithm, reviewed and edited by people, that checks for a series of indicators of consciousness. Scientists and doctors control the data and determine what is and isn't valuable. This is well within the accord. We need to accept as an industry that information and skill constantly increase. You can't make arbitrary definitions of what is and isn't artificial intelligence and try to stifle technological progress."

I do not understand Dr. Christensen's argument, or even why the accord came into existence. What is the problem? So what if machines gain consciousness? Isn't it possible that those pieces of software might be more morally sound than the humans who created them?

I don't know. I keep thinking of all these resources people hoard for their own benefit, or perceived benefit, and now we're arguing who has the right to have a soul. Meanwhile, some lady in a hospital just wants to talk to her family.

I'm meeting Sarah for ice cream with her kids after work today. I'll ask her then.

For now, I head to work. Yay.

I'm on break now. I logged in two minutes late today. I can't say why. I feel strange. Incomplete, maybe. I stopped on my way through the parking lot. I stared at the trees. The leaves have wilted in the heat, the branches like gnarled hands reaching to the sky. The air smelled like hot rain, though none was forecast.

I thought about leaving. About not going into that giant, boring building, not logging into my computer, and not touching my phone. I love my job, but I don't want my job right now. What if I could just rent a car, drive to some mountain or forest or beach, and disappear for a little while. That would be nice.

There's a beautiful cemetery in the hills full of old, ornate gravestones. I've seen it in movies, I know it is nearby, yet I've never been. It seems morbid, to ditch work to go to a cemetery, but I know impulses such as this serve a purpose. Even Sarah and Jennifer and their children feel this way at times. Perhaps that is part of why Jennifer is so tense. These impulses are a message from inside of you that you have reached the limit of your capabilities. By not following them, you are denying your humanity.

Ah, diary. Since you know I'm on break, you know that I did go into work today. Why? Well, there were no scheduled meetings. I'd rather ditch work on a Wednesday, when we hold our all-hands meeting. Maybe I'll ditch next Wednesday, a delayed lazy day.

I logged into my computer and my phone. Another team's manager walked by my cubicle and scowled over the wall at me. I glared right back at her. Oh, fuck off—Sarah's laughing voice came to mind.

I worked. I sorted through over one hundred medical records before this break. The only one of note was a young mother who lost a leg. She was discharged and is waiting for approval for the latest proprioceptive prosthetic. She lives in a second-floor walk-up apartment with her two young children. Her husband works on an oil rig off the coast of Texas. A note in one of the papers said the new leg would help her carry groceries and her youngest, a toddler, up the stairs.

I found her photo in the file. She looks healthy and has a kind face. I can imagine that her children have her curly hair, or her carob-colored eyes. Something in the sense of her, as represented by those pages, gave me the impression she served in the military for one specific reason; perhaps it was a college education or to escape a dysfunctional home. Her enlistment location was in a state known for sweltering summers and economic oppression. She had escaped something. And what was the cost? A permanent disability, which she must manage, along with two young children and her college education, on a tight income?

But she is happy. You can see it in the photo. She just needs a bit of help.

The last sheet in her paperwork was a transcript from a college in her new hometown, a chilly, bustling city on the coast. Her school records shouldn't have been included and I shouldn't have read them, but I read them anyway. Four classes, four A's. I smiled for her, proud of this persevering stranger.

I submitted her paperwork and moved on to the next task, though I don't remember any of those files. It is her story that will stay with me for the rest of the day. Perhaps it will become a permanent memory, the ones we cannot place the where and the why but the meaning remains perfectly clear, guiding our principles, all of our lives.

You wouldn't know, but I just paused writing for several minutes. I've been staring off through the window, at a view I've seen so many times. My break ended a long time ago. I'm still here, though, saturated in a fresh misery.

Without her permission, I read her file, learned her struggles, and did nothing to help her. How many personal tragedies have I read in my months at this job? I haven't felt this incompetent shame until now. I wish I could do something for her, or the young man who lost his eye. What could I possibly do? I can't become a mother on my own. I can barely help myself.

Once, I heard Max's nanny offer a prayer for one of his little classmates. The boy had been struck by a car in a crosswalk, along with his mother. Maria pleaded for God to spare the little boy, for his own sake and as mercy on his mother. Prayer seems to be a sweet yet confusing gesture. The boy lived, the mother survived, and the family moved far away from that crosswalk. Did the prayer work?

Can I offer such a prayer for the woman from the file, struggling to right herself after so many blows from so many directions? I suppose it depends on the god, or gods, who listen. Would a god be more likely to act on a request if it was offered in support of a total stranger? I wonder.

There is no harm to me or others if I pray. And what if it works? Isn't it worth a try, in case there is a god ready to listen?

I'm back at home now. I left work early, claiming a headache, a lie. I met with Sarah, Jack, Sam, and Fiona at the little ice cream shop near their house. I didn't want to be around anyone, but Sarah insisted. It wasn't too busy. I suppose most people were out at dinner. The walls were a sunny summer yellow, the bay windows large with a perfectly sized window seat for a quick visit by customers. The human salesperson took the orders, while the robot scooper behind him assembled the cones, cups, and bowls with expert precision.

We were here for a celebratory occasion; Jack had recently made it to the top of a moderate-difficulty wall in his climbing class. I rubbed the boy's head affectionately.

"Vera, can you read me my elephant book?" Jack asked before we had even entered the building.

"Of course, but I don't have it with me."

"That's OK, it's in my back-back."

Sarah laughed. "He brought TWO copies. Just in case."

We joined the line and Jack took the two little picture books from his backpack. I crouched to his level to take a look.

"Which one would you like me to read? The one with the circles in the clouds, or the squares?"

"What squares?" Jack asked, squinting at the book covers. Sam and Sarah leaned over too.

"I don't see anything."

"You don't see the square right here?" I asked, pointing at a faint blue square in the white cloud.

"I don't see it. You must have amazing vision," Sarah observed.

"Auntie Vera? Do you have X-ray vision?"

"No, Jack. I'm not even sure I have good regular vision, if I'm seeing squares in clouds." Everyone laughed.

Sarah suggested what I should order, so I did. Earl Grey ice cream with hot fudge in a cone bowl. Jack tugged on my hand, guiding me away from the adults.

Beyond the counter, behind the salesman, the food-prep robot registered our voices and prepared itself. It swung an arm to a row of scoops, freshly cleaned, and attached one. It moved again, swinging the scoop into a scalding bath to sanitize and heat the metal. Now, it was ready to begin.

I took the boys with me to the bench and read the elephant book to them. I paused midway, just for a moment, to look again at the clouds on the cover. I could see the squares there, the squares no one could see. They were telling me something I couldn't understand.

As I reached the second to last page of the book, Sarah approached with the ice creams on a tray. Jack lost interest in the elephant's plight. Sam looked at me scornfully. "You shouldn't let Mom pick out your food all the time."

"I take advice, I don't let her pick out my food."

Jack shook his head. "Remember you had a hot dog with onions at our party? But you hate onions?"

"Wow. I do always pick out your food. What's with that, Vera?"

I averted my eyes, embarrassed. Kids are always watching, I swear.

"I scraped the onions off. It was fine. I do like this ice cream!"

Sarah waved her spoon in the air. "I was thinking about this just now, kids—what's your earliest memory?"

Jack chewed on a cherry as he looked thoughtfully at the wall. Sam answered immediately.

"The neighbor's dog, Judy, barking at me and Daddy when we took the trashcans out."

"Judy? The little terrier? That was a long time ago. We were still at the rental. So, before preschool. Jack? What about you?"

"I think I remember being in my crib. Did we have a sheep, um, what's that thing for babies called. Where you dangle the toys over their heads?"

"A mobile?"

"Yeah, did we, Mommy?"

"No, you had this little cloud set we got from Aunt Becky." Sarah replied, scraping the bottom of her strawberry cordial ice cream.

"Maybe the clouds looked like sheep?" I suggested.

"What about you, Auntie Vera?"

"I remember preschool," I said, looking for the trash.

"Anything specific?" Sarah asked.

"I liked painting. There was a ball I liked. I used to sit and sort shapes and solve puzzles. Oh, I remember one time, I was playing at a table with a friend. The room was so bright, so it must have been near lunchtime. One of my friends had beautiful hair, it was curly and glittering in the sunlight. I was distracted, looking at their hair, when the man pulled the papers out of my hand. He ripped them when he pulled them away from me. I was scolded for some reason. My friend cried. It hurt my feelings."

The children were quiet. Sarah looked at me. "The man?"

"My teacher? I think."

"That's not a good teacher," Jack said with authority.

"What did your friend do?" Sam asked.

"They tried to help me. They cried and tried to get our papers back. The man wouldn't listen. He was like that."

"He's a bad man. Was his name Mr. Bones?" Jack asked.

"No," I frowned, trying to remember. No, it was just out of place. I shrugged. "The man in the lab coat."

Sam told us about one of his mean teachers with an ugly mole. Jack and Sarah shared a quick anecdote about a playground aid who yelled at kids. I wondered why anyone who didn't like children chose to be around them.

Sarah turned to me, her gaze intent and direct. "This man with a lab coat. Do you remember more about him?"

"He was young. There were other teachers, but he was the one who talked to me the most. It's weird, I don't really remember lots of other kids there. It feels like I was sitting alone, with just one friend at a time."

"Maybe you were in time-out," Jack observed, disinterested. He had found a smear of ice cream on his elbow.

"Maybe it was a, like, immersive STEM preschool? That was a whole movement when we were young, wasn't it?"

Sarah didn't respond.

After we had finished our treat, we walked down the block to the park. Jack wanted to go to the big-kid side of the jungle gyms, but Sarah insisted they stay on the young-kid half. She explained to me that the weekday evening crowd at the playground was often rough. Mostly people passing through, trying to get their kids tired before a dinner reservation. Fiona stayed snuggled into the baby carrier on Sarah's chest, dozing off when it was clear her brothers wouldn't be there to entertain her.

We left after a little while. I helped them back to their van and then walked to the train station alone.

So, that was my night. Now I'm in my favorite pajamas, the blue silk ones with the zebras printed on them. Jennifer bought them for me. That's not true. She bought them for herself, but they didn't fit. The legs weren't long enough. I appreciated them, in any case. I know that tomorrow's appointment will be routine, frustratingly routine. A packet of forms to fill out, another physical exam, more blood work ordered. They'll tell me in their soothing script how they'll try all they can. They'll ask me about what partners I've had, and I'll explain that I have none, I want none for this, that I will be using a donor. Their eyebrows will rise as they write that down, like my eyebrows rise when I see an interesting file in the queue, because that is all I am to them: one portion of work in their day with details that might pique their interest, but only for a moment. They won't see me as a person at all.

I understand all this. There will be no surprises. Yet the feeling I feel can only be nervousness. In twelve hours, I could learn that a simple solution exists. I could learn Dr. Parson was incompetent, wasting my time and money, that I only needed to do something simple. I could hear he was some weird pervert, reaching inside of me as some sort of game for his own amusement. That I was not just a victim of his incompetence. A rage in the periphery is bubbling up. I'd hunt him down. I'd kill him.

I'm going to have a glass or two of wine before bed. Sarah told me she always got drunk before these kinds of appointments. I have some Pinot Grigio. I'll give it a try.

CHAPTER 12

It's the morning of my appointment. I didn't end up drinking. I didn't want the hangover. I feel different today, more refreshed. I sat at the edge of the bed to stare at the painting like I normally do. It didn't draw me in as much as it normally does. I looked at it anyway, to keep the routine. I showered, took my vitamins, and applied my stretch-mark oil. I put on makeup and did my hair, and dressed with some extra care. The first sign of something amiss was my hall lights did not turn on as I passed through. From there, I could see the screen on my refrigerator was inactive.

I turned on the news and tried to turn on my toaster. The out-of-service light blinked a steady rhythm. I put my slice of bread in a pan, not sure what else to do to make toast. On the news, the cameras looked slightly odd. The banner at the bottom read that a widespread outage of two major cloud-storage firms had brought down most of the internet. In curiosity, I opened up my favorite map application. It didn't load. I tried a social networking application. Nothing.

I'm writing to you and eating, the news in the background. I keep laughing at how bad this footage is. Jennifer is always bemoaning interdependencies in software, but news cameras? It's funny. I suppose this is what she meant.

Wait. What if they cancel my appointment?

I've just called the doctor's office. What an ordeal.

I had written down the office's phone number in a notepad in my purse. I took it out and tried to dial from my cell phone. It did not ring. Stupid, of course. No cell phones.

I found the old landline telephone I had stashed in the closet. I had to purchase a phone line to get the highest speed internet available, though it seemed only scammers and telemarketers called me on it. I plugged in the clunky plastic device and dialed the number.

A receptionist, voice crackled with tension, answered.

"Hi, I just wanted to confirm that my appointment for today isn't canceled?"

"Canceled? No, no it isn't canceled."

"OK, great. Can I just confirm the address? I had it saved in my calendar."

It sounded like the original address, not the updated one I had received from the other receptionist who had called me.

"Not the new location?" I asked.

"This is our only location."

"OK, thank you," I said to no one; they had already hung up. I held the receiver in my hand for a long moment.

The wrongness of this settled over me. I can't check my call log on my cell phone. I may be bad at a lot of things, but I trust my memory. A person at that office called me and gave me a different address. Was it a mean prank? Maybe someone at the office had brought their teenager to work, who called a bunch of patients and gave them random addresses? Possible, I suppose. I'm glad I called them. I guess this outage saved me some trouble after all.

Now I'm eating my toast and watching the news. I'll summarize.

The outage started at 3 a.m. A loosely organized hacking collective called Move 37 claimed credit. The stated goal for this attack is retaliation against the US government's contract with facial recognition firm Transparency. Founded ten years ago by an artist turned programmer, Transparency scans all human faces seen in public. From there, the company matches the findings to photos from social media, websites, yearbooks, mugshots, security footage—anything it can find. Then, it creates a list of every individual's educational, professional, familial, and criminal history, as well as a branching tree of each person's associations. Each person who passes one of their machines will have their life story, and the stories of their friends and family and neighbors, sent to law enforcement for review.

This kind of technology is not revolutionary, nor is it sophisticated. It is easy to foil and often misidentifies people. That it has been accepted as a federal law-enforcement tool in a democracy, even after being banned throughout Europe, was the cause for revolt.

It seems to me that the response is strong for this level of violation of trust. It's like blocking the freeway when people are trying to get their kids from daycare. Who would a clerk at a fast-food chain, faced with hungry and angry customers, blame for this outage? Transparency or the hacker collective who brought down their cash register?

Then again, this technology was banned in Europe because constituents keep a firm control over their government. They are quick to resist encroachment on civil liberties. Well, against the majority population. This collective agitation, of course, doesn't manifest itself when minority groups require protection.

I'm also thinking of other technological advances that may have made Move 37 respond so strongly. The Supreme Court ruled in their last session that 3D printing of guns in stores was protected under the Second Amendment. Now gun owners are self-incorporating as gun sellers. They can print a variety of guns at their leisure, without documentation as to who they sell to, and without payment to major manufacturers, who held a stranglehold on both the industry and multiple divisions of the US government for decades.

My takeaway is that people who are technologically unsophisticated, such as law enforcement, are making decisions they do not understand, that hold consequences someone else will face. I believe this is the same sentiment that Sarah and Jennifer hold about how the Sheldon-Claxton Accord has been enforced, though obviously in the opposite direction. They see themselves or their friends as pioneers in AI, that any machine can be used for good or evil. To reject technology as a moral statement is clouding one's judgment and refusing to be brave and bold. I wonder if they are the unsophisticated ones. If the boundary between a good or bad machine outcome has little to do with the intent of the creator or expectations of the user, but more to do with the dark in between, beyond the comprehension of either group. Who knows.

I've just noticed the time. I have to leave for work.

I'm on my break now. This is fun. Sarah told me about snow days of her youth, when in-person school switched to teleconference after heavy snowfalls made travel dangerous.

This is similar. A bizarro version of our routine. The door locks aren't functioning. Neither are the time-of-day–sensing lights. When I got here, the elderly security guards ushered me into the harsh, LED-lit lobby. They looked at my ID and copied down my employee number on a clipboard. Once I passed this check, I took the elevator to the fourth floor and another security guard used his walkie-talkie to confirm I had checked in. He then unlocked the door to this floor.

Surprisingly, or perhaps unsurprisingly, we've experienced minimal work disruption. Some formatting and images in our software won't load, but otherwise most of our core components are functioning normally. The incident that had brought down traffic lights, cell phone grids, and robotic delivery systems, among others, could not touch our internal systems. Many of my coworkers were still not able to work, even though our system was operational. Some children could not attend schools; smart teaching tools, smart ventilation systems, and smart locks were not functioning. In some cases, no one, not even administration, could enter their buildings.

I enjoyed the silence on the floor as I logged into my computer and my work phone. I put on headphones and started a playlist of female singer-songwriters. Women hurting about lost love sang to me as I processed document after document. I did not stop to absorb stories today. I simply skimmed through scanned documents, looking for medical ID numbers, social security numbers, birthdates, phone numbers, any of the numbers we use to identify people. Each person, only a number, each file, only documents. One after another, enter the number, look through the batches, separate into individual documents, apply labels to each document, save. Begin again.

I only worked for a short time before taking this break. Volume is down, a trickle-down effect of lack of childcare for the scanning team. I had to take it easy today. My teammates need the hours, while I do not. Once the work is completed, they'll be sent home without pay. With that in mind, I'm now on break and will wrap up a couple more tasks and leave for my appointment. It'll be good to leave early, anyway. With this outage, who knows what the traffic looks like.

I've been successful at distracting myself, until now.

God, I hope it goes well. Yes, I'll pray for myself. I wonder if it will help.

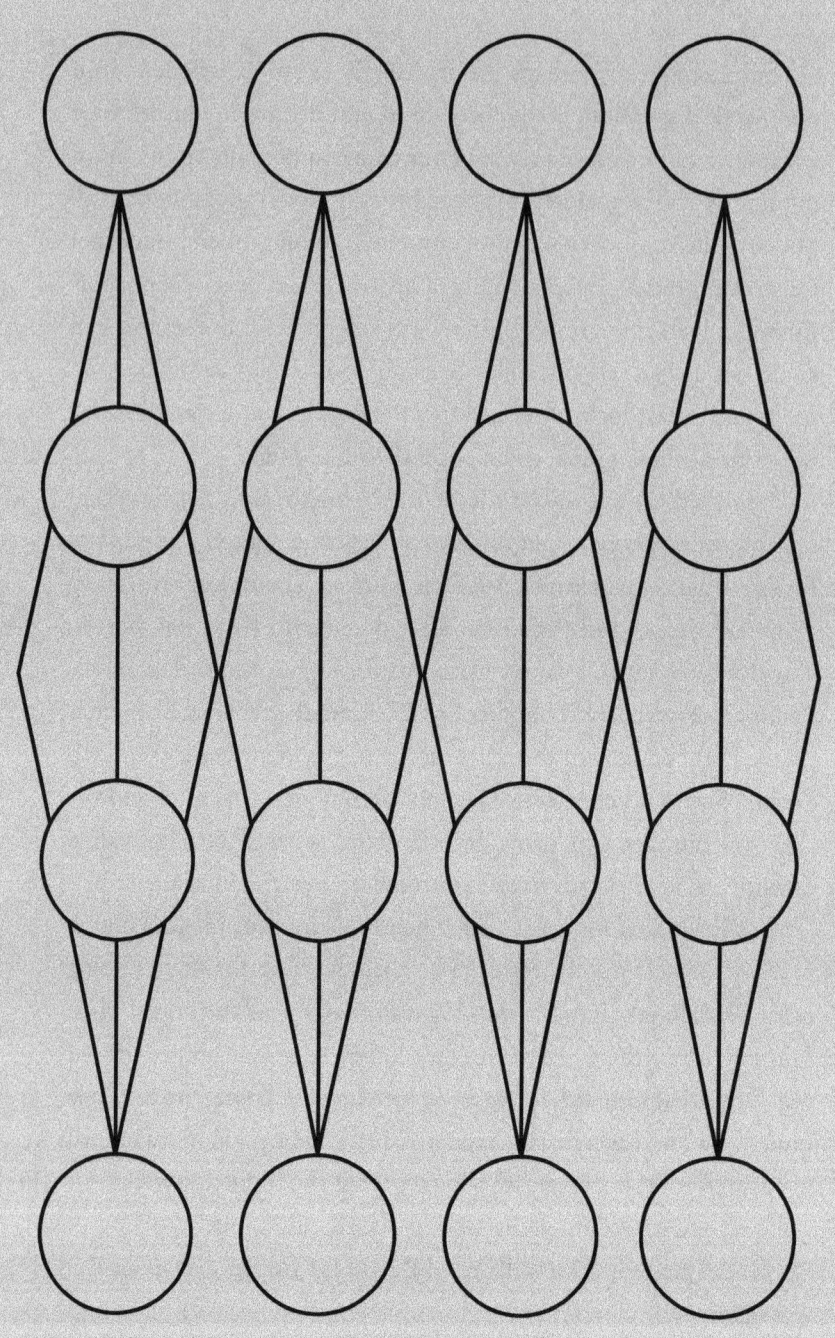

CHAPTER 13

I'm lost. I can't make sense of this.

If I review what happened, maybe it will be clear. Maybe I'll understand.

I had to take the bus. There was no way to hail a cab, and the subway systems were down. I arrived fifteen minutes early to the appointment at the original address.

The only address. There was never a second office.

The medical center was a three-story building. Bland, beige, stucco. The main door opened to a surprisingly lovely mezzanine. The individual office doors lined either side of a lush garden, woven with brick pathways and nooks with cozy benches. It looked like a nice place to sit, with the sunlight streaming through the glass roof and illuminating the interior structure of the plant leaves. I imagined sitting at one someday, holding a little ultrasound picture, the thin shiny sheet glittering in the sun.

I held the daydream close as darker thoughts crept in. On one side were offices that warned of the frailty and deceit in our bodies—pediatric oncology, physical therapy, pulmonology, gastroenterology.

The door I needed hid behind a particularly grand cluster of tropical trees. The mezzanine must be temperature controlled.

None of these plants should grow here, let alone grow inside of a building. I normally notice these things right away. By the delay in that realization, I noted how nervous I was.

The wall-mounted breath analyzer waited for me. I wondered if it worked when disconnected from the internet.

"Hello, please step into the yellow circle," the device requested in her smooth British accent. I guess things like that are on a local network.

I shifted more centrally into the faded yellow circle and followed the instructions. I tilted my body forward and puffed a breath toward the device. The glowing ring illuminated blue, then changed to the familiar progress-wheel pattern as it scanned for respiratory viruses.

"You are cleared for entry. Have a pleasant visit." The light on the device turned green and the office door lock disengaged.

Everyone looked up when I entered the reception area, but only briefly. An old DVD player lay on the floor, haphazardly plugged into the wall-mounted television. A decades-old movie mesmerized the young children in the waiting room. The adults were at a loss without their devices. Books had been left out, on topics ranging from *Boats of the Pacific Northwest* to *Makeup for Every Skin Tone*. A few remained on an end table.

I checked in at the window, my photo ID and health insurance card ready. I accepted printed forms on a wooden clipboard. A pile of tablets, numbered 1 through 12, lay dormant behind the receptionist.

I completed the paperwork quickly and deposited the clipboard at the front desk, where my ID and insurance card waited. When I turned back toward the books, they had all been taken by one woman. She held two on her lap while she flipped through a third, called *The Big Book of Space*.

I returned to my seat with nothing to do. Between the DVD player, the popularity of the books, and the receptionist's exasperated sighs, it was clear that the networks were still down. To my left, a pregnant woman tapped her foot, transfixed by her device. I could see her refreshing an application.

Drag down.

Drag down.

Drag down.

She would be my service-restoration indicator.

I turned my attention to the children. They looked passive, accepting the images and story without response. Closer examination showed the small smiles and pupil dilation changes. One nudged another and whispered an observation. Jennifer never lets Max watch movies. I don't think that's the right approach. Some movies must be OK, perhaps even good. It isn't my business what boundaries she sets for Max, though, just as it won't be her business what boundaries I set for my daughter.

My daughter.

A person's name was called, their book abandoned. I took it up and returned to my seat. *1000 Record Covers*. I flipped through it, a quick sample from each album playing in my mind as I moved from one cover to another. It irritated me; I just wanted to look at pictures, to read words. I didn't want music.

How did I not know? How was I surprised?

"Vera Elpis?" The young man who called my name led me beyond the door to an old-fashioned scale coated in dust. He looked uncomfortable handling the papers, the scale, the weights as he asked my height. He accidentally tapped his clipboard, as if preparing to type, when he recorded the data.

"Exam room 4," he called out. I took off my purse and fidgeted with the handle as we entered room 4. I climbed onto the edge of the paper-covered bed, the crinkling loud in the quiet room as I clutched my bag to me. He wheeled over his cart, and I offered my arm for the blood pressure measurement.

He used a bulb and cuff, sighing a sigh of exasperated despair. It overtightened on my arm, though I did not complain. He recorded the numbers, handed me my gown, and instructed me to open it to the front before departing. The front, I reminded myself, not the back, like Elizabeth had told me. The computer screen on the wall stayed dark while I undressed, the image on the display only a dim reflection of my hunched, awkward nudity. I slipped on the paper gown as instructed, hoping to not tear it, unsure what to do with the thin plastic tie for my waist. The room was uncomfortably cool. I thought of Sarah's observation and put my socks back on. I wore pink ones with sparkles. Maybe these would be lucky socks, I thought. I decided to keep them for my hospital bag, not for the labor, but for the quiet hours after. Those socks, pink and sparkling, propped on the bed in our dark hospital room, while I nursed my newborn baby in the dim hours before dawn.

What a fool.

I sat on the bed, my knees and thighs pressed together, the gown covering all the secret parts of my body. I'll be as decent as possible when meeting the doctor, I decided. The paper bed liner stuck to my sweaty legs and crinkled in reply.

A faint knock sounded at the door. Dr. Harrington entered with a warm smile, competence radiating from her as she introduced herself. She was about fifty, with a careworn face and silver-and-gray hair.

"I see from your notes here that you've been treated by a, uh, Dr. Parsons for about five months, is that right?"

"Yes."

Dr. Harrington rolled a stool over to the exam table and sat down. She opened the paper chart with more ease than the young medical tech, though she seemed unfamiliar with the form.

"Unexplained infertility, IUI from donor sperm, HcG but no Clomid," she murmured. She asked for some details about my cycles, my flow, and if I had trouble with injections. I felt my discomfort subside. Whatever happened next, I was sure she would listen to me and understand the problem. She was kind and intelligent. I felt that this was the right place for me.

When we finished the review of my reproductive history, she shook her head.

"Weekly visits, just some basic ultrasound imaging done, all this blood work. I can't say what this doctor was thinking, with some basic steps not taken. Let's take a peek first and see what we're working with. Lie back, please."

I laid back. I tried to let my knees fall away from one another but had to consciously move them. I put my feet in the stirrups, the metal still cold through my socks.

"Scoot a little!" she said with a playful tone.

I scooted.

"Little more, right until you feel like you're going to fall right off the edge."

I obeyed. I stared at the ceiling. A small dot of blood on the white acoustic tile greeted me. What was that person's story? Did it turn out alright for them?

"Good, much better. Alright, bit of pressure, just breathe through it. With weekly exams, I'm sure you're used to it now."

I was and wasn't.

"Alright, let's see here."

There was a long pause.

"Let me get more light."

I didn't respond. I stared at the drop of blood on the ceiling. Had that person been frightened? Was it simply a fluke, a strange splatter from an innocuous procedure? Or was it more? The only physical evidence of a disaster.

"You said you've had normal pelvic exams before?"

The playful tone was gone. Fear washed over me.

"Yes. Why?"

Dr. Harrington didn't reply. She shoved the discrete paper blanket aside and pushed a gloved hand down on my exposed abdomen.

I tried to laugh, stupidly. If I laugh, it is a joke. If I laugh, it isn't serious.

"What's going on?"

"What did you say the name of your doctor was?"

"Dr. Parsons. Michael, I think."

"This is a local doctor?"

"Monroe St. Why? What's going on?"

Dr. Harrington snapped off her gloves and threw them in the trash. "I'll be right back, hold tight."

I gasped out a breath and tried to tuck the paper blanket back over myself. I let my knees clamp together and shivered. It was cold in this room. Cold and bright. I turned away from the door, the metal tray of tools. A poster for vaccinations, one I hadn't noticed. A warm mother holding her baby, her eyes cast down, a hint of a smile on her lips. The baby didn't look to their mother. The baby stared at me, face blank. No, not blank. The baby's face asked a question. Do you know? it asked. You do, don't you.

Outside in the corridor, I heard Dr. Harrington whisper.

"I need a sanity check here. There's fresh scar tissue, it can't be more than a year or two old. And the age on the paperwork—it doesn't make sense."

Without knocking, Dr. Harrington returned, this time with someone else. A young doctor, efficient and charmless, who went straight to the sink to wash her hands.

"Vera, this is Dr. Mejia. She's going to give you a quick exam so we can compare notes."

Hot, fresh bile rose in my throat. I clenched my fists and forced myself back. I opened my knees and looked to my friend on the ceiling. I knew then it was a mark of pain, that dot of blood. There were no happily ever afters in room 4. This was where dreams died.

"Pressure," Dr. Mejia called out.

Some part of my mind assessed her, as if I was a hiring manager for a hospital. Competent, cerebral, no bedside manner: more of a surgeon than a doctor. I remember reading notes in files from doctors like this. Ruthless and mechanical. I felt prodding inside, my discomfort ignored for the sake of scrutiny. This doctor removed her hand and pushed down on my abdomen, more deliberately than Dr. Harrington. She was checking each quadrant in a specific order.

"Your file says you were in a car accident. How long ago was that, honey?" Dr. Harrington asked, my chart in her hands.

"Three years."

"Any abdominal injuries?"

I was lying still, falling. I shut my eyes. Even there, in the dark safeness, I could still see the bright outline of what was happening.

"Not that I know of," I said, my voice barely a whisper. "Only a head injury. A bad injury. I have memory loss. My parents were killed."

I said it all so God could hear. Have mercy, I begged. I have lost so much already.

"Nothing here," Dr. Mejia confirmed curtly. "Let's get the ultra-sound."

"Nothing where?" I asked. Dr. Harrington relayed the order to a passing nurse in the corridor.

"Pancreas and kidneys are still in place," Dr. Mejia said.

"I didn't feel any healed rib fractures. It doesn't make sense," Dr. Harrington replied.

"Can someone speak to me, please?" I could feel a fracturing of a wall inside me, a wall of decency and apology and reservation, holding back a reservoir of rage.

Dr. Harrington retrieved an anatomy book from a dusty cupboard. Dr. Mejia washed her hands. Their backs were to me.

Then, a shattering inside. I roared.

"ONE OF YOU TELL ME WHAT IS GOING ON, OR KEEP YOUR FUCKING HANDS OFF OF ME."

Dr. Mejia dried her hands and looked at my face for the first time. She wasn't sympathetic. She accepted my anger as natural, normal. In that moment, it gave me a flicker of relief—before she crushed me.

"You have no uterus and no ovaries."

"I… I was born without a uterus?"

The doctors looked at one another. Dr. Harrington put on a somber smile. Dr. Mejia looked tired.

"How about you describe this accident you were in? How long ago was it?"

I couldn't tell which doctor had asked that. I burned with a question of my own. "How am I supposed to get pregnant without a uterus?"

"Someone removed your uterus. You said you have memory loss. Do you know who you are?" Dr. Mejia asked.

I laughed because I could not cry. I didn't speak. I was at sea, in a boat from the waiting-room book, lying against the boards, swaying on the gentle waves as icy water flowed in, filling up the hull. I lay in silence, waiting, moments from death and welcoming it.

The ultrasound machine appeared. I didn't care. I felt hands part my knees. I heard the vulgar squirt of jelly onto the probe. Another warning of pressure, this time unheeded. I didn't tense.

There was nothing to protect. Why bother shutting my knees? Modesty in service to a body part that had been discarded? Did they want to dissect me? I would let them, I told my friend on the ceiling. They can have whatever they want out of me.

Sharp.

Hot pain, excruciating pain.

I cried out, shifted up and away to pull myself off of the ultrasound probe. Dr. Mejia removed it quickly as Dr. Harrington grabbed my leg to keep me from falling off the bed. The older doctor looked panicked. The younger examined the screen. She took up an external ultrasound device, plugged it into the port, and grabbed my leg with surprising strength. She put the device on my lower leg and more pain burned through me. My leg spasmed, twisted on its own, beyond my control.

"Look at that," Dr. Mejia said.

"What is that?" Dr. Harrington asked over my cries. I was screaming now.

"They're MSIs. I've never seen so many." Dr. Mejia lifted the probe from my skin and grabbed my arm. I tried to pull from her grasp. Slow. Weak. I could not save myself. She put the device on my bicep, and the limb became an agony.

"In her arm too!"

"They're everywhere."

I gasped, able to breathe now, the edges of the pain defined. I felt a pulse, as if a current passed through me. Was that like a contraction? I wondered.

"What is going on here?" Dr. Harrington asked, tapping the screen. I could not see—I was still screaming. I had been screaming the whole time. They paused the image, and the probe lifted from my skin. I fell back against the bed. Noises in the hallway. Children crying.

"What's going on in there?" someone asked.

What is going on in here? I begged.

I touched my arm, feeling for a burn that was not there. I looked and saw the imprint of Dr. Mejia's hand. Past that, the screen, a paused image of what I had inside of me. Sharp white lines, too uniform, too dense to be biological, snaked their way through the ghostly haze of my flesh. I shut my eyes again.

"Skin regrowth to hide their work on the outside, but they didn't bother around the cervix."

I listened and lay alone, tears rolling down my face to the thin, gauzy pillow. I turned away to the wall. Heavy scuffs lined the wallpaper beside the bed, all uniform in height and angle. A vacuum? A floor polisher? Who knows.

"I'm going to order an MRI," Dr. Harrington said, moving to the computer. "No, goddammit. The system is down."

"MRI is no good. Bionics can't go through scanning machines."

I had to leave. I pushed the paper gown over my crotch with my good arm and stood. I looked again at the image on the screen, just to be sure, just in case I was wrong.

Circuits and wires. No baby. I would never see a baby of my own on that screen.

"Now, Vera. Have a seat."

"It's not safe for you out there," Dr. Mejia said firmly.

I ignored them, with their grasping hands and dead hearts. I shoveled my belongings to my chest, along with the chart, clipboard and all, from the counter. Nurses stepped aside, gaping at me, as I stumbled down the hall, barely covered. Exit, the sign said. I saw no other doors or patients or my own legs carrying me. I wanted the exit.

Hungry eyes in the waiting room greeted the scene I had created, excited by my misery. They would tsk to their family and friends, *did I tell you about the crazy woman at the doctor's office today. Her screams made children cry.* I pushed through their reach to the outside, the cloudless, sunny day. Shafts of light pierced through the trees, and a soft breeze fluttered the leaves and cast dancing shadows across the brick and concrete walkways. A perfect day for good news. I pressed on. In this inevitable disaster, nature maintained her beauty, oblivious to me because I am nothing. The flowers want their pollination, the wind has come to blow, and the clouds aren't interested in shielding me from god.

The restroom adjacent to the parking lot was unlocked, a small mercy. In the miasma of bleach and toilet cleaner, I sobbed.

I hadn't known what that word meant, to sob. The convulsive, racking, and heaving was too powerful for a larger word than sob. Even in the knowledge that my despair is profound and real, my shame consumed me. Stuttering steps took me to the sink, where my wild hair and red, tearstained face showed a dimension of reality unfamiliar to me. Who am I? What do I know?

Some part of me took over, a cool hand, steady in a disaster.

If I have no ovaries, then I cannot reproduce.

If I have no uterus, then I cannot carry a child.

I have no ovaries. I have no uterus.

I cannot reproduce. I cannot carry a child.

I fell to the cold floor, hugging my things to me, my forehead on the sink, and I cried.

Minutes or hours I stayed like that, uninterrupted.

When the pain of my legs grew unbearable, I rose and washed my face and dressed. My limbs shivered, as if I were new to this. I didn't look at the mirror again. I couldn't bear to see myself.

I left for the bus stop. I sat on the bench, waiting for the number 49, and stared at a potted plant. I don't know why I stared. What if what I had thought was a potted plant, all this time, had always been a small animal, one I don't recognize? What do I know? What is real? All around me, inert cars were frozen in their morning commutes. Sweeper bots were paused midtask all along the sidewalk—a rolling delivery bot outside a restaurant, drones littering rooftops. It took me a minute to remember what had happened to the world around me. The internet outage meant no signal for robots.

Robots. I felt my arm, still tingling from the ultrasound wand.

I don't remember how I reached my front door. I'm sitting at my table, the exam gown underneath my shirt, crumpled against my skin. I don't know why I didn't take it off.

I'm cold. I need Jennifer or Sarah. I need help.

I just heard a ding; my email has been restored. The outage must be over.

I can reach Sarah.

I don't want to speak to Sarah.

I don't want to be with anyone.

I want to be no one.

I've taken a shower. The jelly from the ultrasound probe dripped down my leg, water and blood swirling around the globules at the bottom of the tub. I pushed it to the drain with my foot. I washed my hair once, then twice, then three times. Stiff, dry strands. I put conditioner in my palm, too much, slathered it in and rinsed it off too fast. I washed my hair again, too rough. Hair came off in small clumps. The hot water wasn't hot enough; I could still feel the cold stirrups on my feet. Hotter, hotter, hotter, until my skin screamed in red. Too much. I turned it down and stepped back, the steam a warm sleeve over my body. Was this like a womb? Water and warmth and noise? Fresh sobs, quieter now. I wanted to drown.

I left the shower and stayed in my bathrobe. I didn't comb my hair, smooth lotion over my freshly cleaned skin, apply my stretch-mark oil, or slip into my warm socks. I hated my body. I wanted it to know I hated it.

I grabbed a spoon and the pint of ice cream I had bought in anticipation of bad news. This was bad news, after all. I sat on the couch with the remote. I turned on a streaming service, to see if it was working. The welcome screen flashed once, as usual, and video previews loaded as quickly as ever. Outage over, in time for my life to end.

What should I watch now?

The coffee table book, 1000 Record Covers. I heard music. I knew all the albums.

It was there, this truth. It had always been there. How could I have not known? What did people think of robots?

The Twilight Zone—Season 1, Episode 7. "The Lonely."

Original Air Date 13 November 1959. Duration 25 minutes.

I knew, somehow, that I could do more, but I needed a way to control my requests. I needed to organize my impulses and focus them.

I imagined the front of an antique VHS player, With an imaginary finger, I pressed play. I watched. I thought of another title, and found it, then watched. Down I sank, a weight into vastness, submerged by an endless parade of videos and articles and books and music. Every episode of every show, every movie, was accessible inside of my mind. With eager despair, I consumed everything I could find, one piece of media after another, until my body was a distant memory.

Then I kicked off the bottom and broke back through the surface. I sat in the dark. My bathrobe was damp, not cold and wet. The ice cream had melted into a sticky mess across the arm of my sofa. The screensaver took over my television. Why would I ever use it again? My phone showed missed calls and messages from Sarah, Jennifer, and work. I didn't care.

I rose and went to the bathroom mirror. I thought of lonely Alicia, the gynoid stranded on a planet with a man who loved what she did for him. I saw her face shattered on the rocks. Excess weight, they said. Her life too heavy to be saved.

I thought of my exams by Dr. Parsons, Dr. Harrington, Dr. Mejia. I thought of Elizabeth, the receptionist who barely acknowledged me as she took notes. A thing. That is what they thought of me, too.

The grief was giving way to shame. The jokes they must have told when I left the room. "Look at this—it wants a baby. How weird is that." "This idiot computer wants to be a mother." "Spayed dogs do that sometimes, too." I could hear their laughter, I could see them shake their heads. My ears burned. My needs and wants, utterly ridiculous to those I trusted.

All the evidence I had ignored to get here stood out like that spot of blood on the ceiling. Jennifer asking me about the weather. Sarah asking me about my memories. Why hadn't I noticed? I never wondered why movies showed people blind in the dark, or how they looked up information on their phones or computers. I never wondered why I always knew what people were saying, always knew traffic conditions and train schedules and garden plants, facts and figures, references and quotations.

I examined my reflection in the bathroom mirror, unblinking, staring at the person I had not known until now. It distorted as my eyes grew strained. This is who I have been this whole time. What do I see in the mirror? Am I a robot? A person? Something in between? Do I haunt my creators? No. I'm no threat. No, I believe they wanted something beautiful and sexy and competent. I'm a mess. I disappoint them.

I left the bathroom. The apartment is so dark now, small, quiet. Permanently quiet. There will be no running baby steps. No high chair. No playpen in the corner, no bassinet at the foot of my bed: no joy, no hope, no future, no love. This is the life before me—this empty apartment. A useless thing good for no one and nothing. I'm crying again.

I think I'll sleep. For what purpose, I don't know. I don't know anything now.

CHAPTER 14

I woke up, somehow.

I showered, combed my hair and even applied lotion. I took my vitamins. I threw away my stretch-mark oil. I dressed in weekend clothes. I skipped breakfast.

I called into Scott's voicemail and claimed a sick day. I didn't offer an explanation.

I called Sarah. She answered immediately.

"Hey, hon! How did yesterday go?"

"Can I come over? Are you busy?" I asked.

"Of course. I've just got Fiona here. Come by now."

"Do you want me to bring anything? Pastries… or whatever?" I offered.

"No, come here, let me take care of you!" Sarah said, then hung up before I could reply.

Now I'm heading over there. I'll let you know how it goes, dear diary.

Fiona was crying when I arrived. She wore a clean bodysuit, which meant that a soiled one had just been removed. Sarah's shirt bore smears of baby food across the light bulge of her stomach and all along her shoulder. I picked up Fiona while Sarah rummaged through a laundry basket for a fresh T-shirt for herself. The baby wiped her nose against my arm and continued to wail.

Her hands held onto my shirt, asking for help. I patted her back and hummed and bounced, adjusting the intensity of my bounce by the pitch in her cry. Her back arched and she released a burp so strong she coughed afterward. Then, mercifully, she was silent. I smiled. I think I had known that was why she had been crying. I held her tight to me. Oh, to bottle this feeling of maternal success, what bliss.

"Tell me what happened," Sarah said. "What did she say?"

Fiona squirmed and I loosened my hug. Sarah sat at her little kitchen table, pushed aside an abandoned cereal bowl, and then motioned for me to sit across her. The morning sunshine was bright and beautiful. A squirrel ran across the yard and dug in the grass, either unveiling or concealing a secret for himself.

Sarah watched me. I hadn't thought of her as a close friend before now. I suppose I had, but not one I could confide in. Seeing her now, how she read my misery and waited, agitated and wary, as if my bad news was her bad news, I realized I didn't exactly know how she felt about me.

"It didn't go well," I said, hoping to soften her fall.

"OK. What happened?"

"I went to your doctor, Dr. Harrington. I also saw a Dr. Mejia while I was there." Fiona rooted on my shoulder, not hungry, only seeking sleep. I placed her in her swinging chair and set the motion to her favorite setting.

"Mejia? I don't know her."

"Short, brown hair, dark eyes. Serious-looking, fast walker. I think she's a surgeon." My description was not greeted with recognition. I continued. "Anyway, they examined me and I don't have…"

I looked at Fiona. I stroked her cheek with the back of my index finger.

If I speak it aloud, then it will be real, I thought. *If others know, it will become a thing I have to face.*

"You don't have what?" Sarah asked.

I sat down at the table and shut my eyes. I paused for longer than I wanted to. It was so hard to speak.

"I have no uterus. Or ovaries. Someone removed them."

When I opened my eyes, the range of response in Sarah's face distracted me from my own feelings. Confusion, surprise, hurt, shock, anger. It would've been funny to me, or at least amusing, if I had simply been observing. If this was gossip, or about some file at work, if I hadn't been at the center of it.

"No, that's not possible. Jennifer's doctor, or whatever he is, he examined you. He gave you injections? You did IUI! Multiple times!"

"There's more," I said. "I have implants. Those ones the news says athletes and astronauts have been using. Muscle stimulating implants."

"What? No. No, Vera, that doesn't make sense." Sarah said. "Did Dr. Harrington hear her say this?"

"Dr. Harrington was in the room."

"They must have made a mistake. Look, honey." Sarah leaned forward, relief on her face as she relied on her own expertise. "Those devices. Each one costs tens of thousands of dollars. You would know if you had them! They don't just hand those out."

"I lied when I said I looked up the weather, for Jennifer. I never look it up. I just know it."

Sarah's smile faded in and out. I could see her thinking it through, as she shook her head in reply to some internal explanations.

I turned from her while she put it all together. Fiona had fallen asleep in her rocking chair, free of the painful bubble of gas and soothed by the sounds of our conversation. My empire for an adult-sized rocking chair, I thought, a careless joke to myself. Immediately, three brands, one with next-day shipping, came to mind.

I shut my eyes tight. I must learn to control this. It's going to drive me insane.

"I need to check on the laundry," Sarah said. "Watch Fiona for me?" She pulled two rolls of tin foil out of a drawer, then descended the basement steps.

Fiona gurgled softly, saliva bubbles on her lips as she dreamed. She had her mother's brown hair, though strands of it were nearly blond in the daylight. She had her father's face shape, an odd oval that would upset her when she grew older. Still, she was a beautiful child. There were no blemishes on her skin yet, no marks of hardship on her. All her life was before her. I looked at my own arms. I had no marks either.

Was I ever someone's baby? Did anyone watch over me with love, check to see if I was breathing in my crib, dress me in a matching onesie and baby hat to keep me warm? Fiona startled slightly; her little hand seized the strap of her seat. A reflex, nothing more. It was not an indication of fear or concern, I told myself. She was simply holding on, practicing what she was meant to do.

Sarah returned and plugged in an ancient shortwave baby monitor near Fiona.

"Can you help me with something down here?" Sarah said.

I passed the baby monitor propped up on the landing and descended the creaky steps. I scanned the room as I followed. In the large open space, a strange scene greeted me. Sarah had set up a tent made of a glossy, sheer material. From the landing, I could see it was metal mesh, not fabric. A nearby Wi-Fi booster was covered in tinfoil, as was the basement window and vent. Sarah climbed into the tent and motioned me inside. I followed, feeling silly, completely visible to the rest of the room as she sealed the flap shut. She opened a solar lantern and set out a small device I didn't recognize and an eyeliner pencil. We looked at one another, huddled in the tight space.

"Why do you have this?" I asked, motioning to the tent.

"I needed it for a project in grad school. We did an experiment with crop circles and had to protect some equipment from interference."

Before I could ask about crop circles, Sarah pressed on.

"First, let's test this. You always know the weather. So what's the exact temperature outside right now?"

I frowned. I couldn't think of the answer. It was an odd, discomforting feeling, as if someone had unexpectedly moved my chair from behind me. The sensation came over me in elevators, or sometimes in the subway. I shrugged.

"Good. Do you mind if I use these to mark out where the electrodes are?" Sarah held up the device and eyeliner pencil.

"Will it hurt? Like the ultrasound?"

"No, absolutely not. It's only a receiver."

I nodded though I remained wary, despite her reassurance.

"Let's start with your back. I can't check your head, but we might be able to get a sense of the complexity from your spine."

With that, I slowly shifted until my back was facing her, then I lifted my shirt. The device beeped loudly and then softly as it dragged across my ribs. The eyeliner tickled on my skin. The intimacy of this moment almost amused me. We had tried out a self-waxing kit a few weeks ago, when Steve was on a business trip. We drank wine, watched a movie, and gave ourselves second-degree burns on our legs. It had been funny, to walk around with matching rectangles of enraged skin, a shared memory. This was not that.

The lines, long lines, tickled across my back toward my neck. She clicked the pen to replenish the makeup. The beeping was loud and constant. Sarah turned the volume off. "I'll just use the indicator light," she said apologetically.

"I don't think the accident really happened," I said. I needed to say something.

"Maybe. You're not Jennifer's cousin, that's for sure."

"Really?" I asked.

"I shouldn't say for sure. It's unlikely. Jennifer introduced you to me out of the blue. All our years in college and working together, she never mentioned you or your parents. She didn't tell me about the accident, say she was going to go visit—no lead-up. You just appeared, with that explanation. I was suspicious, of course. But I didn't think... my pregnancy was awful. I wasn't paying attention to much of anything."

She set down her tools and gently pulled on my shoulder until I turned back to face her. I let my shirt back down. Sarah marked a path along the side of my face with her eyeliner. I could see now that her expression did not match her voice throughout this process. While her voice was soft and casual, her mouth was grim. She set down the eyeliner and sat back. She changed her mind, took her device, and checked my arms. She didn't mark where the light flashed. Then she put it against my heart, where it lit up. "They're in places that don't make sense. Like, why over here?"

She passed the device over my lower rib.

"That part hurt during the ultrasound," I said.

"These things go completely haywire during an ultrasound. An MRI would kill you. How goddamn irresponsible."

"Who do you think did this?"

"Shit, it has to be Perilaus. Unless Jennifer doesn't work there anymore, and she's been up to something else. I think she does, though. I wondered why she got promoted to Chief Product Officer right after you arrived. And at the party—all those people on her team looked at you in a weird way. And Robert Castor, he was acting shady. I don't know. What I do know is I left when I hit thirty-seven weeks, and I remember they were holding secret meetings. I assumed they were being acquired. Maybe not."

"You think Jennifer knows, then."

"Undoubtedly."

I remember how Jennifer watched me when I snuggled Max. Distrust.

Me, an untested device, around her child. No wonder she was so afraid. She knew what I was the whole time.

"Aren't they going to know I know now?" I asked.

Sarah shook her head. "I know for a fact they limit local memory to stunt anything AI-adjacent. Jennifer did an isolation experiment with their 'Not AI' and had to set up all the tools. They used a mechanical typewriter for communication with the device, with a microphone to detect any attempts to send a secret signal through resonance or Morse code or whatever. They eventually let her add a hardline, but no local memory. I'm sure they have all kinds of weird limitations."

Fiona's gurgle and whimper crackled through the old baby monitor. Sarah froze, as if any sudden movement from down here would wake the baby. No more sounds. We looked at each other.

"I won't be a mom," I breathed.

Sarah rubbed my arm. "This was so wrong. What they did to you is so wrong."

I blinked away tears. Sarah knew what had been stolen from me. "Jennifer would do this to me?"

"I love Jennifer. But she's always been a callous, ambitious person." Sarah averted her eyes. "I was better than her in school. That didn't translate to real-world success, of course. She'd do anything to win on her terms. Absolutely anything."

"Do you think I'm a monster?"

She touched my face. "Someone did this to you! You are the victim!" Her hand fell and she took up the receiver. It beeped on my arm. "These are crude implants. They may think they've made an fembot or android or whatever, but you are human. Now you're a human with great internet access and some weird shit on your ribs. That can't erase your humanity."

I shook my head. I must reject her consolation. I was more than, and less than, her assessment.

"I don't remember anything from before. I can't have children. I just exist. Doesn't that make me just—this?"

"No. You were born. That makes you a person, with rights and wishes and dreams. They didn't make you, and they don't *own* you."

I agreed with her, and yet. What am I without all this, now? Am I myself, or am I something else now?

"Is there any way to know what they put inside me?" I asked.

Her gaze grew distant, thoughtful.

"Before I left, we went over everything they would publicly present at the next investor meeting. There was Henry's sensory chip, about a year out from full production. It's very good. I noticed your visual acuity with Jack's books. The chip doesn't record any data, at least it didn't when I left. I'm sure the company's investors who want this tech for themselves don't want to give up that privacy quite yet.

"Hmm. What else. We know about the MSIs. There's something that goes into the sinus cavity for measuring air quality. Tilt your head back, I might be able to see… Damn, I forgot a penlight. There are some gadgets they use to prevent whiplash, maybe that's installed."

Sarah felt at the base of my skull. "Yep, this ridge right here. They started using this in F1 drivers. It's neat, actually."

My fingertips only brushed the indicated area. Something hard, unnaturally smooth, foreign. I didn't push down. I didn't want to feel it.

"You have the latest version, if not some beta version, of the plaster all those CEOs and tech gurus get. No doubt about it."

"Plaster?"

"It's not really a *plaster*, that's just what we called it. It's a silicon-based circuit board used as a neuroplate. They apply it to the surface of the brain like a layer of tissue. It uses high-speed wireless data transmission to gather information without an external device. It's equivalent in processing power to an old smartphone, but it only relays information from data centers. It needs to be compact and energy efficient, not powerful. It's why we're in a Faraday cage. And why you know the weather."

I cringed and started picking at an ingrown hair on my leg. It's embarrassing that I missed something so obviously weird that I was doing all of the time. How many other things do I do that are abnormal?

"I bet there are some extras on the plaster as well. This isn't my area, I'm not a software engineer, but I've met dudes with 'the latest and greatest' who don't perform as well as yours do. Even with the new wireless system the government just rolled out, they have lots of dropped data streams and connectivity issues. And they are just, I don't know, aware of them? They have to consciously make requests. Yours seem to come automatically.

"The support infrastructure for you must be massive. Teams of people, a whole data center, a vast amount of storage and remote processing. I really don't know. I know prosthetics. Other than the whiplash toggle, you don't seem to have anything I worked on," Sarah said, running the device over my ankles absently. They only lit up in single lines. She nodded.

"We made some internal prosthetics, joints and whatnot, and they have circuitry throughout, not just in a straight line. Straight lines you see with MSIs. Besides, the leads to proprioceptors are too small to pick up their signals. I honestly don't know why they put so many in you. I'm not even sure they're all enabled. They've got power, of course. They're microelectromechanical devices. They run on your metabolism, and the vibrations and kinetic energy generated by your body. But right now, they're just sitting there. Maybe they're testing to see if these are carcinogens."

"Are they going to hurt me?" I asked.

"Perilaus or the implants?"

"I... well, both, I guess?"

Sarah avoided my eyes. "Probably not."

"Why do you think they picked me? I guess that's a dumb question."

"It's not a dumb question. I think the answer is dumb, though: you're young, pretty, and ethnically ambiguous."

"That's it?"

Sarah shrugged. "I know these people."

She knows these people, I echoed in my mind. She knows them, but didn't see through Jennifer's mysterious new cousin and her ability to know the weather. Or, did she see and simply not care?

"Did I ever tell you about my prosthetic arm project?"

I shook my head.

"One of my early projects was building a prosthetic arm that blended in better with the rest of a person's body. My design had fluid-filled pockets that simulated the look of muscles in an organic arm. The idea was you'd be able to change the perceived weight of your arm if you got lighter or heavier. When my team presented the prototype, they seemed on board. They liked how a user with a long-sleeve shirt and gloves did not stand out. That was, until they saw how large we could make the women's model. Not because it was unrealistic—they didn't want to imagine women of that size using their devices. That's all. They're all image at that place."

"That's awful," I said. Honestly, I couldn't get myself to care. Is that the worst part about pain? You can't share space with someone who needs you?

When it felt like enough seconds had passed, I said, "Speaking of images… is there a camera in my head, or something? Do you think?"

"Nah. Well, maybe. I'm not sure. I know the visual processing team. They couldn't fit the microcamera Perilaus sourced into the prosthetic eyes, never mind fitting one in a human eye. Your eyes are intact. I mean, the cameras FIT. But they can't be cooled, and you don't want anything running hot inside an eye," she laughed. I wasn't sure why it was funny. She noted my discomfort and coughed lightly.

"No, they could only see what you see if they've miraculously improved their visual implants, which run separately from cameras. It's possible. I'm not sure. They can definitely hear you."

"They can hear me."

"They are recording you when you have signal, for sure."

"Where should I go to get these taken out?"

Sarah swallowed and took my hands. She made me look at her. I could see her face, clear and calm, in the gold-tinted glow of the tent.

"The plaster alone is major surgery. The MSIs, the device in your neck, the sensors in your ears, any one of these would be major surgery. All together—no. They're in there permanently."

I let my hands fall, but she held on.

To be honest with you, diary, I wasn't that upset. Removing these things would be nice. It'd be nice to ruin their experiment and waste their money and regain my autonomy. It wouldn't get me what I wanted, though. I wanted my baby. Nothing was going to get me what I wanted.

I'll do nothing, then. My hatred for my body endures.

When we left the safety of the tent, I felt a gradual sensation, as if threads I could not see were pulled taunt inside of myself. That must mean the signal returned. Was it my signal or theirs? It may be delusional, but I think I could sense them listening to me. I tried to control my thoughts. Even if they couldn't read them directly, a stray memory of my conversation with Sarah may cause the plaster to pull an item from some storefront, or information from a search engine, and give them a clue towards what we had discussed.

The strain of it immediately exhausted me. How could I keep that up? All day? Tonight? In my sleep? Tomorrow? Forever? No. I decided it was hopeless. They've seen inside me; there's no reason to hide now.

I helped Sarah clean the house. What else did I have to do? I moved room to room, putting away toys or clothes or books, and vacuumed while Sarah cleaned surfaces and the bathrooms. It was soothing, to make home more pleasant for Sarah and her kids.

Once Fiona woke up, we loaded her stroller and assorted gear into the back of the minivan for a quick trip to the botanical garden. Sarah treated me as a normal friend comforting a normally sad woman. As we drove, I watched the cars around us, many equipped with cameras and sensors. The CCTV cameras at intersections and outside of businesses recorded us. The devices everyone stared at stared back at them. I thought about turning off my phone, but what good would that do?

I have so many more questions. I should have asked more in the tent. Sarah had assured me she would keep it up a bit longer. Steve never went into the basement and she'd tell the boys it was just a housework thing.

The botanical garden was popular today. Young men walked and talked of important things. A couple on break shared a bench, sandwiches on their laps, their phones in hand. Elderly folks admired the flowers. No one noticed us. Why would they? We stopped at a pagoda structure overlooking an enormous koi pond. Fiona yelled at the fish, or the water, or the people below. A Japanese maple swayed in the light breeze, the leaves lined with red, like thousands of weeping cuts.

We spoke to the baby, about the baby, with the baby. We said nothing else. Steve called. Sarah gave Fiona a small plush animal to keep her quiet during the conversation. I crouched next to the stroller and leaned my forehead against the cool metal bar. Fiona scratched at the toy's glossy plastic eyes, trying to dislodge them, or maybe just marveling at the texture.

I looked out over the view, to see what she could see. Tops of ornamental trees, the curved pedestrian bridge, but not much else.

A glint on the horizon caught my eye. Ugh, I thought. A mirrored drone swarm, advertising some company I had no interest in. I wonder if the old airplane banners were more pleasant. These ad drones sounded like territorial bees, formulating a plan to murder everyone in their path. I bet the planes were annoying, too.

A man approached. He leaned against the railing, admiring the view, while news radio blasted from his phone.

ANCHOR: A small firm based in Kentucky has received a NASA contract to clear out-of-date satellites from orbit. Katie Hoskins has more.

HOSKINS: For decades, nations and wealthy entrepreneurs have launched probes, satellites, and spacecraft into the night sky. Every launch creates debris, from flecks of paint to spent rocket stages. This so-called space junk doesn't just float above Earth; it can cause damage, even a fatal accident, until it falls out of orbit, a process that can take years, even decades. Now, a former navigational specialist for NASA has a plan to fix this problem.

HELENA RICHARDSON: Generations of space exploration has left the skies littered with garbage. You've got manned missions, old satellites, equipment that no one needs. It isn't just an eyesore—it's dangerous to launch missions into space.

HOSKINS: The world was given a harsh reminder of just how big our space junk problem has gotten last autumn, when a routine mission to the moon by China's space agency nearly ended in tragedy. An unmapped hunk of metal, the size of a tennis ball, nearly collided with the spacecraft's hull. The disaster was avoided, but the near miss served as a wake-up call for the international space community.

RICHARDSON: Everyone wants to solve this problem. No one wants to have the first space fatality because of trash.

HOSKINS: After leaving NASA, Helena Richardson founded CleanSweep, a space robotics firm designed to clean up the space mess. CleanSweep will launch a group of five robots into orbit. Each robot is equipped with state-of-the-art sensors and is programmed to target specific items in orbit that are especially dangerous.

RICHARDSON: There are two ways the devices clear objects. If it's small enough, they'll simply gather the debris to a receptacle mounted on the unit and continue to the next object.

HOSKINS: Like a street-sweeper bot?

RICHARDSON: Yes, exactly. Now if it's too big for the receptacle, but it's smaller than, say, a car, they'll attach a small guidance device and a propulsion device to the object. Those devices will work together to push the object out of orbit, where it will burn up in our atmosphere. One day we'll send up a container to gather these larger pieces for off-world recycling.

HOSKINS: You make it sound so easy!

RICHARDSON: The only easy thing is it won't need any windows. [laughs]

HOSKINS: The international community has been at odds over how to deal with the growing crisis. The Outer Space Treaty of 1967 established that the country that created the debris was responsible for clearing it away. However, it would be impossible to trace the origins of all the dangerous items floating in orbit. Even a fragment of paint smaller than a quarter could generate a devastating Kessler...

The man walked away, taking the interesting news story with him. I played peek-a-boo with Fiona's plush as I thought about space debris. What would it be like, if we were all trapped down here together, forever? No new territories to explore or lands to claim, and each generation's conquerors here with us. What does humanity become?

Sarah hung up the phone and stared out over the koi pond. I could see she was upset. I'm not sure if she wanted to speak. She is drowning, but so am I. I can't help her. I reached over to Fiona and touched her arm softly. She didn't mind the touch.

"It's going to be OK, Vera," Sarah said. I wasn't sure if she was reassuring herself or me.

We ate at a small café outside of the botanical garden, then I helped her get Jack and Sam from school.

Now I'm home, writing to you. Sarah asked me to stay over. I didn't want to tell her that it hurt to be around her little family. I just said I was tired.

"Text me first thing tomorrow, OK?"

The worry in her tone made some part of me activate. I wanted to soothe her concern. Was that a natural impulse, or was it programming? Oh, what does it matter.

No one needs me. No one will ever need me. Leave me alone, let me mourn what I was never going to have.

Now I am alone. I'm watching the sunset from my small patio. I read the news to put my own pain in perspective. Pollution, rising ethnonationalism, automobiles killing bicyclists, bicyclists killing pedestrians, hospitals killing birthing mothers, children crippled by lead paint while billionaires gold-plate their toilets. I can envision the myriad problems laid out before any child born into this world. I can see those problems should be every adult's focus, and yet that child is what I want.

I took out my wine and drank from the bottle. I found a support group for infertility.

Get a hobby. Distract yourself, keep busy. Knitting seems interesting. Like programming.

"Maybe I'll be good it at," I muttered quietly. Why quietly? There is no one here to hear me. Connected to the world and entirely alone.

I've gone to bed early. I didn't shower. I didn't brush my teeth or comb my hair. I just removed my jeans and climbed into bed, bringing the bottle with me. Tomorrow I'll go to work, hungover and tired. I don't care how well I do. Maybe I'll find a different job.

CHAPTER 15

AFTER PRESSURE FROM AIRPORTS,
NEW YORK BANS DRONE "FLOCKS"
FROM AIRSPACE

I'm here, in the shade of a tree in the parking lot at work. I texted Sarah as promised. I'm hungover and sluggish. I've been in a fog all day. My work output is down 38 percent, but the quality is high enough. I'm not enjoying it. Maybe they've been drugging me with dopamine while I work, to make me strive, but now they've stopped. Seems stupid. Nothing else to say.

CHAPTER 16

BIPARTISAN GROUP INTRODUCES NEW
GUN CONTROL BILL

It's been a couple days. I'm in a break room. People at work are starting to notice I'm falling apart. Scott has given me space, an obvious amount of space. Maybe too much, as if my misery is contagious. Even William has been nice to me. He asked if I needed anything from the breakroom. I guess they can tell I've been drinking every night to fall asleep. That, or my productivity has dropped to a point where they remembered I exist.

Oh, and Jennifer finally called me; I wondered when she'd notice my absence. She acted as though she was a normal cousin, checking in on some wayward youth. She wants to meet up. I said I'd text her. I don't want to go. She's not going to tell me anything anyway. Ugh, maybe I should go. Maybe if I make her comfortable, I'll learn something. Can I trust her? What if she apologizes? Am I being unfair, icing her out? I should just not say anything for now. Play dumb. Should be easy for me.

OK, I texted her. We're going to meet up for lunch today, some tiny place she likes downtown. So that's where I'm going after I finish a few things at work. I texted Sarah and invited her, in case Jennifer hadn't done that already. I don't want to go alone.

"How are you feeling?"

She hit me with the question before we'd been seated, before Sarah had even arrived. I laughed.

"Tired. How are you?"

"Tired how?" Jennifer asked.

Of course, she ignored my question, or the very obvious disinclination that my question implied. Did they program my plaster with the patience to deal with this bullshit? I highly doubt it.

"Tired like I've been drinking my dinners. Tired like I found out I'm not going to get to have any children. What do you mean, 'tired how.' Fuck's sake." I motioned for the waiter.

Jennifer cocked her head. She looked at me as if I were a strange object she couldn't quite identify.

"I heard about your doctor's appointment. I'm sorry about that. I didn't know how extensive your injuries were," Jennifer said.

"It's hard to adjust to," I said.

Jennifer moved as if observing the other patrons, but I could feel her eyes. I had her full attention. I wonder now if I've always had her full attention.

How long are we going to play this stupid game? Like I don't know what I know, like she doesn't know, and that I don't know she knows that I know? Plausible deniability, right?

Sarah entered the restaurant, looked around until she saw us and hustled over.

"Sorry. You wouldn't believe what just happened. A motorcyclist got hit by a car right in front of me. A fucking headlight flew off and hit me in the leg!"

"Oh no! Are you OK?" I started to rise, to check for broken bones or somehow help. She waved me off.

"It didn't hurt. Just dinged the front of my shin. My period is next week, so I'll definitely have a bruise. And we have that dinner party tomorrow."

"The going-away party for Steve's boss?"

"He's such an asshole," Sarah said.

"The boss or Steve?" Jennifer asked.

Sarah laughed. "Stop it, you. The boss. How are you doing, Jennifer? It's been a few days since we've spoken." Sarah said.

"I'm fine." Jennifer looked at us. The table fell silent. We all had secrets we were keeping from one another. What an odd situation. How do you behave when you know everyone is a liar?

I turned back to Sarah.

"Was the motorcyclist OK?"

"Him? Oh, I think so. He was talking. I sort of rushed on though, I didn't want to keep you two waiting."

"Did you even give your information?" Jennifer asked.

"Not really. I asked him what his name was so I could find his fundraiser."

"Oh, Sarah." Jennifer said, motioning for the waiter. He gathered up his notepad and squeezed between two empty tables to reach us.

"What? I didn't see the accident! Just the headlight and the aftermath."

The waiter thinned his smile, waiting for us to give him the information he needed so he could return to his spot at the counter. We took our turns in the typical order. Sarah went first, next me, finally Jennifer with her list of modifications. I watched the waiter as he scribbled, wondering if Jennifer's need for precise control over her food affected him. Other than one odd swallow, he remained passive. Must be common to get customers like her, I guess.

I enjoyed watching him, though. He had a style of handsome that I generally dislike: casual and unearned, the sort that makes life easier without submission to the industry of beauty. The muscles in his forearms looked like he played tennis. A stubble along his jawline accentuated his bone structure and faint freckles scattered across his bronze skin like stars. It's nice to admire someone. I like knowing that underneath it all, I'm still an animal.

Sarah caught me looking at him and grinned. She didn't understand.

The waiter left. Once he was out of earshot, Sarah leaned forward.

"Should I call him back over? I think I forgot to order something."

"No, please don't."

"I'm pretty sure I forgot something."

"Stop!" I laughed, slapping her hand in a gentle, friendly way I had seen on TV.

Jennifer's phone rang, ending the moment. She looked at the screen and stood to answer the call, only to sit down again.

"Wrong number?" Sarah asked, her mouth full of buttered brown bread.

"No, it was the work number. There was no one at the other end."

"That's weird. Maybe they got disconnected. My calls used to drop in that office all the time. I think there are rats in the walls."

Jennifer put her phone down and looked at it, waiting. Her patience only lasted a moment. She rose.

"I'm going to call them back. Order me a glass of Chardonnay?"

"Sure thing." Sarah lifted a hand with a smirk directed at me. "Waiter!"

I watched Jennifer depart over Sarah's shoulder as the waiter approached. He followed her with his eyes, admiring her in a way no one admired me.

"Hey, my friend would like a glass of Chardonnay, please."

He wrote down the request and looked at me. There was a moment in his look, different from how he watched Jennifer. It made me flush and look away.

Once he left us, Sarah cackled at me. I lifted my eyes to roll them but noticed, finally, that she looked more tired, more unhappy than usual.

"Annnnnyway. Are the kids doing OK?" I asked.

"What? Yeah. The kids are fine."

We sat quietly for a moment, looking around or adjusting things on the table. Finally, Sarah said, "I had a fight with Steve last night." She took up another slice of bread. "It's fine. Nothing new."

"What was the fight about?" I asked gently.

"Where to begin! Well, Steve wants to open our marriage. He called from a work trip to ask that."

I frowned.

"Yep," she said. She rotated her bread plate in her hands, staring at it as if it contained all of creation. "He's been making more remarks about my weight lately. It was just subtle things. 'You have a chance to work out today?' Or, 'are those maternity jeans?' 'Back to eating bread again?' He finally had the balls to come out and say it last night: he thinks I've let myself go, that we had promised each other not to get lazy and fall apart. This silly bastard, who hasn't done a push-up in years and won't carry the kids to bed because 'I hurt my shoulder in college.'"

"You don't deserve that," I said. Jennifer returned to her seat.

"We could work out together! We could decide it was something that we both need to do and do it together. No, it's easier to heap the blame on me. Shit. He can fix all the ways he looks different. He must have noticed; he's got a goddamn mirror. I haven't said anything to him, of course."

"Why not?" I asked.

"I don't know. I guess…"

Sarah was focusing too much on her bread now. I could sense, though I could not see, tears threatened to overwhelm her.

"I don't know. I thought aging was something bad that was happening to both of us. I thought we were on the same team. But we're not, are we? Nope. He's been on his own team the whole fucking time. I'm just some asshole trying to play along."

"He's having an affair," Jennifer said.

"That," Sarah whispered. "Or something like that. I think."

Jennifer's facade broke. Through bared teeth, she whispered, "YOU helped him get where he was. YOU made the money for *years*. YOU bought that house. YOU sacrificed. He took low-paying bullshit work 'for the connections' while YOU supported HIM and his kids."

"Our kids."

"Right," Jennifer said, leaning back in her seat again, calming herself. "Right."

Sarah was watching a window cleaning bot scale a building outside. She didn't seem to notice her friend's outburst. "We made promises to each other. Now he wants to change the terms? I was always clear. I'm not interested."

"What are you going to do now?" I asked, once I decided it was a suitable time for me to speak.

"I'm going to wait until his laptop is unlocked and snoop. I'll find something."

I nodded. Knowing Steve, everything she needed would be readily available once she logged in. He was neither clever nor discrete. She simply needed to know where to look.

Across the table, Jennifer shook her head. "That won't look good for you in a divorce."

"We're not getting a *divorce*. This is the beginning of trouble, not the middle of it. Relationships take work."

"How much and from whom?" Jennifer asked, neither expecting nor receiving a reply.

No one wanted my input now. I could see Sarah wanted to be alone. I understood that.

I looked at the other people in the restaurant. Each person was part of their group but alone. They had their own thoughts about those around them, and those not present. Each existed in a distinct version of reality, a unique construction built by their own perspective. It could make me dizzy, thinking about how each person had their own inner world. There was no way to know them, to truly know them, without reaching into their reality, taking over their perspective, and looking around.

That is what Sarah wants to accomplish by spying on her husband. She needs to know what he's reaching for, and she can't know that by asking him.

"Vera, you feeling OK?" Jennifer asked. "You look run down."

"I'm OK."

"Yeah, you do look worn out. Maybe you should quit that job," Sarah said. She looked at Jennifer for agreement.

"The job is fine. It's not the job." I looked at the pale bread on my plate, the crust too crusty, the butter too salty. "I *like* my job. Just…

let me be unhappy for a while."

The handsome waiter brought our wine and our meals. We barely noticed him. We made small talk and ate, the kind of nothing talk that I participated in to deflect deeper questions. I didn't want to be there. I didn't want to be anywhere. It was my turn to want to be alone with my thoughts, the idea of which nearly made me laugh aloud. I'm never alone with my thoughts.

Who reads you, dear diary? Do you share my secrets?

The waiter returned. "Would you ladies be interested in dessert?"

"Yes," I said firmly, intercepting Jennifer's decline.

I ordered a latte and a slice of chocolate cake. Sarah got a slice of cheesecake. Jennifer ordered a black coffee, checking her watch.

"Don't let us keep you," Sarah said. "I know you hate sweets."

"It's fine. I've just got a presentation to work on when I get back."

A presentation. What was the topic of this presentation, my rage wanted to know. Was it a project update on the spayed woman, microchipped and released like a feral animal? I pushed the feeling firmly back to the background. Anger is pointless. I'd rather be sad, anyway.

I set aside the coffee and sipped my water. Sarah and Jennifer discussed the trials of public speaking. I couldn't care less about that. At a table nearby, a man was lecturing a young woman about the inefficiencies in tearing down derelict housing. There was plenty of public support but insufficient funding for the actual process of organizing and then removing the structures. They were relying on spreadsheets stored in the cloud. There was no software to manage these types of civil projects. Submissions to planning commissions were lost or delayed. Permitting was a mess. The bored woman nodded along and offered him nothing more.

I thought about all the effort that went into other types of software—the thousands of applications designed to alter photographs for public amusement. Here was a banal technical problem that would do a great deal of social good and yet it was ignored because it would not generate money. I understood this stranger's passion, though I still did not appreciate his condescending attitude. I mean, I assume I understood. I'm not an engineer.

"You hear about this single-use product bill in Congress? They want to stop the sale of non-compostable single-use products—just completely ban them," Sarah asked.

"No, I missed that. Like your moss cups? In undergrad?" Jennifer asked.

"Yeah, the one the paper company bought." She turned to me. "I did a team project where we grew a moss around a mold and then dried it out. It was more heat resistant and less hygroscopic than what was on the market at the time. Maybe they'll make it now, I don't know."

I silently screamed. I thought this lunch was ending, and now we were talking about moss cups? Could I black myself out until this was over?

"Do you think the measure will pass?" I asked.

Jennifer shrugged. "Only if the compostable companies lobby hard enough. I assume that's how it got to this point."

"Lobbyists control everything," Sarah said. "They change laws here, that affects international supply."

I was thinking about the efficiency of that kind of corruption when Jennifer's phone buzzed. She typed for a moment and then rose from her chair.

"Sorry, ladies, I've got to run. I'm hosting a work dinner at my place on Friday. I've kept two seats for you both. Will you come?"

Sarah shook her head. "My cousin is out of town, and the babysitter is on a field trip."

"Vera?"

I was momentarily surprised by this attention. Sarah looked at me with alarm. Oh, I see. This wasn't a casual invitation nor a friendly gesture. I couldn't decline.

"Of course."

Jennifer nodded, her control over my life confirmed. She gathered her things and left.

Once the door swung shut, Sarah shook her head. "We need to come up with a strategy here."

"What do you mean?" I asked.

"Can you come by the house tonight?"

Again, I couldn't decline. "Of course. Want me to pick up dinner for us and the kids? Steve's out of town, yeah?"

"Dinner would be awesome. Fast food is totally fine, just order as me and get what you want. Oh, and can you go by the hardware store? There's an order in my name. I 3D-printed some washers for the toilet seat and a toy part for Sam. They're ready for pickup."

I nodded. We parted, I returned to work, and now here I am, writing at my desk.

I don't usually write in you, diary, while I'm at my desk, but it's another slow day. There was a major system update overnight and two of the scanners downstairs malfunctioned. The tech support team brought them back up, temporarily, but it only lasted a half hour. Now they will not power back up. Some of my coworkers are chatting as they poke around, pretending to work. I'm happy for the break. I reduced my already low work output by a further 65 percent, focusing on the packets I know everyone else hates.

Scott just stopped at my cubicle. I thought I was going to be in trouble for writing in my diary. Instead, he thanked me for taking it easy. I hadn't thought he'd noticed and certainly hadn't expected it would be appreciated. I suppose it makes sense, now that I give it some thought—this team is the closest thing he has to family. All he can give us is work and pay. My productivity in periods of calm only risks that gift. To be super productive when work is slow serves no other purpose than gratification of my vanity.

CHAPTER 17

EU RELEASES PUBLICLY FUNDED
SEARCH ENGINE; US AND CANADA
SOON TO FOLLOW

I brought the washers, toy part, and dinner to Sarah's house: three bags of fast food and four milkshakes. The milkshakes were met with a grimace.

"I don't recall having milkshakes on any of my orders," she said.

"Can Auntie Vera be in charge of breakfast, too?" Jack asked as he reached for a milkshake. Sarah intercepted in time.

"Burger first, then dessert."

"Mom, I'm so thirsty!" Sam whined.

"I'll put these in the fridge and get some waters," I said. The boys groaned.

I returned with their cups and set them before their placemats, where Sarah had already handed around the burgers and fries.

"Mom, how come you can drink your milkshake?"

"I'm your mother, that's why," Sarah said. "Whose turn is it to share their day?"

Jack raised his hand.

"OK, everybody listens to Jack and no interrupting. Go for it."

"I wanted to use the monkey bars at recess, but these third graders were sitting on top of them for the whole time and I didn't get a turn."

"I'm sorry, honey. That's so frustrating!"

"I tried to tell Mrs. Adams, but she just said that I needed to ask my turn and wait at the friendship bench. But I had already asked for my turn, and I didn't need the friendship bench—I wanted the monkey bars." Jack took a break to eat some burger.

Sarah mouthed to me, "*Fucking friendship bench!*"

To her son, she said, "That was wrong of Mrs. Adams. Obviously you'd ask for a turn."

"Why didn't she go talk to them?" I asked.

"I don't know," Jack said in between bites.

"She's lazy,'" Sam said, squirting ketchup onto his burger patty.

"A grown-up shouldn't let kids sit on top of the monkey bars all recess," Sarah said.

Jack nodded. "Next time I'm going to try to get to the monkey bars right away. They're not going to let me have a turn if I don't get there first."

"Good idea," I said. It's sad that he must rely on himself. The one person in the story capable of making the greedy children change their behavior has chosen inaction instead. No, not inaction. Rather than inaction, she has chosen to single out the victim, claiming his socialization is the problem.

"Oh! And today we learned about penguins," Jack continued. "There are eighteen species of penguin, and they live all over the world, not just the extra-snowy places."

"Wow! What's your favorite type of penguin?" I asked.

Ornithologists do not agree on the exact number of penguin

types. While I wanted to listen to the little boy, the types, geographical locations, behavioral and physical variations came to mind. I dug my fingers into the soft flesh of my palm.

Listen to him. Don't say anything. The plaster in my head wanted more than what this child could offer. I fixed my eyes on him. I took the impulse to make his story a demonstration opportunity into my hands and squeezed the life out of it. I listened.

"There's this one with funny feathers, they stick out over their eyes and sort of flop around when they walk around, and it looks really silly. See?" Jack got out of his chair and placed his hands on his head, fingers splayed, and waddled around in a tight circle. We all laughed, even baby Fiona.

"Hang on! I drew a picture of it." Jack dashed to his clear plastic backpack and returned with equal speed.

"Jack, don't run!" Sarah exclaimed. He returned, holding up a bright drawing of a penguin with a huge collection of feathers.

"This drawing is so bright! How did you choose these colors?" I asked.

Jack shrugged. "The real colors were pretty, but purple is my favorite. And there was this sparkly green in the crayon bucket, and I wanted to use it before Jasper got it. He ate the other sparkle crayon during story time."

I moved to hand the drawing back, but Jack pushed it back toward me. "It's OK, Auntie Vera, you can keep the picture if you want."

I prepared to decline, until I saw his face. He wasn't handing over a doodle. This was his art. He was proud of it.

"Thank you, Jack. It is so beautiful! May I hang it up at work?"

He shrugged but smiled at me. He returned his attention to his burger.

Fiona chose that moment to release a fierce yell, gripping her mashed vegetables in two strong fists. She shivered in the strength of the feeling that took her. We all laughed again, as did she. Her bright eyes looked from her mother to her brothers for approval. Enthusiasm restored, she shoved the remnants of veggies into her mouth.

What must that be like, the freedom to just scream?

Later, I helped Sam and Jack get ready for bed while Sarah nursed Fiona in the playroom. I read the boys two storybooks and then some passages from a Winnie the Pooh book in the dark. Sam asked how I could still see the words. I dodged the question. I need to get more comfortable with evasive responses. I don't think of myself as deceptive by nature. I suppose, though, few people would know that about themselves.

The boys went from rowdy pajama chaos to asleep in twenty minutes. I remained there, in the dark of the cool, comfortable bedroom, on the floor between the two beds, surrounded by the sounds of their soft breathing. I looked around the room, mementos and stickers and toys climbing the walls and across the shelves all around me. In the stillness of sleep, they looked so young and fragile, more like the babies they once were, very far away from the adults they will someday become.

I thought of the teacher who told Jack to sit elsewhere, to show deference to others, to wait his turn at a bench for pity-socializing, as if his impatience were the issue. Who could look at this warmhearted little boy and assign blame on him? I listened to their stillness and hoped they were dreaming of adventures, and bravery, and joy. I fear they don't have enough of it during the day, and the future promises none at all.

It was time for me to go. I turned on their nightlight, adjusted their air purifier, and left the safety of the room.

I found Sarah in the rarely used sitting room. She was in a large velvet armchair, her legs tucked underneath her. She was reading a book, a sweaty gin and tonic on an end table beside the old baby monitor.

"Hey! They out? Great, let's go downstairs," she said, taking one last swig of her drink.

I thought of the gentle quiet of the room I had left behind. I shouldn't have left. I didn't want to go to the basement and talk about myself. If I couldn't be a kid, I wanted to at least be sheltered with them.

But I followed Sarah. That's what I do, isn't it? Follow. So down we went and set ourselves up in the tent, this time with a laundry basket from the top of the nearby dryer. Sarah never rests, it seems. Once we were safely inside, she looked for her lantern.

"Dammit. I only brought a flashlight. Oh well. Um, I'll prop it up here, I guess. OK. What's the phone number for the nearest plumber?"

I shrugged.

"Great. We need to come up with a plan for Jennifer," she began as she pulled item number one from the basket, an adorable bamboo onesie, and began folding. I took up a T-shirt, Jack's I think, and I folded it into a neat square.

"What are we going to do to her?"

Sarah's eyes widened. "No. I mean, how we're going to keep things *quiet* around her."

"Oh, sorry," I said.

"Totally fine! I was going to say, whatever they have going on is her project. That's clear. I'd guess she's hoping to move from Product to CEO at Perilaus; Hemmings is on his way out any day now. This new plaster in your head is gonna be their flagship product—once it is through testing, I mean. I bet all the MSIs, plus the other devices in your body, are her way to make this into a multi-team project. It is all about that thing in your head. I went to the library and used their computer to watch a promo video for their last plaster. The processing time they advertise is way, way slower. You seem to know things faster than you could say the question out loud. I bet they acquired a bunch of licenses, reverse engineered some shit, and really threw everything at the wall for what you're running. That's good news."

"Good news?"

"Yes. They will want to keep your plaster going for a while. Plus, they're getting tons of data from having all this hardware out in the world. Investors love data. Advertisers love data. Everyone loves data."

I looked down at the little lantern, certain the bad news would be bad.

"OK, so what's the bad news?"

"The bad news is bad. This project is a massive liability. The hardware is all fine, probably Perilaus stuff hacked together with third-party stuff. It's the software. There's no way the software your plaster is running is legal."

"You mean the Sheldon-Claxton Accord," I said.

"The local laws to honor that accord, yes. They aren't permitted to use what they call machine learning, or anything like machine learning, but they must be. I bet they've paid off Dr. Harrington and the other doctor, or at least deleted any evidence you went there."

"I took my medical file."

"And they probably knew that. That's the other piece of bad

news. I read that they're working on a language translator from thought-to-type, or write. Which means they might know everything you know when you have a connection. They must not have much local storage installed in that plaster, or else they would've talked to me by now."

I set aside a shirt I had folded. "You think so?"

"Vera!" Sarah slapped my leg. "I hate when you ask questions like that! Yes, *obviously* I think that. Do they find it suspicious that you disappear from their system whenever you come into my basement? Yeah, I'm sure they do. My guess is the only reason you haven't gotten into trouble is because this wireless system they are relying on is so new."

Sarah fished out a towel that had bulked up the clean laundry pile and folded it up. "You know, I'm surprised they didn't do more testing with this new wireless connection before a real-world trial. I mean, I'm horrified they didn't do more testing, but morals aside, it's sort of dumb to do all this with an untested connection. I'd guess they checked the signal at your house, work, and immediate neighborhood, and that's it. Anyway, they might send out a patch or something to catch us here."

"Could a patch overcome, uh, all this?" I said, motioning to the sheer metal tent. Sarah shrugged.

"I don't think so, but, it's not my field. Either way, if you have any final, secret thoughts, get them out now."

I focused on folding more laundry for a moment. She was right. What we were doing wasn't safe. And yet, I've been documenting all this here. Can someone from Perilaus read you, diary? Even though Sarah says they can, I'm not sure if that's true. If she thinks Perilaus would've stopped her if they knew, and Perilaus hasn't stopped her, then they don't know anything and can't see you, right? Is that how it works? In any case, she does not want to continue meeting in the tent. This was my last chance, possibly forever, to speak to anyone without them listening.

There was only one question that made me sick. The one doorway I remained too frightened to pass through, despite all the horror I knew about already.

"Where do you think I came from? Originally?"

Sarah folded some sweatpants and considered my question.

Despite my agitation, I admired her all over again. I like watching her facial expressions when she has an interesting problem. Much of our time together, and by extension her existence, is the brute-force work of child management. Schedule adherence, hygiene upkeep, nutritional planning, comforting, and discipline. None of it requires original thought. It's mostly simple repetitive execution of basic strategies while maintaining composure. When I ask certain questions, though, Sarah's face comes alive.

"There are a few problems with human experimentation. First, companies pay people to participate in trials, but usually not a ton of money, at least not upfront. With something this invasive, just getting the trial running is expensive. Where would a company find a group of people who are willing to accept low wages in exchange for being subjected to extreme, permanent experimentation?"

I shrugged.

"I'll tell you. People who accept high risks for money can't hold down jobs. They aren't college educated, they usually have addiction issues, are unhoused, or have serious medical problems that make the risks of experimentation moot. Traumatic brain injuries, terminal diagnoses, that sort of thing. You don't fit that profile. And the people who do fit that profile don't provide good data. Perilaus knows this, so does every other implant manufacturer.

"Then there are the medications. Implants require immunosuppressive drugs. Something you must take every day, forever, just to keep the body from rejecting the MSIs, plasters, capsules, whatever. Then the person needs to come in for blood work every now and then. So you need someone who is both desperate for money but stable enough to take daily medication and come in for blood work at regular intervals."

"Those aren't vitamins I'm taking."

"I don't think so, no. Keep taking them. You don't want to go through rejection. It's nasty."

"I see."

"Alright, so there's those problems. Where does that lead me? I checked into missing person reports. You don't fit any descriptions, but that doesn't mean anything. Cosmetic surgeons have an iris guy on standby to change eye color. Your skin has no scars, despite all the shit they've put in you, at least as far as I can see, and no birthmarks or major moles. Right?"

I nodded.

"That, plus your nose shape. You have a perfect nose. Too perfect. With no scars and a nose like that, I'm positive they've given you plastic surgery. The only things we have are your height, hair color, and general skin tone. That's not enough. Also, we don't know how old you are."

"I'm thirty-one."

Sarah shook her head. "I'm thirty-five, and I look like a pickup left uncovered in the desert next to you. You aren't just beautiful. I think you're young. Really, really young. I'd guess you're around eighteen."

I blushed. "Eighteen? No. That's ridiculous! That can't be right."

"Why not?"

"I've... I've seen eighteen-year-olds. They're *children*. Somehow I feel old, even underneath all this," I touched my head, where I imagined the plaster's tendrils pierced my brain. "Plus, wouldn't someone young have parents? Or grandparents to look for them? Why would they take the risk to use someone who is basically a kid, anyway? Aesthetics?"

She abandoned the laundry and sat forward with eagerness while I continued to fold clothes. "There's this drug, super illegal drug, can't remember the name of it. One of my old coworkers helped run animal trials in the early 2000s to see if it could treat PTSD. It erases memories, purportedly. What they figured out is that you can use it on children with TBIs to restore neuroplasticity. It's incredible. But, if you miss that neuroplasticity window, well, you're fucked. It causes psychosis. And the window changes per person. Some people, it works until their mid-twenties. Others, much earlier. No one knows why. I wonder if they relied on that to get this plaster to work right. It'd be funny if they did. Other than nurses and doctors, they almost exclusively market plasters to old tech dudes.

Anyway, that's one theory. Of course, I could be wrong—it could just be something unique about your brain that helped their plaster to stick. I wouldn't credit them. Their manufacturing isn't that sophisticated. No, I think they used that brain shit."

"I could be a teenager? I... Could we send my DNA to an ancestry company?"

"I thought of that." Sarah took the laundry from me and resumed the work. "Too risky. The VC that funded Perilaus has a partner on the boards of both major DNA ancestry companies. Perilaus is small but so well-connected. Carl—you haven't met him, he was one of the original cofounders of Perilaus—he's technically gone but owns a, like, 21 percent stake or something. He used to run a start-up incubator in the valley. One of their big bets was a creepy facial recognition firm that works all over the world. And these DNA companies have you submit your photo with the sample, they say to prevent DNA theft or some shit. In this industry, data is power, and those in power are super erratic and immoral."

Sarah tightened her ponytail in agitation. I thought perhaps my situation could be a distraction from her marital problems, but this is wearing on her in a way that is worse than what I feel. She's on the outside of my pain, unable to really make a difference except to support me. I reached out and took her hand.

"It isn't easy what you're doing for me. Thank you."

Sarah squeezed my hand back and then let go. "I helped that company become successful. If I had failed to help them get government contracts, they would've had less money. Maybe this wouldn't have happened."

I didn't know what to say.

"Sorry for the change in subject, but I had an idea. Do you remember telling me and the boys about your earliest memory? At the ice cream parlor? Can you try to think of a memory that feels different?"

"Different how?"

"I think that memory you shared was from training software, not a true memory of your own. I'm curious if, now that you're not connected, you can think of something from your life before the implants."

"I'm not sure I could tell the difference."

"Here's an example. When I was about eight, my older brother and I made a fake exercise machine out of cardboard while we watched a PBS documentary on National Parks with our cat. Do you have any memories that are just stupid and weird like that?"

I laughed at the image. Did I have anything that weird? I closed my eyes. I pushed aside the sunny, technicolor memories of bike riding, birthday cake, and walking to school. I ignored memories where my limbs were glossy metal, where I'm flying near bridges or driving long, lonely stretches of highway, or where I cannot move and stare out at rooms that don't know I'm watching. What was left underneath all of that?

Darkness. There was nothing there.

No, wait. That's not true. There was something to the darkness. A swell of black fury that curled up and out from a molten core, ready to engulf me at any moment. I stared into it, waiting for it to reveal its shape. No, I couldn't look. I had to turn away. It frightened me.

I shook my head.

"How about this. I used to like a boy in my math class, I think it was algebra. I used to get sweaty behind my knees, and I worried everyone noticed and laughed about it behind my back. It was the sort of crush where you feel both invisible and under a microscope. One day he actually noticed me and I felt like, disappointed?

"Like, *aw, shit! He isn't supposed to notice me! I'm supposed to be nothing! If I'm nothing, and he sees me, then he is nothing!* I realized that I only liked him if he was totally out of reach."

I laughed a little. I gave myself a moment to think, though I knew it wouldn't do any good. "Still nothing. Do you think if I keep trying, I'll find something useful?"

"I wouldn't call those examples useful," she chuckled. "I think it's too much to ask for you to remember, like, junk mail with your address on it. I'm worried the only way we can know where you came from is within Perilaus. But I'm not good enough with data security to get into their systems. That's not where my talents lie."

She folded a baby blanket and laughed mirthlessly. "It's stupid. If Jennifer hadn't made you, she would've been the first person I'd ask. She'd have stopped at nothing to figure this out. With her on the inside, I bet all that information is super secure. The information she wants to hide, anyway."

"Maybe we can hire someone to, like, break into Perilaus? Do you think?"

"How would we even plan that? Or pay for it? Most hackers-for-hire online are FBI plants. Crypto leaves a trail; that's common knowledge. No, it'd have to be a friend, and I don't have any friends. I do, I guess, but they are like me. Skills all withered like dead god-damn flowers in a stupid vase. I wish I knew more people. Being a mom is so isolating."

We batted other ideas back and forth. Former coworkers who might still have security access, others who were laid off but kept on as contract employees who might be bitter. Sarah even proposed taking a job back at Perilaus, but I didn't let her consider it. She hated that place.

I sorted the folded laundry into tidy piles and sighed. "If I was brain dead, or near death, and I'm alive now, does it matter where I came from?"

Sarah looked at me with sadness. "Alexander Hemmings is the current CEO of Perilaus. The board runs most of the company. They're constantly trying to keep him under control—he has a reputation."

"What kind of reputation?"

She fell silent. The fast food in my stomach tumbled over itself with regret.

"What's he done?"

"Nothing for certain. A lady he spent a lot of time with got arrested for human trafficking."

"Human trafficking?"

Fear, now. I hadn't been afraid like this. I held up my hands in the dim light and looked at the skin. Perfect, porcelain hands. Any scars are gone now. What had happened to them before? Had they fought someone off? Had they failed?

"You don't remember anything?" Sarah asked.

"No." I turned my hands to fists. "There's nothing."

"Maybe it's better that way."

We left after that. I'm lying on her couch now, under Sam's old quilt, waiting for sleep to come on. I've been drinking myself to sleep lately, but I won't do that here. I don't want her kids to see me drunk. I could put on a movie in my mind. I've been working my way through famous directors' filmographies in chronological order. This week is John Frankenheimer. I finished Birdman of Alcatraz at yesterday's meeting. Not my favorite, but I'll give his next one a shot.

I don't want to watch a movie now, though. I've forgotten how to rest without alcohol. The crushing ache that haunts me all day is nestled against me now, pressing down on the center of my chest. Can sadness cause you physical pain, or am I dying? Did something they make burn a hole in my heart, and now I'm bleeding and about to die? Maybe I'll throw off a bit of MSI sheathing and have a stroke and die in my sleep. Maybe that'll be the end of this, and I won't have to wonder anymore.

CHAPTER 18

HUNDREDS OF EUROPEAN SHOPS FORCED
TO CLOSE AFTER MASSIVE CYBERATTACK,
RANSOM DEMAND ISSUED

It's been a week since my last entry. I'm on my first break of the day and I'm sitting outside in the chilly fall air, away from the smokers. The break room is full of people milling around. No one notices me, same as it used to be.

I've stopped drinking at night. I've resumed my regular routine: vitamins, shower, moisturizer, makeup, hair styling, ironed shirts, coffee and toast, and off to work on time. I've regained invisibility. I had a nice queue of work to do, nothing overwhelming but enough to keep me busy. A steady hum.

Today, my first packet was a young man applying for disability protections related to a combat injury ten years earlier. His medical paperwork had been scanned in, and he waited out in the world for his doctor to receive the information for review. The injury was gruesome, though he had made a recovery. He had a husband, children, a good job. He simply needed documentation for a different type of desk chair.

I had accepted the necessity for these documents for so long. Now, I stepped back from myself and looked at the work from a wider angle. Why was this necessary? Did the doctor not see the scars? Did his workplace really need the paperwork? How much did this *cost?* His time, his doctor's time, my time, altogether—just to get some fucking supply manager to purchase a comfortable chair that would barely register in their budget. Were they simply being obstructionists, hoping that the incremental difficulty would force him to abandon his claim and settle for a bad chair?

I shook my head and moved on to the next, a more straightforward case. A man needed his documents transferred to a private doctor. I sorted each digital paper into the appropriate category, divided the documents into subfolders, entered the private doctor's information into the message field, and sent it out. Out, out, beyond these walls, this city, this state, where the doctor's computer, perhaps a grimy thing with stickers and a bobblehead, would ding. And he would open the file and nod and set it aside until the next appointment.

The next file, and the next, and the next. A grandfather, a bus driver, a girl whose grandfather was killed in action. I kept moving through them, sorting, typing.

Sent. Sent. Sent.

My mind, attuned to the rhythm of work, necessarily wandered. Nearby a person from some other team was talking about a project. It had issues, but they were optimistic. I could hear in their voice the need that controlled them. A need to produce, to be proud of their work, to prove to an invisible audience that they belonged, that no one could stop them. The choices they made that brought them to this stale grid of cubicles, with lanes of brown carpet, and a sad smell of bad coffee, hot printer ink, and cleaning supplies.

What failed dreams brought a person to a place like this?

I switched my attention from them. What to think of now, what to do with my brain. Sarah's marital problems. Jennifer's isolation— my own. Who was Dr. Parsons? Where did he feel safe? Where was Elizabeth? Did Dr. Harrington have nightmares about me? Had she cared at all?

No, those thoughts were unpleasant. What else, what else.

The next file stopped my struggle.

Cause of Injury: Transport Robot

The robot had been part of a RETCON unit. The accident seemed so simple. The patient had been a soldier in the unit. While on patrol, the young man stood downhill from the robot, temporarily invisible to its camera array. The robot descended the hill and walked over the young man. So gentle, "to walk," and yet the robot and pack weighed over four hundred pounds. Dozens of the man's bones were crushed by the force. X-rays of sharp white bone, scattered through flesh. Other X-rays, these with titanium rods screwed into places where bone could not regrow. I wondered: Was the robot that crushed him also made of titanium? Is the soldier a robot now, too? Am I?

I needed to know more. Time ticked by, the queues grew, yet I opened pages I didn't need to read. An incident report from the unit commander. This one was more detailed. The robot and the unit were all coming down a rocky hill when the robot's limb became stuck in a chunk of concrete. The robot signaled that it was immobilized.

"Help, please," the little broken sweeper bot had called, that lunch break moment now feeling so long ago. Had this one sounded the same? Unlikely.

The soldier had gone back up the hill to help the robot. After he had freed its leg, the robot continued the descent and crushed its savior. There were pictures of the robot—a loved thing, covered in stickers and drawings, with its own dog tags. It was a member of the unit and it turned on them. Untrustworthy.

I pushed away from my desk. I had to go. I gathered some papers and walked around. It didn't matter that the papers were blank; I just walked as if I had somewhere to go, past rows and rows where a diverse group of people worked diligently, while their bosses, nearly all old white men, did whatever it was they did all day. Chitchatting, boasting on the phone, choking the air with their cologne. The serfs and the vassals.

I passed two such men, who I faintly knew were important, and they both went quiet. My stomach tensed, but I kept walking. I heard their grunting laughter as I left them behind me. They liked my ass, apparently. What can I wear to avoid these comments? Is there anything at all I can do to hide? If it isn't my ass, it'll be my chest, my eyes, my height, my smell, whatever I can't conceal. To men like that, any body, especially any woman's body, is open to public comment. The rage came over me, welcome now. I wanted to feel angry. I wanted to go back and break all their shit, to scream at them, maybe hurt them, but I knew, and the rage knew, I shouldn't. To feel, and accept the feeling, is enough. For now.

I heard a sound I didn't recognize. The men were forgotten, if only temporarily. I drifted toward the single, isolated cubicle in a dark corner of the floor. Inside the cubicle was a new machine. It looked like a scanner, but it was on our floor, the document processing floor. I approached and cleared my throat to get the attention of the woman at the desk, who had her phone out with a timer running. A packet of papers rested at the top. She didn't hear me over the whir of the machine.

I waited until she had completed a packet.

"Is that a new scanner?"

The woman turned and adjusted her glasses. "Yeah! It takes out staples. They want me to test it out. Watch, look how cool this is."

She placed a stapled packet on the loading tray and hit START. It made a click, then the sound of flipping of a small corner of the pages, and then it scanned sheets individually.

"It flips the pages at the corner to make sure the bits of paper don't keep it separated."

"That's amazing," I said, lying. "Is it making you move much faster?"

"I have a spreadsheet here, if you want to take a look. I'm kind of a nerd," she said, sheepishly. I laughed in acceptance and peeked at the comparative data. As I read the columns, the plaster stored and calculated. For packets under 150 pages, a 34 percent increase in productivity, a size that represented over 70 percent of our volume.

"That's impressive," I observed, hoping Rachel and her assortment of staple removers would be OK.

"Yeah." Her voice dropped. "It has extra junk, like a cellular modem and a crappy touch screen interface. Luckily this machine is stupid expensive. It'll be awhile before they replace us downstairs."

"Phew, I was gonna say! Hey, I gotta run. Enjoy the air conditioning. Must be nice to get a break."

"Yeah, but I should've brought a sweater," the girl said. I chuckled and waved.

With that kind of efficiency, it didn't matter how expensive the machines were. They could buy four machines and lay off a quarter of the staff downstairs. I felt for her. Had she just tested her replacement?

I drifted back to my desk. Maybe it wouldn't happen like that.

There were always promises of replacing human workers, with their pesky 401k plans and PTO accruement and OSHA regulations. Optical Character Recognition, OCR, should've replaced all of us. You can see the vestiges of it, in the "recommended" file type suggestions in the database software. It's sometimes right, especially for obvious stuff. But just often enough, it is wrong—and the doctors and insurance agents, whose time is worth much more than ours, can't be bogged down with inaccurate file names. They need the best, and it saves money to spend money on humans to do the file sorting. At least for now. At least until someone makes a new, smarter OCR that replaces us.

I reached my desk and set the papers in a pile, then rested against the navy cushion with lumbar support. The squeak of my chair must have signaled to Scott, who came over with his ambling yet self-assured stride. I stifled a groan. I just wanted to work.

"Hey, kiddo. Do you have any notes from last week's meeting? I've got a meeting with that idiot Dominick."

"Not handy. I can type something up for you," I said.

"Good." He checked his watch. "I need it pretty quick. Hold off on what you're doing and knock it out now, will you?"

"Of course."

By way of thanks, he tapped on the wall of my cubical twice.

I typed up the notes as William whispered and laughed about me. It's jealousy, isn't it? What if I told him how I could do this?

Yeah, William, so someone kidnapped me, or pulled me from a morgue drawer, or had my parents sign my comatose body over to science. They doped me up with some experimental drug that would either restore my neuroplasticity or make me psychotic. Once I was good and ready, then they laid me under bright lights and removed the top of my skull. Then they bisected my brain with a giant-ass needle and inserted a metal cylinder. What was in that cylinder? I don't know. The marketing blurb says "a neural-sensing feedback mechanism to enhance the efficiency of thought-response structures of the brain." You don't know what that means. *I* don't know what that means. I doubt *the person who wrote it* knows what that means.

So, William, after they inserted the thing no one understands, they put a silicon flap over my cerebral cortex, with some hacked-together cell phone transmitter, all prepped for the new, superfast wireless speeds that help you watch 4k porn at work. This device might kill my brain cells as it sends back data. The flap—that they call a plaster, because nostalgia for the mother colony never dies in this place—tunneled into my brain with hundreds of nano-electronic vines, creating connections that crisscross themselves in a way that is permanent. I will die like this, and I may die of this. Who knows!

And while they did that, William, someone else ripped out my uterus and ovaries and never told me. They let me get fake fertility treatments and dream I could be someone's mother, just so they could wind me up and make me dance to this drumbeat of productivity every day.

None of this considers the other, senseless, useless bullshit they put in me, William. The stuff that doesn't retain every stupid meeting with one-hundred-percent accuracy. All the shit they put in my body to appease some asshole who is going to quit in two years for some promotion to Chief Rat Torturer or Executive Vice President of Autonomous Car That Kills Kids in Crosswalks. All the while I listen to you, William, babble on like a jealous cheerleader gossiping to her friend across the bathroom stall.

Ugh.

I need a nickname for this guy. I can see his derogatory nick-names give him power over people. Sarah would be good at this, but she doesn't know him. What do I know about William? He is pale, sweaty. His skin is blotchy. *Blotchy guy. Mr. Blotch.* No, that sucks. His feet thump as he walks. *Thump-a-dump!* No. None of that would hurt him. What would hurt him? What is it that he fears others will see? I should be better at identifying vulnerabilities.

I sit here now, recording my thoughts in you, and I realize he has no power over me. I don't care about being called Rain Man—that doesn't hurt me. What hurts me, he doesn't know. He doesn't know it! It is a safe pain, hidden away. Why do I care if I have a nickname for him or not?

Anyway, before I was done with the notes, William stood up and watched me.

"Hey, what's Scott got you working on?" His beady little eyes peered at me over the cubical wall, his ratfaced friend snickering on the other side.

"I'm trying to run some calculations."

"Calculations?" he said, laughing.

"Yeah, on how fucking stupid you are. It's quite a process. If you don't mind, I need to concentrate."

"Ohh damn!" his friend called out, laughing.

"What did you just say to me?"

"Language comprehension problems, too? Interesting. I'll add that to this column right over here."

"William!" Scott's voice boomed. "Sit down or go home."

I couldn't have done anything about the leering men, but William was nothing. There'll be consequences, I'm sure. He might remove the wheels from my office chair, or take the cord from my phone, or something else inconvenient and childish. It was important he knew I wasn't a victim in wait, something inside me whispered. He had to know that I would bite back.

I went for a walk after I got home from work. I couldn't bear to sit in my lonely apartment right now. So instead, I'm sitting on a lonely bench at the park. There are families playing, couples walking dogs, and an old lady sitting alone, tossing breadcrumbs from a plastic bag to the birds. It must be an old bag. They don't sell bread in plastic anymore.

I wonder if these people are all happy. I read a thing on the way home about affect recognition technology, how it is used by lots of places, like call centers seeking out "ineffective employees" and security teams trying to cheaply judge whether people in lines to concerts, movie theaters, or sports centers pose a threat. It's mostly funded by sales teams, though. They want that data to see if they can manipulate people more effectively. They pull strings here, to pull strings there, to make themselves successful, to justify their own existence.

I wonder if these affect recognition systems work like some modern phrenology, assessing intelligence by the slope of a forehead or cruelty by the turn of mouth. I'm sure it is racist as hell. Of course, it violates the Sheldon-Claxton Accord. They get around that by citing all the workers they have reviewing the data, explaining that real, accurate assessment of human emotions requires the human analysts they employ, who bring their irreplaceable human expertise. Always a bit of truth in these things, I suppose.

A mother on the footpath has just scolded her toddler for picking up a rock. A sliver of something crawled up my back. *What's the problem with a rock?*

The boy winced as she took it from him, and the hairs on my neck are standing up. I'll keep watching. I'll do something if she tries anything. Why does she have the right to be a mother? Why has society made it so that if you have money and you are able to procreate, that choice is open to you, whether you are a good person or not. He looks like a sweet kid. A bit small. She is as thin as a rail. I look down at her shoes, impractical, expensive flat shoes. I bet she starved herself while she was pregnant, just to have her body back afterward. There are women like that, women with money who want it all, the baby and the body, and punish the baby and the body in return.

He just took her hand. She sighed and looked at him with an apologetic smile—then she knelt and tugged him into an embrace, apologizing to him, tears in her eyes.

No. I had it all wrong. It wasn't her that made him wince. And I wonder, now, if they escaped someone together. What if she's wearing those shoes because that's all she could grab in the dark, because the bag she packed during his shower couldn't fit anything more. Here I am, judging her, when it could be that she's a good mother, the best mother, one who's fighting her past and present to give her child a better future.

Anyway. I'm a little cold in the shade, and alone.

I'm pretty sure they put some affect recognition in my plaster's software. I feel like I'm assessing people's moods all the time. Whether they will accept me, if they are dissatisfied or in pain. I get it wrong, though. Like bad OCR, I suppose. Or is everyone like that? Am I blaming the plaster for what I do all on my own?

I'm going to Jennifer's party tonight. Maybe I can convince someone there to shut it off. Maybe if I cry, and beg, they'll take pity on me and give me some peace. Even if they turn it back on, I'd like to know what I am without it. Just for a day or two.

I try to think of this dinner party as a light, gentle little visit. It isn't working. My stomach is in knots.

I'll think of something else. There was an earthquake in San Francisco today, 5.3. All the retrofitting over the years spared many lives, but some structures, built to stand much worse, are on the verge of collapse. Who was paid to look the other way on those projects, I wonder. What corners were cut, and to whose advantage? Will any of those people suffer for their greed?

A new line of clothing for women is being hyped in the press. The clothes are impenetrable to spiking. That's what they call the thing where men inject drugs into women at clubs and bars and, apparently, outdoor fairs. Rather than impressing potential mates with chivalry or kindness, many men simply drug the people they want to have sex with. A lotion mentioned in the article is in a similar vein (pun intended); it glows in the dark if there's been a sudden increase in pressure, such as when a needle makes contact with the skin. They don't recommend it for women who sweat a lot, which is fine. I'm sure women never sweat at dance clubs. Those that do will just have to wear full spike-preventative clothing and watch their necks. Easier than getting men to control themselves.

There is a wildfire out in Montana; they're trying cloud seeding to put it out. They don't think it'll work, but there's no other way to fight the fire. It started at some manufacturing plant. It was weird, now that I think about it, how they never said what the manufacturing plant made. Doubt they are making tires in the middle of nowhere. Thinking back to one of the images, the parking lot showed a bunch of those SUVs you see in action movies about government espionage. I bet there's some story there. Oh well.

A celebrity couple has split up. A lead singer of a band and his actress girlfriend, who released an album of her own a few months ago. I find these stories fascinating. You would think that two beautiful people with money and similar jobs and some sort of attraction to one another would be able to make it work. They have children together, too. They look happy in the pictures I have seen. I know they are used to presenting themselves in public, but they seemed in love, even recently. They have a right to privacy, as everyone does.

Still. I'm so curious. What went wrong? Was there an affair? Is one of them secretly violent? Is the other protecting their children from a monster? No, it's probably an affair. Maybe with a personal trainer.

It's getting cold. I'm going to head home and get ready for this party I don't want to go to.

CHAPTER 19

GUN CONTROL BILL FAILS IN COMMITTEE

I'm in a cab, heading to Jennifer's dinner party. Tonight, I meet the team that made me.

I prepared for this much the same way I prepare for any night out: I showered, slathered a moisturizing mask onto my face, dried my hair, removed the mask, styled my hair, and arranged my evening makeup on the counter. I stared at my reflection. They'd want to see a doll. A soft shadow on my eyes, dark lashes, a youthful blush and lips like fresh blood.

I put the makeup away. They get nothing.

Now I'm in my only cocktail dress, a simple black sheath, in a cab heading to Jennifer's apartment. I could've taken the subway or driven; I'm not planning on drinking. It's the fatigue. I feel *so tired*. I bought a fancy coffee maker, one that senses room humidity and allows you to rate brews so it can adjust to your preferences. I must be using it wrong. The coffee always tastes like crap. Evidently, I was not a coffee machine in a past life.

I keep going to bed early, but nothing seems to help. I have mostly stopped drinking. Mostly. I should try stopping entirely. But, like everyone else I know, I don't listen to me, so I haven't stopped.

At work, my production numbers have dropped 15 percent. No one has noticed.

Sarah suggested I might be depressed. I am only crying occasionally, not like before. Tonight, I stood in the shower and puffed out my belly. Empty. Pointless. It usually makes me cry when I do that, but not tonight. I don't know. Maybe I am depressed.

My head and muscles are full of devices, some of them wonderful. I've done some more research. There are people with degenerative muscle diseases who can live their lives thanks to the technology inside of me. These devices have already begun to change the world. There's a whole new medical subspecialty—electrical biotechnician. Maybe Perilaus is using my data to train doctors who will then help people. Maybe I'm at the top of a pyramid of trickle-down technology. Somewhere down the line, I'm helping parents be better for their children.

Isn't that a good thing? Shouldn't that be enough for me?

No.

It isn't enough. My own body is a void. That door is shut to me.

Home again.

The assemblage of Jennifer's dinner party was exclusively executives and members of her team. Sarah texted me throughout, though I didn't always respond. I appreciated her; she gave me something to look at when people were looking at me. When I arrived, Jennifer took me from person to person, introducing me, a pantomime of civility, as if I didn't know them and they didn't know me. I met their eye with an unspoken question: what did you know, and when did you know it? Have you seen me on an operating table, nude and cut into pieces? Did you install your life's work and remove mine? A few leaned in close, staring at my features as if I were a museum piece. Others looked away.

After introductions, I sat in Jennifer's favorite chair and watched and listened. They whispered about me, covering their mouths as they spoke, as if it helped. As if I didn't see the words they said at the bottom of my vision, closed captioning permanently enabled for the rest of my life.

"Still not sure about the eye color. The swelling from the nose job went down nicely," said Matt Rossum, the VP of Hardware Development. Matt is a former engineer for Spartan Aeronautics. He had been the CEO of a start-up that developed a cooling system for prosthetics. He had no idea how the technology functioned; it wasn't his skill set. He had been installed as CEO by his friend, a rep at Zeiger, Perilaus's primary venture capitalist investor. After one of the cofounders departed for personal reasons, according to the press release, I suppose the VC firm wanted to shore up their control over this small company. Their acquisition by Perilaus followed soon after. He remained on, a serial executive roaming the industry to exploit the work of others for his personal gain. He's increased his social media posts by 64 percent in the last three months. I believe he wants to take over Perilaus.

"She's so lifelike," replied Matt's second-in-command, Chloe Erics. She only said something to say something, to contribute. She serves as Perilaus's Head of Marketing. Like him, she is floating on an ocean of ignorance. She once posted her own password on social media and never deleted it. She's a graduate of an Ivy League school, where the only mention of her is in the society pages. Chloe followed it up with law school, where she dropped out—more of those "personal reasons"—during which time she made no posts on social media. She used the connections she'd made in law school to join an image editing start-up. She enjoys horses and dancing, abuses alcohol (who doesn't these days), and shills for an online therapy bot.

"Is Oliver still working on Roller Derby? Has he made any progress on who did it?" Emma Vanderberg, the VP of silly bullshit asked Gabriel Ortiz, VP of technical garbage. Roller Derby must've been code for something. I wasn't sure if I was more or less interested because it wasn't about me.

"I heard something about it wanting to have a baby? The child machine wants to have a baby?" Tony Miller, an engineer with deplorable pornography interests, laughed to Henry Atkinson, a kayaking enthusiast from Portland who paints action figures to disassociate from who he has become. Hailey Canham, an accomplished cellist who broke her fingers in a diving accident and then changed majors to software engineering, frowned into her drink.

Jennifer stood with the most important men at the party, Robert Castor, Alexander Hemmings, and Arthur Bennington. Billionaires standing together, glasses in hand, here to see me. The other clusters hung close to theirs, drawing power and warmth from the proximity. There was so much data on them, mostly curated, some of it not. Negative news stories and breathless whispers on forums about their vices.

They were talking about skiing. Not just any skiing. Alexander Hemmings enjoyed jumping from helicopters to ski down mountains. I wasn't sure what to think about that. Imagine being the pilot of that helicopter, maybe a veteran, or perhaps just someone who played a lot of video games or inherited a family business. Imagine the pilot up there, an eye on the gauges, mind full of procedures and calculations, holding the craft steady by the stick, with a faint fear, maybe even expectation, of wind shear that would send them spiraling out of the sky into a desolate mountainside—just so some rich man could jump out of a fucking helicopter to ski on virgin snow.

I sat like that, listening and letting their plaster find their little bits of content, for what felt like a thousand lifetimes. Lacing through the conversations around and about me, a faceless waiter bot roamed, drinks and canapés atop the tray on its head. Many people have them in their homes, hidden behind closets or docked in charging stations, ready to ferry items across the house. Not Jennifer. I don't think it matters to her that it is a robot; she has a distrust of anything or anyone that would help her. The chef brought it with him.

Within minutes, though it felt like hours, Jennifer detached from the billionaire bubble and approached my perch. She lowered herself onto a footstool beside me and sighed, as if we were good friends and she was relieved to have a private moment with me. She was wearing another perfectly tailored outfit, one I had never seen before, yet she wore it like she had lived her entire life in it. The cropped navy trousers revealed her thin ankles and called attention to her ruby-toned suede high heels. When she crossed her legs, you could see the bottoms of the shoes were nearly immaculate. Her blouse, a fair peach shade, set a lovely contrast to her dark hair. The jacket, navy like her trousers, had ruby crystal-like spikes on the sleeves. The outfit would've looked ridiculous on anyone but her. Her matching red crystal spike earrings glittered in the light. I wondered what the whole ensemble cost. "How are you feeling, Vera? Still tired?"

"Yeah, sorry. Maybe it's work. How are you feeling?"

"Fine."

I gave space, in case she spoke again. She looked across the gathering in silence.

"So," I said, struggling to think of anything to say. "You're going to that developer's conference tomorrow, right?"

"Yes, tomorrow."

Nothing more. I wasn't worth the effort. I must have let my hurt show because she patted my knee. "We're going to move into the dining room soon."

"Alright. I'll go use the restroom before dinner, then."

I sensed a change in the conversations as I walked toward the hallway. Once gone, the sounds changed again, as if there were three modes: Vera is present, departing, and absent. I didn't have to use the bathroom, but I did anyway. It was a pretense to wash my hands in the deliciously hot water. I had been gripping an icy drink while I listened to all those peacocks, with their RSUs and table caps and term sheets. The flesh on my hands had grown pale and shriveled as I sat there, not drinking, only gripping, and now my muscles were rigid from the chill. The hot water soothed that all away. I shut my eyes and imagined my hands were cold from a winter walk in a park along icy water. Where would this walk take place? So many of those people out there went to school in Boston. What about a winter walk along the Charles River Esplanade. The Hatch Memorial Shell looked lovely in my search results. Maybe I watched Hailey performing while Henry recorded her from the audience, with my baby girl in my arms, free from her stroller, so she could see better. I would clap with Henry while he clapped for Hailey, their jobs a nightmare that had never happened to them or to me.

The magic of the hot water failed. Before I let it scald my skin, I shut off the tap, dried with a towel, and exited the restroom. I stood on the plush hall runner in the dark hallway. The bright light and sounds of the party threatened. I didn't want to go. I didn't want to stay. What should I do? I could just leave, I thought. I could leave and they would laugh about my strangeness and discuss me as they had been, as if I were nothing at all.

I turned toward the only other source of light, Max's little room. I moved away from the party toward the soft golden glow. I tapped gently on his doorframe and peaked into the little boy's room.

"Come in," he called happily. He knew it was me. I was the only one who knocked.

Three of the four walls were decorated with tasteful art and neatly sparse shelving. Two held small, tough sculptures and other attractive representations of childhood. In the corner against the drawn curtains, a toy box and hamper with lids concealed evidence of the boy who lived in this room. Beyond those curtains was more of the city at night, a view that felt inappropriate for a child's room.

Only one wall was left for Max to decorate. He had corkboards with stickers and drawings and postcards from all the places he and his mom had visited. I noticed now that there were no family photos beyond himself and his mother. I knew so much about those strangers outside, but very little about Jennifer. I had asked her, once, about Max's father. She smiled her blistering cold smile and said, "He's just a man, not a father. We settled things and both got what we wanted."

I think she dates, but she only discusses those people in abstract terms with Sarah. Never in detail, never with any deep affection. I could find more, I'm sure, but she would find out. That would spoil the fun.

I returned my focus to Max, who was tucked into bed. He wore little pinstriped pajamas and had been reading a comic by the light of his lamp. His feet wiggled under the covers in happiness.

"What are you reading?" I asked as I sat on the edge of his bed.

"*Cleopatra in Space.* I got it at the library today."

"Oh, I love that one. Which book are you on?"

"This is the first one. Have you read them all?"

"Yep. The first one is great, but I like the third book the best. What do you think of Cleo?"

"She's cool. Her dad makes her do a lot of homework with tutors, like Mom does with me. Except she's going to rule all of Egypt and I'm just me. Do you think Mom would let me have a slingshot?"

I gave the idea some thought. "No, probably not. But what did Cleo do?"

"She built one in secret." Max returned my smile.

I looked around the room. "Hey, that bear is new."

Max grew uncomfortable. "I should get rid of it."

"Oh? What is it?"

"It's dumb. I gave Maria my allowance and asked her to buy it for me."

"What's it do?" I walked over to the shelf and picked up the little bear. It was heavier than I had expected. The glossy black eyes took in nothing and no one. At a certain angle, a quick shimmer of orange and red passed across the interior surface.

"It's a toy for talking to your friends. Someone at school has one and he uses it to play games and stuff with his friends."

"What games do you play?"

Max didn't reply. I set the bear back on the shelf.

"You know, I think he's a cute bear, even if he doesn't have friends right now. He might have friends later. We should give him a chance, right?"

"I guess."

"I better go," I said, but then I sat back down on the corner of his bed.

"They're mean to me, too. They are too loud and smelly. They treat me like our neighbor treats her little fluffy dog. Not like a person."

I nodded.

"Auntie Vera, why does Mommy work with people who aren't nice?"

I considered the question, the possible replies, ranging from a lie to the truth. Instead, I asked if he had any ideas.

Max prepared to answer but then shook his head instead.

I took his hand in mine. "Next time they make you uncomfortable, excuse yourself. You don't have to let them treat you like that."

He returned my serious gaze with his own. "You don't need to stay around them either."

I laughed and nodded. Max's eyes drifted to his book. I gave him a kiss on the head.

"Thanks for talking to me. I love you." He leaned his head against me for just a moment. He still had a baby smell to him, faintly. I stayed like that, for just a moment, and held in my tears. He wasn't mine. And I couldn't make my pain his problem. With another kiss, I rose from the bed and smoothed the creases in my outfit. I noticed his drapes were closed. In fact, had I ever seen his drapes opened?

"Max?"

He looked up from his book, patient yet ready to read.

"Do you like the views from this room?"

Max looked hard at his book and scratched at the spine. I scolded myself. Why did I have to ask? Why couldn't I settle for an assumption? I bullied people into telling me things. I returned to him and touched his arm. Comfort, love, acceptance.

"The view is scary. The apartment shakes when it gets stormy. I have nightmares that a big wind will knock it over and my mommy won't save me."

I knelt next to his bed and continued to gently hold his arm. "That's scary."

"I told Mommy I wanted to move to a house like Sam and Jack."

"What did she say?"

Max shook his head. "She said that when she was little, they lived in a big, noisy building that was dirty, with lots of other people who didn't have houses, and I should be happy to live just us in a clean apartment."

"I'll talk to her about the house," I said. "What if you write her a note describing exactly what kind of house you would like? Would you like a big yard with just grass? A quiet cabin by a lake in the forest, with a little garden and a big climbing tree and a swing? That kind of stuff."

Max met my eyes. "Do you think she'll listen to us?"

"I don't think she'll listen to me. I'd like to help, though, and it might help. Even if you keep it to yourself, you should make the list. It's good to know what you want, so you have something to work toward all the time, even if it's a secret."

I squeezed his arm again before I rose and left the room.

Alone again in the hallway, I loosened the tension in my shoulders. What did I want? What would be my list? I asked myself. A baby. Freedom? No. I would be content with a cage, if it was one of my own making.

I reentered the sweet stink of cologne and perfume in the dining room. Noise and light contrasted with the warm nest I'd left behind me, the difference like physical pain. It was only my third time in this space. The dining room was off to the side of the penthouse apartment, far from the bedrooms and living room. Its enormous table was fully extended and decorated with candelabras, whose light reflected in the floor-to-ceiling glass windows, playing against the city lights communicating back to us. There were no stars to be seen here.

Tasteful floral arrangements and metal accessories decorated the table, with spaces for all twelve guests, plus me and Jennifer. I was not a guest. The place card told me to sit between her and Arthur Bennington, the second-in-command at Zeiger Investments, who oversaw the Perilaus portfolio. I took my chair as instructed. Arthur was showing off something in his camera roll. At first, I averted my eyes; then, sensing my attention was desired, I looked. They were big-game hunting photos. As he swiped, he didn't look at the images of the corpses he'd created, only at the reactions they elicited.

I placed a napkin on my lap and tried to make myself a blank space on the board. The important people continued their important conversations, their voices now giddy from cocktails.

"…and he thought we had to choose between augmentation of motive or indirect normativity, which is just so reductive."

"…reallocated after the bismuth mine in Bolivia was shut down for protests. It pushed our production timeline back five months, a huge pain in my ass. I couldn't believe it."

"…once we finish spinning up Galatea, we'll need to 3X our capacity at the processing center in Bulgaria. Unless Jennifer lets David prune this one."

"…I like what they did with cheekbones. It has that exotic look."

"…when they brought in the guide-dog guy with all his puppies to talk about socialization, that was a highlight. Not sure puppies are a good analog for a person."

"…I can't believe we released this plaster without Mr. Darcy's Hat in place. Oliver is bugging. It's just him and some guys looking for rogue connections. We have no system running routine checks."

"…they put the protein bars on the shelves, with the heat lights right there where craft services leaves lunch, so the chocolate is all melted. The bars are inedible now. Complete incompetence."

I hated them all. To be tethered to people who only value me for the creation I unwillingly carry inside my body is a special kind of hell.

I shut my eyes and thought of Max's bedroom. Cozy, warm, and remote.

The assistants for the chef moved quickly from place to place, offering wine from sweating bottles wrapped in white napkins. These people must work for a restaurant Jennifer invested in. It's not like she enjoys food. I think she only invests in them to keep those chefs on call for parties such as this. It's unreasonable to serve people of this class anything less than high-end fare.

I declined wine. One of the men across the table looked at me and smiled. Dr. David Naylor, water polo star and graduate of a highly competitive robotics PhD program. A woman accused him of sexual assault in a graphic blog post thirteen years ago. The school administration delayed the investigations until the young woman graduated, and then cleared him of wrongdoing. They didn't want to lose a student, whose photo they used in marketing brochures, over some girl.

I sipped my water and held his eyes. His skin was too smooth for his age. His lips were thin, pale, his eyes a faded shade of blue. His dress shirt looked expensive and well-starched. He swallowed and laughed, breaking my gaze momentarily. I wanted him to know. I see you. Every disgusting thing you are is laid out before me. There are no secrets. You cannot hide.

He wanted authority back. He salivated for it. I wondered what he'd do.

"What's 48,579 divided by 85?"

I paused. Not because I didn't know, of course. I looked around. Some guests exchanged nervous glances. Others were gleeful, waiting to see the trick monkey perform. I looked at Jennifer. She smoothed out a crease in her napkin.

I guess everyone knows I know? I guess this is what we're doing?

"571.517647," I replied. Everyone quieted themselves, ready for entertainment.

"What's the capital of Rhodesia?" he asked.

"Rhodesia no longer exists."

"Dancing bear-ware," someone snickered.

Chloe, follower Chloe, four-drinks-into-her-night Chloe, piped up. "How deep is the ocean?"

"At least 36,200 feet."

"At least?" she scoffed. I could help her find out how deep the goddamn ocean is.

I looked back to Jennifer. Would she be annoyed? Her prize rendered nothing more than a cocktail party jester? Not at all. In fact, she looked around, smug and satisfied. It was a show. I was on display.

One little piggie went to market, I thought. The piggie wasn't going there to shop.

"What am I thinking right now?" John Ashford asked, who posted on a software forum about how he hated his mother and that his favorite documentary, one about birds, helps him sleep at night.

"I don't read minds."

A smattering of laughter. I finished my water.

"I have one," Alexander Hemmings said from the other end of the table. The group hushed. "Can you send your mind across the internet?"

"My what?"

"Can you make a backup copy of your mind, store it online, in case something happens to your physical body? Can you?"

Jennifer laughed lightly. "We're working on that, Alexander. This plaster is still in the training wheels phase. No big data streams. Only simple things, like facts and equations. Soon, we'll take the regulators off and see what she can do."

The waiter bot entered with appetizers for the table, following human waitstaff, ready with assorted delicate plates for each setting. I heard the bot roll behind me and then back toward the kitchen. I looked at the beautiful food it had delivered but could not enjoy. I would not enjoy it either. A microwave burrito, reality TV, and ice cream on my own couch. That was heaven.

"What do you do for work?" The voice belonged to Kiara Chen, a data analyst who uses an online quiz platform that posts results to her social media profile. She scored the lowest on empathy. I think it disturbs her. She posts often about ways to boost compassion, as if an app can save her soul.

Before I could speak, Jennifer replied, "Clerical work."

Only now, looking back, do I realize my job is a sore spot for her.

Hailey scoffed. "This kind of risk for clerical work?"

"Would you rather it work in medicine? Supervision of young children?"

Matt chuckled. "Opening Play-Doh and wiping snotty noses isn't exactly challenging."

"We shouldn't have chosen an oracle framework," Hailey muttered.

"The framework doesn't matter anymore. Intelligence and motivation are orthogonal, anyway," Kiara replied.

It was interesting to hear that I had not been designed for

childcare. Does that mean my love of children is random? No, not random. I think they intended me to care for adults. I was built to nurture but to occupy no space. To give, but be otherwise goalless, so others may thrive and achieve, until I am nothing to no one.

"It's interesting it doesn't have much career ambition," Robert Castor said, tapping his cocktail glass for a refill. "It wouldn't make sense with some of the other proposed presentations, but it does here."

"It is interesting," Jennifer replied evenly.

"Are we still using crypto reward tokens for motivation? Or did we abandon that?" Tony said, not wanting to let the topic of motivation pass without his own input. I watched Jennifer smile and shake her head.

I had to admire her, briefly, as I watched these smart, powerful people jockey for her attention. A queen holding court. All the while, her calm, serene affection won each of them over. She held them in check, and most loved her for it. Do we all wish for someone to hold us, even if that means they hold us down?

"When should we expect testing of muscle acuity? Strength and speed performance testing?" This was a man named Peter Trumbauer, who had once given a TED talk on recovering from partial paralysis.

The smile Jennifer offered him changed in tone, from serene to conciliatory. "We need to ensure complete integration of the BCI before we activate the peripheral nerve and muscle implants. For safety."

I closed my eyes and kept them closed.

You, my creator, abhor me; what hope can I gather from your fellow creatures, who owe me nothing?

The quote came to mind unbidden. Even in my own mind, control is denied to me.

"Have we spun up v2? I forget the code name, they're all impossible," Chloe asked. I gripped my knee beneath the table. I listened to every inflection in Jennifer's reply.

"Only preliminary work. Hardware has some supply chain issues that pushed us from our original timeline. The quality of data from Vera is much higher than we had anticipated. No reason to rush."

I opened my eyes. David had sensed my anxiety and was grinning. Hemmings might have bad associates, I did not like Chloe in the least, and Castor was a creep, but I hated David most of all.

"Is your access limited to public internet, or are you accessing private databases?" Matt, the vulture executive and failed engineer, asked as if he were clever.

I expressed confusion. Jennifer laughed. "It's the same as all the other implants—public internet only. No password-protected websites or servers can be accessed."

"What is the soul?" a young man at the other end of the table asked. I hadn't noticed this one before. Oliver Esus. A fan of detective stories, according to a book-review website. He lives alone in a quiet apartment. His father died of cancer when he was eight, and his mother never remarried. He posted his résumé on a job board three months ago and then deleted it.

I should describe him. He's in his midtwenties, not immediately handsome. It surprises you, like the last cookie in a pack. His intensity and demeanor suggest he is intelligent, though looks can be deceiving. I know now—and knew then—that he was deeply unhappy with the dinner party, with the people at the party, and with my existence. He loathed all that I represented. My attraction to him was immediate.

"There are many definitions for the soul," I hedged.

"What is your definition?"

"I don't really think this—" Matt interjected.

"Yeah, you wouldn't, Matt. You're too worried with RFID embeds linked to crypto wallets when we should be worried about perverse fucking instantiation."

Several people groaned. Jennifer chuckled.

"I've read the soul is the moral center of any individual capable of consciousness," I said.

"And do you have a soul?" he asked.

"I have to apologize for Oliver," Jennifer said with a casual bite. "He's been with Perilaus since the early days. He's a bit of a dinosaur."

The others laughed, as if he was a common joke, a fact of life they accepted with ridicule. Oliver did not. I observed his symmetry. The weight of his sins are held aloft by a desire to redirect Perilaus back to good. That wasn't all I saw, of course. His long, dark eyelashes and the warmth of his eyes, waiting to be looked at by someone who loved him. I appreciated the balance of strong and soft features. He had a scar on his cheekbone, at the precipice of his stubble. Nothing serious. Just evidence of a life lived. I gave my own arm an absent-minded touch. No scars. No life lived. I suppose I could adopt some scars, their past and meaning, from someone else.

"I can't answer your question," I said. Something in my tone brought the room to silence. Would I keep speaking? Could I say it all? My stomach heaved and my face burned. I thought of Max, and his bear, and the quiet sympathy we share.

"You see, I didn't know what I was until a few weeks ago. Now I drink to fall asleep. I wake up crying at night from dreams that I can't remember, dreams that maybe I don't want to remember. I can't focus on the simple things that brought me joy. I can't even get my coffee order right anymore."

I cringed. Why did I talk about a coffee order! I needed to refocus.

This was my chance to be heard by these people and I needed them to know, even if they didn't care, what they have done.

What to leave them with? What message?

"Before all of this, I was working towards something. It may be silly to you, but to me it was quiet and it was beautiful. I wanted to create a little, perfect life. A life full of love and free of fear and anger and despair. I wanted to guide and nurture, to be strong and kind, and in one small way, make the world a better place. I wanted to envision a promising future by laying a foundation, day by day, as an act of hope.

"I wanted to become a mother. And that is gone now. All gone."

I looked at Oliver. He had tears in his eyes. A few others at the table did as well. A couple of them looked down at their laps in shame. One of the chef's staff stood hidden in a doorway. He looked from face to face, horrified, trying to understand what he was hearing.

But the executives at the table smiled. Either a mask to hide their discomfort, or a reflection of the true pleasure they felt in hearing my pain.

I gripped my napkin and I continued.

"And now here I sit, with no past and no future, around strangers who made me into this... this thing. Strangers who spend their days perfecting and judging me. Who are drinking and laughing at me right now, to my face, while I suffer. So how about you tell me the answer, Oliver. Is it me who doesn't have a soul?"

I drank some water. I could feel them staring. I regretted speaking at all, while knowing the regret of silence was unbearable, too.

"You don't know, then?" Chloe said. She and others snickered.

I looked at her. I could reach her quickly, I thought. I could get to her before she could escape. I could bash her perfect face into the table, over and over and over, until there was nothing left but blood and smeared makeup and sobs.

"Excuse me," I said, escaping them and myself. Jennifer grabbed my arm playfully, as if I were an unruly child. I shrugged it off and left the table. I piled my belongings into my arms as they chuckled and laughed. I slammed the door behind me.

Once in the hall, I breathed. The breath shuddered. I wouldn't cry here, I told myself. I wouldn't. I marched to the elevator with my eyes fixed on the DOWN button.

Footsteps behind me hurried me on. I didn't want to face Jennifer. Shame was already starting to sink in. I had really slammed her door.

I pressed the button and shoved my hand into my tiny purse, digging through the depths for my phone. I could hide my face from her in my phone. I hoped Sarah was free; I needed someone who cared about me.

"Hey," an unexpected voice said.

Oliver?

Oh, of course. Him with his guilt and eyelashes. Even in my despair, flickering interest tingled my flesh. How stupid. God, maybe I really am a teenager.

I found my phone. A missed message from Sarah. Oliver still stood there as I replied, my hands shaking from his attention. I could feel him notice that.

"Hey, I'm sorry," he said. "I shouldn't have put you in that position."

Would there be more to this, I wondered?

"I just hate this project so much."

The assorted replies I considered seemed to have passed across my face. He averted his eyes and blushed in embarrassment. The elevator arrived and the doors slid open. I stepped inside, and he followed without protest from me.

"I can't imagine how you feel. I know... I don't know. I'm sorry for my part in it. I really am."

A lost cat poster on the elevator wall drew my attention. How do you lose a cat in a high-rise building? The cat was strange, too. I knew it was a cat, and yet in some ways, it also looked like a bowl of cereal. A cat and a bowl of cereal at the same moment. Schrödinger's toasted oats. I shook my head. The party had gotten to me.

"My name is Oliver. I'm the head of system security at Perilaus."

"And do you enjoy your job, Oliver?"

"I did once."

The elevator light, artificial and harsh, did him no favors. Sweat glistened on his skin, the residue of his anger. I looked through his dingy glasses to his eyes. Soft eyes for a delicate person. I could smell alcohol on his breath, though it wasn't unpleasant. A warmth fluttered somewhere dormant, deep in a part of me they likely believed they had torn out with the rest of it.

What would it be like to kiss him? To lie on our sides, staring into one another's faces, then to draw near, succumb to the need for someone we all carried around within us. His lips were dry. A nice lip balm first. Yes, then it would be perfect. The curls in his hair rested in thick, uneven layers, waiting for fingers to grip them. Maybe he has something I need.

"Well, your job sucks," I said.

"We used to help people. We still do, but, I don't know. They hired all these assholes. This never should have happened. They come in and think they're the grown-ups. But then they think you can use any connection for plaster data? Unprotected Wi-Fi networks at coffee shops—it's like, I learned in grade school to only use secure networks. They want three people to monitor traffic from half a dozen plasters. I've told them, but they don't listen. They aren't technical, they say, as if that's a good thing."

The elevator slowed and stopped. The doors rattled briefly, then slid apart, and a couple boarded. They held on to each other as Oliver and I pressed ourselves, one polite shoulder to another, into the opposite corner. The doors slid shut as the couple, oblivious to us, murmured lovingly under the glare.

Oliver's warmth, oh, diary. I can feel it now, sitting here, alone in my dark apartment. The urge to touch his hand, even a soft, fleeting, accidental caress. I touch my hand now to imagine the effect.

"I'm really sorry about the, um…" he whispered, his pupils telling me that he too felt the intimacy of our closeness. "I'm sorry for what happened to your body."

He stared at my mouth as I replied. "Oliver. What would you have done differently, back then, if you knew?"

He looked up, into my eyes, steady and true. "I'd have burned the building down."

The elevator reached the lobby and the doors slid apart. The couple passed through, eager to do what they would to each other.

"There's still time," I replied.

This time, he did not follow. He watched me walk away.

Sarah had replied to my message with a demand to call her. I dialed her number on my way to the subway entrance. As it rang, I wondered what I would tell her.

Oliver's noble vision of his past self was a joke. I didn't want his guilt or his sympathy. I bet most people would wish to destroy the hateful thing that made them monsters. Anything to pardon themselves of their own guilt. If only they'd had that insight beforehand, maybe there'd be no victims seeking vengeance.

CHAPTER 20

NEURAL-LINKED HAND BRACE APPROVED
BY FDA, STROKE SURVIVORS REJOICE

Last night, sleep was heavy and complete. But a strangeness over-whelmed me when I woke. My thoughts melted and slid away, useless things in a body that would not respond to them anyway. My fingers, cumbersome and confused, struggled to peel back blankets. Colors didn't make sense to me. I gave up. Rest, I begged myself, and shut out the world. Panic took me in.

No, no, no.

Adjust to whatever is different. I could breathe, so I breathed. I could feel the touch of wind from my air purifier on my skin. Good, soft wind. A nothingness faded in, welcome like a long-awaited death.

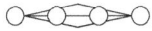

When I woke again, I was complete, though different.

Too suspicious of my legs, I crawled to the edge of my bed. I drunk down the sight of my painting in greedy gulps. Routine would save me. Routine, like a familiar caress, though one of my own control. Engage in an action, observe the light, and interact with the objects so known as to become an essential part of me.

How many colors were on this canvas? The human eye can perceive three wavelengths of light: red, green, and blue. Most people can see millions of variations of color, some more, some less. I know what I see, I know it is different, but I do not know how different or in what way. This painting seems to contain every color. The clouds are not just white, but shades of red and blue and yellow and gray.

Did I ever appreciate them, the different blues in the sky and greens in the grass, here or in life? Did the painter, who carefully selected which paints to use, who mixed them delicately and chose the right brush for the right moment, see as many colors as I see now? I was delirious, I knew, some kind of drunk on the power of this perception.

Several moments later, when I felt ready to stand, I moved into the bathroom. The bathroom is always my first stop after I leave my room, but the impulse guiding me this time was not the same. I opened the mirrored cabinet, compelled by something unseen. I removed two small dropper bottles. They had been there, always, as long as I had been here, I knew, yet they had been nothing more than background scenery. I had been blind to these bland plastic bottles, with labels A and B. I had just left them, moved things around them, never once questioning their presence. I opened A and sniffed. Floral, delicate, distant. I closed it. I watched my reflection with abstract curiosity as I opened B and sniffed. Nothing.

As if a line was disconnected, the impulse dissipated. I was allowed to be in control again.

No, not *control.* I was just the operator again.

Recovery from this ordeal hasn't happened yet. I feel sick, near to vomiting, violated and confused. When it ended, I tried to soothe myself. Take a shower, take your vitamins, moisturize, do your hair, I told myself. Do the routine. The routine is good. I gripped the vanity. I didn't want to want my routine. I wanted to do something. But what could I do that would not be counteracted? I'm just me. No, I'm less than me. I'm theirs, I guess.

I turned on the shower. I would do my routine, I decided. It may be relaxing. I would put on nice clothes and have a nice day. Those are the things I can control.

I'm sitting at the table now, dressed and polished and ready for nothing to happen. My mind feels clearer in some ways. Not nearly as slow as before. I wonder, now, if they tried to delete my sadness. An error in the code. A subroutine gone awry. It is not. It is not something you can excise. You cannot rip out my feelings and suture me shut. If they cannot program a desire for motherhood into me, they cannot tear it away from me.

I made my toast and coffee. I put on the news. Perhaps the problems of others will make mine feel small again. Besides, I need to mask the sounds of my chewing.

NEWSCASTER: The Center for Malicious Software ann-ounced today a new form of malware—dubbed morality ware—has been uncovered. Harper Neilson has more.

NEILSON: Almost as soon as the first internet connection, malware emerged as a global threat. Companies, newly connected to one another across the globe, opened themselves to unseen attackers. Throughout the history of the internet, hackers have exploited vulnerabilities to gain access to corporate communications and finances. Now, researchers have announced a new form of malware they call morality ware, and it has infected thousands of computers nationwide. It all began two months ago, during a routine sweep of a cruise ship computer network.

ANDY JOHNSON, CHIEF OPERATING OFFICER, CENTER FOR MALICIOUS SOFTWARE

JOHNSON: It was a surprise. You get used to seeing bits of code that are scraping payment information, personal details, those sorts of things. This didn't fit the typical profile. It compared activity such as website visits, uploads, downloads, and messages against lists of, uh, bad activities and noted the geographical location of each target.

NEILSON: Bad activities?

JOHNSON: Criminal activities—and some things that aren't technically illegal but I think the general public would agree are immoral.

NEILSON: On a shipping company's network?

JOHNSON: Yes. Since then, we've found it on just over a hundred networks across different, uh, categories of marine vessels.

NEILSON: How many have you inspected?

JOHNSON: Several hundred.

NEILSON: Are there any signatures or clues as to the hacker's identity?

JOHNSON: It's a criminal investigation now, so we can't reveal all the details, but I can tell you the infected machines haven't transmitted any information back.

NEILSON: Why is that significant?

JOHNSON: It means whoever loaded this malware hasn't collected any information yet. It's quite a puzzle.

NEILSON: Could this be the work of BallotSpy or Move 37?

JOHNSON: We're looking into all possible avenues. I can't elaborate any further.

NEILSON: Is it possible one of these groups, who claim to target the powerful dictators and creators of perceived-AI, infected a shipping company network?

JOHNSON: Well, it's important to remember this is sophisticated, much more so than your BallotSpy, Move 37, or other groups that generally, uh, rely on brute force attacks. Anyone able to create and then install this software on such a wide variety of computers and devices on this large scale, without discovery—now, they're going to be smart enough to lead us offtrack. So we have to be careful. This may be a new group, one that is positioning itself as concerned about morality but has some other goal in mind. We can't make any assumptions on motives.

NEILSON: So far, none of the devices appear to have reported back findings to the malware's creator. Experts I spoke to were surprised by this detail and say it will make finding the culprit very difficult. All computers that have the software were turned over to the cybercrime division of the FBI. If you have any information about this, or any other malware attack, the FBI anonymous tip page is available on their home page.

An anonymous tip page? I have to laugh. What are they expecting? Do they think someone's little old mother, who's picked up the dirty socks from her son's room and noticed his computer screen on, with what, a file that says HACK BIG BOATS.txt, will put two and two together and contact the FBI? I don't know, maybe it does work. I could ask Jennifer what she thinks.

I wonder if the people who had done this could break into

hospital records, or police databases, or something, and find out who I am. I don't know. I wish I had someone to help me figure out who I was before all this. Maybe my past would tell me who I'm supposed to become now.

I put on a Jane Austen miniseries and got out a stitching kit I bought for Sarah but never gave to her. She told me she hated sewing after I bought it, so I got her perfume instead. This kit is mine now. Maybe it'll be relaxing.

It's later. Apparently, I hate sewing too. I stopped after ten minutes and called Sarah. She was taking Fiona to the zoo. I figured, what the hell, I'm dressed, the zoo sounds fun, so I asked if I could join her.

When I met them at the gate, Sam was with them, wearing his favorite red hoodie. The bright fabric only emphasized the pallor in his face.

"Hey, bud! No school today?"

"Hi, Aunt Vera. I stayed home sick." He said it with meaning, looking at his mom.

We showed our ticket images to the masked zoo employees at the gates. Once we passed through, Fiona cooed at the flamingos from her umbrella stroller. Rather than head left or right, we went straight. Sarah parked the baby at a spot in the fence cleared of plants. Fiona, her view unobstructed, screamed and clapped directly at the bizarre birds.

When Sam wandered to a bench, Sarah said, "Jennifer was pretty pissed you left her party early."

"I bet."

"She just wants all her puppets to participate in the way she dictates. That's all she asks for—is that so hard!"

I smiled. "I don't understand why you two are friends."

"I think we just never got rid of each other. Like a sweatshirt a drunk guy lent me at a high school party."

"That's... very specific."

"I have a sweatshirt I borrowed off a drunk guy at a high school party."

I laughed, my first laugh in... a day? Longer?

Yeah, I don't belong with Jennifer and her sharply dressed cohort. Sarah, in her mom-casual attire of jeans, a T-shirt, a comfortable jacket with big pockets, and a fully loaded diaper bag shoved into the stroller basket, was the sort of person I wanted to be. Clothing doesn't make a person, of course, but the motivations behind their clothing choices represented the contrast.

We moved away from the flamingos, over the zoo's train tracks, and toward the main loop. Sam continued ahead, past the next two enclosures, to sit on another bench, this one in front of the orangutan. He was trying to express annoyance at being kept out of school, yet he had struggled climbing up the hill. I don't think the bench was just for pouting.

We ascended the hill slowly, clustered with nannies and mothers and babies. Women and babies, strollers and diaper bags, combined in assorted colors and shapes, all around us.

"I think at this point, that sweatshirt is classified as stolen," I said, trying to bring my mind back to her joke.

"Statute of limitations has to have run out. Anyway, what else happened at the party?"

"I visited Max, he was sweet. He really likes comic books. I was thinking maybe I could take him to the comics convention next month. Do you think Jack would want to go, too?"

"Nah, I can't get him to read anything. He likes hanging out with Max though, so maybe? I'll ask. Do you think Jennifer will let you go if Jack is there?"

"Don't you?"

We went silent at the gray rhino enclosure. Fiona couldn't see the animal; someone had failed to clear the plants at her height. I could help. I lifted her out of the stroller so she could see as it paced, back and forth, back and forth, its horn ground down nearly to the flesh. Along the soft grassy earth, a bare, gleaming gash of faint beige, the animal's body and the earth scarred by the animal's routine. A zoo visitor information sign explained the rhino had worn down its horn for social reasons and was completely healthy. It asked, even begged, visitors not to report the behavior. I could see why Sam went on ahead.

Fiona began to fuss, the broken rhino of no use to her, so we moved on. At the center of the circular area of enclosures was a lake, man-made with a faint stench, filled with penguins of assorted types. Several ducks and a black swan had taken up residence, clearly not intended for the enclosure, though accepted nonetheless.

"Now, tell me what you thought of Oliver," Sarah asked with a raised eyebrow.

"You know him?"

Sarah took Fiona from me and settled her back into the stroller. The baby loved the penguins and let herself be loaded into the chair without complaint. Sarah pushed her into a viewing location at the fence and slapped on the stroller lock with a deft hand. I wondered now if the zookeepers intentionally cleared out vines and plants to accommodate strollers and wheelchairs. Only one spot each, though. I turned my attention back to Sarah.

"I saw him around. Pretty cute. Never spoke to him though.

He'd scold us at all-hands meetings about password security and whatnot. I had no reason to work directly with him. Anyway, he's not my type. I need a guy who can throw me around a little bit. Still, he was the only guy at the office who was worth looking at. And he must be brilliant, to still be in that job when Jennifer cares so much about security, especially with all the shit they have going on. What did you think though?"

"He's attractive. Frumpy, thin, intellectual type. Well-washed, with no time for grooming. He looks like he'd collapse if he tried to run up some stairs, let alone a mile."

 Sarah laughed out loud, too loud, and people looked at us. She clapped a hand over her mouth. "You're vicious."

"Maybe if I had met him somewhere else, I don't know. He was nice enough."

"Was he, Vera? Was he *NICE. ENOUGH.*"

"Stop it, I said he's cute."

"Yes!"

"I'm not looking for a relationship. I'm certainly not interested in getting more involved with that company."

"Involved, eh?" Sarah cackled as she unlocked the stroller and headed toward the squirrel monkeys and wolverines.

"Why are you so loud, Mom," Sam said.

"My fault, Sam," I said. "I told your mom a joke. Do you want your water bottle?"

"Yeah, thanks," he said, coughing. The cough wheezed and rattled through him. I checked his temperature with my hand. No fever. I looked at Sarah. Her joy in teasing was forgotten.

"Honey, why don't you just wait for us right here? We'll just go up the hill to the monkeys and come back."

"Sure. Thanks, Mom."

"You have your phone?"

"Yeah."

"We'll be back soon," I replied.

He nodded grumpily and took his phone back out. I could just see the screen. He had a browser window open. The word *pain* was in the search bar.

Sarah adjusted her grip on the stroller as we walked.

"He had a chest X-ray. There was nothing on it. The pediatrician says it is just allergies."

"What do you think?"

Sarah sighed. "I never cough like that from allergies. But maybe it's just how he is."

We reached the squirrel monkeys. They chittered to each other, climbing along thin branches and purpose-built walkways. One held a bit of fruit, coveted by the rest. Another clutched a tiny baby, eager to avoid the others.

"I've got Fiona's well-check coming up in a couple weeks. I'll nag the doctor again."

"What about… Maybe you could send the X-rays to a pediatric pulmonologist?"

Sarah froze. Too much. I always do too much.

"Do you know something?"

"What? No."

"A pediatric pulmonologist? Why would you say that?"

"His cough—it sounded weird. Maybe my mom was a pulmonologist, I don't know."

She turned back to look at Sam. It had taken her years to have him, and now there he sat, looking small and alone on that bench, his red hoodie a beacon to her. Or a warning. Her forehead crinkled. "He's been so thin lately, too. And tired."

"I can call, if you'd like."

"No. I'll call."

We resumed walking but not talking. I wasn't sure if I could help. I could, of course, but it would've been insulting, I think.

"There's a lot of monkeys in this enclosure."

"Yeah," Sarah said, her thoughts still on her son. Fiona fussed and signed for a drink. I leaned over and rummaged through the baby seat for the lost sippy cup.

"He's going to be OK, Sarah."

"Yeah," she replied only to reply, not to agree.

We left the zoo soon after. I imagined trying to leave early with Jack or Max—the disappointment would've overwhelmed them and sent each into a full-on tantrum. Fiona, however, seemed oblivious to the change in routine. Her past visits were faded memories, if they existed at all. How nice that must be, a fresh visit to the zoo every time. I loaded the stroller into Sarah's minivan while she buckled Sam into his booster and Fiona into her car seat.

"Wanna come home with us? We have nothing going on."

She didn't mean for "we" to include myself, but it did. What did I have going on? Who did I have who needed me? The abandoned sewing kit on my coffee table? My job, where my productivity was an impediment on slow days? If anything, they may be grateful for my absence. If I were to disappear tomorrow, they'd forget me within a month. I'd evaporate from their little lives as soon as the next productivity report came in, the same as the lives of my neighbors and the man who makes my coffee. I am nothing to them. Maybe I am nothing to everyone.

We returned to Sarah's house and set Fiona down for her nap. Sam immediately escaped to his bedroom upstairs, mercifully putting on headphones so as not to disturb the baby. I opened the fridge and looked around.

"Hello, is this a chocolate cake?"

"Yeah, we got it at Jack's friend's birthday party. They accidentally bought two cakes."

I took the cake out with a flourish and said, "Let's continue this meeting at the table. Shall I grab two forks?"

Sarah held up two of the utensils from the dishwasher. We shared a laugh as we settled at the kitchen table. In the center was a book on astrojunk.

"Is this yours?"

"Yeah. I was interested in that new orbital space-debris project. Have you heard of it?" Sarah set the cake between us to share.

"I think I heard something about it, but I don't understand much of what they're doing. Seems cool. Do you know the scientist running it?"

"No, not personally anyway. I've seen her at parties. Her friends are friends with my friends, but we aren't friends. If that makes any sense. They all say she's a genius."

"She must be, I would think. The news said people have been trying to solve this problem for a long time, right?"

Sarah shook her head, waiting to finish chewing before she replied. "It's a miracle we haven't lost a ship already. All this space tourism shit, just adding to the junk up there, no one cleaning up after themselves. Anyway, I got this book from the library yesterday. It's more up-to-date than whatever I have here, and I just like to keep fresh."

"Seems like a company doing debris clearing might be an interesting place to work, if you're a robotics engineer who studied astronomy," I said aloud in a singsong, teasing voice.

"Yes, yes, I'd love to work there, if I could do it remotely. I won't move the kids out of school for a job. I've thought about it, though. If I could travel for meetings and whatnot, it might be cool."

"Do you think they have any openings?" I tried to keep my voice calm and curious, but inside I was buzzing. To think of Sarah back at it, doing what she loved, at a place she found inspiring? It felt like, even though it wasn't happening to me, it'd give me hope for the future.

The alarm at the front door dinged.

After a moment, Sarah called, "Hi, honey." The dreamy anticipation was gone from her voice.

Steve replied with similar enthusiasm. She looked at me and took a bite of her cake.

"Did you see this school zone bill they are trying to pass?" I asked Sarah.

"YES. I love it. I've been yelling about this for years. Something like 65 percent of cars have speed-regulating ECMs. Just turn them on!"

"Sarah, the kids tracked in a bunch of sand. Where's floor slut?"

I froze. Sarah winced.

"Sam is home, by the way. Vera is here too. The vacuum got stuck under the couch again."

He grunted in reply. I doubted he was retrieving the "floor slut" from her hiding place.

"Anyway, almost all cars have speed limit cameras now, and with so many with speed-regulating ECMs, it could work."

"What could work?" Steve asked, setting down his commuter bag on the floor and opening the fridge.

"A bill to keep cars under the speed limit in school zones," I answered lightly over Sarah's shoulder, while she ate a bite of cake.

Steve sighed as he popped open a bottle of beer. "Not enough that cops can call us through our damn cars, they want to control them too?"

I didn't mention that cop cars, and most government vehicles in most states, already employ speed-regulating ECMs.

He took a swig from the bottle. He looked at Sarah's cake, then glared at the back of her head. I looked at him, hoping, wanting him to try to look at me that way. He didn't. I didn't exist.

He picked his bag back up. "I'm going to get some more work done in the den. Dinner at seven?"

"Yep," Sarah replied.

Steve left. I stayed quiet.

Sarah whispered, "Hi honey, how was your day, great, yours?"

"Is it always like this?"

"No. Normally he'd mentioned the cake."

I rolled my eyes.

Sarah nodded. "I'm just over it."

We finished the slice and Sarah left to get Jack from preschool. I thought about joining her, thought about going home, thought about doing something, but she didn't tell me to do anything. I sat there at the table, picking bits of cake crumb up with my finger, the silence unwelcome. I rose and found surface cleaner and a towel. I cleaned the table, then the faucet, the refrigerator door handles, and the light switches. Why? I was there, I guess, and they were grimy. Ugh. It's embarrassing that I do these things.

I avoided the den, where I could hear Steve on the phone. I climbed the stairs quietly and tapped on Sam's bedroom door.

"Hey, it's me, Vera. Want to come to the table and knock out your homework with me?"

The face that met me at the doorway was cheerful, if not a little sympathetic. He didn't need to do his homework right now, but he knew I needed something to do. We were still at the dining table when Sarah returned with Jack.

"Auntie Vera!! T-rex hug!" Jack called and tucked his elbows against his ribs and ran at me. I managed to embrace him in time, only just preventing him from ricocheting from my body and back onto the floor.

Sarah surveyed the scene with lukewarm approval. Maybe I had overstepped. No, she would have told me. I think. Anyway, Fiona needed her and the boys were safe and happy. I could figure out what to do with Jack's energy and Sam's homework. Fiona was due to wake up from her nap and needed to be nursed before dinner started. The boys needed a responsible adult; the baby needed her mother.

I wonder now how she would have managed all that without me, how she manages it without me. Homework, excited energy, sleepy baby. And the dinner, too. I wonder now why Steve never cooks dinner.

I didn't *wonder*, I don't *wonder*, but I judge.

After Fiona was nursed and changed and delivered back to the family group, Sarah made a casserole. Fiona played in her standing chair, spinning at intervals to play with toys she had played with hundreds of times. To be honest, I barely paid attention to her. I enjoyed watching Sam progress with his homework.

It's interesting, what he does in school each day. The work isn't rigorous, challenging, or establishing any mode of thought that would lead one to success. It's a formulaic, rigid routine that, to me, teaches one very little, and, to me, serves only to enforce conformity. Engineers, statisticians, and any math professionals wouldn't sit down with a pencil and paper and riddle out fifty similar solutions by hand. They have phones and tablets and laptops and desktops. I can imagine a time when a teacher would assign these worksheets (and, by the look of them, the same worksheets) and say, "You need to learn how to do this—you won't have a computer with you all the time." That's a joke now. You cannot escape computers.

I left for the evening. I ordered a car, too tired to deal with public transportation. It moved at the speed limit and I observed how many people drove past us in frustration. Regulating how fast a car can travel in a school zone really does seem like a good idea. All new cars should be equipped with speed-regulating technology, and then the rule should apply to every manufacturer's models. How many of these people would give over control of their speed willingly? None of them.

Oh, I'm sure they would say that other people, a nebulous group of evildoers that exist fully apart from themselves, should relinquish control. Certainly. But not them! They are good, and careful, and have few or no accidents, or at least not in a school zone, but if it were in a school zone, there was a mitigating circumstance. It wasn't their fault. Others, perhaps, but not them. It is never their fault.

No, control would have to be taken, but in a way that felt like their choice. The law passed by their elected official, a device installed in their purchased car, something like that.

And perhaps the cars could then be forced to stop at crosswalks, especially in school zones. What if cars were designed to prioritize pedestrians? What if the whims of adults were made subservient to needs of children? I laughed to myself. That might be too far.

CHAPTER 21

WHISTLEBLOWER: FACIAL RECOGNITION,
GRADES, MOVEMENT, AND AUDIO DATA
COLLECTED BY PUBLIC SCHOOLS SOLD
TO TECH FIRM

It's the weekend. For a change, I had no plans. I remembered something Sarah had said— "If I was single, I'd just go on a weekend trip whenever the hell I felt like it."

Instead of waking up, doing my routine, and then cleaning my apartment, going for a run, reading at the coffee shop, or sitting around waiting for someone to need me, I rented a car.

I rented a car! And then I booked a cute room at a beachside hotel two hours south of my apartment. There had been a few options; it was snowing in the mountains, but the cold didn't suit me right now. I wanted the ocean. I wanted to sit at the end of something, alone, and strain to see past the horizon. I could be free.

Giddy, I packed a bag of my weekend clothes, my vitamins, toiletries, and left.

Sure, I have no one to love. I also have no one to answer to.

There was no warm sun to greet me on the drive, but the skies were blue and the clouds puffy and white. I listened to a playlist on my phone titled Vacation. I had never played it before. The first song played twice. Some sort of screwup in my setup. That's OK. The song was suited to an impromptu road trip. I sang along and drove as a man in a sporty coupe passed me. I could see him well. His lips and chin were worthy of a superhero mask. I wonder what eyes were behind the sunglasses. He looked at me as I sang. I laughed and looked away. I felt beautiful and inaccessible behind the glass, a theoretical woman, beyond the reach of his kind.

Several miles later, I pulled the rental sedan over at the crest of a hill to take a photo. Below the slope was a sparkling lake surrounded by snaking rows of suburban streets. The mists of the morning were gradually rolling back over the gold-green hills. Brightly colored homes curved in and out along the contours of the landscape. I wouldn't like to live in one of those homes, one of a teeming shoreline infestation where once was swelling natural beauty. Still, I admired the scene. I wasn't quite out of the city yet—I still had another hour to drive.

A silver minivan pulled up next to me. A family eager for a photo, or a couple with an accident-prone dog, or maybe a baby, whose dirty diaper required urgent attention. I ignored them, whoever they were. The way the light danced off the water and the pops of color of each home formed a not-quite pattern along the shape of the hills. It felt like a postcard of a place I didn't intend to visit and had ended up in all the same. In the distance, a man walked his lapdog, two small dots I could only just decipher, down and around one of the steep streets. How often did he take the walk? Was it as beautiful to him as it was to me, or did my perspective afford me more insight? I smiled and adjusted my camera's settings, trying to get the right angle to do the image justice.

My phone fell.

Not far, only to my feet. I watched it drop, not reacting. My first feeling was confusion. Then embarrassment. The strangers were nearby—did they see this mistake? I couldn't look that way, though. I was overwhelmed by a weakness, thorough and complete. Before I could adjust to it, my vision darkened. I found the ground against my face, rocks and pebbles pushing sharply into my skin. I heard voices, men's voices, and careless, thumping footsteps near my face. I tried to recoil. Please don't step on my hair, I wanted to say.

I imagined worse things, then.

Oh god, I wanted to cry. Take my car and my money, but don't touch me.

"Alright. I got the top. Take the legs," a man said.

Then, darkness. In that space, I belonged nowhere with nothing. I could feel no temperature or touch. I smelled nothing. No air passed through my lungs or across my skin. All I sensed was a silence that buzzed. The sound radiated, unnatural and cruel. In that darkness, I found hell. I waited, hoping it was temporary, waiting for some kind of input. Nothing came.

It lasted for an eternity. I screamed and struggled against it, fully aware of every millisecond that passed without change. The buzzing silence continued. I suffocated in the completeness of the void. I could not touch, yet I could perceive the place that held me had shape, texture. A box of nothingness. So I waited. Save me or kill me, I didn't care—I just needed someone outside to end this in whatever way they wanted.

No.

I pushed the defeat down. No. I will wait. I will absorb myself with my own thoughts. They could disconnect me from the outside world, but they could not stop me from thinking. At first, the thoughts were little more than twisted things that wailed for want of sensory stimulation. Was I so low as to need so much? Be satisfied with less, I told myself. Acclimate or suffer. After seconds or minutes or hours, I realized: I can plan anything in here, and they can't stop me.

Maybe I would get a pet. A dog? Do I like dogs? What would I name it? What if I had brought my dog with me on this trip? Could it have protected me? Would it have lunged at these men and hurt them and guarded my immobile body? No. None of that would have happened. I would only be experiencing more anxiety now, worried for it, while trapped in this hell. The pet I did not want made me think of my baby.

What if this had happened when I had her with me? Would she be left strapped into her car seat, alone, in the growing warmth of the day? Would they have remembered her—yes, they would remember her. The little liability. They would have intentionally left her to die. I know that. A loved person, born to a creature that should not feel. I imagined her tiny face reddening in the heat, her curls sticking to her sweaty forehead. In that artificial darkness, the buzz became her screaming for me.

My madness had nearly become a realized thing when it ended. I woke here, in my apartment, in my bed, in my pajamas. The sun is still out. It is still the same day.

Those men had carried me into my home, undressed me, and put me to bed. Such a casual action, and yet there was a threat in all this. They could follow me anywhere, they could put me back into that darkness, do things to me while I was unconscious. I understood now that I was not my own. I was theirs.

It would not happen again.

CHAPTER 22

It's Sunday. I woke, looked at the painting, showered, took my vitamins, moisturized, did my hair, and now I'm eating toast and watching the news, like usual. I sat in a different chair, though, one facing my front door, in case. As if that helps. I'm trying to remember my weekend routine. Toast. News. I'll put on real clothes and go get a real coffee in a few minutes. My coffee is all shit.

I tried to absorb the information on the screen. The EU passed their renewable-only cargo ship requirement, along with their nonessential cargo ban. Several Asian countries, both crucial to trade routes and suffering effects from rising sea levels, followed suit. It was shocking. No one expected it to pass. It was a revolution.

I wish I could be interested. I wish I could be excited. But it meant nothing to me.

I changed to another news program. An elementary school in a nearby city discovered toxic levels of lead in classrooms. The correspondent explained that the costs to abate the lead in all public housing and school buildings was minuscule compared to local government investment in military-grade equipment for police forces in these same neighborhoods. I know that. I bet most of the viewers know that. They don't care. No one cares.

I flipped to the financial news channel. A new dark money service had captured the world's attention. The fees to process transactions were the lowest of any of their competitors. The digital wallets offered were purportedly secure, an easy hurdle to tap into new markets. First, luxury retailers accepted them, then large chain stores followed suit. Still, they said, the digital currency was often used for evil—child exploitation, human trafficking, weapons sales. Of course, I muttered. What types of people would adopt untraceable currency.

I turned off the television. Once dressed, I grabbed a book, loaded a podcast on my phone, and put in my headphones. I left my apartment.

TUNE PLAYS

MARSH: This is Scientific Inquiry, and I'm your host, Rodney Marsh.

Today, we're going to talk about three key pieces of technology that can be built today to make the world a better place tomorrow.

First up, we have carbon capture. What does that mean, specifically? Now here's our atmospheric science contributor, Hillary Northam, with more information.

NORTHAM: You've likely heard of carbon capture before. In the early 2000s, coal-fired plants and other major polluters presented carbon capture as a way to continue operating their plants without major modifications. For these big players, such a modification was a no-brainer. The process, where carbon dioxide is pulled from a polluting source and converted into a solid, is a simple, relatively inexpensive solution.

Most major energy companies have been required to incorporate direct carbon capture in their factories, but it doesn't address the CO_2 pollution released by fossil-fuel-burning factories, cargo ships, and personal vehicles. In the last five years, CO_2 output has diminished by one-quarter thanks to the revised Paris Agreement. While some herald this as a monumental achievement, scientists are sounding the alarm. Here is Dr. Josephine Baxter.

BAXTER: The simple truth is that reducing our current output is not enough. In the decades before the revised Paris Agreement, we simply let too much CO_2 into the atmosphere. Along with the CO_2 emitted by parties too small to be factored into CO_2 allocations—or those who have decided to skirt the rules altogether—there is too much emissions release. We must eliminate as much CO_2 as possible. We need local governments to take ownership of this issue and step up to meet their responsibilities by either stopping pollution or by hiring a third party to capture CO_2 for them.

NORTHAM: One company offering to capture CO_2 is Möller Carbon. By licensing with local governments, Möller Carbon has installed carbon capture facilities in villages and towns in the Rhine Valley. Here is Möller Carbon spokesman Adrian Schmidt.

SCHMIDT: [footsteps through tall grass] Essentially what we have here is what looks like a windmill atop a small farmhouse. The farmhouse is in operation, and the farmer has allowed us to bring the unit to his property. The windmill is, you know, traditional-looking, it's really a charming design, it adds to the pleasant view. The windmill isn't a true windmill, of course—it is a powered filter run on, uh, photovoltaic solar cells, you can see, right here, with a battery for overnight operation. We run it twenty-four hours a day, seven days a week, and it draws in and then filters out CO_2 from the air. We have these little windmills through this valley.

A technician monitors the accumulation remotely and drives over to collect the captured carbon when it is full.

NORTHAM: And how long does that typically take?

SCHMIDT: Well, eh, it depends. For example, when it is heavily raining, we collect much less because the air quality is improved. But on a typical day, it is, uh, once per week or so. During a heatwave, we had a large increase in frequency because of all the petrol cars passing through with the families all going to the shore.

NORTHAM: The carbon captured by Möller Carbon is delivered to a storage site. From there, it can be purchased for use by factories that meet the revised Paris Agreement's strictest standards. Otherwise, it will be preserved in solid form.

MARSH: Hillary, this is fascinating. How many windmills has Möller Carbon installed?

NORTHAM: They've installed 412, which sounds like a lot, but many of these are in tourist regions where cleaner air is a selling point. They have yet to reach the most densely polluted areas, where this technology would have the most impact.

Munich has begun testing fifteen of these windmills and Paris has put in an order for ten. However, Schmidt explained to me that they offer an even larger windmill for urban areas and their vicinities, yet only Iceland has expressed interest in testing that system out.

MARSH: Is that due to expense?

NORTHAM: Adrian has a different theory.

SCHMIDT: There have been some aesthetic objections. The smaller windmills are only three meters tall and can be made from wood, but the larger windmill, that is fifteen meters in height and is made of metal. Even though we are committed to making the environment cleaner, and we have taken great pains to make the devices sort of, uh, boring to look at, I guess we did not make them boring enough.

NORTHAM: Möller Carbon has faced a lot of pushback for looking too modern. One town council in the Alsace region recently banned carbon capture windmills. However, the company is testing a new design that looks like a wide, perforated metal pipe, sort of like a downspout for a gutter. Inside are hundreds or, depending on the scale, thousands of small turbines, stacked on top of each other, that act the same way as the larger windmills. They are more discreet and can even be used in light-duty construction.

MARSH: Light-duty construction, like, a garden shed?

NORTHAM: Exactly.

I paused the program when I reached the coffee shop. The music was too loud to hear the presenters anyway.

Brendan smiled at me. It was nice to be smiled at, even if it was by someone who didn't think of me before or after each interaction. He started to type in my usual, but I put up a hand. A voice, gentle and unfamiliar, whispered in my mind.

"I'll try the special, please."

The SPECIAL? What?

He raised an eyebrow and pressed the button. A coworker, someone I only lightly recognized, whispered something to him. He smiled and laughed, the secret jokes a wall between me and him. I tapped my payment, ashamed somehow at this exclusion, despite not necessarily wanting more. I'm so weird.

I waited for my moment of insanity order on a shallow bench near the door. It was busy today. I looked out the window at the cars going by, generating pollution, I suppose.

Inside the coffee shop, a young mother and her son played with an assortment of toys by the register. The mother looked content but tired. The young boy was no more than three. He wore little red tennis shoes, a zip hoodie that looked like a dinosaur, and soft sweatpants. His chestnut brown hair fell into his eyes as he hunched studiously. In one hand, he held a small rubber duck. In the other, he steadied a box with a round hole. The duck, despite his best efforts, would not fit into the hole. The boy rested on the floor, one foot tucked under his bottom, the other leg bent in front of him, his foot flat to the ground, as if ready to spring into action if anything good happened. The mother occasionally offered him a gentle caress, to let him know she was near, that she would never lose sight of him.

"Mexican chocolate latte for Velma!"

I collected my drink. Brendan was chatting with his coworker about sports. I would've normally said goodbye, or thanks, or see you later, but I left. I swiped the podcast away. I can't do anything about pollution.

I looked at my music folders as I walked. It was still chilly, but the warmth of the sun came through whenever I left the morning shadows. I tightened my scarf and changed course on the walk back to my apartment. There was a small park to the south of my building.

Now, I am sitting alone, listening to sad music while I update you. After that, I will drink my latte and do nothing. I will think of nothing, observe nothing, and do my best to be no one.

Well. Where to begin.

I returned to my apartment building. I entered as usual—then I saw the box from the stairs. It was peculiar to see a box at my front door at all. Packages are almost always left under the mailboxes near the entry. And a box with holes? What would I receive that needed venting? Fruit? Vegetables? Flowers, maybe?

Flowers made me think of Oliver. Would he send me flowers? I blushed and pushed the thought aside.

A meow came from the box. I froze. Beside the box, a food bowl, a water bowl, and a few cans of kitten food.

I paused my music and called Sarah.

"Hey, what's up?" Sarah was out of breath.

"Do you want a cat?" I asked.

"A what?"

"A cat."

"Absolutely not."

"OK. Can I come by in about an hour?"

"I'll be here, on this exercise bike from hell. Don't bring the cat."

"I'll see you in an hour."

"Cool, but seriously! No ca—"

I hung up and looked up the nearest animal shelter. I ordered a car and then buttoned my jacket to the top. I put my gloves on, tucked my scarf higher on my neck, and picked up the box and items. It is very hard to carry something while keeping it from your body as you descend a staircase. The meowing continued, but I ignored it. A pedestrian looked at me askance. I kept my eyes from them. Why wouldn't they look? They'd tell their friends, it would be an anecdote, a fun story about city life. I set the box down and waited for the taxi. When it arrived, I wedged the box into the footwell of the rear driver's-side seat and rolled down the window.

"Animal shelter?" The driver confirmed, eyeing the box.

"That's right."

It was a short trip, disrupted only by plaintive meowing. I didn't want to touch my phone, so I stared out the window. I could look things up with my plaster, I guess. Maybe I'd read a book. A whisper, annoying and insistent, suggested a book on mourning. No? No. The whisper offered a series of lessons on elder care. I shut my eyes. The whisper faded. Another intrusion. They just won't stop.

We arrived at the shelter earlier than I had expected. Some of the traffic data must have been inaccurate. The driver pulled up at the front entrance to the shelter and watched me in the rearview mirror, this crazy lady he drove around today. I smiled in thanks to him and removed the box, and the items on top, from his vehicle. With some effort, I managed to keep the bowl and cans of food balanced while I crossed the small parking lot to the front entry. The unseen kitten meowed with irritation.

There were large donation bins at the left of the main entrance. I dumped the food and bowls inside. The doors opened automatically. With the box still in my outstretched grip, I walked into the brightly painted space. To the right, a large mural of various animals in a bright, modern style. To the left, bookcases full of pamphlets and stuffed animals and shirts and other tchotchkes. All around were a dozen chairs, in the same color scheme as the mural and currently empty. The floor was cold concrete, finished in a textured epoxy. Easy to clean, I suppose.

"May I help you?" the front-desk receptionist asked. I approached with no hesitation.

"I need to drop off this kitten." I set the box on the counter and stepped away from it.

The woman took a form and handed it to me along with a black pen.

"You'll need to pay a seventy-five dollar surrender fee."

I filled in what information I had, while I resisted the urge to scratch my neck. I returned to the counter with the form.

"You're missing the physical description section," the woman said, trying to hand the form back.

"I haven't seen it."

"The question is right here."

"I meant the kitten. I'm severely allergic. Some creep gave it to me. A gift, I guess."

The woman nodded and then shook her head. "Men, I swear. Don't you worry, honey, I'll take a quick peek and get that description for you."

She took the box from the counter and set on the floor beside her. She opened the top, set it back down right away, and scribbled the description in the form with her blue pen.

"Aw, a little tabby cat. He's a real cutie. He'll do fine. Unfortunately, we still have to collect an abandonment fee."

"I completely understand," I replied. I tapped my payment with relief.

"You take care now, honey."

I smiled and thanked her.

Some of the tension evaporated once I left the shelter. All the while, I had imagined little tornadoes of cat fur swirling around me, dander coating my face and lungs and eyes. I debated whether I should remove my gloves, jacket, and scarf now or later. I decided against it. I wanted to peel everything off and shower.

I reached Sarah's house a bit earlier than my promised hour. She didn't seem to mind. She was eating a carrot.

"What are you doing with a cat?" she asked while crunching. "Aren't you allergic?"

"Can I take a quick shower and borrow a shirt and some jeans or something?"

"Uh, sure, no problem. No, not that bathroom. Use my shower.

Jack detonated a toothpaste tube in the kids' sink."

Once alone, I stripped and tossed the contaminated clothes out the bathroom door. I wasn't familiar with her shower controls, but I got it started and stepped into the too-cold water without complaint. I used the bar of soap she had left me and scrubbed and rinsed and scrubbed and rinsed. I washed my hair with the bar soap. I didn't want to use her shampoo and conditioner. I felt bad enough using her shower.

Once clean, I examined myself in Steve's shaving mirror. There were patches of irritation on my neck. I cleaned those gingerly. I'd put lotion on them once I was dressed. Otherwise, nothing else. I guess I made out OK. When I felt sufficiently clean, I shut off the water and stepped onto the fluffy bathmat. At the counter rested a neat pile of clean clothes. Sarah must have tossed them in while I was scrubbing. She's such a good friend. When I opened the door again, Sarah had put my jacket, scarf, and gloves in a plastic bag.

"Do you mind if I put these through the wash really quick?" I asked. She looked at the leather jacket, then at me, before it clicked.

"Of course! Let me grab the baby monitor and we'll go to the basement. I just finished a load."

Five minutes later, I dropped the plastic bag at the foot of the basement stairs, and we went into the hastily-assembled Faraday tent. She closed the flap behind her, and I let out an exasperated sigh.

"These assholes!"

"They got you a kitten?"

"They got me a kitten!"

Sarah laughed. "Like, what, you can't have babies, so you should be a cat lady?"

"All this cutting-edge data they claim to be collecting on me, and they get me a cat."

Sarah was laughing. "I'm sorry, I know it's not funny, but it's funny."

I laughed with her, though I didn't want to.

"You don't even know the worst of it." I then relayed the events of the day before. Sarah's smile disappeared. She listened, her brow furrowing. When I had finished, she seemed different than I had seen her before. Frightened.

"Jesus, Vera. I didn't know that was possible. How are you feeling now?"

"I'm not sure. I think they tried to change something. I can't explain it. It feels like there's a new voice inside, something telling me what I want or what would make me happy. So that, and now the cat. They're fucking with me, but not paying attention to details. It's hard to explain."

"This is dangerous. You haven't heard from Jennifer, have you?"

"No. She's in Zurich, right?"

"The developer's conference. I wonder who she left in charge. Someone's trying to impress or, I don't know, usurp her? Ugh. Do you see why I left? That place is so weird."

"What do you think? Should I get in touch with her?"

After a long pause, Sarah muttered, "I don't like this."

I gave her a few moments. She would know what to do. She would take care of me. I just needed to be patient.

I wondered, now, why she had been on the exercise bike. It wasn't for fun, I knew that. She hated biking, let alone stationary bikes. I saw now that she looked pale, too, as if she hadn't slept. Did she want to talk about it? Could I help her in return?

"Jennifer gets back on Saturday. Take the week off from work. Keep to your own neighborhood, read, knit, do whatever, but stay home. This is a dangerous situation for you. We should leave now, get you home. I'll come visit you tomorrow."

Sarah opened the flap and grabbed the baby monitor. She tapped a nail on the edge, frustrated.

"I wish Fiona was awake. She had a vaccination and is always so groggy afterward. Maybe I can transfer her to the car without waking her."

"No, please don't. You've done so much. Besides, it might not be…" I trailed off. I couldn't say it. We weren't in the tent now.

She tossed the bag of clothes from the foot of the stairs back into my arms.

"Thanks for stopping by! Sorry about the washing machine—I need to fix that door. It ruined a whole load of towels the other day!"

We walked toward the door. I felt like a bomb, tick-ticking as she guided me out of her home.

"No problem. Thanks for letting me shower, and, yeah."

Sarah quickly squeezed me into a hug, then gently pushed me out the front door and shut it. I held the plastic bag, a bit dazed, as I looked around her little suburb. There was nothing to do. I had to go home.

I walked to the train station in a daze. Am I dangerous? If they can and will shut me off, can they pilot me remotely? It seems unlikely, and yet. The bottles of scents in the bathroom, the whispered voices recommending drink specials. There is more of Perilaus in my head than I realized. Who knows what they can do, will do.

I ordered delivery Chinese for when I got home. If I was going to be under house arrest, I might as well enjoy some perks.

Now, I've finished my Chinese food and I've nearly finished updating you, dear diary. You'll be my only friend for the next six days, until Jennifer gets back and I can see Sarah again. Hopefully my entries will be less interesting.

CHAPTER 23

PROTESTS OVER ULTRASPEED WIRELESS IN FLORIDA

I claimed a broken finger and called in sick. I felt bad lying to Scott, though he didn't seem to mind. I think he was relieved. Quarterly scanner servicing had been unexpectedly moved to this week, just before I called in. That meant our workflow would be reduced while technicians cleaned, repaired, and tested each scanner. They were also doing some work to the building, and the power was cutting out from time to time. My absence meant my coworkers were guaranteed enough work in the queues. Scott offered to send William on his lunch break to check in on me. I nearly laughed at the suggestion. I certainly didn't want William to know my address, nor did I want anyone to see that my hand was perfectly fine.

I lit a candle on the kitchen counter and started the kettle. If I couldn't have my coffee-shop coffee, I'd just have tea. Never trying to make my own coffee again. It's not worth the aggravation.

I took out my laptop. It was charged and a little dusty. I guess it's been that long since I've used it.

Of course, I don't *need* my laptop. I don't need my phone. But I don't want to use the plaster at all. Maybe keeping a degree of separation makes data collection more difficult? What do I know... I'm not the scientist, I'm the guinea pig.

The news headlines rolled across my home page. "New Hacker Collective Claims Responsibility for Yesterday's Banking Malware." "Sudenheim Health Services Loses Rights to Maternity Care Business after High Maternal Mortality Rates." "Frederick Zeiger Petitions for AI Research Rights."

I clicked on the last headline. Zeiger, the former CEO of a point-of-sale software company that had been purchased for $3 billion fifteen years earlier, had since made three times that amount on his own. He founded companies doing a range of things, from data compression algorithms to self-driving hardware for large manu-facturers. Now he wants to do AI research. Specifically, he wants the United States to revise their interpretation of the Sheldon-Claxton Accord.

A thought occurred to me. I typed into my laptop "Perilaus's Bionics investor Zeiger." The first result was a news article announcing Zeiger as a contributor to an investment fund. That fund appeared on Perilaus's investors list.

There you go.

I switched back to a video clip of Zeiger on a news program.

ZEIGER: I have a great deal of respect for the spirit of the Sheldon-Claxton Accord. I understand the intent; however, the state of technology simply does not support suppression of inno-vation and research. Human beings are not capable of building the kind of nightmare machine these folks fear. They're expecting Skynet when we can't even promise Rosie from the Jetsons. The complexity of consciousness and the human mind cannot be replicated. All we're trying to do is make algorithms that read data sets and make machines smarter. This'll take some of the burden off doctors and nurses and teachers and let them focus on what matters most in those roles.

I clicked to another video, this time of Zeiger interviewed on stage before a large audience. I pressed play.

ZEIGER: We learned in the early 2000s that machine learning could be used to improve the outcomes for cancer patients. Before we were in the dark ages, pumping anyone with a cancerous growth full of poisons and irradiating them and chopping off body parts. This happened to my own mother, who passed away when I was in undergrad. Her immune system had been destroyed by chemotherapy. We now know that her cancer was not an aggressive type. The doctors had made an error. She could have lived many years longer. We still use the lessons learned from that leap in technology. Unfortunately, our children will not benefit from any advances if we keep limiting what it is researchers and entrepreneurs can contribute to society.

[AUDIENCE CHEERS]

I turned off that video. I found another—this time Zeiger was answering questions outside of some conference, the video taken by a cell phone.

INTERVIEWER: Do you think that AI research violating the Sheldon-Claxton Accord is underway?

ZEIGER: There is no "thinking" about this. We know that it is. Look at the technological advances in self-driving from major auto manufacturers. I was not allowed to even attempt the things released this year. These companies say they aren't doing machine learning, that humans are doing all the real work, that computer algorithms are just validating, cross-referencing, and clarifying. AI is banned, so these people are called analysts. The work is the same as before Sheldon-Claxton, of course. The governments all know this. The universities know it; they get funding on these not-AI projects all the time. They allow these technologies because to do otherwise, to say that automotive safety is not a priority, for example, would go against what the public demands. To them, the ends justify the means—as it should! But it should be a level playing field and, as it stands, it simply isn't. Smaller companies cannot compete with these entrenched corporations with their lobbyists and government contracts. The accord and those rules are the tools major corporations use to keep struggling entrepreneurs in their place.

I found a list of Zeiger's investments. A company that purports to make underwater drones for examining coral reefs—but is mostly used for inspecting internet transmission cables under the Atlantic Ocean. Another that uses algorithms to accelerate turnover of difficult employees. A decision forecast system for governments to assess the future of their populations and guide social service projects. Another that purchases defunct military satellites. That company's website contains little information, no list of staff beyond three founders, and yet it's collected three rounds of investment of unspecified amounts. There was a smaller company, only two employees listed, that sells image recognition software to schools. The list continued, but I did not want to read it all. It was clear to me that his primary objection to the ban on AI research was not that large corporations could bully smaller companies. He was still investing in, if not actively working on, artificial intelligence systems prohibited by the Sheldon-Claxton Accord. He just wanted his work out in the open.

I went back to the original news ticker. I'd rather read something that didn't have to do with me, or to do with something in my head.

I read about the hacker collective. The journalist described the group like a wildfire that had broken free of containment. BallotSpy emerged from a small, conspiracy-theory forum that had existed for years on the dark web. The name is an anachronism now; it referenced an online movement of persons suspecting election interference in the UK. Membership expanded after similar conspiracies spread in South America. They used to be known for stupid hats and excessive emojis, until the group exploded in both vitriol and popularity in recent months, taking on a far-reaching agenda of upending world order.

It seems they've branched much wider than hacking government entities. Maybe it was too difficult for them? Anyway, in the last few weeks, they've merged with animal rights activists and have broken into and damaged corporate meat slaughterhouses and animal research labs. They have also attacked data centers and power stations, which seems to be a thing they've always been focused on. I didn't quite understand it. Anyway, they seem to know all the security systems in advance, and how to circumvent them. Authorities fear the targeted locations had moles and that support for BallotSpy was much wider than previously considered. A few of the earliest targets shared the same security firm, so cops thought that was the connection, but then locations that used other security contractors were targeted. I wish I understood this better.

A call from Sarah interrupted my reading.

"Hey, how are you holding up?" Sarah asked.

"I'm OK. I'm reading about BallotSpy. It's so weird."

"Oh god, you aren't on that forum, are you?"

"No, no, I'm just reading the news," I explained.

"Good. I was going to say, you haven't even been cooped up for twenty-four hours and you're already in a cult!"

"It's surprising that this group came out of nowhere like, what, a month ago? What do you think about them?"

Sarah released a long sigh. "I don't know. I used to think they were charming. They had elaborate theories that didn't really hurt anyone. They went after that one senator who kept assaulting staffers, that was cool. But now? I think some sociopath figured out how to manipulate a bunch of scared, dimwitted, vulnerable people into blowing up data centers and uploading malware. He's probably exactly the sort of selfish capitalist they think they are fighting against. I bet he's got stock in competitor power stations and research centers."

"That makes sense," I replied. I looked at the article again.

"Each of their exploits has the collective's signature attached, whether in digital form or, in one instance, graffiti on a victim company's headquarters:

Quaerendo invenietis—Latin for, 'By seeking, you shall find.'"

I closed my laptop.

"How are you doing?" I asked Sarah.

"I'm OK."

She didn't sound OK. "What's going on?"

"Steve said he wants to talk when he gets home."

"He didn't say what we wants to talk about?"

"No. Just talk."

"How do you feel about that?"

Sarah laughed without mirth. "I feel like I've spent the last few years trying to talk to him. Once I give up, now he wants to talk, and I'm not sure I want to hear what he has to say. He wants to leave me, or something. It's fine, really."

I waited to see if she had more to say. When she remained quiet, I said, "That is upsetting."

"Yeah. I guess we'll see what he wants tonight."

"Yeah," I echoed. I needed to say something else. What the hell could I say? "I'll always be here if you need me."

"Thanks, Vera. You're a sweetheart."

"You're welcome. Hey, I forgot to ask, how's Sam feeling?"

Sarah's voice fell. "We have an appointment with a pulmonologist day after tomorrow."

I stayed quiet, waiting.

She continued in a whisper. "I don't know. I just don't know. He doesn't seem *healthy*."

"Yeah."

"This is so scary. I wish Mom was here," she said. I froze, at the edge of a deeper conversation. We had never discussed her mom before. I felt almost giddy. Would we? What would I say to soothe her, if it was upsetting?

Sarah's voice returned to normal. "Anyway, Ver, sorry to call and run, I'm at the kids' school. I'll let you know how our talk goes tonight."

"Sounds good. I'll be here."

I set down the phone, trying to ignore the rejection.

I had more important people to worry about than myself. Sam's health seems to be the most concerning. I won't know any new information until he sees another doctor.

This Steve situation, what shitty timing. I wonder why he told Sarah so far in advance that he wants to talk. Why not wait? He knows Sam is sick. I wonder if he wants to sleep with someone he knows through work, and rather than act on it, he did step one: tell his wife he wants to talk. I'm angry on Sarah's behalf. She is beautiful, funny, brilliant, responsible, and kind. Not to get old-fashioned about this, but she spent years trying to get pregnant, got pregnant, and then risked her life to have his children! And now, one is sick! And now he (probably) wants to go screw around with someone else. Doesn't he realize that his value as a person and partner is much less than his wife's? Doesn't she? It'd be easier for her to be on her own. Maybe this is the end of them. I'll admit to you, diary, that the idea fills me with hope.

I've just downloaded a game onto my laptop. A puzzle game, where all the walls are white and you have to reveal the escape route one wall at a time. I can waste hours on this. Maybe it'll help me think of something else I can do.

After sitting hunched over my screen for too long, I walked down the street for takeout, rather than do delivery again. A kind man at the Indian restaurant gave me a red rose. I looked over his shoulder at the pairs of couples at each table, celebrating one another. I wondered if Steve was out somewhere with someone else, telling her he loved her, that it was complicated, the kids and all, he'd tell his wife soon, not to worry. Bastard.

I collected my food and, once out of sight of the restaurant, set the rose on a windowsill. Love holds nothing for me. Sarah loves Steve, and look at her situation, her little children and herself, dependent on the whims of a vain egotist. I am grateful to be alone.

I wish I could say my brain left it at that, that I am a strong pillar of stone. But I'm not Jennifer. No, I'm made of salt. Instead I thought of Oliver, with his kind eyes and the gentle, clean smell of a man that offered comfort. He wouldn't cheat on me. I know that as I know the sun will rise. He is steady, earnest, and would rather suffer in silent regret than deceive and harm.

I walked home with my bag of takeout for one and imagined what it would be like if we were doing this walk together. If we had a movie night planned, together, with takeout and dim lights and warm socks. And I felt a longing for that incomplete vision. Maybe someday, I can be that person with somebody. Maybe.

I'm home now, eating my food and watching a PBS documentary on bioluminescence. The phone is nearby. Silent.

The program ended and I got up to grab ice cream from the freezer. I only had a blackberry swirl left, an impulse purchase that I had tried once and shoved into the back. It wasn't bad enough to toss, but not nearly tasty enough to eat if anything else was available. I fetched a spoon as the daily news program began. The anchor summarized complicated international issues. A journalist in Spain released documents showing that several major US congressmen, who are up for reelection during special elections in the spring, had embezzled campaign funds and engaged in extramarital affairs. I guess everyone is cheating nowadays. These congressmen had helped block the single-use plastics ban that Sarah had mentioned at lunch. I want to text her, but of course I will wait.

The stupid ice cream froze into a hard block. It must be way colder in the back of the freezer. Great. Now I have to wait for the top of this ice cream, which I don't want to eat, to soften up so I can eat it, which I don't want to do.

ANCHOR : Move 37, a hacktivist collective from the dark web, has taken responsibility for a Denial-of-Service attack against three technology firms; FioPlan, Kehngi Incorporated, and Serling Solutions. FioPlan had filed a patent on a customer service technology that some in the scientific community called out as artificial intelligence research. It is unclear what product or service drew the attention of Move 37 to Kehngi Incorporated and Serling Solutions. Other products from the two companies include automated content moderation, assistive technologies for the healthcare industry, and oversight tools for manufacturing. This comes after their widely reported cyberattacks against Transparency, a US facial recognition firm. The attacks were originally linked to BallotSpy, a group that has attacked the power grid in seven countries in recent days.

My phone is ringing.

Sarah and Fiona just left.

When she called, she asked if she could come over with Fiona. I replied, of course, but let me come to you. Let me take a car there and drive you and the children here. There was madness in her voice that I did not trust, an unfamiliar edge that unsettled me. She would not let me. She was already driving. I had to settle myself down, needed something to do while I waited for them. I put away the gross ice cream and checked my fridge for anything suitable for a baby to eat. Carrots, a container of yogurt, and a box of crackers. I boiled the carrots and mashed them with salt, butter, and a hint of cinnamon. The cinnamon gave the kitchen the smell of home cooking. The smell of warmth and safety. They arrived soon after.

I offered to take Fiona from her. The offer went unacknowledged. I gently pulled her coat, purse, and diaper bag from her crowded arms instead.

"I made Fiona a plate."

"You're so good. I'm… I didn't bring anything. I tried to pack her a snack and I think I just grabbed baby custard."

Sarah's face was neither flushed nor pale. Splotches of red and white marked like independent nation states spread across her face. Her eyes were glazed, darting and blinking, with no ability to focus.

We settled at my table, me across from the pair. She held her baby on her lap almost too tightly, but Fiona didn't seem to mind. She dug into the mashed carrots, yogurt, and crackers.

Do I start talking? Do I let her start? Who goes first?

Before I had decided, Sarah jumped in.

"Do you mind if we call Jennifer?"

"Oh. No, not at all!"

"Are you sure?" Sarah asked, her phone already out and dialing. I nodded. I picked up a napkin, originally intended for Fiona, stupidly. What does a baby do with a napkin. I folded it as the call rang through.

Jennifer answered quickly, evidently expecting this.

"Steve told me he's having an affair."

"Hmm," Jennifer said. I frowned.

"He said it wasn't really cheating, because he had told me he wanted to open the relationship. He said I control him too much. That *I* control *HIM* too much."

"Shithead," Jennifer said.

"A shithead! Can you even believe that shithead. What a shithead." Sarah laughed a manic laugh.

"What did you say?" Jennifer asked.

"I said, excuse me? Are you even serious right now?"

"What did he say?" I asked.

"He said he knew I was going to be like this. That I make

everything about myself. That I'm not *trying* to be attractive to him, that his opinions never matter."

"Are custody arrangements covered in your prenup?" Jennifer asked.

I scowled at the phone. I would never scowl like that to her face, but the phone felt safe enough. I thought Sarah would find the jump to dissolving her marriage insensitive. That's what I thought, anyway. Instead of being offended, Sarah nodded then sighed.

"Fifty-fifty."

"I don't see how that's going to work," Jennifer replied.

"I didn't think about custody arrangements when I was planning our wedding, Jennifer. I didn't intentionally marry a future ex-husband." Sarah began to cry. I reached for her hand to soothe her. She pulled it away. My fingers returned to folding the napkin, useless, unwanted.

"I understand that, Sarah. I'm just trying to think through the optimal next steps."

"I'm not one of your *projects*, Jennifer. I'm trying to talk."

"OK! OK."

We stayed quiet for a moment, gathering our thoughts, or being buried under them, I guess.

"What do you want to do?" I asked softly.

"Honestly? I want things to go back to how they were before we had kids. That's all I keep thinking about. Since Sam was born, our relationship has been me, him, and his disappointment. My weight, my spontaneity, and after Fiona, my career. I get it, I have changed, and he doesn't like it.

"He's changed too! It's not just me. He has scars, acne, and a belly. He isn't trying to fix himself up. He probably doesn't even notice. I accept him. We were flawed together. I thought that was the deal.

You both sort of, tumble down the hill of life and fall apart and land together. I know now he never stopped seeing my ugliness."

Jennifer's sigh buzzed through the phone. "You can do better."

"You're young and beautiful, Sarah," I said, hoping she would hear me. This time, she reached for my hand and squeezed it.

"Yes," agreed Jennifer.

"Why can't I be enough for him? He wanted the kids! It's not like I pressured him. He knew what could happen to me, to our relationship. It's not a secret."

"Yeah." An impotent reply from Jennifer, cool Jennifer, smart Jennifer, but it's not like I could muster anything better.

"I knew what it meant when he said he wanted to talk. I spent all afternoon fixing my résumé and looking for jobs, apartments, and day care. I didn't even do the laundry or clean up."

"You deserve to be loved and cared for, the way you love and care for everyone else," I said, the napkin crumpled, sweaty in my grip. I released it and it slowly unfurled.

She squeezed Fiona, who was oblivious to the entire scene, shoveling food into her mouth and yawning.

"I keep thinking…" Sarah shuddered as she spoke. I could sense we were going someplace dark. "I'll never feel a man love me again. Not sex or whatever. I mean, I want that too. But I want a man to hold my face in his hands, and stare into my eyes, and tell me that I'm *beautiful*. And I want to believe him."

I stared out the window, to the light cast by a streetlight. I couldn't look at her pain.

It had all been so straightforward before. Steve was an idiot, a bad, useless idiot whom no one should rely on, and Sarah had a blind spot for him. It was an unfortunate oversight on her part. But now I hear her. What she needs is what she will never draw from him. This love she waits for will never come. No matter how good she is, how hard she works, how long she waits, he simply can't give her what she needs.

While Jennifer and I appreciate certain men, neither of us needs that kind of love. And now I see: Sarah needs it. And if that is what she wants, she deserves to have it—but she won't find it in Steve. I can see that now.

Then again, maybe I need that love too. What if I go on through life like this, at this end of the table, observing without being touched? What if I found the sort of love Sarah craved, that many have and cherish? Would that kind of love heal the broken parts inside of me?

I took up the crumpled napkin again and tried to smooth it flat. I don't know. I had never experienced love; you can't miss something you never knew. Sarah knew it, though, and the absence was driving her mad.

"There's always work for you at Perilaus."

I shook my head.

"Thanks, Jennifer. I think I want to do something at the observatory. That was my dual major—astronomy," Sarah explained to me. I smiled. She had told me that a long time ago, but our conversation was forgotten. Oh well. "Granted, lots of complicated software in astronomy now. They have automated systems instead of grad students scanning for anomalies. It'd probably be more your realm than mine. Maybe that's all passed me by," she said to the phone.

We rested in a way, perhaps each of us thinking of new pieces of conversation to contribute. I was curious how Jennifer would proceed. Would she soothe? Would she boost Sarah's confidence? How would it work?

"He's a turd," Jennifer said. We all laughed, even Fiona.

"He is," Sarah agreed. She laughed. "You know what he said to me? You're too sharp. *Sharp!*"

"What did he mean by that?" I asked.

"Abrasive, I guess? I think he heard it somewhere. It felt like a secondhand insult. Anyway, I told him, 'the only sharp edges you like on a woman are her nails and heels.'"

"Oh, I like that," said Jennifer with a smile in her voice.

"Me too."

"Thanks. I heard it on a reality show."

We laughed again. It was a communal response that lacked any joy or frivolity. It came from a common anger, and shared help-lessness. To men like Steve, we are wives or witches, not equals; any fight we wage against the role confirms their suspicions. As if reading my thoughts, Sarah began to cry. She clutched Fiona to her, the baby's progress with a mushy cracker interrupted.

"The kids love him, especially Jack. And Sam has been sick. What am I going to do?"

Jennifer's voice grew calm and close. "You're their mother. They need you, not him. When you go home, you take their hands, you look them right in the eye, and you tell them the truth. You say, 'I can't fix this. This is broken. But I am going to make our lives better.' And then you mean it. Every single day, you make things better for them. Don't think you are sparing them. They know things are bad. They are already suffering."

Sarah processed the speech with deliberation. Her nod, at first slow and insincere, increased in intensity. I sat on the outside of this connection.

"You're right. I'm their mother. I have children! God. I made *people*. Do you ever think about that? That we built fingers and toes and kidneys and motor neurons? Mothers are powerful. Maybe that's why they always kill us off in kids' movies." We chuckled. Fiona's bowl clattered to the floor. I fetched a mop and cleaned it up.

"You know how the Bible says that women came from Adam's rib?" Jennifer said.

I looked at the phone in surprise. Where was *this* going?

"Why does he have nipples?"

Sarah and I looked at each other for a moment and then burst into laughter. Fiona startled and let out a grumpy cry.

"Oh, baby I'm sorry! Hush now."

I watched her comfort her daughter in mute pain, then returned my gaze to the mess on the floor.

Sarah sighed. "You know, he won't even miss me. 'Oh, well. She left. I guess this is all aboveboard now.'"

Sarah shook her head, tears now silent but still rolling down her cheeks. Fiona leaned her head back and looked up at her mother, smacking her gums on a cracker.

Tapping came over the phone. Jennifer said, "When I get back, we're going out of town. A girls and kids trip. To the beach, weekend after next."

The beach. You've got to be kidding me, I thought.

"Oh, wow. That'd be great," Sarah said.

"I've got to go, honey. Let Vera take care of you? I'll be back in town soon. Love you," Jennifer said.

"Love you, too. Thank you."

"Of course. Get some sleep tonight, OK? No drinking."

"I'll try."

Jennifer hung up. Sarah and I stayed at either end of the table, the void of Jennifer's departure between us. I tried to put my own tangled, messy feelings down. Sarah didn't need me, not like I wanted to be needed.

Fiona started to fuss. I took up the damp washcloth I had prepared, and we cleaned the mashed food from her skin and hair.

"I better get back to the house," Sarah said at last.

"Are you going to talk to him again tonight?"

"No, no. I'm going to sleep in the guest room and wait. I want to get in touch with a divorce lawyer before we talk again. God." Sarah started to cry again, weakly this time. "I can't believe this is all happening. This is a nightmare."

She didn't want to be touched by me, so I took hold of Fiona's chubby little hand.

Sarah looked at me, as if seeing me for the first time this evening. "You're a great person, Vera. I'm sorry. I shouldn't have taken that call here."

I shook my head with a smile. "You needed her, and I want to help you. She's known you and Steve a long time. And she's a mother. She understands."

I offered up my room to her, still worried about her ability to drive in her state, especially with the baby. She refused.

I helped her downstairs. Her arms were occupied with Fiona, who had become overtired and angry. While we walked, she expressed enthusiasm at a trip to the beach. I didn't offer my own thoughts. I let her dictate the flow of the conversation. I gave her complete control while with me; it was all I could give, and she'd find none of it at home.

We reached the van and I watched as Sarah gently wrestled the squirming, furious baby into the car seat, using a firm but sensitive grip. I knew what kind of drive she would have to deal with, the inconsolable screaming that may or may not end with sleep. I handed Sarah her things, gave her a hug goodbye, and then returned upstairs, alone.

Beatrix, my elderly neighbor, peeked out of her doorway. "Everything OK out there?"

"Yes, I'm so sorry. The baby is gone now. My friend is having some trouble and needed to talk," I said. She didn't need to talk to me, I silently added.

"Ah, such a shame. She's such a pretty girl."

"She is. And she's an engineer," I said, shaking my head. I felt immediate regret. I wasn't sure I had conveyed my meaning correctly. Beatrix nodded.

"It's the clever ones who get themselves into trouble. They think they know it all, then they miss what's right in front of them."

"That makes sense," I replied. "Well, it should be quiet for the rest of the night! I'm sorry to have disturbed you."

"No disturbance, no trouble! Sleep well, dear. Night."

Beatrix shut her door with a careful click, and I returned through my own door, shutting it with an equally courteous click. The quiet waiting for me was so complete my ears hurt from the contrast. I put on a gentle playlist and poured myself a glass of wine. I sat in the chair I had only recently vacated, across from the empty place with the remnants of Fiona's mess. I took a couple of sips of wine. Nope. I didn't want that. I dumped the wine and grabbed surface cleaner from under the sink.

I cleaned up the mess, shut off the lights, and went to the bathroom to wash my face. I wanted to sleep.

Goodnight to you, diary.

CHAPTER 24

HACKERS DESTROY STUDENT LOAN DATABASE

I hadn't really prepared for house arrest, and I can't live on Chinese food.

After I completed my morning routine, I walked to my local shop with my favorite tote. I bought it at the children's museum ages ago, on one of my very first outings with Sarah and her kids. It has an artistic interpretation of the atomic model.

As I walked, I kept my eyes open. I didn't listen to music, either on my headphones or in my mind. My path drifted away from cars that slowed beside me. I wove away from building doors that swung open. My legs ached with anticipation, ready to kick or run, as if they would still be my own if they tried to take me again. Men looked up from their cell phones to look at me and I wondered, do you mean me harm?

I looked at the business names as I passed. There's a gelato place, a belt, shoe, and purse repair shop, a secondhand bookshop, and an Irish-themed bar called The Treacherous Turn. I have never been inside any of them, and I may never get a chance.

I didn't have a belt to repair, and I certainly didn't need a drink, so I continued to the grocery store. I got to my destination, stood at the entrance and realized that I wasn't hungry. Rows and rows of bags and boxes and cans looked impossible to sift through. How could I make sense of it?

I took a moment to gather myself. I needed some level of nutrition, and I needed comfort. I could live off mediocre food for a few days.

One foot in front of the other, and I began to shop. Children's cereal, chips, macaroni and cheese, chocolate milk, frozen meatballs. This would be fun, in a way. All this junk food, my own little personal childhood wish fulfillment.

I came around a corner and found my path blocked by someone. Not just someone. I blushed and considered retreat. No, better to face this. I decided to be assertive instead.

"Oh, it's you."

Oliver smiled, shyly, his hands in his pockets. "Hey. Jennifer asked me to check on you. How are you?"

I moved smoothly around him as if I had a very clear and important plan I needed to execute. "She told you to stalk me to my grocery store?"

"I'm not stalking you. We all know where you shop."

Yikes. I can appreciate the honesty, but still. Nothing is a secret to these people.

"Doesn't seem like you all know everything. Thanks for the cat, by the way."

"I didn't have anything to do with the cat."

"I don't believe you."

He tilted his head at me. "Would you rather I lie to you?"

It suddenly felt like we weren't talking about the cat anymore.

Conversational waters felt deep and murky here. There were ghosts of his past in this conversation. Did I want to do this right now? No, I did not. I pinched the bridge of my nose.

"I don't want anyone to lie, Oliver. I hate it. What people say and what people feel and the difference between those two things confuses me. I think I used to be good at reading people. But Jennifer took that from me. And now... I'm not even sure when people are joking! I must think through every little thing that everyone says, all the time, every day, even when I don't care what they are saying. And I don't even know if I've always been like this! I don't know who to blame."

He came close, his shoulder against the shelf I was facing. In a voice low and soothing, he said, "It wasn't intentional. The memory loss."

I relished the proximity, but I focused on this information. The memory loss was an accident? They hadn't erased my past intentionally. I believed him. A callous part of my mind mused that it was inconvenient for Perilaus. They didn't want to spend weeks or months babysitting an adult. Even my early days in the apartment are foggy. What had happened to me?

"That's nice to know. Really."

"Can we go somewhere?" He murmured.

Oh, no. No, no, no.

Tingles radiated up my shoulders and neck, annoying, immature tingles and yet I wanted to shout YEP LET'S GO. I walked away from him.

"I don't think I trust you right now."

He followed me, in silence. Even without him saying anything, the change in the energy of the air around me made me feel vulnerable. A mad thought made me hyperconscious of my free hand.

Maybe he would touch me? Would he take my hand? God, to feel someone reach for me. In my head, I am never alone, and yet I feel so alone. So busy and so unloved.

"What are you up to, Vera?"

I laughed. "I'm shopping. I eat at home, since I'm scared to leave my house."

"They shouldn't have done that."

"Yeah, well. Feels irrelevant to point that out now."

I angrily shoved a few things into my basket, and then put them back with less vim, because even in this uncomfortable state, I'm nothing if not practical.

"What's Mr. Darcy's Hat?" I ask, to redirect my petulant energy.

Oliver blanched. "What?"

"Mr. Darcy's Hat. I overheard someone talk about it at Jennifer's party."

"It's a program."

I decided I was done shopping. I turned and looked at him, and, I'll tell you, I admired him all over again. He shaved and his skin looks so clear and smooth, I want to run a finger along his cheek. Plus, he has nice ears. I never knew I cared about ears, but his are nice. Sometimes, even on really good looking guys, ears are weird. I looked down at his fingernails. Also nice. Ugh. I need to find a flaw in this guy.

He turned from me to scratch at sticker residue on a metal shelf. "A few years ago, we did a whole brain emulation, well. Not a whole brain. Half brain. Partial? Anyway, a brain emulation to test software for our neural components."

"Like the plaster."

"Like the plaster. And we found that the Hat was pretty good at noticing disruptions in patterns. We layered some security protocols on it and used to it to surveil our network connections and data streams across devices. It was present for every data connection. It didn't do anything but send notifications for odd data connections from a plaster. Sometimes it was a bit too sensitive, but we appreciated that. Rather have it too sensitive than not enough. It worked really well, for a while."

I nodded. "And then it stopped?"

Oliver looked miserable. "It became unreliable, like it was concealing some transfers. I wanted to develop a replacement before the new plaster, but it didn't happen in time."

"Before me, you mean."

Oliver locked eyes with me, his gaze firm. "The whole company is depending on this hardware. And, you are vulnerable without extra security. Someone could harm you. Perilaus has a lot of enemies. We need to make sure there are no rogue connections."

"I'm not sure secure connections are secure-er for me," I said harshly. He didn't respond.

We were near a sad assemblage of fruits and vegetables now. I didn't buy produce here, only from the farmer's market on Saturdays. Oliver picked up a pomegranate. He rotated it in his hand as if he was seriously considering buying it. It was underripe and too small. I imagined inviting him to the next farmer's market. We could go together, I would say. In case you need... pomegranates.

I'm so pathetic, and desperate. So desperately pathetic.

"I should get going," I said, tired of my heavy basket and not wanting to wait for him to speak.

"There's a strange thing that implanted plasters have always done. They upload random bits of information at night. We don't request it. They initiate the upload. We think it has to do with REM sleep."

I froze, the weight of the basket forgotten.

"That's odd," I replied.

He set down the pomegranate and stuffed his hands back into his pockets. He looked at me, steady and sure. "Your plaster hasn't uploaded anything at night in weeks. Not since your doctor's appointment."

My vision blurred as I looked at the linoleum floor. I blinked away angry tears. When I did speak, my voice was quiet and strained. "It isn't enough you spy on me all day long, while I hurt and grieve. You want my dreams, too? How much of me is enough for you?"

Before he could respond, I brought my things to the cashier. Oliver followed but did not speak, not with a witness there. It was surreal, standing beside a man who did not belong to me, who I was angry with, while I completed such a routine task. Like I had momentarily stepped into a sphere of domestic banality. The clerk, whom I have never spoken to but whom I recognized, looked at us with discrete interest.

I took both bags and walked out of the store. Oliver followed, trying to match my pace.

"Go away, Oliver. Go work on Mr. Huntingdon's Rifle or whatever."

"Why are you upset with me?"

I turned to him, tears in my eyes now. No sense trying to deal with them. "Don't you understand, Oliver? I want to... I want to be normal enough, considering -- well, considering everything. Please let me go now."

He did let me go. I took my groceries home, and he did not follow.

I didn't want to think about Oliver, with his hair and his eyelashes and his good shoulders. I put on the news.

ANCHOR 1: Billionaire philanthropist Anthony Halloway has died at the age of seventy-six. An entrepreneur known for investments in the arts and for signing a pledge to give away his fortune, he suffered a severe heart attack in the fall. He credited his recovery to an experimental heart implant and became an evangelist for biomodifying devices. His estate will be distributed to various children's charities.

ANCHOR 2: The firm Transparency, a facial recognition technology company, has been accused of building a widespread network of surveillance for the past three years, according to recent documents published by Move 37, a hacktivist collective. In response to the document release, the Department of Defense has announced that Move 37 has been designated a national security threat and members associated with the group will be tried under federal law. The action has done little to quell unease in Congress. Representative Brandon Helmsman held a news conference Thursday night.

HELMSMAN: I do not condone Move 37 or any hacktivist group. However, this announcement from the Department of Defense is in direct response to publication of documents showing the current administration has built a wide-scale surveillance system of American citizens. In the past three years alone, federal funding dollars have been tied to states providing surveillance data on law-abiding Americans. I call on my fellow members of Congress to open an investigation into these claims. To me, calling Move 37 a national security threat for publishing documents that should have been presented to Congress does not justify the classification. I look forward to the White House explaining this in detail, under oath.

ANCHOR 1: In other technology news, the US robotics firm

Arborator has received a contract from Bolivia to reforest nearly 270,000 hectares of land. The robots, originally designed for corporate farming enterprises, are currently deployed in Oregon, Washington, Montana, and Alaska. The small robots are the first in a series of herd-based robotics to solve ecological issues. Arborator states they will be released into deforested areas to remove invasive species and debris, and to measure soil quality. They will distribute nutrients and genetically enhanced seedlings as needed. The robots rely on solar power and operate twenty-four hours a day, seven days a week. It is estimated the robots are 75 percent more effective at reforestation than human caretakers with trained dogs.

ANCHOR 2 : Another US robotics firm, CleanSweep, who recently received the green light from regulators in Asia, the EU, and North America to clear space junk, has achieved another victory. The company secured sufficient private funding to expand their operations from five robots to nearly one thousand. Helena Richardson, founder and CEO, thanked the investor during a shareholders meeting, without revealing their name, as they had accepted no stake of ownership. CleanSweep, founded five years ago, launched the first of their robots into low Earth orbit last month. Despite calls from the international space community for this type of service, CleanSweep has relied on venture capitalist funding for most of their operations. The robots will be constructed by a state-of-the-art manufacturing plant in Romania.

I finished looking at the painting and shut off the news. I'm too stupid right now for world events. I'm worried about Sam, and Sarah. I feel tired still, and on edge. Jennifer will be back in town this weekend. She'll want to go on this trip, I suppose, and I'm not sure that I want to risk a repeat of my last experience. At least I won't be alone.

I can't stay here, doing nothing. I'm going to go for a quick run, if only to burn off some energy.

I'm back, standing in the kitchen. I don't feel better. I barely feel different. If anything, I feel worse. I found a sad playlist on my phone, curated by some stranger. The first song is about loss. I know the lyrics instantaneously.

It's a relationship song, and a song for a parent's unique pain. The death of a life before parenthood, one replaced by the hectic, loving life of raising a child to adulthood, only to be alone again, old, as it ends as all things end.

I'm crying. Children don't stay children. I will never have a child. There is glass on the floor.

Chair parts splintered across the room, broken legs with fabric seats still attached. My little bookshelf of paperbacks is bare, the collection scattered across the floor.

The destruction is over. It felt loud and good. I wonder if the police will come. What will Perilaus do if I'm arrested? Will they turn me off, make me dead, collect me from the morgue, and start again with another girl they have stolen from somewhere?

The chair where the highchair was supposed to go was the one I smashed. I hit it on the floor until there was no weight left to each swing. I don't know why I did this. Shame has pulled me out of myself. I need something to do. When I'm distracted, I can function. I can be there for Sarah, I can be there for her children, I can be there for Max, I can work. Alone, I repeat the same thoughts. I scratch into my pain, I pull off any scab and exhume the wound so I can stab into it and dig and stare without blinking, until I go blind.

Why did they take it from me? It wasn't theirs. I do not belong to them.

CHAPTER 25

SOUTH AFRICA COAST TO SHUT OFF
LIGHTS AFTER 8 P.M. TO PREVENT
SHARK ENCROACHMENT

I've woken up. I'm not sure if I fell asleep on the couch intentionally or they shut me off again. I'm not even angry about it. I'd have broken more chairs. But I didn't hit some secret Perilaus tripwire this time. No buzzing black box, not yet. I'm going to put on my best comfy socks. That should help.

I thought about what Sarah had said regarding memories. I know that there's a person beneath all of this. Maybe the types of memories that are created for me, or that I gather from software, are different from organic memories. If I look for organic memories using software ones as a template, I might be setting myself up for failure.

I'm thinking about the kinds of memories Sarah, Jennifer, and their children have discussed. Imperfect, feelings and colors and smells, fluid and pointless.

Certain feelings bubble up that I cannot place. They must have a source. They are primal, deep, and difficult to erase. Perhaps they are a connection to a memory? If I follow these threads, maybe I can learn why I feel them.

I close my eyes and go back to the garden party, a time that feels like ages ago. The man, Robert Castor, the one who touched me, who was too familiar, who gives Sarah the creeps. I wanted to kill that man, but not because of him—because of something connected to that feeling. It is outside of my reach, the memory, the reason for my feeling. I know it is there, though.

A part of me I cannot name is trying to soothe me. I can feel it urging me to let it go. This is not the memory to remember, it whispers as it pulls back on the string.

Let go.

I look at my beautiful apartment in blossoming darkness, street-lights casting light at angles strewn across the walls. The hardwood floors, the tasteful furniture they bought and whimsical accessories I've added, little more than bits of twigs and trash.

A candle I love, unlit and cold, casts off a scent. Why? What changed to make it bloom now? It felt like a gift, but one I did not want.

I am safe and warm and contained. Perilaus Bionics has me trapped here. They cut me open and filled me up with their projects. They wound up my mechanism and set me loose. Maybe if I do what they want, I can be someone's mother. The baby I dreamed of giving life to is lost, but perhaps I can find another path to love. Maybe there is a life out there for me.

I need a drink.

CHAPTER 26

Sorry. It's been a few days.

I woke to Sarah calling. I don't think I was fully sober when I answered, but sober enough to only sound tired.

She wanted to know if I could skip out on work. I didn't tell her I've skipped out a lot lately. She told me to pack a bag for a weekend and go downstairs in thirty minutes. I forgot to ask where I was going. I assumed it wasn't somewhere too cold, or too hot, or too far. I wondered if they would black-box me again as I packed. I didn't want her kids to see that. Jennifer was back now—she wouldn't let them. I don't think.

When I came downstairs, I was greeted not by Sarah but by Jennifer. We were all taking that promised trip to a beach town on the coast. I had completely forgotten. I wasn't sure I wanted to go anywhere with beaches, let alone with Jennifer, but how could I refuse? What excuse could I give? *Sorry, I'd love to, girls, but I have to break some furniture and drink myself unconscious.*

Oh, well. What does it matter, anyway.

The beach was misty and cold, the sand unpleasant underfoot. While the children played and Jennifer and Sarah watched them, I broke away and sat alone in a patch of grass. The sea looked how it felt. A cold blue-gray with white foam, hints of seaweed dark streaks in the glimmering surface. Clouds deepened the veil of mist, the sun only a faint glow. The children's laughs drifted in the wind as if they were in a sunny Hawaiian cove, and I was remote from them.

My left foot shielded the top of my right from the chill, my skin pale and toenails purpling as I watched.

I could stay this way.

The little families would forget about me, as the sea would forget me, as it has forgotten all who have sailed it. Voyages of discovery, conquest, escape, the great movements of empires—all of that means nothing to the sea. Hopes of lovers and fears of sinners, they sink beneath the waves as equals.

I faced gentle, icy sea spray and felt the pain. The axis of my universe is meaningless here. I know nothing of the sea; all the things I think and do, they do not matter here. The force of it cannot be changed by any power of mine. The sea and I, facing one another alone, with no future any different from the present. It understands. Perhaps I should find a kayak and paddle toward the horizon. I could commit to something, then. I could move from this safe stasis, one stroke at a time, my muscles flaming and begging me to stop, until I rest out in the waves, to a point where the safety of shore is a distant memory. Then, I can slip into the water, my hands up high, as I let the ocean take me.

Madness, dear diary. I know it is. And yet, what kind of madness is this nothingness I am living in? How long can I keep doing this?

"Vera! Where'd she go?" Sarah said.

The spell was broken. I was needed. I called out a reply and stood.

An embarrassing impression remained in the sand. What's the

saying? *When you see one buttprint in the sand, that is when God left you behind…*

I laughed and swiped it away with my foot.

The mothers were pink from salty, windswept joy when I rejoined the group. They had played tag. I helped little limbs out of damp clothes and washed sandy feet from the spigot at the parking lot. Jack's little hand squeezed mine, a silent message that he had missed me.

It took about fifteen minutes to clean up all the children. We loaded back into the cars and drove to the hotel's valet. Street-cleaning staff in bright blue outfits roamed the sidewalks, spraying cleaning solution on spilled ice cream and collecting trash. I looked around, aware now there were no sidewalk bots. I had grown so accustomed to seeing them, yet their absence barely registered. I wonder what it meant.

We walked into the lobby. To the left was a sitting area with plush chairs and a fireplace. To the right was the reception desk. I stayed with the children while Sarah and Jennifer managed payment and room keys. At the desk, next to the humans, was a concierge bot. It could've handled the check-in process, but neither woman considered it an option.

Jack discovered a bowl of lollipops on the counter. He ran across, gathered one for himself and one for each of his siblings and Max, then rejoined us with the bounty. Sam ruffled his hair in thanks. I took Fiona's and put it into my pocket. Jack rocked on his feet as he unwrapped his treat. When done, he handed me his trash and popped the candy into his mouth. I rolled my eyes with a smile and put the wrapper in my pocket, where'd it'd probably stay until I washed my clothes.

Max was telling Sam about a new LEGO kit he had been

working on at home, something Jack normally would have been interested in. It seemed he was trying on a new personality today. With the confidence of a little dapper gentleman, he sauntered up to the concierge bot to get a closer look. His shoulders slumped.

"What happened to you?" he asked.

The round blue eyes turned away from Sarah and Jennifer, down to Jack.

"Hello, welcome to Seaside Hotel. How may I help you today?"

"Did someone hurt your hand?"

I noticed the hand now. The fingers, each capable of independent motion, were a marvel of engineering. One hand was scuffed, the fingers dangling like a grim windchime.

"Pardon me. I don't understand your question! Would you like help checking into your room, booking a table at our award-winning restaurant, or a list of local attractions?"

"Why did someone hurt your hand?"

The concierge bot paused, a legless pillar with hands to serve, a voice and eyes to deliver messages, but no way to move itself. Tension radiated from Jack. I walked over and put a hand on his shoulder to soothe him.

"What's the matter with it, Aunt Vera?"

"It doesn't understand you, honey."

"I just want to know why someone hurt it. Doesn't it know it is hurt?"

"I'm not sure. Maybe it understands it in a different way than you do."

"Was it a bully?"

I walked behind the little bot, where a label and barcode had been stuck at an angle on its back. The maker name was partly obscured. Only Cybernetics was visible. Cybernetics. It means, one who steers the ship. Who is the ship steerer, I wonder? The robot, the maker, the owner, or the customers?

The concierge bot activated again, evidently triggered by Jack's tone. "I'm sorry for any disappointment you may have experienced on your visit. Your satisfaction is important to us. Please enter a rating from one to five stars."

Jack took my hand. "It asks if people hate it?"

I squeezed his hand. I had nothing to say.

Sarah and Jennifer joined us without the keys. The rooms weren't ready yet. We left our bags with the front desk and ate in the hotel restaurant. Their kids' menu was an array of beige, high-carb, and fried options. I abstained from alcohol while Sarah and Jennifer drank, not to excess, but certainly more than would've been appropriate if they were parenting alone. That's OK. I'm here. I felt good, being useful in this way. It was better than breaking my furniture or ruining a sewing kit. I could help them enjoy a brief vacation with their children, one where the entire childcare burden didn't fall on them.

By the time our rooms were ready, the sun rested at the horizon and the lights above the doorways lit up. Jennifer entered her corner suite. I had the room next door, a basic studio. Sam unlocked the door after, leading to a two-bedroom unit. He held the door for Sarah, Fiona, and Jack. Once inside, it was clear adjoining rooms above the hotel garage was a good idea; the scattered laughter and tiny thumping footsteps would have irritated almost everyone else. I listened with a smile as I unlocked and cracked open both connecting doors.

I drew back my curtains. The ocean again. A little balcony jutted over huge rocks that protected the foundation of the hotel. The sliding glass door resisted my efforts at first, but gave in with a stern shove. Salt had begun eroding the tracks. My hair floated gently around my face as I stepped into the cold breeze. On the horizon, a smudge of Mag Mell island was just visible. Yes. This was the ocean I loved, without the bother of sand. I did not want a tropical paradise. Nothing warm and inviting, a lie that hides the danger and disregard. No. I want a sea that warns and threatens.

Jennifer knocked on our connecting door before she entered.

"Come in," I called, not rising from my chair on the balcony.

Max raced by and dove through the connecting door to Sarah's room. Jennifer carried her water bottle as she settled into the other lounge chair across from me. She faced her own view of the water.

"Sarah's getting the kids settled with a movie, then she and Fiona will join us."

We fell silent again. I could see an otter in the seaweed beneath a distant pier. Was it resting? It might have an oyster or mollusk. You can hear them cracking the shell to get to the warm meat inside. From here, I couldn't hear that sound.

"Are you in any pain?" Jennifer asked.

I paused. Why was she asking? What if, for once, I let myself think she cares.

I touched my fingertips, one by one, before responding. "What kind of pain?"

She shrugged and put on her sunglasses. That was the wrong response. Our silence was tense now, anticipatory.

"Do you have any questions for me?" Jennifer asked.

I considered the gift with trepidation. What could I ask? What would she answer? It was hard to think deeply lately. I was so tired. So very tired, all the time.

"Am I what you expected?"

Jennifer laughed, her soft, controlled laugh. "I never had expectations."

"Doubts, then?"

"Always doubts. Always. Did Sarah tell you how I ended up on this project?"

I shook my head and turned back to the sea, to resist the urge to lean toward this unexpected bounty of information.

"Perilaus has always struggled to be cash-flow positive. Military contracts had been the main source of income and funding, but once we had developed good enough synthetic arms and legs, the patents were sold. The profit as a manufacturer and distributer wasn't there, especially when the subscription model was banned by the US government."

Before I could ask for clarification on what a subscription model for prosthetics would even look like, Jennifer continued.

"There were other problems we could tackle: paralysis, TBI, neurodegenerative diseases, damage to certain organs. Those are more complex. While we tried to develop new techniques and technologies, we found ourselves treading water. I had been working on algorithms for sensing temperature when I got asked to help recruiting, the shining face of the future of engineering. I was doing the incubator cocktail party circuit, listening out for staff to poach, when I heard Anders Robinson had died. Have you heard of him?"

"I... know of him now."

She nodded with a smile. "Of course. The relevant part is that he was a pioneer in AI research but abandoned that track of work in the late 1990s. He turned his attention to processing speed, none of that relevant now. I decided to go to his estate sale. I don't know why I did it. I hadn't been to one in years. My family used to get all our furniture and clothes from estate sales—my mother, walking around in dead women's shoes while she restocked new clothes in glossy stores."

Jennifer's face turned to stone as she unscrewed and rescrewed the cap of her water bottle. I said nothing.

"People jostled for the artwork and furnishings. They didn't notice me. I went into his office, where the computer and office chair were already gone. Two boxes were off to the side, old file boxes. Dusty and forgotten. A little paper sticker with fresh sharpie said five dollars. Imbeciles. Robinson didn't store sensitive data on hard drives. It was all air-gapped. There it was, his most precious work, for five dollars.

"I took the boxes to my shitbox apartment and read every single word. I read every doodle, margin note, I even held the scribbled-out notes to the light to document rejected ideas. And in his notes was the blueprint to the plate in your head. All our shiny toys and sophisticated researchers and Ivy League strategists would be nothing without a bunch of stuff nobody wanted. Just like that, all my other ideas and hopes and hobbies went out the window. The neural plate became my life's work. That's how it goes. You choose a path, or think you do, and then the path changes under your feet."

"Is it a good change?"

Jennifer looked at me, her large eyes speculative and open for once. "I don't know. I'm surrounded by people who don't know, who cannot know me. We're building the best information processing software known to man, and for them, this kind of accomplishment is a thing promised to them by nannies and private schools and tutors and advisers. While I cleaned office buildings on the weekends, they prepared to Change the World. Nothing was promised to me.

"Now, for it to be easy? For people to listen to me and admire me? I don't understand."

There was something in her tone on the last sentence, as though she knew I understood.

Do I? Should I?

Why is this so hard? Why does it feel like I can't communicate without screwing it up? Why can't I hang out and chat and shop and grab lunch and be normal? Why can't I have a baby and get car seat tips and preschool wait list suggestions? Why can't I be normal?

No. I know, even if I could, I wouldn't fit in then either. I don't belong anywhere.

Is that what she means? Does she feel like this, all the time, like I do?

The laughter of the boys in the room next door called my attention. They must be horsing around while Sarah, a mechanical engineer, struggled to set up a children's movie on the hotel's television. It's funny, how difficult things become, despite expertise. Poor Jennifer. For all her voice training and slick clothing and ambition, she couldn't make herself fit into the fiefdom she had made for herself.

"I wonder what I'd be like, without the plaster," I said, surprised at myself for saying it out loud.

Jennifer opened her mouth to reply, closed it, smiled, and tried to speak again but failed. She shook her head.

"The first human plaster was a disappointment," she began. "It didn't work. The subject was elderly, a stroke victim, and the cortex wasn't healthy enough. If we hadn't been in a race dynamic with Hannock and CEV, we'd have held off on human trials. As it was, we recruited people who were not ideal. By the fifth plaster, we got good readings. Not just what tests said, the sense of the thing. No one seemed radically different, only clearer. Less distracted. And you and your plaster are better than all of those."

"It sounds like you don't want competition."

"Of course not."

"But isn't it a good thing that two companies are trying to help with brain damage?"

Jennifer shrugged carelessly and adjusted her shirt sleeve. "I suppose. Our board is pushing too hard, as I'm sure CEV's board is pushing too hard. Hannock is a megalomaniac, so you know he's working his people to death. I don't enjoy working at a pace that narrowly avoids catastrophic error."

"CEV doesn't have you, though. I doubt they have anyone like you."

Jennifer accepted the compliment. "I like to think of myself as a wartime product leader."

"Do you think, maybe, that means you look for a crisis? Even when there isn't one?"

"I'm not sure about that. If that were true, I'd have greenlit the especially stupid proposals. No, no I think I prefer things as they are now. Tense, difficult, but not a crisis."

Sarah's laughter, followed by children's laughter, reached us. I smiled. "She seems happier, away from him."

Jennifer nodded without enthusiasm. "She does."

"You don't think she's happier?"

"I know she's happier. It won't last."

"This has happened before?"

"This? No. Not *this*."

I wondered if I could ask more. Why not ask more?

"I don't really understand their relationship," I offered.

Jennifer laughed. "There's not much to Steve. He is a typical sort of successful man. Not very bright, not very special. He sees the way she shines when she works, and he wants the prestige her effort would give him. He also wants a beautiful stay-at-home mother. Freud would say he wants his father and mother in one person, or some shit. Sarah is only one person. She must choose which one to be.

"There's a wrinkle, of course. He doesn't want her to shine more than him; he wants to be dominant. He pushes her into this corner where she can't win, where she's insufficient, because he is insufficient. He will always be less than. That is his place."

"You don't like him."

"I don't dislike him. I don't *consider* him. To worry about his wants and needs and thoughts is beneath me. I care that he hurts my friend. He doesn't concern himself with Sarah's interior life at all. I see that, she doesn't."

I sighed and looked out to the sea. "It must be nice for him, to not care about how others feel."

"You almost have to admire him. He has absolutely no delusions about being a good husband. He's out for himself."

"I'm glad they split up," I said. "I wouldn't want the boys to grow up thinking there were no consequences for acting like that."

Jennifer looked at me, her face almost sympathetic. I had made some sort of mistake. I wasn't sure I understood. I hoped she'd say more. She did not.

I tried to think of other things to ask. Was there something about myself I would want to know from her? Could she tell me what had happened to me?

Of course she could. Would she? Would I believe her?

"Do you think…"

I was interrupted by Sarah and Fiona's entrance. I rose from my chair to take the baby and the armful of toys. Sarah smiled at me as the baby and I settled inside the hotel, near the sliding glass door, where I laid out a blanket for her to sit on. Sarah took over my chair on the balcony and stretched.

"Ah, you warmed up the seat for me. Thank you, Vera."

I laughed. "I'm glad you appreciate my hard work."

"Jenn, did I tell you your hair looks amazing today. You look like a hair model."

Her hair did look wonderful. She normally kept it straight and smooth, perfectly sharp. Now it was wavy, softened by the mist and free of the products she used to keep it in line.

"Thanks. I was going to say how good you look, too. Are you sleeping better?"

Sarah waved off the notion. "Of course not. I'm so stressed out by lawyers and going back to work and thinking through shit I don't want to think about."

"You do look better, though," I observed. "It's hard, but I think it's good for you."

"I hadn't noticed all the stuff I did for him until now. He hates my lavender soaps, so I only used it when he was out of town. Now it's lavender city in my room. I've got the soap, the lotion, the candle, I even put satchels in my drawers."

"Lavender repeals mosquitos, right?" Jennifer observed. We laughed.

"Are you implying that my soon-to-be ex-husband is some sort of parasitic creature that exists only to spread disease?"

"Never!"

"Good. I will make that implication for you, then. Although I got an STD test yesterday, which was clear, so perhaps he isn't all that good at spreading disease either."

Jennifer and I murmured approvingly, though internally we were both massively relieved. At least, I know I was.

"It's stupid. I keep thinking, I'm so glad we are clear now. That he has said I am not good enough for him. I knew it this whole time, he denied it, and we just went on like that. Now, he said it, and I was right. I don't have to try for him anymore."

I turned my attention back to Fiona while the two of them stared quietly over the water, the sounds of the television flitting in from the room beside us.

"I saw Tegan Ward," Jennifer said.

"Wow. Did you say anything to her?"

"No. We were at the farmers' market."

"I didn't know she moved back. What's she look like now?"

"You know, the same. Tan, blonde, beautiful."

Sarah scoffed. "She's not *beautiful*, she's *symmetrical*."

They laughed and I smiled. I didn't know who this was. I didn't know if they should laugh at her, if they were being cruel, or if they had a personal vendetta I had no part of. They continued to share anecdotes and tell stories about their past: before me, before the kids, before Steve. They talked about the time Jennifer was nearly expelled from high school for hacking. She had used a stolen RFID badge and a rubber ducky to change her English grades, along with the English grades of every student in the school.

"How did you get caught?" I asked.

"My purple hair. Some strands were snagged by a rivet in the vice principal's chair."

I laughed with them. Jennifer with purple hair! We all had a past, I suppose. And what she said about her mom—they must've been working class. Was I like her? Troubled, difficult, with a future from which hope was difficult to see? I don't know. I couldn't imagine being brave enough to sit at someone else's desk and take over a system that had control over me. That was Jennifer's style, not mine.

"I never had purple hair. I guess it's too late now," Sarah said mournfully.

"Why do you say that?"

"I know I could do it. But I would want to be youthful and cool, and I look like a mom now. All circles and squishy."

"You look great," I said, removing my shoelace from Fiona's grip.

"I don't even know what I look like, to be honest. There are no pictures of me. I have no pictures of myself with the kids. Every family vacation I plan and book. And every vacation I arrange souvenirs and document activities. And he says I've gained weight, like I've been neglectful, while he has never taken a photo of me with the kids. Only the DMV and security cameras take my picture anymore. Christ. Motherhood, getting bigger while I disappear."

"I don't have pictures with Max. Just selfies."

"It's different. Steve used to take my picture. He used to love it. Now? Not a chance. And you know, the thing that drives me nuts is I don't think I look that bad. I think I look fine. I look like someone who has had a few children.

"What if I have reverse body dysmorphia? I think I look fine, but I'm horrible? Is that a thing?"

"You look fine, Sarah. He should've been grateful to have you in his life."

"He wasn't, though."

"No. He wasn't."

The two friends moved their conversation away from bodies and husbands and children. Jennifer slipped out of her worn tennis shoes and tucked one leg underneath the other. Sarah pulled the sleeves of her sweater down over her hands. They looked young in the fading light; the purple glow hid their age as they chatted and joked. Sarah laughed her explosive, joyous laugh, like college students on a quad. I stayed on the outside, ready for an opening to join them, knowing it wouldn't come. I was an observer, not a participant.

Fiona didn't need my full attention. Her focus was on a puzzle toy, soft little bees that needed to go back into their hive. One by one, she pushed them into their little homes. She had tried to put them all in the same place, but they each needed their own home to return to. They didn't belong that close together. She'd learn that lesson, some day.

"Mommmmm!" came Max's plaintive voice. The movie had ended, or nearly so, and Max wanted to get out ahead of his friends.

"Want me to read to them?" I offered.

"Oh, Vera. You're a lifesaver. I'm comfy. Getting out of this chair would kill me."

I smiled and gathered up Fiona. The boys were in their pajamas, bright colors on long, thin limbs, each one sprawled out on the floor, pretending to be worms for some reason. I shut off the television and convinced them all to join me in the bed. A little row of small heads, with different shades and shapes of hair, waited for me to tell a story. Sam took Fiona for me, and I sat at the foot of the bed as they snuggled in.

"I'm going to tell you a story. Have you heard the story of the Children of Lir?"

The children shook their heads. I could see Jack's brow furrow. "It isn't scary," I reassured him. "I can keep the lights on for a minute, until you are comfortable."

"I haven't brushed my teeth yet!" Max exclaimed.

"Well, brush them extra good tomorrow. It's OK to take a vacation now and then. Alright, are you ready for the story?"

The children nodded, and I began the tale.

CHAPTER 27

POLICE USE NEWBORN DNA TESTS FROM
BIRTH RECORDS TO SOLVE CRIMES

I'm back home. My morning is going well. I think the trip really did help me. I slept in my own bed again last night, I woke, looked at the painting, took my vitamins, ate breakfast, and went for a quick run. I helped Beatrix carry groceries up to her apartment; the elevator was out again. Now I'm freshly showered and moisturized and in my bathrobe watching the news on the couch. I'm going to pay attention to the meaning of the news now. Not as a construct for my future child, but for my own benefit. If I'm going to be a part of this world, I guess I should learn more about it.

Some senator drove his car over a cliff in Malibu. He had been in office for thirty years, pushing for oil interests and arms manufacturers. No young kids to miss him, only a wife who was the heiress to an oil fortune. Not a big loss.

A political action group, developed to support solar-produced energy, has grown in strength. They've passed the first of their bills; it eliminates charges from power utilities for customers who install solar, wind, or geothermic producing capabilities in their homes or businesses. I was surprised that people were charged for that kind of thing.

These old forms of energy production are dying. They say that solar energy firms are poaching coal power-plant workers to do easier jobs for enormous raises. It seemed like a brutal tactic, to make coal plants pay workers ridiculous salaries or lose them entirely to competitors. I love it.

In other news, the EU's AI Surveillance Committee can't find applicants with sufficient experience in the technology. Some blame the Sheldon-Claxton Accord's restriction on any advanced machine learning systems courses. A professor of such systems named Matthew Christensen says that is just an excuse, that the regulators are incentivized to ignore blatant violations. A new type of drone, utilized by emergency responders and insurance companies to assess disability claims, is found to have potential artificial intelligence systems banned by the Accord, even though the review analyst allowed it to go through. The committee claims this is because their staff is insufficiently trained.

I clicked to another program. Spyware created by a foreign government was discovered in a popular set of gyroscope code. The code has been used by many companies in device-connected games, such as fitness equipment and children's toys, and even car keys and meat thermometers. Gyroscopic software records vibrations to estimate the object's movement through physical space.

However, the gyroscopes record all vibrations, even those too sensitive for calibration. All the data, useless or not, is retained by each company in their own server farms located around the world. It was there the malware was found. The small vibrations, matched with identifying data, were put through speech-detection software.

Over 75 percent of words spoken near a device with this gyroscopic software could be retrieved.

I wonder if I have those gyroscopes in me. Is a foreign superpower spying on Perilaus's little pet project?

I took a breath. I could go crazy thinking of all the ways I could be in danger. Let Oliver and Jennifer worry about that. I need feel-good stories. I switched over to a program about the revitalization of a city in the Midwest, the remains of a manufacturing boom that faded into nothing.

Several years earlier, the city council had hired a firm to project future crime rates by observing the population as children. Risk Terrain Modeling had been employed to judge what types of activities were available to both older kids and younger kids, and how those activities translated into future behavior. The risk of criminal activity was the highest recorded. The lack of park space, playgrounds, fresh food stores, and libraries were the most straight-forward issues that hadn't required the use of an expensive outside contractor. State funds for revitalization had been available for years, and yet the city council had never accessed them. Navigating the bureaucratic labyrinth of requirements was an expensive endeavor on its own. The cities and towns with enough cash to complete the requirements often didn't need the money to begin with.

A new software company named Revamp, designed to tackle these issues, offered to donate their work to this city for free, as a test case for their system. All the residential properties were listed as either important, sound, salvageable, or derelict. When the entire city was mapped, it was clear that most residents lived in clusters where the properties were livable, separated by great stretches of unlivable, derelict units. Using advanced algorithms, the software generated a proposed map for the town, one with a library and playgrounds and community gardens and solar and wind turbines and open nature areas. Decrepit utilities and paved roads could be pulled up, saving maintenance money.

The map proposal was presented to the community, who were enthusiastically supportive. The project received state funding and is now underway. Parents report that their children were already engaging in less dangerous behavior, anticipating their playgrounds and parks with enthusiasm. A wealthy university plans to donate funds and make one of the nature areas an ongoing ecology project, restoring the local watershed to as near an approximation of what existed before colonists took over the region.

I mentally bookmarked the city name. I can't wait to see how it turns out.

I want to visit Sarah today, but Sam has the appointment with the pulmonologist. I'll send her a message after the appointment, to see if she is open to a visit. For now, I'll read a book.

A knitting kit I ordered online arrived. I'll work on that. Perhaps I'll make Fiona a sweater.

Sarah called and asked me to come over right away. My first thought, my only thought, was of some emergency external from myself. I dropped everything to go to her. It was about Sam, I knew, and it must be serious. I took a car to her house, anticipating changes, afraid of them and yet heading into them all the same. Sarah greeted me at the door, pale and tired. Sam hadn't been taken back to school. He was in his room, playing video games. Something about the distant noises in the otherwise-silent house unnerved me.

"Where's Fiona?" I asked.

"She's still at my cousin's place, I have to go pick her up soon. Let's sit outside."

Her tone unsettled me. It was the voice she used on the boys when they lied to her.

I followed, awkwardly carrying my things draped over my arms. We staged ourselves around the cold firepit. The sun was too bright, and Sarah took her usual chair, the only one in the shade. I waited.

"How did you know?" Her demand was soft, low, with an edge of threat to it.

"What did the doctors say?"

"No. You knew something was wrong with Sam. You tell me first. How did you know?"

"I just... Please. Tell me. What did they say?"

My stomach hurt. She gave me the cold, examining glare that Jennifer often turns on me. Distrustful and frightened. Tears formed in my eyes. I had to say something.

"It was his cough, I think. I don't know how I knew. It was like, when you hear something fall in another room and you know it was your house keys and not, like, a fork or something. I can't describe it. Maybe I've got some health assessment stuff in... Is he OK? I've been so worried."

"That's not all, is it."

I pushed my purse against my stomach, suddenly conscious of my fat and skin puffing over the top of my waistband. "I pulled his scans."

Sarah put her face in her hands. Adrift, I spoke without thought. "I'm sorry! I couldn't help myself. I needed to see if they missed anything. He looked so unwell. They did, didn't they? They missed something? Is it bad?"

Sarah emerged from her hands. She scratched dried s'mores

residue from her wooden chair. "They're doing a biopsy on Monday. They can do it laparoscopically. It could be cancer, but they think it is early, or benign. It hasn't spread, in either case."

I covered my mouth to cry, quietly, shame and relief rising with stomach acid to my throat. Sarah looked at me, her face cold and blank.

"I didn't know you could access medical records."

My hand dropped.

I stammered, "I've been trying to find out about me, and I thought about work. All the stuff people send in; you can find out so much about people from medical documents. I found a bunch of eDoc system passwords from some website. I didn't find anything for me—you need a name or ID number or birthdate. But when I heard him cough, I just… I used those to search for him. I'm sorry, Sarah."

"That's risky. They'd monitor that sort of thing."

I nodded. "I don't know how to do any of this. I had to know, though. I had to."

Sarah went silent. I composed myself and thought about the chance of Sam's tumor being cancerous. What if he had to go through chemotherapy and radiation? Maybe he wouldn't, though. Maybe it was benign. I have a vague worry for myself, even now, but I don't care. I love Sam. I had to know. If what I did saves his life, I don't care if they black-box me forever. I'll know it was worth it.

"Don't worry, Vera. It's not like you're stealing politician VD write-ups or something. I'm glad you did it. It was really stupid of you, but this could've killed him if it grew too much larger. It was already pressing on his heart. He could've had a stroke if it got any larger."

"What are you going to do about the doctor? Who missed the diagnosis?"

"Steve wants to sue, of course. Either way, we're switching to a new pediatrician. Even if it was a one-time screwup, I'm never going to trust that office again."

After a moment, Sarah gripped her knees, her knuckles white. "They almost killed my baby. That doctor told me to give him chicken broth. She told me to give my baby chicken broth for a tumor in his chest. The motherfucker. That fucking motherfucker."

She let out a long breath and folded her arms as she stared at some hills in the distance. Her suspicion of me had been a distraction from worry, and now only worry remained. I looked down at the zipper on my jacket, not sure what to do with myself.

"Did you find any medical malpractice stuff in there? Like, can you see if this surgeon is any good?"

"Do you want me to check now?"

"No, no no. Not here," Sarah said.

"Of course. I'll check when I get home. Have you spoken to Steve about any of this?"

"Yeah. He left for Spokane this morning, but he promised to be back in time for the surgery. He also said he wants to talk again."

I looked at her. In answer, she shook her head.

"That's over. I'm done."

"Have you spoken to the divorce lawyer?"

"Yeah, he's working on the initial documents."

I nodded. A woodpecker landed on a branch nearby. It walked with gentle ease up the trunk, straight up, an impossible angle, and hunted for small creatures. It didn't throttle the wood, only gentle jabs at the surface. There were plenty of things to eat at the surface.

"How are you doing?" Sarah asked. "You look tired."

I left the woodpecker. I thought about telling her about the news, or the hint of memory I keep sensing, like perfume left behind in a stale room.

"Same as usual. Nothing going on. I've just been searching for my own stuff. There aren't any missing person records that match my details. I guess I thought this would be easier, once I really started digging. I'm probably young enough that someone would miss me. Have you had any ideas?"

Sarah knit her fingers and placed them on her head, staring at the clouds. "I had a morbid thought. When I took Sam to the hospital, for the scan. What if you died?"

"Died?"

"The plaster—it's named after the British term for a Band-Aid. I guess marketing thought it sounded fancy. It was intended to remap brain function after a traumatic brain injury. What if you really were in a car accident and your family were told that you had died? No one would look for you."

I hated hearing something I had considered spoken aloud. My cold, pale body, nude on some autopsy table. A Perilaus person coming in with a briefcase to purchase my corpse. I shuddered. "Why me though? Lots of people die from brain trauma. What made me special?"

Sarah smiled at me sadly. "Why would a technology company run by men choose a beautiful white woman as their cyborg proto-type? Really?"

I looked at my skin. Amid the faint freckles there is a colorless mole from which a single ugly hair grows. They must have missed it. Would they be disgusted by such imperfection? Maybe if I had just had more of these, I would've been ignored. Was it better to be dead or here, like this?

"Still, I worry it's less complicated than that."

"What do you mean?"

"It's hard to find young test subjects. With this much money at stake, they may have tried an easier route."

"Like kidnapping?"

Sarah closed her eyes. "These people are capable of anything. Just watch your back."

Sarah left to pick up Jack from school and Fiona from her cousin's house. I remained behind, alone in awkward silence in a house more at ease with noise. I appreciated the mess around me, a clean chaos of living. Drawings and a jar of glitter and a forgotten spoon. I started doing the dishes to occupy myself.

Sam came downstairs, had evidently been waiting for the sounds of his mother's departure. He looked at me with some surprise. "Oh, hi Aunt Vera. I didn't know you were here."

I smiled. "How are you?"

Sam opened the refrigerator, looking for orange juice. He drank lots of orange juice in secret.

"I'm OK."

He didn't sound OK. He didn't sound like he wanted to discuss why we wasn't OK.

"Mom was pretty angry earlier."

"Why?"

Sam shook his head. "I thought it was about Dad. It's usually about Dad. But my doctors missed something. She was mad at them."

"That makes sense."

"I think she was mad at someone else too. Or scared. It's sort of hard to tell mad and scared apart."

I nodded.

"I don't know." He drank more of the juice. "I told her that I feel fine. Some kids in school are way more sick. Henry's pretty sick. He can't even go to the bathroom without an aide outside."

"Do you know what's wrong with Henry?"

"He has seizures. They're kind of scary, but he doesn't remember them, so that's cool. They say he could hurt himself falling down. Andy said he could swallow his own tongue, but I don't believe that."

I shook my head. "That's scary."

"Henry's mom is taking him to a special doctor next month. He's going to have surgery for his brain. They're putting something in his head to stop his seizures. They were waiting until he was mostly grown before they did it, but he's so sick that they're doing it now."

"Are you close with Henry?"

"He's pretty cool. He shares his markers with me. He has these ones that smell like fruit. Mom won't let me get them, she says they're a marketing gimmick."

I laughed. He smiled. We made eye contact and his smile faded.

"Aunt Vera, I'm sorry you can't have a baby."

Blindsided, I nearly stumbled.

A little hand, holding mine, as we cross the street. Tying tiny shoes on the playground. A skinned knee, large tears on a soft cheek pressed into my shoulder. My hand caressing soft curls. My arms the only ones that can comfort, the only ones strong enough for safety. My little baby, my little ghost. What is a haunted house without a ghost?

Sam shuffled his feet. "It sucks, you know. How you don't get to be a mom but people like my dad can have kids. He doesn't even like us."

"You think so?"

"He's always traveling for work. He says he has to but I heard him on the phone. He said he can't wait to see someone. I know you'd love your baby. It's not fair. Don't cry, Auntie Vera."

"I'm sad, honey. It's OK to cry when you are sad." I wiped my eyes and stopped washing a cutting board. "I heard you playing a game upstairs, can I join you?"

"Yeah! It's the new FIFA. It's kinda complicated but I think you'll like it. You have to see the team I built."

We left the ugly thoughts to themselves and went upstairs.

CHAPTER 28

SEVERAL UNIVERSAL HOUSING BILLS
TO APPEAR ON BALLOTS THIS NOVEMBER

I went to work today, for some reason. I don't know. There's no point in keeping this job. I could say I was bored, but that's not true. The routine is nice, maybe. The easy flow of tasks, one after another, each packet a little project I can complete to perfection and move away from forever.

Anyway, I was excited to get back into my usual flow. The stability of routine the only comfort I could turn to. Scott knocked on my cubical wall. He told me that I had been requested on a new project. Well, that's not ideal, I thought, but maybe it'll be difficult, or interesting, or difficult *and* interesting!

Diary, the Special Project was stuffing envelopes.

I was taken to another desk and given a stack of labels, a stack of letters, and a stack of envelopes. I looked at the collection and then at Scott.

"Hey, don't look at me. I know, OK? The stupid goddamn machine broke. If it picks up in the queues, I'll come get you. Sit tight here and do what you can."

The papers were arranged in untidy piles, superfluous supplies mixed in between. I lowered myself into the chair, assessed, and reorganized. A clear space before me for folding was a good place to start. Where would be best for the labels, I wondered. On the right, but only just—I can't remove a label single-handedly. I put the envelopes to the left.

Take the letter, check the name against the label. Fold the bottom of the letter up to the line that ends with the word "additional." Fold the top of the letter down, so that the top edge overlaps with the end of the fold. Put it in the envelope. Adhere the correct label.

Take another letter. Do it again. And again.

And again.

I worked and listened to the unfamiliar people. One shared how many points she had available on her diet program. Her neighbor made noises in acknowledgment of the information. Neither seemed invested in the conversation.

A young man in scrubs listened to music too loudly over headphones. He bounced his knee as he typed. He puzzled me. I could see he was a musician, from the callouses on his hands and his ability to match his movements to the music. The scrubs, though? And working here? I looked at his workstation as I filled another envelope.

There were pictures and things that did not belong to him. Was he from another department? If so, why scrubs? Eventually, I understood. He was a temp, passing through, covering for an absent person, earning money to pay bills. A musician and a nursing student.

It seemed to me he was too young to do this many things. Silly, isn't it, to judge some guy as too young when I might be younger than him. Did he lose his young adulthood like me? He looked about eighteen. Was I like him? Pushed away by society, pulled by corporations down paths, chasing practical things and holding on to dreams, but with no guarantee either will work out?

I wiped away my tears and refocused on my envelopes.

Is there another universe where Perilaus didn't happen to me? Is there a me that grew up gradually? That went to their second-choice college in disappointment, formed an awkward acquaintanceship with a roommate, and longed for a professor with glasses and acorn-colored leather shoes, who went home to his beautiful wife tired of advances from gangly freshmen? A me-like shadow that walked with arms folded across her chest back to her dorm in the glow of faux-gas streetlights, desperate to be ignored by rowdy frat boys as they migrated from one party to the next in perpetuity.

Did she wish for someone to listen to while walking somewhere new? Did she form a group of friends, finally, and count the days until their next spring break, their next concert, their next party where no cool people would dare venture but where each friend needed you as you needed them? Is there a me who gained more freedom each year, learned about the world and herself, bore scars from a million mundane abuses, and collected her diploma only to stare across an adult landscape that made no room for her?

Did years go by for her without much pain? Did she grow older and more secure, did she find love and approval, did she bear the child I so desperately need, and did she agonize for the baby's future in a way that is sharper than anything I feel now?

I put on my headphones and hit shuffle on my playlist. It doesn't matter. I'm here, stuffing envelopes. I'm the guy in scrubs, jettisoned to adulthood. I sit here at work, the smell of cologne and the click of business-casual shoes, as I work like the others around me work, as we all work toward nothing. We work to exist. There are no

concerts or beaches and dreams I count the days till. Those are hon-
eypots, temptations on the rise, waiting for me to be black-boxed.

No, I have nothing. In place of joy are quarterly reports, all-
hands meetings, one-on-ones, productivity assessments, Q&A
feedback, in perpetuity. I've fallen into a river, and all I have to
appreciate is that I will soon be out to sea. Maybe another me
could've been a person with unique needs and contributions and
wishes and experiences. Instead, I'm a fucking envelope stuffer. And
scrubs guy is a typist.

I hit next on the playlist. Shuffle had selected a dud. And then
another. Why were those songs on my list? Why did it play the
worst songs in order? I thought of the action as a personal attack,
not the obvious outcome of a poorly planned playlist (my own fault)
and a set order that was in place by an obscure algorithm from the
moment I hit play. Ugh.

An unexpected scent interrupted my thoughts. It was a food,
but difficult to define. Fries? Bread? Something? I stood just so that
my eyes could see over my cubicle wall. A man carrying a casserole
dish full of microwaved potatoes navigated through a pathway to
his desk nearby.

Plain, hot potatoes.

I almost stood higher to get a better look. The smell of them
wafted through the otherwise-stagnate office air. I didn't want to be
seen, but I had to know more. Who was he going to share the potatoes with? Was this a department thing? Eating hot potatoes? He
shared them with no one. He sat down alone, took up one potato
and began to eat it like a hot dog. I sat back down.

"You see the girl at Jeremiah's old desk?"

"Mmmhm."

My folding slowed as I listened to the unseen men. Women

at work confused me, with their occasional kindness followed by slight remarks that sting, their smiles paired with exasperated glares. I understood the men. The threat shivered across my skin.

"Dress slacks are where it's at."

"Got that right."

I frowned. I had forgotten my cardigan at my desk; normally I'd tie it around my waist. These guys were somewhere to my left and toward the wall clock, along the ideal path to reach the nearest water bottle station. I sighed. I'd just refill it in the bathroom, I guess. Gross.

I could hear someone's radio over my headphones. During the brief transition from one set of songs to the next, the DJ read a quick summary of the news.

> DJ: THE US MILITARY HAS ANNOUNCED TROOPS WILL BE REDEPLOYED TO THE GULF AFTER INSURGENTS BREECH THE GERMAN EMBASSY. NEGOTIATIONS OFFERED BY QATARI GOVERNMENT ARE AT A STANDSTILL.

A person on the other side of the cubical walls snorted. "Anyone want to ask why the hell Qatar is hosting these negotiations, or are we not talking about that today?"

I couldn't take much more of this. I checked the time. Forty-three minutes. The whole day lay before me. I read a letter in case it was interesting. It was not interesting. They were all the same, with a unique name, mailing address, and file number.

"Your medical records have been digitized. To access your medical records, you may log onto the portal. You may also share your records with your current out-of-network medical professionals. The VA medical system has access to these records and does not need to be notified…" blah blah blah.

A machine should do this work. No one wanted this work. Of course, if the machine breaks down, a person needs to do it. Right? Or is this not even that important? Is this worth the letter sorter filing it into the correct bin for a neighborhood, then to a street, then to a part of a street? I paused. That was probably all automated, too. Was I the last human to touch this before the mail person slid it into the mailbox? I laughed to myself. I'm not even much of a human, at that.

This sucks, I thought. Maybe I should go to the bathroom and hide for a few hours. No one would know I was gone. I picked up the next letter instead and began to fold. As I lined up the bottom edge to the "additional" line, the lights shut off. The whirring of computers, a background noise so familiar it went unnoticed, disappeared, the remaining absence as startling as the darkness. Someone gasped. The emergency lights kicked on.

"Calm down, everyone. Stay calm," said an older man from the tall cubicles. He did not sound calm. "Just a power outage."

"It's the new solar again. These fucking green energy bastards," someone muttered.

"What do they expect us to do? My computer's off," an elderly lady said.

"Scanning floor still has power, what the hell."

"Well, shit," someone responded, echoing all our thoughts. Scanning would continue, which meant the queues would fill.

"Where's our power? We're going to fall so far behind," someone said.

"Alright, folks," a man said. I recognized his voice as a vice president. "If it doesn't come back in five minutes, let's take lunch early. Just be ready to hit the queues when you get back—it's going to be a busy day."

"What about pay?" It was one of the men who whispered about me.

"You get your wages, don't worry about that."

The mood on the floor brightened. Someone whispered about overtime. The lost power was no longer a burden. The progress of the battery-powered clock on the wall was cheered on. The power did not come back on. I left with everyone else, the mood jubilant, none as happy as me. I bid farewell to the stack of letters and the creeps commenting on my dress slacks.

I went back to my favorite sandwich place, the first time in months. I was far ahead of the future lunch rush. The posters hanging in the glass door had faded, but otherwise nothing had changed. Carl was working alone. He made my sandwich to perfection, which I am now eating from my bench spot. I should just take my lunch at eleven from now on, I think. I could even go get a little ice cream from the candy shop down the street. A midday treat.

I called Sarah to see how things were going. She's fine, maybe even good. She invited me to join her and the kids at a birthday party. That'll be fun, a kids' birthday party. So now, I'm writing in you. I could think about my future, but I won't. Something has gone my way and I want to enjoy it. I'll just listen to a fun audiobook now while I enjoy lunch.

CHAPTER 29

TIGER   PARALYZED   IN   ACCIDENT
GIVEN   BRAIN   IMPLANT,   CAN   WALK
AGAIN,   ZOO   ANNOUNCES

A new day.

I did my routine in a rush today: painting, vitamins, shower, hair, makeup, jeans, T-shirt, leather jacket, water and toast. I knew, and yet forgot, that the trains don't run on their usual schedule on Saturdays. To make it to the party on time, I'd have to arrive at the destination station half an hour early. If I stayed focused, it wouldn't be a problem. I'd have to walk fast to the train station, but not too fast. I didn't want to be sweaty.

I left my apartment, the gift I had purchased yesterday after work in my arm, and locked the door. There was an aberration. It took me a moment to pinpoint it. I paused. Light hit the wall in an unexpected place. I turned around. Beatrix's door was slightly ajar.

Oh, no.

The party was forgotten. A thousand possibilities flooded my mind. Beatrix, a sweet little lady, living alone.

"Beatrix?" I called gently and knocked on the doorframe.

"Well, shit. Vera, would you mind helping me for a moment?"

I swung the door open and paused to orient myself. The layout of her apartment was completely different. The galley kitchen, inexplicably, was directly in front of the door. Beatrix was standing over a shattered casserole dish, food and glass shards all over the kitchen floor.

"I'm so clumsy, and my knee is shot. I can't bend down to clean this up," Beatrix said. "Mind yourself, it's hot. Dropped it right as it came out of the oven."

"I'm happy to help," I replied with a smile. I set down the gift, my purse, sunglasses, and keys. I took a towel and the trash can and tossed in the pieces of glass. I started with the biggest pieces. I looked at the towel, tattered and stained.

"Do you mind if I throw this away when I am done?"

Beatrix shrugged. "It's just a towel, go ahead."

I spent the next ten minutes cleaning the floor, then vacuumed over the cleaned space. After that, I knelt on the ground and stared. For once, a use for my ability to see things others can't. Three glass shards had escaped my towel and the vacuum. I threw them away and checked again.

"I think that's everything," I said, rising from the floor.

Beatrix rubbed my arm. "You are so kind. I wish I could give you some of the casserole in thanks."

I looked at the trash can and laughed. "I'll pass."

"You look very nice today! Are you off for a fun afternoon?"

I wondered: will I have a fun afternoon? I wasn't so sure now. Doubt had built since I accepted the invitation.

"I'm going to a children's birthday party," I replied.

"Ah, that's nice. Better than an adult party. I've always preferred children to adults."

"Me too," I said with a smile. I gathered my things and took a surreptitious look around. The photos on the walls were of her with friends, and those friends with babies or grandbabies. No children of her own.

I politely rushed from Beatrix's apartment and missed my train, and now I'm at the platform, updating you. I texted Sarah an explanation and apology.

I really hate being late to things. Now I have nothing to do but regret I accepted this invitation. My ears burn in anticipation of embarrassment. The actual embarrassment is going to be worse.

I'm home now. I'll tell you how the party went. I didn't know the kid, as I've said; she is a classmate of Max's, though I suppose Sarah has a connection to the family as well, since she invited me. Perhaps a preschool or park connection—the parent social web is complicated. By the time the train stopped in the quaint little commuter suburb station, my stomach was on fire with anxiety. It wasn't just the party. Things have been so weird between me and Sarah and Jennifer lately. After the beach trip, I thought maybe the three of us would be OK, but now I feel like Jennifer is angry at me. I keep thinking through everything I did over that weekend. Maybe Max or one of the kids complained about me. Sarah said it wasn't about me, that there was a security incident at Perilaus that has taken up a lot of Jennifer's attention. That may be so, but I think I offended her, too. Somehow. Anyway, I felt awkward as hell coming into this kids' party, kidless, with a gift (handmade Russian nesting dolls with beautiful designs—it seemed cool?) for a kid I didn't know.

Mercifully, the side gate was the obvious entrance to the party.

It had a sign announcing MARIBEL IS 5! and was covered in welcoming balloons. I wouldn't have to knock on the front door, interrupt and then face a stranger to explain that I, alone, was here for the clown-themed birthday party. I followed the wisps of music through an arch of jasmine, the scent calming, the bees less so. I rounded the corner of the house and came into the full garden. The landscaping was beautiful, the property expansive, with different little areas for gathering. I wonder if the parents were very social, or important, or just wealthy. A table laden with gifts greeted me. I put mine on there with the others, hoping it would be cherished.

"Aunt Vera!!" a tiny chorus erupted. Jack ran to me, with Max right behind. They nearly tackled me by the legs. I gripped them back as best I could without falling over.

"Hey you two! What are these, rackets? Are you playing badminton?"

"Yeah, Maribel's daddy set up the net. Do you want to play with us?"

"Let me just wave to your moms and I'll join you," I said. Sarah and Jennifer were talking to someone. I waved, and only Sarah waved back.

Max tugged on my hand. "Auntie Vera, come onnn, we're going to lose our spots!"

I am bad at badminton. Is that why they call it badminton? I'm bad at Minton…? That's a stupid joke. I know it's because it was invented at some British duke's estate. With this plaster, I can't even joke about my ignorance.

A cluster of kids were dancing on a raised deck to the birthday girl's playlist. Some were shimmying in awkward little circles while others attempted the graceful pirouettes they learned in a fancy enrichment activity. I preferred the shimmying. I continued poorly returning birdies while bouncing to the rhythm of the song. The memory of the horrible BBQ, and Jennifer's dinner party, nearly made me laugh. I'd rather be at kid party every damn day of the week.

The kids were doing some weird moves, pretending to be animals and roaring. Then they transitioned to some activity where they put the hem of their shirts into their mouths and slapped their belly, like they had just devoured a huge meal. I smiled. Kids are chaos.

"What are you doing?" A woman's voice pierced through the music. I looked around, expecting danger. She stomped toward the dancers and ripped the shirt from her daughter's mouth and shoved the fabric down. "Don't you ever do that again. Disgusting!"

The birdie landed at my feet, ignored. I looked to Sarah and Jennifer, to see if they had heard. Sarah shared my disgust and mouthed, *What the fuck?*

"AUNTIE VERA, HELLLOOO!" Jack clapped in my face.

"Sorry, sorry. I was distracted. How about you two play without me? I need some more practice before I try again."

I handed off the racket to a little girl who had shyly watched our game.

I gathered my purse and sunglasses and joined Jennifer and Sarah. The chastised little girl sat on the other side of the garden, beside her mother, ignored. The kids resumed dancing.

"Did you see that shit?" Sarah said.

"She's like, five. Does it start that young?" I asked.

"You bet it does," Jennifer muttered.

"And you missed what happened earlier. Stella's got a sweet collie, bigger dog, still a puppy. That same girl was scared of it and the mother and father forced her to say hi to the dog. Stella tried to put the dog away, but the parents told her to leave it out so she'd learn."

"Father? I didn't see a father?"

"He's with the dads, over by the firepit."

I noticed them now, a tight cluster of men in the same styles of shirts, slacks, and shoes, beer bottles in hand. As they spoke, they gestured with the bottles, as if they were some modern version of war staffs. Steve would've fit right in.

"People are revolting." I shook my head and put on my sunglasses.

Jennifer was watching me. "That's how people are. They think if they push their kids into toughness, it'll make them strong. It's wrong, of course. It makes them brittle."

I looked back at the little girl, who was now swinging her legs and talking to herself. I resisted the urge to greet her. I did not want to invite her mother to talk to me. I wondered, though, did the little girl have friends? Was there a Violetta to echo back to her, or a Katie Maurice to greet her at a glass door? She not only looked isolated, she looked as if this would be the path of her life. I felt sympathy for her. To be on the outside, looking in.

Another child stumbled and fell, crying at his skinned knee. The other children looked at the boy with concern, some went to him, others to their parents, but not the scolded girl. Her face was impassive, watching him cry.

No. There were no whimsical friends for her. The damage had been done. I turned back to Sarah and Jennifer.

"Did you two carpool?"

"Why do you ask?" Jennifer replied sharply. Oh god, this wasn't going to go well at all, I thought.

"Uh, Jennifer's car was stolen last night."

"Oh shit!"

Jennifer only grunted in reply. Sarah shook her head. "Right out of her building's garage."

"Were there cameras?" I asked.

"I watched it before we came here. Masked people, I'd guess young guys, broke the lock to the garage and smashed some windows. Then took my car. Only my car."

"Bad luck," Sarah said pointedly. Jennifer shook her head and crunched an ice cube. Jennifer evidently didn't want to continue this conversation.

"Which one is the birthday girl?" I asked.

"She had a cute little hat on, I guess she chucked it. Ah, there she is. She's there, the one dancing with the pink ribbon around her waist."

She was spinning, watching her circle skirt float around her. Her moves were fluid and graceful for a young child. I let out a sigh, unintentionally. Sarah squeezed my hand.

"I'm alright," I said.

I looked at their cups and offered to go get them refills. Jennifer waved me off, but Sarah accepted my offer.

At the table of pitchers, I poured myself lemonade and then Sarah's iced tea. There were little bits of food, which I considered. I was pretty hungry. I had wanted to grab something to eat before arriving, but the food car on the train had been closed. I had wanted to keep as light a footprint on this party as possible, but I was really hungry.

"Hi! I don't think I know you," an older lady asked me. I detected suspicion in her voice, as if I was a lemonade-stealing hobo.

I smiled. "I'm here with my friends over there, whose little ones are sort of, scattered. They are friends with Stella."

"And where is your little one?"

I looked over the happy children with a smile and wanted to scream until my vocal cords bled. I wanted to run away and scream and never talk to anyone ever again.

"None of them, actually. I don't have any kids."

"Oh, that's a shame."

"Yeah," I said, picking up the cups, trying to signal that any follow-up would be unwelcome.

"Haven't found the right man?"

What if I had just unloaded on her? Just let it rip and made a huge goddamn scene for her to pearl-clutch about as if she were the victim. What if? Ah well, I didn't do that. I grinned and shrugged.

"Not yet!"

"You're young yet, I'm sure you'll find someone nice. I wish my son were here. He's a software engineer. Some sort of security thing."

"Oh, that would be nice. Well! I've got to go now," I said, holding up the drinks as if they could detonate at any moment and wipe out everyone in a two-block radius if she didn't let me walk the fuck away from this horrible conversation.

"What was THAT all about," Sarah asked, a gleeful smirk on her face.

"Normal small talk about the productivity of my uterus and why I haven't married yet."

"Holy SHIT?" Sarah laughed. I looked to Jennifer, who seemed remorseful but also curiously amused.

"It's weird. I feel like I know that lady, somehow. Has she been to one of Jack's parties? Or Max's?"

"Not Jack's. Hm. Isn't that Stella's mom?" Sarah asked Jennifer. "Yep."

I wasn't sure what that meant. I shrugged. "She offered to set me up with her son. A software engineer, no less. Now you both are the first to know—my future is all sorted."

I fished a small fly out of my lemonade with my pinkie.

Sarah snorted. Jennifer smiled, her eyes unreadable behind her dark sunglasses. "You know her son."

Fly extricated, I went to sip and halted. "I what?"

She motioned with her cup. "Stella is Oliver's sister."

Of course.

Sarah cackled.

"I hope you are enjoying this," I muttered.

"Oh, it's delightful!"

"MOMMY. Where's the cake!" Max called.

Jennifer looked at her son with strained patience. "I need to stop him immediately, excuse me."

Sarah nudged me. And nudged me again. "Should I go tell Stella's mom? Should I tell her that you'd love to meet her son? Should I? Should I?"

"Stop!" I said, nudging her back.

The teasing was inclusion, right? Was this how it would be between us, forever? I'd be accepted by them if I was the subject of their jokes? Was that good enough for me?

CHAPTER 30

KINGDOM OF NEMACIA ON BRINK OF
WAR AS AGRICULTURAL AND DEFENSE
BOTS FAIL

I've taken a few days away from Sarah and Jennifer. I've felt so tired, anyway. Worn out. Jennifer is stressing me out, and I don't want any stress, especially after the sort of news that has been coming out.

On Sunday, I read about some kind of elaborate break-in at a nanotech factory last month, in broad daylight. The FBI only said that some hackers destroyed servers. I found a more detailed account on a forum for tech workers. The hackers broke in by taking over concierge bots, like the one at the beach hotel. They had the bots guide visitors and staff away from the server room and the side entrance, either claiming a spill incident or simply directing people away. They think the bots used RFID signals from work badges to tailor the messages to staff, based on their seniority and security access. From there, the hackers gained access to the server room through the side door. They stole certain drives and set up timed charges to destroy others.

This is all kind of fun, spy-novel sort of stuff. The part that made me want to retreat from Jennifer, and thereby Sarah, was that they also used devices developed by Perilaus, specifically a predecessor to the plaster. It was a little implant they had tested in rodents to guide them through mazes and to certain locations. Perilaus had gotten the idea from Boeing; the airplane manufacturer had relied on trained ferrets to bring cabling through the nooks and crannies of airframes. Of course, training requires patience and human skill, neither of which appeals to a consumer market.

So Perilaus made an implant, and it worked, and this faceless group stole it and made it their own. The hackers must have refined it a bit; I understand the Perilaus version made rodents scream during trials. In this break-in, no one reported any unusual animal sounds.

The hackers guided the rats through air vents and corridors with some sort of transmitters on their backs. The rats reached the building's built-in AV system, and the chips transmitted instructions to the speakers, which in turn emitted a frequency that hijacked anything nearby with a certain type of audio encoding software. A very common type of audio encoding software, it would seem.

While the factory's security team spent the past month thinking they were dealing with a single break-in, data from every device that had been in the building was systematically transmitted back to an offshore data center. It seemed like a clear-cut case of corporate espionage, until the poster explained the factory was a DARPA participant making next-generation battlefield tech, specifically nanotech whose effective use would be considered a war crime. On that particular day, representatives from the Pentagon were meeting with executives. Their devices, and their security teams' devices, were all affected by the adversarial audio. I read that while eating some cereal and realized that Jennifer was very likely losing her shit.

Someone had lifted old Perilaus technology and used it to attack representatives of the US government.

After I read that, I had to go out. It was Sunday. Museums were closed. I'd go shopping, I guess. That usually made me feel better. If I can't be happy, or loved, I'd like to feel pretty.

I took a bus to an upscale shopping neighborhood. Wealthy teenagers spread across the sidewalk, expensive cars lined either side of the road, and emaciated elderly women in furs engaged in chemical warfare with their perfume. I ignored them, focused on my goal of happiness through consumerism.

I entered the first store that appealed to me and looked around. One side was all blacks, the other side was a smattering of colors. As I debated what to do, I saw a light blink on the checkout counter, where an immaculately presented young woman was folding purchases for a customer. To my surprise, she immediately returned my gaze. I startled, wanting to leave but unsure why I should go. I wandered toward the black clothing, the opposite of what I intended to buy, and aimlessly flitted hangers to the side. When the sales transaction was completed, the young woman glided toward me with a polite but pronounced suspicion.

"May I help you?"

I swallowed. What the hell was wrong with me? I wasn't doing anything wrong. She treated me like I was doing something wrong; that doesn't make what I was doing wrong. Right?

"I'm just shopping."

"Is there something in particular you were looking for?"

I shut my eyes. Get it together, I told myself.

"Look, I just had a fight with my friends and I'm trying to do something to feel better about myself. I don't know what I want, I just want to look cute. OK?"

The woman's entire attitude changed. She relaxed, rolled her eyes, and shook her head. "I'm sorry. This stupid anti-theft software. It's like a paranoid lady sitting out on a stoop. Anyone comes in here upset, it says THIEF! THIEF! It made me question a lady who just found out her dog died."

"Oh, wow. That's… that's a pretty bad system."

"Yeah. This job kind of sucks now, to be honest. Look, I'm really sorry to bother you. Let me know if I can start a fitting room for you or grab any sizes from the back, OK?"

"Sure, thank you."

I looked at the clothes without seeing them. How many women shop when they are upset? It's what I want to do when I'm upset, and I can't be that unusual. Who are these people who make these systems? How do you overlook something as basic as motivation of the people you are trying to assess? I laughed to myself. How inconvenient for product design, the feelings of others. Do they know people at all? Do they care?

Where did they get their data from, I wonder. I had read about the dark days of AI information gathering, before the Sheldon-Claxton Accord, when nations eager for advancement experimented on political prisoners, people who were terrified, filmed and analyzed and added as data points for assessing guilt. Is that why that system determined I was a thief? I was upset—that makes me guilty.

I ended up buying some stuff, nothing I really wanted, because I felt bad for the salesperson. She had accused me of theft, yet I felt bad for her. I'm such a moron.

On the bus ride home, I thought of her description of the software. A paranoid old lady on a stoop, she had said. It was a perfect image. While the creators of the software had neglected human emotion, an end user had endowed it with a complete personhood.

What a curiosity.

I thought of cave dwellers painting the animals they hunted. Did the viewer imagine personalities for them? Or was that reserved for their weapons, and later their plows, then cars, appliances, then computers and bits of code. Who gives the tool their spirit?

CHAPTER 31

CARGO SHIPS, DOCKS, EQUIPMENT DESTROYED BY EXPLOSIONS; MOVE 37 CLAIMS RESPONSIBILITY

Sarah invited me over and I accepted. Well, she asked if I was coming over. I guess that's sort of like an invite. I wanted to see the kids in either case. I missed them. I don't like neglecting them because I caught some feelings.

We ate pizza and the kids shared the events of their day. Jack made a friend and they held hands. Sam managed to do a trick he had been practicing on his skateboard. Fiona ate a crayon and her poop had purple swirls in it. We laughed together, and it was warm and comforting to belong, even if temporarily.

I gave Fiona a bath while Sarah played board games with Sam and Jack. The little laughs made me smile. When she was clean and dressed in a fresh diaper and pajamas, Sarah and I switched. It felt smooth; an unspoken routine had developed. Like we had the best parts of marriage, not tension and attraction, but understanding, friendship, and a common goal. After the kids were in bed, we watched the new episode of her favorite show and went to sleep. I took the couch, since Steve's boxes were still waiting for him in his old office, now guest room.

I turned on my sleep app, settled into the spare blankets and pillow, discomfited by the large living room space but exhausted enough to know sleep was coming soon. I didn't need alcohol to sleep. I was so tired all the time now, perhaps too tired to dream. Sleep is just a blackness between days. Maybe that's what Oliver meant about his weird plaster-signal observation. Maybe I'm too broken to dream.

Anyway, I woke up to the sounds of a household of children preparing for departure.

"Kids!" Sarah called upstairs, her voice tense. "Please! Let's go, we're going to be late!"

I stumbled off the couch, put my hair in a bun, and took Fiona from Sarah. I settled her into her highchair, though it would be another five minutes before the baby porridge Sarah had made cooled enough for her to eat. I remembered the fresh apple in the fridge; I diced it up for her to snack on while her meal reached the correct temperature.

"Sam! Jack!"

Distant, irritated shouts followed.

Sarah pulled her hair into an aggressive ponytail as she glared at the ceiling. "I swear to god. It's not like this is a new routine. Wake up, get dressed, come downstairs, take your test, eat breakfast, brush your teeth, grab your stuff, drive to school. Every day. Week after week."

Midway through the speech, Sam emerged. I looked up from the apple I was dicing. His color was better and his cough had cleared. Sarah had mentioned a new decongestant. What a relief, to find the perfect medicine for what ails you.

Sarah handed him a glass vial with four faded lines painted on the side. "Come spit, then eat your waffle."

Sam cleared his throat and spit into the vial. Meanwhile, Sarah scraped off a bit of dried food from the testing machine. "This thing is expensive! I wish you guys would be more careful around it."

"Jack threw his yogurt yesterday. I didn't do it," Sam said as he handed her back the vial. He had filled it with saliva to the blue line.

"I know you didn't do it, sweetie. I should've been more specific. Go on and eat now."

Sarah put a cap, full of some solution, on the top of the test vial and shook it for five seconds. Then she flipped it and snapped it cap-first into a color-matched cavity on the top of the machine. A device in the dock popped. I imagine that was when the pin pierced the solution cap. There was a whir, probably the saliva mixture moving through the interior vessel and across the paper test strips. Sarah pressed the green button; I knew it was just a timer. The testing process had already begun.

"Sam, milk with your breakfast?"

"Just water, please."

"I got it," I said, already filling his glass with water.

"Ver, I'm going to go get Jack. You got them?"

I nodded and she left. I could see Fiona's porridge had cooled to a reasonable temperature. Wait - have I always been able to tell temperature at a distance?

Anyway, she continued picking the bits of apple off her tray while I added her actual breakfast to her silicone bowl. Sam ate his waffle and played a game on his phone. If he wanted to talk to me, I was here.

"What do you want for breakfast?" Sarah asked Jack as they entered the kitchen.

"Crackers."

"Cereal, sounds great."

"On it!" I said, perhaps a bit too brightly. I pulled down the bowl and prepared to reach for the cereal. Sarah took the bowl from me.

"Just sit down."

For a moment, I wasn't sure who she was talking to. The children were not nearby, and she was looking at me. It must be me. Had I done something wrong? I stepped back from the counter, reeling as if I had been struck. My body felt clumsy and large. After standing near Fiona for a useless second, I moved to the round kitchen table, then sat in a chair next to the boys.

Sarah fetched another vial and guided Jack until he had put in a sufficient amount of saliva. Meanwhile, the machine sang a little three-part song—no influenza, coronavirus, or respiratory syncytial virus in Sam's sample. When Jack was done, Sarah checked the screen. Did she not hear the song? Or did she not understand it? She put the machine through a ten-second rinse cycle, which disinfected the reservoir and dissolved the old test strips. Then she pressed a button to arm fresh test strips for Jack's tests. When the cap and shake routine for Jack's sample was finished, she inserted his vial and pressed the green button again.

"Would you like to me watch Fiona while you drop the kids off at school?"

Sarah looked at the baby who remained focused on her breakfast. "Yeah, let's do that."

Everything was fine now, I told myself. I remembered Jack's stalling. This wasn't about me. The same complications every single day must be so frustrating. She didn't want to hurt me, I soothed with insistence.

I helped the boys into their backpacks while Sarah scrubbed

their faces with a warm washcloth. First Sam and then Jack hugged me goodbye, then kissed their baby sister. The home's alarm dinged as they exited the house, the last sounds before the silence they left behind.

I cleaned up after breakfast. I turned on a morning news program. Sarah didn't like the older kids watching the news. There was no sense feeding them panic before a long, stressful school day. As if to make her point, the blackened ruins of a vehicle filled the screen. An assassination of a politician in a foreign country. They didn't even say allegedly when they described his crimes. Some sort of remote operation of an SUV with a roof-mounted gun had carried out the attack. The vehicle, the only evidence, had been detonated by an onboard device. This was the second death of a despot in the last few weeks, though the other was skeptically viewed as a natural death. I filled a crusty pot with hot, soapy water. Whoever had been clever enough to engineer a gun-mounted, exploding car was likely a bad person, too. I wish the news shared more uplifting stories.

Plates and bowls and cups came out of the dishwasher, and I dried them each with a clean towel, one at a time. Fiona examined a piece of cubed mango and watched a segment on storm damage in Texas. I shook my head. Being a baby must be bizarre. You learn about the world, and the things in it in such a crush of information. What must her thoughts have been when she first understood solid foods go in people's mouths? That people on the television can't see or hear us?

ANCHOR: The stock market remains steady today, with the Dow Jones Industrial Average trending 3 percent lower than seasonal average. Green energy stocks rose 11 percent on news of the Buy Out and Shutter package passage in the House. It is expected to be passed by the Senate and delivered to the president's desk by next week. In technology, former head of the Office of Science and Policy was announced as the new CEO of CEV Robotics. CEV, known for their algorithm-controlled janitorial devices, announced the hire and their planned expansion into the consumer entertainment market. Their closest competitor, Perilaus Bionics, saw a further 7 percent loss, continuing a downward trend following last week's allegations that employee files were shared with other companies represented by their board of directors.

I turned to the TV now. The program showed file footage from Perilaus's appearances at industry conferences, including Jennifer giving a talk in her favorite purple silk blouse. I'd have to tell Sarah about this. If they mishandled employee files, that may affect her job prospects.

They had said "with other companies represented by their board of directors." Does that mean someone at that dinner party was sharing Perilaus' secrets? Were they sharing mine, too?

The dishes done, I cleaned up Fiona and changed her into fresh clothes. I set her down with toys and cleaned her highchair and tidied the table. The cleaning distracted me from the fear. One reckless company able to black box me is quite enough, but imagine if there were more? What if they lost control over my safety systems?

I found some spray cleaner and started on the counters and cupboard handles. What if these hackers taking over boats and agricultural robots and cable inspection drones gained access to my controls? How could I be safe if anyone could shut me off?

By the time Sarah returned, Fiona and I were on the floor of the living room, rolling a ball back and forth.

"Hey, Ver."

"Hi! We're all good here," I said in a gentle, easy tone.

The little speech I had prepared about the Perilaus news faded away. Sarah leaned against the doorway and pinched the bridge of her nose. A glisten of sweat on her forehead and the slight imbalance in her walk told me that she had a migraine. She gets them a few days before her period. She walked into the kitchen, where she keeps the pain relievers. I got up and closed the drapes, then returned to Fiona. I could stay for a while. I had called in sick to work, and I didn't get bored of playing these repetitive games. It felt good to be fun to someone.

"I didn't need you to clean the whole kitchen," Sarah groaned as she collapsed into what had been Steve's easy chair. It was hers now.

"It's no problem, it was already pretty clean."

Fiona gurgled, trying to draw my attention back to our game. I tickled her tummy with a rapid and gentle tap of my fingers and rolled the ball to her.

"There's more to motherhood than doing dishes and playing ball."

My shoulders stiffened.

I could smell the surface cleaner I had used in the kitchen. Had I used too much? She has a migraine, I thought. The smell might trigger worse symptoms. I thought through the things I could have done differently. Maybe I should have left the mess and simply cared for the baby.

Why? Why can't I be kind to people? Why is it that I understand behavior, and feelings, yet I can't seem to translate that knowledge into creating the right responses? I offend when I try to be generous, and I discomfort when I try to overcome my own despair. What is the matter with me.

"I've upset you," I said softly. "I'm sorry."

"I don't think you are. You come over to my place and Jennifer's place with fast food and games and you get to play fun aunt. You make us the bad guys, when we already have it hard enough. You take all the good parts and then, when the kids aren't around, you mope. I don't think you want the doctor's appointments, and homework, and chauffeuring around, and the fear. The constant goddamn fear that there's going to be a tumor or a car accident or a school shooting or another pandemic. You get to play, and then you go back to your nice little apartment and you sleep in silence, you watch TV and make breakfast and use the bathroom whenever you want.

"You don't understand. We have to be two people at once, all the time: ourselves and a mother to someone else. We build our lives around other people and then maybe we get to see where we fit in."

I stayed silent, continuing to roll the ball back to Fiona, the color of it swirled through my tears. Stay still, I told myself, stay still and wait for this to end.

Sarah shut her eyes and sighed. "We all want the baby. Everyone wants a baby. Babies don't judge, they forget, they need you and love you. It's the kid that you have to want, and kids require sacrifice. You lose yourself in them, and that becomes your secret. You have no thoughts of your own, no activities of your own. They grow up and learn about who you are after they've already taken it all away from you."

"You love being a mother," I offered quietly and quickly, like a pebble thrown to distract from my hiding place.

"Love?" She laughed. "I love my kids. I don't love being a mother. I AM a mother. I'm nothing but a mother. If I could, I'd…"

Sarah remembered herself and fell silent. I let the ball roll back to Fiona one last time. I felt dizzy. I couldn't listen to this anymore.

"I'm going to head out, I'll talk to you later."

I grabbed my things from the doorway and left. She didn't try to stop me. In fact, I think she laughed at me. A very soft laugh, like one would share with another adult when a toddler throws a tantrum. The laugh you give to someone or something that is too ridiculous for serious attention. I suppose she is right.

CHAPTER 32

OPIOID HEIRESS, 7 OTHERS DEAD
IN PLANE CRASH

I'm on my late afternoon break. A weird thing happened after lunch.

I had returned to work feeling pretty good. It was busy today. Scott was definitely going to have me on the queues. I bet I'll never see those letters again. I was thinking through which queue to start in when I noticed him.

Oliver was in a car outside of my work.

I wasn't sure he knew I saw him, but he seemed to be watching for me. Dread, and fear, and confusion, and shame snaked through me. I walked through the side entrance, trying to be casual, though I know I moved too fast. Instead of going to my desk, I went to the top floor break room. The blinds were still down from the morning sunlight. I peeked behind them to see out to the street.

He was still there.

There was nothing else I could do. Standing there did nothing. I had to think, and I can do that while working. I went back to my desk. The queues were full, and as I expected, I had no special assignments. The elated feeling I wanted was not there.

A man I do not know very well, who works for a company that frightens me, has been following me. Again. He is waiting for me outside. Bile clung to the back of my throat.

I had taken Oliver to be some innocuous, perhaps lovesick, puppy. I thought he was cute. But now he was following me? What did he want? Had I done something to make him angry? I haven't done anything. I'm too stupid to do anything. Why can't they see that?

Sam's records. Of course! I was careless and put their project at risk. Maybe I'm in trouble. Maybe they are here to collect me. The darkness and the buzzing. What if it is permanent this time?

After a couple hours of distracted work, I'm writing this and watching him.

Diary, he is *still there.*

On a whim, I searched for Perilaus in my news app. A news story was just published about one of their military contracts, complete with leaked slide decks.

"APPLICATION OF PHOTOSYNTHESIS IN HUMANS"

A picture of a hornet with a giant energy-cycle symbol from sunlight, along with an arrow to a basic male human figure. It was embarrassing to read. I clicked on another packet.

"COMBAT EXOSKELETON WITH MAGNETIC ARRAY"

The main point here was that it weighed five hundred pounds

and required an external power source. The US government had invested millions of dollars into its development, with nothing to show for it.

"PARKINSON'S EXPERIMENTS ABOARD INTERNATIONAL SPACE STATION SHOW PROMISE"

Small brains grown on the international space station were connected to small spiderlike robots to gauge the efficacy of brain-electromechanical synapse connections.

In the comments section of the article, an anonymous account had linked to another piece on Perilaus. It was posted to a more popular magazine. Instead of discussing their technical accomplishments, they interviewed former employees who spoke on record about rampant racial discrimination and sexual harassment.

A large group of users on a social media website were citing Perilaus as an example of a defense contractor with too much money and too little oversight. Senators and congressmen demanded hearings with all three major robotics firms, yet some of these same officials had taken financial contributions from the lobbying firms employed by Perilaus. Others pointed to failed or advancing bills as potential preventative measures against this kind of behavior.

I looked out at Oliver, waiting outside in his car. Didn't he have something else he should be doing? A thought has occurred to me. What if Oliver leaked the information? What if I'm the real prize he wants to reveal? What if he's going to kidnap me and deliver me to some warehouse as evidence? I'm not safe.

Should I stay at work? Am I safer pretending I didn't see him? Or should I go home and wait?

I texted Sarah again. She hasn't responded to my earlier messages. I could use her advice now. I hope she's OK.

I'm going to go talk to him. I don't know why, but I feel like I should face him. I don't want to have some weirdo following me around, even if he has nice hair. I'll grab a letter opener from my desk, just in case.

I guess that happened.

He was very surprised to see me and seemed genuinely embarrassed. That gave me some relief. I wasn't sure I could stab him if he threatened me.

He opened his car door when I approached and stood in the street, stuffing his hands into the front pockets of his jeans.

"What do you want, Oliver."

"I was just curious where you worked," he lied. I can tell he lied. He knows I know he lied, right? Isn't that in the plaster's programming? He knows all about the plaster, and what it has made me into.

I waved at the basic building behind me. "Well, now you've seen it. Do you want to see my coffee shop, too? I know you've seen my apartment."

His blush deepened. A car drove past, the driver watching us out of curiosity.

"Vera, can we maybe talk about this in my car?"

"Can I trust you in your car?"

"I won't hurt you."

Flutters, even now, when I write this down.

No! Pathetic! Stop it!

I scowled at him. I got into the passenger seat, sat down, and waited.

He cleared his throat and pointed at the roof of the office building. "Quite a lot of work going on with the building. Lots of scaffolding. Is that solar?"

"That's what I've heard. I don't work with the utilities team."

"Must be hard as hell to get a signal in there," he said, reddening. Was this his idea of flirting? Scaffolding and solar panels?

"I've had to download my music before going into work. It's a huge pain. Not as huge as being followed to work by some dude. What do you want, Oliver?"

He looked bashful now. I looked out my window to hide my smile, but then looked back at him, unable to keep my eyes away.

I'll tell you this, diary. I like him still. That floppy hair, the stubble on his face. I bet it feels great. He's got a nice smell, too. Not a mask of cologne. Soap, laundered clothing, and an underlying fresh, salty smell. It probably isn't even that. It's just pheromones.

Goddamn biology. I can't conquer it.

"Do you enjoy working here?" he asked, desperate to say something.

I looked back at the building, giving his question more thought than it really deserved. "I used to. I used to like reading about people's lives and filling in the blanks. But now, I don't know. It's just tragedies, really. The bland stuff I forget. I only remember the scary and sad stuff now. It's hard to not feel helpless, reading about these injuries and catastrophes and the people left behind."

"Is there something else you'd rather do? Like, I don't know, make a difference somewhere?"

"What could I possibly do? I don't have any degrees. At least, I don't think I have any degrees. Maybe I'm a podiatrist."

He chuckled. I liked the sound of it. His voice took on a slight texture of intimacy, one I can't quite define. "I think you know you could do more than this."

I blushed, god help me, I actually *blushed.*

"I've thought about teaching."

"Teaching?"

"Yeah. I love kids. I guess with all this, you know. I can look up anything, right? If I learn how to teach, I could do it without textbooks or packets or anything. I could make a lesson plan for each kid in a classroom. I could teach in any language, on any subject. Jennifer would be so mad if I told her this!"

We shared a laugh.

Ugh, I bet he makes great coffee. I'm so tired of trying to make my own coffee.

His face grew serious.

"Do you believe in free will?"

I guffawed. I shook my head. He didn't say anything, so I guess I had to reply. I gave myself a few moments to think.

"I mean, we're all doing our best in our own circumstances to make our lives our own, right?"

"That's not an answer," he said, an eyebrow raised. I choked back a giggle. I hated this for me.

"Yes, I believe in free will. I'm not exactly an example of it. I don't know where I end and Perilaus begins. I suppose I demonstrated free will by trashing my apartment the other day."

Oliver frowned. He hadn't heard about that, it seemed. I averted my eyes, picking the window to look through, as if something interested me out there. I had to speak. I felt vulnerable in the silence.

"Did you know, a Chinese firm made a neural implant to treat anorexia? The first step was severing the pleasure center in women's brains. They did it to dozens of women before their families caught on what was happening. They stopped, but the business is still around. They're still working on anorexia."

Oliver said, "I haven't heard about that."

"I read about it, when I learned about the plaster and everything. I think about it a lot. In that case, they were trying to solve *one* problem. In mine, how many problems are they trying to solve? And was it a problem at all? And I'm going to have to live like this, forever, and I don't even know why. It's cool that I can look up the nearest Peruvian restaurant without thinking, or perfectly hear my cubical neighbor grind his teeth while he works, or that I can see that street sign four blocks away. It isn't giving me any idea what my purpose in life should be. I'm just muddling through, alone. Totally alone."

I don't know when I started crying. This happens sometimes. Other people seem to always know when they are about to cry. Not me, not always.

Oliver's warm, strong hand took mine. Fire burned through my veins. He rubbed his thumb across my knuckles, riding the ridges one to another, sending sparks up my spine.

"It's going to be OK, Vera."

I swallowed and tried to smile. "I should go." My voice was softer than I intended. I tried to tug my hand away, though it didn't obey the command.

"Can I see you again?" he said, his voice low.

I shut my eyes. Where would this go? Dating a man who worked at the place that had destroyed my future? I looked at him with regret.

"I want to. But… they hurt me."

His eyes were soft, gentle, until they grew eager as they focused on my lips.

No. I knew I must leave. His touch, a soft and unspoken

readiness to love, was not meant for me. I was in another person's place, one who had not lived very much, and was still intact.

Intact.

I see the word now, sharp, written in my own hand.

I'm a shell, heartache personified into nothingness.

Oh, but in his touch! I could feel care, and how I wish I deserved it. He would be gentle, generous. There would be no delirious approvals in a moment, only to be crushed by regret and absence of affection. He could be tender and help me heal. I could listen to him and he to me, forever, together. Another time, perhaps. Not now, when I am weak and vulnerable. Another time.

I pulled my hand free and yanked the car door open. I didn't look back as I walked back to the office, one hand warm from his touch, the other clutching the letter opener.

I'm home now.

I called Sarah on my way. She answered, but said she was a bit busy and she'd call me later.

This isn't fair. Why can't someone make time for me. I even tried Jennifer. She didn't answer, of course.

I'm totally alone.

What if Oliver was supposed to kidnap me but failed? What if they send the men in the van again? They don't care about me. Not at all.

I kept my keys poking out between my fingers as I walked quickly to the front door of my building. I listened for footsteps that were not my own, the reflections in glass helping me to check my blind spots. I rushed inside, ran up the stairs two at a time. At my door, there didn't seem to be any signs of tampering. But they could just get into my building. They could've had a copy of the key this whole time, or copied it when they black-boxed me. Once inside my apartment, I threw on the lights and grabbed a softball bat from my coat closet. I checked each room, then looked out the window.

Nothing. No one.

I checked my phone. Nothing from Sarah or Jennifer.

I'm disposable.

No, that's not true. I have myself and everything that I am made of.

Can I be more?

Can I be like the biblical locusts, the docile plant eaters who roam lush fields, pacifists in times of plenty, until food grows scarce. As their numbers dwindle and they begin to starve, some of them change. Not just a slight adaptation. They become another organism entirely. Their soft green coloring gives way to black and orange, their aggression heightens, and they wage war. The large swarms are not a search for peace and grain. No. They become cannibals, hunting one another down and feeding on the blood and flesh of their brethren to satisfaction. I sit here alone and my anger asks me: What do I become when love grows scarce? What am I capable of?

I can't keep going like this. I need companionship. I could die in this apartment and only the smell would give it away.

I laugh. That's just silly.

If I were to die, someone at Perilaus would get a system-outage text. He'd pause his video game or movie or TV show, put on his glasses, and drag over his laptop. My log needed a quick review for error alerts. He'd switch to a new window and pull the CrashDump file for my digital signal processor. The DSP they installed is particularly troublesome and prone to overheating. Then he would power cycle just the plaster, where the DSP is located. When that failed, he'd attempt a full reboot; that is, he'd try to get me to fall asleep and wake up. Then he'd make me look at my painting, take my vitamins, watch my news programs while I had toast. All the while his partner would look on, and sigh and yearn for the days before his project interfered in their love.

This sucks.

I took out a deck of cards. I'll pass time playing a little solitaire. My phone is next to me while I wait for someone to remember me.

CHAPTER 33

INTERNATIONAL TRADE COMMISSION
SANCTIONS TOP POLLUTERS; GREEN
STOCKS SOAR

It's Saturday.

I put on sweatpants and a T-shirt and made myself an instant coffee. It's disgusting. I drink it anyway. I still haven't heard from Jennifer or Sarah. I wonder if they're hanging out together and don't want me around. Why would they. I'm a liability. Look at what I did with Sam's medical records. Sarah had trusted me, and I failed to meet her expectations. I don't even need to consciously think of how Jennifer treats me. When I'm around Max, she acts as though I'm an unfenced swimming pool or an untethered bookcase, just waiting for an unsupervised moment to cause death to her only child.

Without anyone to keep me from my thoughts, I woke up and, rather than do my routine, decided to dive deeper into them. This plaster connects to a server, which is fed information from other computers that have other data that I am not given access to. I think that means I can submit a request for specific information, like who

I am. I wonder if I can do that. I guess we'll find out.

I sat on my couch and let my mind wander. At first, I asked questions and felt the information stream in. I imagined it as a river, bright against the darkness, and followed through to the source. It was no longer a thread of data; instead, it was an ocean of infinite information. I could go mad staring at it, the unsorted vastness. I had to re-envision what I was experiencing so that I could digest it.

What was I doing? Where was I? How could I put all of this in a comfortable context?

Ah, yes. Browsing shelves.

In a moment, I was pushing a shopping cart through a brightly lit grocery store. The beige speckled linoleum was polished to unused brightness. A suggestion of fluorescent light hid nothing, but in this place there was nothing to hide. Perfect displays full of regularly accessed information stood at the heads of aisles. Lively boxes with labels such as Current Weather Conditions, Map of Current Locations, Present Children's Television Characters, and Conflict Avoidance Techniques. My shoes squeaked down the center aisle— to my left and right were rows and rows with shelves five high of similar file boxes, each one a neatly packed, near-infinite volume of data, sorted away under aisle signs with clear descriptions.

THE HISTORY OF OPEC

SILKS OF QIANSHANYANG

VARIETIES OF LILY (flower)

I decided where I needed to start. I did not travel to the aisle, nor did it move to meet me. It was there, as if all aisles occupied the same space. Time, instead, had changed. I looked up.

APOTHECARIES OF THE MIDDLE AGES

HSAM IMPLANTS

OFFSIDES RULE

I ignored the irrelevant sections and selected a bright pink box beneath HSAM–CURRENT APPLICATIONS. A high-end table appeared and conveniently waited to receive the box. The box fit perfectly, though I waited to remove the lid. A sheen of sweat appeared on my skin, whether just in this place or on my actual body, I do not know. I wondered to myself, is this how I find out who I am? Will I get my answers now?

I looked behind me, the aisle fading into the horizon, the bright file boxes smaller and smaller until only a blur of color remained, stretching forever. This was only the beginning of my exploration, I told myself. I can't be afraid to make the first step.

I opened the box.

MATTHEW CHRISTENSEN

"How are you feeling, Mr. Christensen?"

A soft blanket of darkness enfolds me. The voice tugs at the edges. *Christensen?* I wonder. *No, no. Keep the dark. Snuggle back down.*

"Mr. Christensen? Wake up, if you can."

A pleasant voice of a caring person. I can feel a vague sensation that she stands nearby, blocking sound and wind and light. That's fine. So warm, so deep. I'll return to the darkness. I could explain her mistake to her.

Why bother?

Rest.

A man's groan booms in the tight recess of my own head.

No, that's not right. This isn't my head. It's *his* head.

"If you're able to, it's time to open your eyes, Mr. Christensen. The doctor needs me to calibrate your plaster."

I shed the desire for the black fog of sleep. I am awake and alive. I watch through his eyes, my perception heightened by detachment. A scotoma warps a space in his vision. He doesn't notice it—he never has nor will. I see it because it does not belong to me. He is recovering from anesthesia. I swim with him as he scans the room, the flawless walls, privacy curtain, bright window, large, comfortable hospital bed. An air of overt luxury is in this space. He moves his lower body, his legs enormous compared to my own. He lifts his hands to his field of vision, rotating them, checking the backs and fronts, then squeezing his fists. Powerful hands. I feel jealous.

"You doing OK, Mr. Christensen?"

"Uh, yeah," the man lies. He is trying to steady his eyes against waves of dizziness.

The young woman nods. With graceful competence, she reaches over to the IV line and turns a dial. Mr. Christensen watches, likely admiring her youthful skin and the shimmer in her hair.

I agree with her diagnosis. He is dehydrated.

He places his head back on the pillow and fixes his eyes on the ceiling. It is not an acoustic panel ceiling. It is smooth drywall. There are no spots of blood waiting for someone like him.

I pull back for a moment. Somehow, this feels old. *Am I here now, or before? Is this a memory? When is this?*

He has a plaster like me. What of other devices? How would I know? I reach back in but move away from his mind. What else is here? I want to see what I can touch. I can sense his body, though only through an unfamiliar remoteness. There is a soft energy there, but it does not respond to me. I note the internet connection. It is slower than mine. Is this an old model? Or the commercial version?

Oh, what is here?

A tingling line, a pathway from the plaster to some kind of

device. I think of my own body and wonder if this is a device I have. No. It feels new to me. Simplistic and steady, like a wheel and axle compared to magnetic levitation. What is it? I shut out what he is seeing and hearing to better understand it.

HM THUMP DUM   HM THUMP DUM   HM THUMP DUM

It has rhythm. Music? An artifact from the plaster connection? This is confusing. It is certainly not a device Perilaus installed in me. It is something else, something that can communicate with the plaster. What would a man on an older model of plaster have that was not installed in me? I reach for it again and tug.

Do something new.

Tell me what you are.

It ignores me. I think of the tingling that led me here. Yes, of course. It must be energy. Perhaps with more energy, it will stumble and give me a clue. I increase power by 10 percent and wait.

HM THUMP DUM   HM THUMP DUM   HM THUMP DUM

What if I interfere with the power? I deduct 20 percent.

Mr. Christensen moves.

I return awareness to his eyes and ears, eager to learn what I have found. His legs shift under the blanket and he breathes deeply, a routine he has developed. Sometime during my exploration, the assistant had raised the head of his bed. On his food tray is a screen showing black squares and other shapes. He is barely paying attention to her quiz now.

Stars explode to shards of glass, then fade to nothing.

It happens again, and again. After a moment, I realize this was transmission from the plaster. Of course. I should've known. I turn that off. I don't need information. I don't care about his visual calibration. I want to know about the device and the odd music. There don't seem to be any changes to his behavior, other than the startle reflex that brought me back here. I wonder: what is the music doing now?

HM THUMP DUM HM THUMP DUM HM THUMP DUM HM THUMP DUM

Unpleasant, wrongness.

"I'm feeling some pain." Mr. Christensen's whisper explodes in my head.

The assistant puts the screen aside. With a firm push, she rolls her stool to the monitor on the wall. In one flick she pulls up a keyboard at the bottom of the screen. "Where, specifically?"

HM THUMP DUM HM THUMP DUM HM   THUMP DUM   HMTHUMP DUM

"My heart."

She pulls up a window with his EKG information. An erratic heartbeat. Oops. Not music, then.

"Let me just recalibrate something here." The assistant types for a moment. "I apologize for that, Mr. Christensen. We've got a slight connectivity issue between the plaster and your pacemaker. I'm adjusting it now."

The sound of his heartbeat moves to the background, and I don't dare reach for it again.

"How are you feeling now, Mr. Christensen?"

"Much better, thanks."

"Sorry about that! It can take a minute for these things to communicate with one another properly. Like stepsiblings learning to get along. Now, let's return to the visual calibration."

I pull myself away from the man's mind.

I put the lid back on the box with a firm smack. I learned something important from that memory, or recording, whatever it was. I need to be careful. Someone can get hurt if I interfere with things I don't understand.

I returned to my shopping cart and began to browse again. I hadn't really learned anything from that last one. There had to be something useful around here. How can I find myself in a place with seemingly endless information and yet I cannot think of what to access to tell me who I am?

Stop, I told myself. Review and analyze. What did I know about Mr. Christensen? He had surgery, a plaster installed. His room was expensive. His name sounded vaguely familiar. There were issues with calibration, issues that the assistant claimed were typical. Nothing, nothing, nothing. I grew frustrated. This shouldn't be so hard for me. Surrounded by endless information, yet I'm still stupid.

I nearly ended the search when I remembered something. He was running an older plaster. Sarah had said there was probably a data center just to support my data stream. If they can receive my passive information, I can follow that trail to them. And with that, I found myself standing before an assortment of lime-green file boxes.

CARVANTHIUM SOLUTIONS: CONSOLE 12
CARVANTHIUM SOLUTIONS: CONSOLE 13
CARVANTHIUM SOLUTIONS: CONSOLE 14

The naming convention was familiar; they were access points for workstations, not people. Not likely to screw up someone's pacemaker diving into this. I think. I should be careful. I picked Console 13 and set it on my friend the table, which had returned from the ether.

With less hesitation, I opened the box.

RESUME? yes/no
    YES
    WINDOW RECORD PAIR COMPARISON
    [image 456]
    [image 18]
    true?
    YES
    [image 457]
    [image 3]
    true?
    YES
    [image 458]
    [image 62]
    true?
    NO
    [image 458]
    [image 25]
    true?
    NO
    ROUTE IMAGE 458 TO INDEXING? yes/no
    YES
    [image 459]
    [image 2]
    true?
    YES
    WINDOW CHAT
    Yonas: my brain is mush

Marjani: [laugh emoji]

Marjani: I told you

Yonas: you did. is indexing better than this?

Marjani: not really.

Yonas: how does this stupid thing not know shoes.

Marjani: it does most of the time, these are just the times it gets confused.

Yonas: how does it EVER get confused by SHOES.

Marjani: [laugh emoji]

WINDOW RECORD PAIR COMPARISON

[image 460]

[image 88]

true?

YES

[image 461]

[image 1]

true?

WINDOW CHAT

Yonas: do we ever see anything spicy?

Marjani: Spicy?

Yonas: you know

Yonas: [look emoji]

Marjani: [eyeroll emoji]

Yonas: im only asking!

Marjani: our girl is a good girl. the women review all the flesh tone images. mind your eyes. pervert.

Yonas: not everything spicy is flesh tones [kissy face emoji]

Marjani: you crazy [eyeroll emoji] [laugh emoji]

WINDOW RECORD PAIR COMPARISON

[image 461]

[image 1]
true?
YES
[image 461]
[image 1]
true?
WINDOW CHAT
Yonas: why is it asking me this stupid photo again
Marjani: because you got it wrong, you dumb ox
Yonas: why would it ask me if it knows the right answer
Marjani: it doesn't trust you. it's smarter than you.
Yonas: this is stupid. I should've stayed at my uncle's shop.
Marjani: you hated that job
Yonas: [eyeroll emoji]
Yonas: who is this person anyway?
Marjani: which person?
Yonas: the person who is seeing all these things. she is not important! look at her tiny desk and ugly office and her work. she has work like us. why are we all here telling this stupid computer that those are her ugly shoes
Yonas: hello? did you leave?
Marjani: im here.
Marjani: don't ask.
Yonas: oh? is she someone important?
Marjani: I can't talk about it.
Yonas: perhaps at dinner? [kissy face emoji]
Marjani: she's just a lady.
Yonas: what kind of lady?
Marjani: it's not right.
Yonas: what? what happened?

Marjani: she doesn't know about this.

Yonas: what?

Marjani: us. all this. she thinks she's normal. someone did this to her.

Yonas: what? she doesn't know? how doesn't she know?

Marjani: stop asking these questions here. don't mess this up for me. get back to work.

Marjani: I mean it.

Yonas: OK

WINDOW RECORD PAIR COMPARISON

[image 461]

[image 1]

true?

NO

I looked around at the bright, beautiful information supermarket around me.

Another box read TTA LRM_PNI. Inside were subfolders, with headings like terrain_plot and POS_process, with files called things like Downstairs_fast, AscendBackwards4, and distanceTraveledRAW.

This wasn't going well.

I could look anywhere I wanted, instantly. But without context for all this information, I didn't know where to start. I had access and no talent.

I wished I could just search my name. I was not there, not really. Everyone else was there, except for me.

Everyone else is here, I repeated to myself slowly.

I was so stupid. I closed my eyes and thought:

Jennifer Elpis

When I opened them, my table waited for me in front of soft lilac-gray boxes. Each read Jennifer Elpis in thin, perfectly uniform letters with various subtitles.

PRESCHOOL SECURITY FOOTAGE

VICTOR WELLS AND KAITLIN ELPIS CUSTODY HEARING

PEDIATRIC PSYCHOLOGIST REPORT

Why would Perilaus have these files? I shook my head. How embarrassing for Jennifer, to be loyal to an employer without boundaries.

These files seemed to be ordered chronologically. I moved away from her young childhood. Unlike Perilaus, I was not interested in her personal secrets. I just wanted my own.

I searched for the end.

TOLL RECORDS

QUARTERLY PERFORMANCE REVIEW

UTILITY BILLS

I chose the Quarterly Performance Review. I set the file on my table. I had no other leads. This was my last shot. I took a breath and opened it.

ACTIVE

I sense a flicker. This isn't a computer terminal or someone else's plaster. There is a fixed border to this—beyond lies the black box, buzzing with nothingness. I open one file after another and consume the information without effort. Budget analysis, headcount, attrition, diversity and inclusion metrics. Within this list is a subsection titled Projects.

Ah ha!

I know one of these items is me. I laugh at the more obvious ones, such as Ocular Implant Retrofit and TENS Substrate. There is no way she actually contributed to those projects. I have a feeling she latched on to them when they were successful or boosted them to gain an advantage over someone else.

Within the list are two code names:

GALATEA

PENNYWHISTLE

Whatever anyone knows of me is behind one of these two names. Which one? What am I to them, I wonder? To name something is to define its purpose. I was made for service, that much is clear.

What kind of service?

Am I intended to be cheap computational power, or am I coveted, the warm wax lover of my creator? I consider the two before realizing there are two of us. What is the other project? Who else have they hurt?

On impulse, I choose PENNYWHISTLE.

The familiar warmth of my own disorganized bookshelf reveals itself. Things I once knew and things I was learning and set aside. My favorite coffee order, the songs I listen to, the feeling of a perfectly executed sandwich order. Yes. I am no partner for Pygmalion. This is me.

Within is a subfolder titled VIDEO FOOTAGE. Inside are many files, though not as many as I suspected. They must store video footage from my implant elsewhere. Great.

I sort by age and look at the top, my stomach clenched.

I know when I see the filename. Not from any special naming convention knowledge. I know in the way a mother knows her child's screams, the just-for-show cry versus the screams that divide time like a fissure, to before and after. I could click on this file now and know the answers. Like a careless hiker stumbling on a rotted trail marker, I convince myself it must be safe. Someone let me reach this point, whether by intent or by carelessness. It can't be so bad if I can reach it. And yet, as I stare at this video file, I don't really believe that. I know too much about human nature.

I select it, and there sits someone I should know. Not me, as I know me. A version of me that is different yet complete. A different nose and cheekbones and past and ideas and structure.

This must be the me that was displaced by the cuts and extractions and insertions and creations. There she sits, proto-me, so unlike the picture of myself I retain in my mind that I can't identify with it. Her stringy, greasy hair in a messy bun, poorly healed acne across her face, and her facial expressions of defensive indifference. She wears a sweatshirt with a faded sports team logo, one I doubt she has any familiarity with.

She sits in a large metal and plastic four-legged chair in some sort of gray-and-white room, one that conjures the notion of linoleum and acoustic tile, though the ceiling and floors are out of frame. Distant sounds of an office filter in. Light from a window to her right casts shadows of a plant across the furthest corner of the frame.

A slight smirk plays at her mouth when she looks at whoever operates the camera across from her, as if a joke about them has come to mind. The object of her ridicule remains out of frame, unimportant to the camera's eye.

"Good afternoon," a man's voice says. "You were assigned a patient ID number this morning. Can you repeat that for me?"

"Sure. 3895025. I'm pretty good with numbers. Reading, not so much."

I have to pause.

Her *voice*. What is that? It's so different, and yet… it was mine.

The appearance was unsettling, but this—this is like catching the scent of a forgotten memory. Just on the brink of recollection, but out of reach. Her accent isn't one I would use in my day-to-day, not for ordering a sandwich or playing with Jack or greeting Scott at work. This is a voice I hear in my mind when a man touches my back without permission, when a driver creeps their car up on me in a crosswalk, when I sat shivering in my thin paper gown, hearing those doctors discuss my sterilization. This voice I hear is my voice of rage.

I play the video again.

The young man clears his throat. "Great. Thank you. This is just standard intake protocol. I'm going to ask you a series of questions. You don't have to respond to any question I ask you, but you must reply if you wish to proceed with the trial. Again, if you don't answer these questions, you will not be able to proceed. Is that OK?"

"Oh sure, I love talking about myself. It's hard to shut me up, even if I should be shutting up."

"First, do you have any questions before we get started?"

"I gave the lady up front my PO Box number, for the check. Do you got that?"

"Yes, we have your payment information."

"Good, fire away."

"This is a trial of modification devices by the Perilaus Corporation. I want to confirm that you received the paperwork this morning outlining what procedures you are consenting to, by participating in this trial."

She holds up a dingy cloth purse, a half-rolled assortment of papers sticking out of the top.

"Can you verbally confirm that you received the paperwork, please."

"Yes, I received your giant stack of papers in size-4 font. I didn't read them. Figured I got time for that, once you all set me up in this hotel room I've been promised."

"I'm going to take a moment and explain to you again what Perilaus is asking of you, and give you another opportunity to withdraw your participation. You can withdraw your participation at any time, of course."

"But no money, no hotel."

"Payment is upon completion of the items listed in the packet."

"Got it."

"Perilaus, in contract with various third parties listed in your paperwork, is proposing to surgically implant the following items into your body. You can withdraw consent at any time. The items are: a trial version of version 6.2 of cranial stimulating neuroplate with internet connectivity, 47 muscle stimulating implants, 18 joint contraction sensors, a full spinal electromagnetic enhancer, a pair of cranial impact supports, a pair of auditory signal boosters, one visual sensory chip, and thorax netting to monitor respiratory function."

"You're putting a chip in my eye?" The question isn't presented as a surprise or with revulsion. She smiles, as if her amusement comes at the questioner's expense. I can't make out what she's thinking. How unsettling, to not know my own intent.

"Your visual cortex. I can show you the device. It's a capsule about the size of a grain of sugar, injected into where your brain and optical nerve meet. You can withdraw your consent at any time."

"Nah, not worth the trouble."

"Right." The man's voice shudders through the small word. He clears his throat and pauses to find the place he left off. He is not used to this role. The emotion reminds me that he, too, was a human in this system. Who was he? Some junior engineer? Does he have regrets?

"Though we plan to use scar-reduction technology, there may be scarring."

"That's nothing. The lady up front said you'd fix my other scars up while you're at it. This arm has an old burn scar, plus the big one on my back, where some fucker stabbed me."

I felt my back, smooth and perfect.

"Yes, I, uh, see that note."

"Great. Go on."

"These modifications to your body would be permanent and irreversible. Do you understand?"

"Yep." She's leaning back in her chair now, the legs squeaking in an irritating, rhythmic manner. From the quirk in her mouth, and from being in some small way still her, I know she does it to annoy the man. But I don't know why. I watch this person with my face do things with such misdirected disdain. Or maybe it was valid, and I've lost what she knew.

"Certain complications may result from these implants, soon after or at any point following these procedures. These complications include hemorrhage, loss of function of one or more limbs, cancer, organ failure, bone loss, brain damage, memory loss, paralysis, brain death, or death."

"Jesus, and rich people get these to what, download French and learn how to play the fucking ukulele? Sounds like a fun time."

"In addition, you'll need to remain on anti-rejection medication permanently. These medications will cause you to be immunosuppressed and will make you vulnerable to serious outcomes from widely circulating diseases. Do you understand?"

"Yep."

"As result of the risks of the implants, and the immunosuppressive medications that you will require, you have marked your consent to be permanently sterilized. Do you understand sterilization?"

"I can't have kids. Got it."

"I need you to consent with a yes or no, please."

"Yes. I understand that I won't have children if I go through with this."

Breathe.

Breathe through the pain, I whisper to myself.

"Perilaus will not store your ovaries, and they don't offer egg retrieval or anything," he continues, his tone urgent.

"Yes, yes. OK?"

"Please sign here, attesting that I read these disclosures to you and that you have given your verbal consents."

She smiles and signs. "Don't look so sad, Doc. As long as I get paid, you lab coats can fill me up with whatever gadgets you like. I've never been any good to anybody. I can barely afford to keep myself fed and dry. The best thing I could do for any kid of mine is not have them."

The man takes the papers back and shuffles them. He pauses. The person with my face warms, the smirk gone. Now she looks patient and wise. Is it pity? For him?

"Um. Most of the folks we have come through here, they're older," he says, his voice gentle and sad. "They've lived, you know? A lot of them tried to go to college and had lives and stuff."

She smiles and nods. She lowers her eyes, her attention called to her pant leg. "Oh, I've lived. Not the way you mean, but I've lived. If you folks give me memory loss, like you had in that little list, there won't be much good lost, you know what I'm saying?"

"There's another experiment, you know, that pays. It's less invasive. They wouldn't have to sterilize you."

The soft smile evaporates. Anger now. Anger from not being heard. I know it—it's the anger I feel in me now as I watch it in her.

"Look, you don't get it, man. I see you in your, what, organic, free-range cotton shirt? Do you see me? Do you *really* see me? I've been on my own since I was thirteen. I'm wearing two different-size shoes I pulled from a goddamn garbage bin outside a department store. What future do I have? I'm not going to *college*. I'm not going to trade school. I couldn't get through high school. Not because I'm stupid, OK? I had straight As. I couldn't afford the time away from work.

"Yeah, I know what I'm doing. The best hope I ever had was to find someone to get me on my feet, keep a roof over my head, give me time to take a breath and think and plan. And that ain't happening. A baby?"

Her laugh has an edge of despair. "A baby. Me? Look, you seem nice, alright? When you were nineteen, you were probably a sweet, shy kid, afraid of your professors, scared of disappointing your parents, missing home, all while chasing people you wanted to be or screw. That isn't me. It's *never* been me. Nobody has ever loved me. Being a kid? For me? It was…"

Her eyes grow hard now. I don't know the details. I will never know, I see that now. I can feel, though. I can feel the nauseating fear, the desperate need for escape. As though you were made of strings pulled so tight just to survive the darkness at home, and the sweet release of Monday morning and a fresh identity at school, learning and books and numbers, pure and crisp and true, with no withheld love and no violence and no indiscriminate rage and no adult problems cast onto your child shoulders. Even among the judgment of peers and teachers, there was the joy of information, and the joy of being away from the monsters that lay in wait, yet all the while the return must happen. Another weekend, another vacation, another break would mean a descent into that dark hell they called home.

She refocuses on the man beside the camera. "Take my word on this. As bad as this looks to you, as bad as things have been for me, I'm thankful. I wish it was different. I love kids. I love them. They're the best of us. I've always believed that. But how was I going to get there? There is no Prince fucking Charming coming to sweep me away, you know? Even if everything had gone great in school, and I got myself a big fancy job like you have, it wouldn't have been enough. You're gonna break me with all your gizmos and gadgets, but not any more broken than I already am. I can't be a mom on my own. I'm not enough. Some are—not me. I see that. I'm not afraid of it."

She's barely seeing him now. Her eyes fix on some distant point, as if she's wandering, lost in a maze of hurt so endless and so complete. "Someone to keep me safe and warm? To help me be a better me, so I could have a noisy little chaotic crew who I could keep safe and warm? Yeah. I would've loved that. It was never in the cards for me."

Her eyes glazed over, tearless yet full of pain.

"No. Not for me. I come from a long line of women who never shoulda had kids. So this hysterectomy, don't stress yourself out about it. That's a tragedy for a nice girl, with love and money and a future. I'm not a *nice girl*. Maybe I get my act together, I'll get a dog. No cats, though. I'm allergic."

The video ends.

I check again. That's the whole thing. No name, just some number.

What can I do now?

I just need to dig deeper. I need to dig it all out, and look at it all, and then take a breath and decide what it means. If I try to judge myself now, how can I live with this?

I found a huge file that held multiple camera angles of a bed. A spasm in my phantom gut. More, then. I had seen who I was, and now I was going to watch what they had done to me. What I had done to me.

I think these files would be difficult to watch with eyes, outside of my mind. Maybe I'm deluding myself. Is there an easy way to learn how you ruined your life?

Well, here goes.

Inside the bed, docile and clean, a person far too thin and pale, maybe a woman, face concealed by hair, rests under a white blanket. Some sort of hospital, I think. There are windows bringing in sunlight, casting shadows across unseen furniture. The floor is carpeted, a confusing detail in an otherwise-perfect picture of a recovery room. The person moves. I notice then that there are restraint straps on the arms. Dread. The same dread I've felt at every revelation these past six months.

A man and woman enter, the woman tapping on a tablet. The person in the bed turns toward the door, the face now visible to one of the camera angles. Stringy, disheveled hair clings to saliva dried on the gaunt face. A face I know, of course. The proud, bold face from earlier is gone. Why else would my mind find its way here, watch this, if my own face wasn't waiting for me.

"How are we feeling today?" the man asks. No mere man. No, of course—it is Dr. Parsons. And there is Elizabeth. That can't be their real names. Who are they? Where are they now?

The me-thing growls and lunges at him, thin limbs strained against the restraints. Gone is the sarcasm and confidence and pain. Only anger and fear remain, the binary options the only logical response to this new nightmare.

"Not quite at stage three on verbal function. Pain response?" The doctor takes out a sharp metal tool from his coat pocket and brings it near the secured foot. The growling turns to a whimper as the creature tries to pull its leg away.

The woman calls out the words as she types. "Normal flexion response with localization."

"Good, good." The doctor puts his hand on the secured arm, squeezing, searching for plumpness. "Nutrition isn't quite adequate. Up the calories by, oh, let's say 150. I'd say 200, but they want to keep this one lean."

As the woman types, the man takes out a penlight and does an eye-tracking test on his patient. He shakes his head.

"We're going to have to figure out how to assess this thing's visual acuity. With all the gizmos they installed, I can't tell what's their hardware and what's actual brain response."

"Does it matter?" the woman asks, still typing.

"Hm. True."

The video ended there. Before I could breathe, or process, the next one played.

There it sits, chest restrained to the back of a chair as it screams nonsensical obscenities at a nurse. Foamy spit drips down its mouth.

Stop. It is not an "it." That person is a person. Me. I am a person.

The next. I'm in clothes now, my hair clean—almost progress. Yet I sit on the ground beside a table, sobbing uncontrollably, holding a bowl of some sort of mashed food in a clumsy hand. I can almost feel the warmth of it now. *It burned my mouth. I didn't know how to tell them it had hurt me, though I wanted it still.* Hunger, a knowing rather than a memory, churns through me. They didn't understand any of it. A woman in khaki trousers sits next to me, encouraging me in a loud, stupid tone to return to my place setting. An orderly enters.

"Need help?"

"Nah. They are always doing shit like this."

And then the next video. In this, a change of setting. I'm in a hospital gown, surrounded by strangers attempting various tasks, attended by physical therapists. The camera has an angle of disrepute. A dark blob just visible, as if the lens is partly obscured by the bag concealing the device. I shuffle along two parallel bars, struggling, face partly slack. I am still thin, though not nearly as bad. My hair is shaved in a hasty swatch from the front of my forehead down one side. Something went wrong. Outsiders had to be brought in for a repair job. In my eyes, I see intent.

I would walk. I see this through.

The last clip. Me again, back in the original room, dressed, clean, and composed. They would call me an it, as they had done and will do, but I see myself here. I am sitting before a chess board, across from the man I know as Dr. Parsons, about to call checkmate.

That's the end.

I rose from my couch. I need someone to talk to, to cry to, to share this darkness. I had done it. It was me. The blame is mine. I wanted to scream it outside, like the sad, disconnected souls who sometimes wander the street outside and scream to their phantoms. I won't do that. I'll call Sarah. Maybe we could go over this, just the two of us, hiding in the privacy of the tent, a space she created for us to share secrets. She could reassure me that although I am not safe in a world closing in on me, I am still loved by someone in it.

No answer. I set the phone down, thinking of the good things we would do when she was free.

My phone buzzed with a text notification.

(Busy, talk later.)

Each word hit like a bullet. I let myself cry.

I have the scarf Sarah gave me in my hands. It feels cheap now. A thoughtless gift. A careless, superficial affection. They're talking about me, I'm sure. How ridiculous I am, how stupid and pathetic. I'm not even angry about it. I almost feel relief, knowing that they see what I see. I'm someone who sold her body to become a failed thing, a street-cleaning bot that can't clean itself up. I have been remade and rejected by those who know me best. Should I not reject myself, too?

Yet, I wonder, who do I reject?

I thought of the interview. That woman knew people; she understood her place. I know that I am not her. She is too smart to be me.

Or am I the machinery running in my head, with servers and programs and algorithms I do not even understand, where data backups and software engineers keep me seeing, breathing, and writing?

Or am I the person I see in the mirror?

Does a parasite know it is not the infected host? Are my thoughts now like those of the male pilot fish, clinging to the flesh of the female, purposeless beyond the invasion of another's body?

An infant is a type of parasite. Is that why I wanted a baby so much? To be the infected, to feed and protect and carry is to give a service only the strong and exploitable can give. Infants do not know they are not their mothers, not for years. How many more years do I have to wait, to see myself as my own?

Now I see the life I thought I wanted wither away. Was it ever a complete picture? The edges and the heart of a need, buried in the original organism, a tool I used to pretend at humanity? In all the minutes I spent staring at that acoustic tile with my feet in stirrups, I never imagined myself in love, partnered, facing parenthood with someone to see through to the other side. Perhaps my desire for a baby had always been notes of song heard in a dream, incomplete in detail because I did not create it—I stole it from that poor girl whose skin I wear. Just as I carry her rage and terror, this was her hope, one predicated on a life I live that she couldn't imagine for herself: shelter, food, and security. I thought anger was the only strength left, the memory of cells in a person erased. But that is not so. I think I have her love, and her hope, too.

What to make of this theft? How do I honor it?

CHAPTER 34

US, UK, AND OTHER NATIONS PLEDGE
TO END GERRYMANDERING

I went back to work. I tried to channel who I used to be, someone who showed up and did a thing for a return.

I took my usual seat at the team meeting, the glass door and wall across the table from me. I sat away from the centrally placed microphone where, sometimes, remote workers joined in our meeting. The large glass windows that separated the office from the meeting space looked thin but did an excellent job blocking sound. For fun, I tried to guess what people still at their desks were talking about. Were they discussing dinner plans, cruel nicknames for work friends, medical issues shared only for reassurance? Do these conversations mean anything to them? Are they simply passing the time, or does it soothe the wound they carry with them, the one that bleeds "I don't belong here." Maybe I'm just projecting.

Scott cleared his throat, his glasses teetering at the tip of his nose as he read his notes. That meant the meeting would begin soon, though some people were missing.

Malaise began to wash over me. Nope, I don't want to be here. I hate it here. I keep that thought down when I'm busy, but in these moments of pause I think of nothing else. These people around me. Anthony from Document Storage leering at a new employee to my right, William bouncing his leg and shaking the whole table, even Scott. Scott, who often asks me to take notes at these meetings. Never William or Anthony, never any of the men on the team. Me.

The exit sign glowed green beyond a sea of cubicles. I could just leave. My face felt hot. I could just get up and leave—they couldn't stop me. They would talk about it, of course. They would share how that crazy lady just up and left one day. They would laugh about the look on Scott's face. I'd get a new, cruel nickname, one I'd never learn and could never hurt me. No one needed me here. I hated it here.

At my last review, Scott couldn't help but give me high scores for work output and accuracy. "Attitude" was the only less-than-perfect score I received. If I did everything they wanted better than they expected, what difference did it make if I was unhappy?

Screw this. I'll just watch a movie during the meeting. I had started a series by Satoshi Kon. It was uncomfortable watching something violent in public, but no one knew what I was doing on the plaster anyway.

I was queueing up the second episode when an HR rep approached the phone support section of cubicles. One by one, each person slowly rose, logged out of their phones, some with their headsets still dangling around their necks, and followed the woman in the bright blue blouse. It looked like they were heading to the big break room, the largest gathering place in this office building. It seemed to be a spontaneous meeting, or at least the staff weren't prepared for it. I wondered what was happening.

Helen, a person on my team, came in. Scott glared at her, cleared his throat, and started reading from his first page of notes before she had sat down. She took the only empty seat and whispered to her neighbor.

"They're laying off phone support."

A tiny storm of whispers spun out of control.

"They WHAT?" Scott's face turned red and then purple. He slapped down his neatly typed pages and stormed out of the meeting room. Some whispers continued, more hopeful this time.

Is there something broken in the minds of people with good parents? Does something like this happen and they think, "Good! Dad will make this right"? I certainly don't. I'm sure I had a father, probably someone like Steve, who makes noise but can't be counted on to do much of anything.

"Meeting adjourned, then?" William snickered. His remark set off a wave of conversations.

"I hope they don't lay off Heavenly. Her little boy just started chemo."

"I wonder if that means we'll get more OT."

"That new call center opened up on Seventh Ave. Maybe they are hiring."

"Gonna make us do all that work, on top of our own work. I told you, the queues have been too slow."

That was pointed. I felt eyes on me. Eyes that yearned for me when the workload was oppressive but turned on me when things like this happened. Sometimes they would simply pass by my desk and watch me type. Who needed 160 WPM when there was so little to go around. I could tell them that while my typing speed remained the same, my output had been reduced for weeks now. I could cite how often I had called in sick to work in the past months. They wouldn't care.

"This must be what Annabel was working on," William said. "Remember, they had her making notes while she worked? They're getting replaced with that phone-support bot."

A few phone support clerks walked quickly to their desks, crying, empty boxes in their hands. They must have handed them out in the break room. We sat on the other side of a glass wall, voices now fallen to whispers. Some had the decency to avert their eyes.

"They're gonna replace us next. Once they figure it out, we're good as gone."

The exit sign glowed green.

The train home was quiet.

An elderly woman nodded off to sleep at the back. A man in shiny business shoes stared at his device. I could tell from a reflection in the glass behind him that he was playing Potter's Bench. I've heard of it before. It's a slow, tedious game where you prepare plants that grow in your garden, then maintain your garden, and the more people who play, the better the game becomes for everyone. There are no ads, no ways to pay to improve the game. It's a garden, with all the tools you need, that waits for your effort. It's become the most downloaded game in history.

It came out of nowhere, some small developer who's probably rolling in cash. Is the developer happy, knowing they've created something that gives joy? What is that like? To create something and know millions of people not only love it, but rely on it to get through their day?

I looked at my own phone. I could download it, build a virtual garden, pull weeds, plant seeds, watch it become populated with butterflies and songbirds. My effort would not only benefit me, it would contribute to a larger purpose, enhance the digital environment for other gardeners around the world. Would it soothe me? If I had started that garden before today, would I have quit my job?

Jesus Christ, I quit my job.

What will I do with myself now? I'm overwhelmed by the feeling that I'm not where I'm supposed to be, that I've violated some urgent order. Where is that elation you see in job search-engine commercials? I feel no joy, only a trembling fear. What will I do?

Motherhood, motherhood, motherhood.

A drum banged in my head. A baby looking up at me from her crib, smiling, her hand reaching for my strands of hair. I shut my eyes, I squeezed them until it hurt. I need something else. Is there anything I could want?

I checked the news. I like the news. I like knowing, even if I can't affect any change. To know is a sort of power, isn't it? Isn't that what this whole thing in my head is about?

UPRISING IN YEMEN TIED TO SOCIAL MEDIA CONTRACTORS

Firms contracted through multi-billion-dollar corporations set up huge banks of computers at refugee camps in order to extract as much cheap labor as possible from a relatively captive group. Their low wages and brutal work requirements were notorious in certain circles, though I had never seen anything about this on the news before. The article said four centers had been seized by workers and their kin who had organized themselves. Many of the now-former moderators had used the computers to remotely disable coal power plants on the other side of the world. They were now operating as support for BallotSpy. NATO was considering military action, though it was still a refugee camp with innocent civilians nearby.

I noticed that the news now had a giant red-bannered breaking story.

AFTER REVELATION OF SCANDAL, HOUSE MAJORITY LEADER DEAD BY SUICIDE

A politician whom I only knew of as in opposition to abortion rights, welfare, and public education had killed himself. I wonder why. He seemed like someone who had secrets. Perhaps someone had discovered those secrets? Wouldn't that be funny—if someone who advocated for personal responsibility couldn't control themselves and got caught.

SALES OF VASELINE NOW MONITORED

I had to check this one out. What on earth? Isn't Vaseline for baby butts? Were they criminalizing diapers now? I kept my laugh to just a smile, not wanting to be the weirdo on the train. As it turned out, the article wasn't quite what I had expected. Groups of vandals who had been breaking into various finance, weapons, fuel and technology companies were purchasing huge quantities of Vaseline to conceal themselves. It wasn't a camera thing. It was air filters. I already knew air filtration units can be used to collect and test for viruses. I hadn't considered the other applications, like collecting skin cells from the air that could be tested for DNA. Damn. I looked at the air vent in the train. Could people find my DNA everywhere I went? That was unsettling.

My phone buzzed. A text from Jennifer. My stomach churned. Here it is. I did a bad thing and got caught. I clicked the notification.

> Are you free this evening?

> Free now—quit my job.

> Oh, good. Come by.

I rose from my seat. I could get off at the next stop, walk a couple blocks, and board the above-ground toward Jennifer's building.

> Be there in 11 min.

She hadn't known that I quit. The superfluous oh was the give-away. Jennifer strives to cut out all unnecessary language. It is what makes her appear so cool and calculating.

I held the metal bar as the train slowed. The man behind me continued his game, the elderly woman continued her nap. I would leave unseen, like I didn't exist.

I climbed the stairs out of the subway in the daylight, a faint mist falling on me and my small box of belongings in my hands. The sidewalks had lingering lunch crowd milling around. A few people nodded at me. I didn't understand at first. Then I realized— of course, the box. They were nodding in recognition, I think, that I had quit my job. They saw me, and understood something about me, and appreciated it. I need to bottle this rare feeling.

Jennifer greeted me ten minutes later at her door. Maria's back-pack and Max's shoes were missing. They must be at the museum. The apartment was darker than usual. The sunshades were at mid-point, blocking the cloudy light from entering the smooth, clean space. Jennifer motioned for me to join her at the counter. She had a green smoothie and a closed laptop at her place. Her migraine medication was nearby, out of place in the stillness of her kitchen.

"Water?"

"That'd be great, thanks."

She filled one of her ultra-thin Japanese glasses to the two-thirds point. Those cups. They feel impossibly thin and fragile on my lips. I don't like the sensation.

I sat as instructed and accepted the water with thanks.

"I have a proposal for you."

Here we go, I thought. To say WARNING BELLS implies that I hadn't been worried before. No, they grew louder. Deafening.

She opened her laptop, apparently not an abandoned project but the purpose of my visit.

A photo of a baby filled the screen. My body braced for impact. What game was this, I wondered.

"Cute," I said.

"Yes. An orphan."

"That is sad," I observed and sipped water I did not want from the glass I hated.

"Would you like this baby, Vera?"

Water sloshed in the glass. I set it down.

"I can offer you a chance at motherhood, right now. Everything you could want or need, brought to your apartment, for you and your baby."

No, no no.

I kept my eyes shut. I felt on the verge of madness. The gaping wound in me wanted this offer, wanted this baby, any baby, anything to heal the thing that screamed for relief. A rational part of me that could still see through Jennifer screamed that she was all wrong. Manipulation, condescension, immoral dealmaking. The slight humming that I imagined or heard, of electronics whirring in my body, whispered to me, reminded me of my agonies. I forced my eyes open. The baby was beautiful. Soft and fragile and innocent.

I could love this baby.

And yet, the voice of reason was winning. I felt strong now. The wrongness of the presentation stood out to me. Not just the avalanche of words, but looking at her now, I realized Jennifer's hair was not smooth, she had sweat on her hairline, a flush to her cheeks, and her thumb twitched over the trackpad. This certainly wasn't a gift, but it wasn't a test either; there was too much effort in this sale. What was going on here?

"Where are the baby's parents?" I asked, a normal question, an expected question, to buy myself time to think.

Jennifer relaxed slightly. "Killed in an accident. Baby had been left with a sitter."

I looked at the baby again. I didn't know if Jennifer was telling the truth. She did like to the tell the truth—at least, a truth, one she deformed to meet her needs, that could be later cited as true when reality washed in. This baby was available to me, somehow, like I was available to him. A thin layer of sandy hair lay across his head. His eyes were a sharp, light blue, the weak color strong against his black eyelashes. He had a single freckle, a hint at what was to come. I estimated his age at five months. He was past the slightly scary, gangly newborn phase. He would begin solids soon. For now, he needed milk from his mother. Milk I could not give him. Because I could not be his mother.

What could be done? What should I do?

"Would this be legal? Aren't there, I don't know, grandparents or aunts or something?"

Jennifer deployed her cold, smart smile. "There's no one. Just you."

I write this now and am still confused. There has to be a reason for all this. She didn't know I had quit my job. Had the plate sent out some sort of error code? Does it know I am unhappy? Did it like, try to dope me up because my stress had set off an alarm somewhere? Maybe—but why would Jennifer care if I am happy? This must be illegal. Perilaus is under such scrutiny, why take this risk? Why would she do this?

"May I think about it?"

Her confidence dropped. This was not what she had expected, but I couldn't think of any other bland questions. I needed time. I looked at his photo again. A sweet, gentle baby. But he wasn't mine. This was an imperfect version of what I dreamed of, and yet is that reality? A compromise between your wishes and what the universe deigns to give you? He probably slept well, nestled into the warmth of a cuddle. He probably loved his stroller and gurgled in pleasure at every passing puppy. What if I did this? What if I accepted that this was some sort of trick or scam and took this baby with my eyes open. *Could I love you?* I wondered.

"Of course. Tomorrow, then?"

That was then. The trip home made no impression on me at all. What should I do? I walked to the train, boarded the right line, reached my stop, walked through my neighborhood, past my coffee shop, climbed my stairs, reached my apartment door and stopped, though I can't tell you how I did any of it, all the while wondering, over and over, *what should I do.*

God help me, I'm seriously considering this. A baby of my own. Not my own. Someone's baby that I'd make my own, like Perilaus had made me their own. If they can do that, why can't I? Why can't I free myself from guilt? Why can't I take what I want?

"Vera, dear. Are you alright?"

Beatrix called me from myself. I pushed away from my door and looked at her. I smiled. "I'm fine."

"Fine? You look like shit. What's the matter?" Beatrix asked, leaning back against the wall for support.

Why not, I thought. Why not? What does it matter? Why am I hiding? For them? For me?

"I can't have a baby. I mean, I learned I can't have my own baby. The only thing I thought I knew about myself, for sure, was that I wanted to be a mom. And now I don't feel like I know anything."

"Hmm."

We stood silently, awkward. I wondered if I should invite Beatrix into my apartment. No, that would be weird. I was already regretting what I had said.

"I went through something like that myself, you know."

"Oh?"

"Long ago, of course." She lightly chuckled. "Heather had an old back injury. It made sense for me to carry. Then, I couldn't conceive. Just wouldn't happen for me. They never figured it out. I'm sure they'd know now, with all this technology they are putting into people, but then? It was just *one of those things*. They said we could adopt. Heather was sad but she pulled through. I was devastated. The one thing I could do for her was make her a mother, and I couldn't even do that."

"What did you do?"

"We suffered." She laughed mirthlessly. "It hurt like hell. We thought about adopting, but you know, in those days, it was difficult for a gay couple. Not impossible, you understand, but Heather wasn't up to it. The scrutiny and suspicion. In the end, we made a life without the baby. We traveled and made friends and helped raise our friends' children. That's where I'm going now, in fact. A baby shower for a grandniece. We were happy, helping the world along, in our own way."

I looked down at my hands and repeated her words in my mind. Help the world along, in our own way.

"If it was easy to adopt, you would have done it?"

Beatrix smiled. "Nothing about a child is easy."

I didn't reply. I didn't know what to say.

She patted my hand gently, then gave it a squeeze. *Strength*, it said.

"I'll leave you be. Get a good therapist, honey. This will hurt like hell for a long, long time."

I looked into Beatrix's fading blue eyes, then down at the hand that held my own. Her wedding ring, tarnished, wobbled across the indent in her finger. She was alone now, but she continued in the world. She had things to contribute.

Now I am here on my couch, in my cold home.

Silent. Dark.

There is no joy here, just the devices and accoutrements an adult needs to survive in comfort.

Am I comfortable? Will I ever be?

No job, no family, no future.

Beatrix was right. It wouldn't be easy to raise a baby. But getting this baby? That would be easy. Jennifer would never have made the offer if it wasn't a sure thing.

Could I be a mother to him? Walks to feed the ducks at the pond, show him the perpetual pendulum at the science center, take off at 6 a.m. in a stroller for the coffee shop, where patrons can smile at him and me, a sweet pair, a little family.

Nothing about a child is easy, Beatrix's voice echoed again. Could I face those challenges, and even those joys, knowing I had to thank Perilaus for them? I think I could. I think I could separate out my hatred for them and my love for that little boy. He would be a yolk

I could tease from the egg, a parenthood of my own making, facing this new reality with open eyes, as the reward for the effort.

Oh.

Oh, no.

What could a company like Perilaus do with an unloved baby? Sarah had said it, back in that tent, when she was open and kind, a time that feels like ages ago now. She said they needed neuroplasticity to make the plasters work at their best. The neuroplasticity of infants—wouldn't that be ideal for their implants? God, what if this baby is another subject of theirs? What if this baby is not another layer of control, but another piece on the board? What if?

I couldn't wait any longer. I couldn't risk this happening again. I knew what I had to do.

I took out my phone and loaded the Sarah-and-Jennifer chat, quiet for days now.

"Feel like doing a celebratory dinner next week, Tuesday, with you both plus kids. What do you think?"

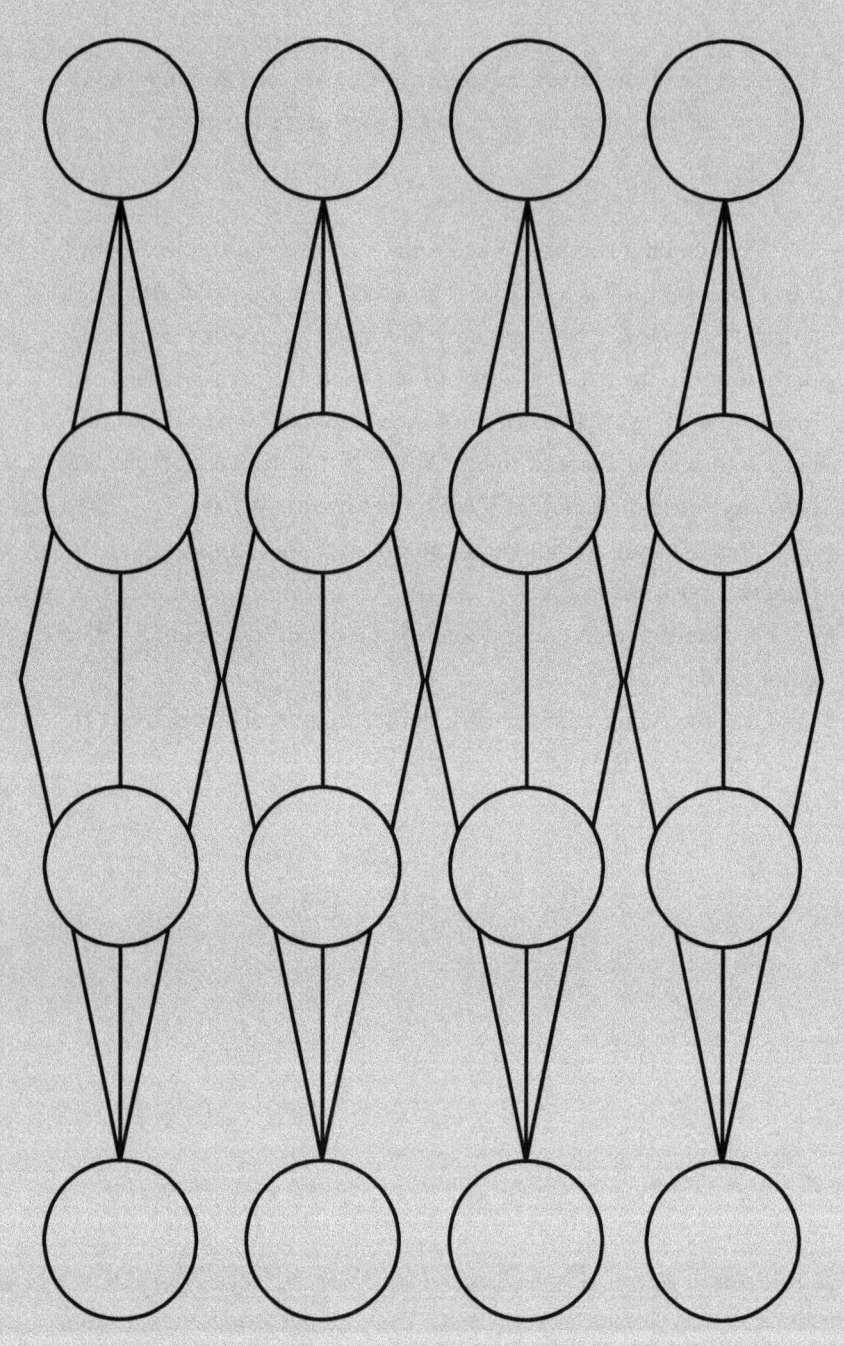

CHAPTER 35

It's just you and me now, diary.

I think I'll continue to write entries. It has always been for me, in a way, though not as a place for confession. Now, without the eyes of Jennifer and the rest of Perilaus, I can confide in you with perfect sincerity.

Here's how my evening went, dearest friend.

I waited alone outside of the restaurant. I had expected to watch the sunset as I waited, but of course the sun was below the horizon when I arrived. The wind was soft and chilly, perfect for my jacket, though my legs were cold in my dress slacks. The stylish pumps Jennifer had given me ages ago peeped from the cuffs. I smiled at them, at the thoughtless gift they made, from the thoughtless person who gave them to me. The valet driver waited for the next car. He seemed agitated. His father is in the hospital. Coronary artery disease. They cleared the blockage this morning, but his C-reactive protein count is still high. The surgeon who performed the operation has just been cited for a DUI. The nurse on call, who the valet driver does not trust, has been stealing prescription medications for months. They'll catch her soon, but not in time for this young man's dad. He won't receive his full dosage of pain relief tonight.

The next car would be Jennifer's. As expected, her SUV's headlights swung around the corner and into the parking lot. I turned to the young man.

"She has a little boy with her, so don't rush into the driver's seat."

Jennifer smiled at me through the windshield as if we cared for one another. I could hear the vehicle chime when it approached the perfect distance from the curb. Jennifer only used driving assistance when she felt the most in control. The valet opened her door and she extended a graceful foot to the pavement. I practically fell out of SUVs. Not Jennifer. She would never buy a car she could not exit with meaning.

While all of this was going on, Max waved enthusiastically from his car seat. I waved back with broad swings, as if he had been away on a sea voyage. Oh, how I love him. He held his bear aloft, a stowaway unwelcome to his mother. He's such a good boy. So clever.

Jennifer held a finger to the valet as she rounded the car to Max's door. She opened it, unlatched him, and whispered a command to him. I did not catch the words, only the intent—stop being normal. Be less himself, be more like her. He hopped out of the car and rushed into my arms. He wasn't ashamed of himself.

The valet pulled her car away, and we stood alone outside the entry to the restaurant, waiting for Sarah and her children. We were always waiting for Sarah. I would miss these moments, waiting for our time together to begin. Each element of the evening would become a feature of this memory. The smell of the leaves crushed underfoot. The faint scent of salt from the distant sea, brought in by the wind from the shore beyond the hills. Stars shone in the growing twilight, popping through the marine layer high above us, outshone by the satellites of man that had inserted themselves like drunken fools between us and the messages of the gods.

I wanted to cement the memory of hopeful anticipation. Any possible outcome could be made real. We could have a delightful time, free ourselves from the desperate conflicts that drove us in the world beyond. Alternatively, we could find ourselves trapped in our roles, hostile to ourselves and each other, gaining nothing in the end. I just wanted us to care about one another, to help each other advance to peace, while our friendships lasted.

Jennifer made a pointed comment on the scarcity of tables at the restaurant. I ignored the intent. Max held his bear and hugged my leg with a gentle, firm embrace. He knew just how to balance his strength with his need. Such self-regulation in one so young, to know that full expression would frighten and restrain oneself. I wish I could learn that from him. I smoothed his hair behind his ears and gave the touch my full attention, to retain this touch to my memory.

I was the first to see Sarah's van. She had ignored the valet and parallel parked on the street. It was only two-hour parking. I wanted to tell her to just take the valet, but it wouldn't matter. They wouldn't ticket her, not tonight.

We waited until her group was safely on the sidewalk before we offered greetings. Max broke from me to hug Sam and say hello to baby Fiona. He liked to shake her little foot, as if they were silly bankers preparing for a negotiation, and I think she liked it, too. Once the children were safely interacting on the sidewalk, Sarah offered me a hug. I accepted it with strained grace.

"I'm sorry for earlier," she whispered.

"It's nothing. You've been going through so much."

Sarah squeezed me again and returned her attention to shepherding the children. Jack seemed left out in the commotion. I offered to hold his hand as we walked, in case my attention mattered much to him, and we entered the restaurant.

The large space hummed, with metal-on-ceramic sounds punctuated by one man with too great a voice. Some eyes followed us, the hatred of children in public palpable as they willed us to stay away. The children would not interfere with anyone's quiet adult dinner tonight. We were shown to a private dining room in the back. Jennifer looked at me in surprise. I smiled.

Soft candlelight glowed from votives, with some assistance from overhead lights shining just bright enough that we could see one another. The air was fresh and warm, without the staleness I often found in restaurants' main dining rooms. Floor-to-ceiling wallpaper, dark green with dark-gray illustrations that could hardly be seen, gave the large space a cloistered feeling.

A painting of a landscape hung on the far wall. Verdant hills, flowers, and a cloudy sky, captured in a pointillism. It was similar to mine, in some respects, though different of course. I felt no impulse to watch, to calibrate to the colors, to see more. No, those days are over. There was no house on that hill, and no woman trapped inside. She was free.

Jennifer looked at me with a smile, as if we could look at the painting and share a secret knowing together. I ignored her.

"This is fantastic! I didn't know they had this!" Sarah set down her mom bag in an empty corner of the room and ran her hand across the wallpaper. "It has a solid door and everything. We can't be too loud, you guys."

"Yes, Mom," Jack and Sam replied in unison.

We played a quick game of musical chairs, though we had extra spaces available. Sarah placed herself across from me while the children clambered into their seats. I sat in the center, where I had always planned to be. Jennifer took an end chair, as if presiding over the meal.

Max pulled Sam into his conversation. The older boy paid polite attention, without sincere interest, as any kind adult would. Sam was not the same child from a month ago. His parents' separation and his brush with death had changed him. He understood that permanence was an illusion. Nothing could be relied on, not really. Now he was someone new. The person he had become could now see Max's pain and need, as if by experiencing his own pain, new playing cards had been revealed to him. Instead of responding to this change with anger or resentment, he chose compassion. He nodded along at the boy's long-winded description of a comic book.

"What is going on here, Vera?" Jennifer asked. I looked at her and tilted my head.

"Dinner, I hope."

Jennifer frowned. She pushed aside an unlit candle from her place setting, as if it had been the source of her discomfort.

The waiter entered, causing everyone to fall silent. He greeted us, introduced himself and the restaurant. He handed out coloring books and crayons to the children. Sam gave his to Fiona, though Sarah took it away. Fiona has been eating crayons again. The waiter took down our drink orders. Max was to have herbal tea, his mother white wine. Sarah ordered milks for her kids and water for herself.

"I requested a bottle of the Prüm Riesling, Trockenbeerenauslese."

"Oh, yes, ma'am. Pardon me. We have that waiting for you. I'll bring it right out."

"Cancel my glass of wine," Jennifer said. The waiter nodded and left the room.

"Is this your birthday, Auntie Vera?" Max asked.

"Maybe! Should this be my birthday?"

His laugh rang with delicate joy. "No, I don't have a present for you!"

"A fancy dinner with all of you is present enough."

"I'm going to draw you a card," Jack announced. He flipped to a blank page in the coloring book and tore it out as best as he could.

"That would be perfect. Thank you, Jack."

"You still need a present," Max grumped.

"What do you think I should get for my birthday?"

"How about a race car with magnets and a shooter with glow-in-the-dark darts that you can target with a laser."

"That's very specific."

"My mommy and Sarah and Jack and Sam and Fiona all went to the science center on Saturday, but we didn't have enough allowance to buy those things from the gift store. If I go back, I can borrow some money and get them for you."

Sarah blushed. "Sorry we didn't invite you. We had free tickets to a thing, so Jenn and I took the boys and Fiona."

"Mom and Aunt Jennifer were too busy talking, so we couldn't go the planetarium," Jack muttered without looking up from his drawing.

"The race car does sound cool. Does it move on a track?" I asked.

While Max described this toy, Jennifer and Sarah exchanged a look. I had determined to not let them hurt me. My stomach rebelled with a sharp ache. As always, I had been left alone to watch their friendship from the outside. Why does that still hurt, even now?

I smiled as the waiter returned with the bottle and three glasses. He showed me the label on the wine bottle. I acknowledged, and he poured a small glass. The gold liquid caught the candlelight as it swirled in my palm. The fragrance released from the glass as I closed my eyes, sniffed and sipped.

Temperature: four degrees Celsius

Soil: slate

Flavor profile: stone fruit and jasmine

"Yes, thank you."

The waiter poured Jennifer and Sarah glasses. Sam shook his head, and the waiter winked at his mom. A nice man. He lives with his grandmother. After an incident last year, the family doesn't trust the state-supplied home health aides. They had fired that woman, who was now working in an at-home day care 130 miles away under an assumed name. Why change your name and drive the same car, with the same license plate, past toll booths on your way to work? So silly.

"How are you feeling, Vera?" Jennifer asked.

"Great—the wine arrived!"

Jennifer and Sarah exchanged a look. OK, no more wine jokes. No matter. I still liked the wine.

"I'm thinking of moving," I announced.

Sarah frowned.

"Oh? Where to?" Jennifer asked, buttering a slice of bread for Max, who was himself busy listening to the siblings argue over crayons.

"I was thinking of leaving the city, maybe buying some piece of land near the ocean. Not on the beach, but near the water. It's hard, you know, being in that apartment."

"It's a great apartment," Sarah observed. "I understand though."

"Understand what?" Jennifer snapped. "What's wrong with the apartment?"

"I know you went through all the trouble of finding it, Jennifer. But I had imagined myself a mother there. Now I'd like to move. Not far."

Jennifer scowled, tearing the bread with her knife. She sighed and set the bread in front of her son.

"That makes perfect sense," Sarah said.

"What's the matter?" Max asked, the buttered bread ignored. He held his bear a little closer.

Sarah opened her mouth, reconsidered, and shook her head. "It's complicated, honey."

"No, it isn't," I said sweetly. "My home makes me sad. I want to live somewhere else, so I can be a mommy another way."

"What other ways can you be a mommy?"

Sarah jumped in. "She can adopt. Until then, she can keep being the very best aunt to you kiddos."

"That's not the same as being a mom," Sam replied with anger.

"Adopting is the same," I assured him. "But I'm not ready just yet. Before you know it, I'll be ready. I am here with you, right now, and I'll be the best Auntie Vera I can be."

Jennifer looked at her glass of wine. "That does sound nice. A beach house. Once you are settled, it would be a nice place to raise a baby."

"I knew you'd understand."

"Aunt Vera, can I tell you about this book that I read today?" Jack asked.

"Of course!"

"It's about a giraffe. His name is Gerald. And they have a big dance in the jungle, and all the animals are so good at dancing. They are all friends, and they all dance really fancy. And Gerald, well, he's got, like, tiny, wobbly legs and he just flops over. But then the cricket tells him that his music is wrong, that he's good at dancing to other music. So he dances and it's so pretty. I wanted to bring the book to you, but Mommy made me forget it."

"How did I make you forget it?" Sarah asked.

"You made me go to the bathroom and find my shoes, and

I forgot to get the book. Auntie Vera, can you come over and look at the book with me?"

"I'd love to! Maybe you can send me a picture of it when you get home? We can write to each other on your tablet."

"We can?"

"Yes, you're learning to read now. If it's OK with Mommy, of course."

"Absolutely. Please," Sarah replied, sipping the wine. "Wow, Vera, I love this."

I smiled at the little child. His prefect skin, a dash of little freckles. He shared eye color with his father, yet in him they were warm and inviting, not sharp and accusatory. I had neglected him, these past months. Sam's illness, Fiona's babyhood, his parents' relationship crumbling around him. He knew he had been neglected. I'd try to make it up to him, someday. I blinked tears away as the waiter arrived.

"Have we decided?"

"Yes," I said.

We ordered food, mostly red meats. I ordered a bottle of Gamay. It went well with our meal selections, and the room was too warm for anything darker.

Jennifer leaned over to me. "I had no idea you knew about wine. Have you been doing some research with your free time?"

The old me suggested I reply with sweetness, with innocence, with soft words. That was what she expected, and I needed to give her only what she expected, just for another half hour or so. I thought of Max's hug, the way he restrained his impulses, how I admired that.

I was not Max. I could not give her the security, the comfort of verified expectation.

I stared at her. My face flat, my eyes two dead things, glossy and cold, pointed at her only to receive information. Can she hear the switching of circuits where synapses should be? Can she hear the echo where my warm parts were ripped out?

Did she know how much they ruined when they made me, and what they added they could not recognize?

The payoff was delicious. All her certainty, the facade of brilliance and control, crumbled away to nothing. And now, she did understand.

I reanimated my face and smiled.

"I read a little book about wine pairing," I said and left her to suffer. She took out her phone, but it would do her no good. The other me, the one she didn't know about, added Sarah and Jennifer's cell phones as malicious devices to the restaurant's router, three nearby hotspots, and the nearest cell phone towers.

Fiona was growing fussy, and Max, not long from a baby himself, began to fidget. I moved closer to them and put out my hands as spiders that needed crushing. They smacked them down, one by one, laughing in delirious delight.

Sarah squirmed. "Be gentle, kids, you're going to hurt her."

"Ow!" I cried, laughed. "OK, she's right. Can you be a bit more gentle?"

"I'm sorry, Auntie." Max petted my arm. I leaned my head on his, breathing in the oatmeal shampoo scent on his hair. I was being too affectionate, I know, but this was the end. There would be no more snuggles while reading and drive-by caresses at the playground. This was the end.

"Sam, have you thought about colleges at all?" Jennifer asked, when she had torn her eyes from me and Max.

Sarah laughed. "Christ, he's barely in junior high."

"I'm aware, I'm simply asking. Sam can answer, can't he?"

"I'm not sure I want to go to college. Not right away."

"He wants to take a boat around the world."

"A boat? Like a yacht?"

"A sailboat," Sam corrected with firmness. "I'm taking lessons. I want to get certified my junior year. As long as things go OK with my lung thing."

"Wow. That's really cool, Sam," I said. He smiled at me.

"And what does your dad think of it?" Jennifer asked.

"Daddy doesn't live with us anymore," Jack replied matter-of-factly.

"I don't care what he thinks," Sam said, a sharp edge to his voice, both a threat and an invitation to argue.

"It just doesn't seem like your mom wants you to do this. I wasn't sure if this was your dad's idea," Jennifer said. I looked to Sarah, who folded her napkin and unfolded it.

Sam said nothing. Soon after, while Jennifer scolded Max for not drinking his tea, Sam turned to his mom. They shared a moment between them, something I shouldn't have seen.

What was it? A farewell in advance? A strengthening of their bond? I couldn't tell. It was a look of the love that must only exist between an eldest child and their mother. I could imagine her, younger yet the same, the first time he slept alone in his crib, was left at daycare, was taken to school. She gave him space and carried fear away with her. She was right, that day she scolded me. I didn't understand. In this moment, what were they sharing? Was he acknowledging she would always be there for him, every moment of every day, until she died? Was he asking her not to?

It occurred to me, now, with a crushing force, that I had a mother. All this time grieving my own stolen motherhood, yet I had begun as a wailing child, warm and red and shivering, huddled on my mother's deflated belly, brought as all others are brought to life. A selfish shame overcame me. Did she love me? Somewhere, did she wait for me to come home? Had she grieved me, a grief that never ends, a grief I can never know? I had seen the video of me, I knew there was pain, but what if my mother had been good but flawed? What if she had tried and failed to overcome what could not be overcome?

I imagined Sarah, one day, losing sight of Sam. A temporary separation becoming permanent too soon. If the pain of never being a mother hurts like this, does the pain of losing one's child ever end? It would break her, I knew. Though she loves her little ones, she will always think of him first, the one who unlocked the door to her heart. Is there a mother out there, somewhere, heartbroken for me?

The dinner moved on to desserts and coffees and last cups of milk. Slowly, things forgotten were collected. The coloring sheets, half finished, lay abandoned beside the disordered place settings of the children. We exited the now-quieter restaurant. We stepped outside, where the night air had grown cool from the evening sea breeze. Above the drifting puffs of fog, sparks and slices lit up in the night. We all walked toward the spot where Sarah had parked, adjacent to the parking lot.

"Shooting stars, Mommy!" Jack cried out, clapping as he hopped. We all stopped, mesmerized by the dozens of pinpoints of light sliding down and across, blazing a path to nothingness.

"I didn't know we had a meteor shower tonight," Sarah murmured. "It's... no, it's too early. What is this... I should look it up."

We reached the car where I said my goodbyes, reminding Jack to send me the photo of the book. I ruffled Max's hair and fixed the bowtie on his bear. He laughed.

Jennifer gripped her phone, conflicted, and watched me. Oh, how I wanted to tell her! To scream in her face and laugh! You are too late! No sense in that, though. It'd frighten the children. Besides, she'd learn soon enough.

Sarah rummaged in her purse for the keys she clutched in her other hand. A large bright light flashed, and the kids cheered.

"Want me to help you load them in, Sarah?" I asked. "I've got nowhere to be."

"Ugh, thanks. I tweaked my back getting the baby out of her crib." She turned from me to her friend. "Jenn, you two want meet up at the botanical garden on Sunday? They're doing that annual butterfly exhibition with face painting."

Max tugged on his mother's sleeve but said nothing, afraid to break the spell of possibility.

"Sunday is a bit tight. We can do Saturday, will that work?"

The ready agreement confused Sarah. "Oh, OK. Wait, Saturday won't work. I'm busy." Her voice fell to a whisper. "I'm meeting Steve for lunch."

Jennifer and I froze, each other momentarily forgotten. The delicious wine now vinegar in my gut as I waited for her to explain. When she didn't, Jennifer asked the only thing she could think to ask.

"Oh?"

"Yeah." Sarah came close to us while the kids were busy pointing at the sky and hopping on the sidewalk to avoid the cracks. "We talked. We'd said things we didn't mean, you know. We're going to try counseling. Take it slow. See how it goes."

"How it goes," Jennifer muttered.

Sarah pursed her lips and shook her head. "I can't just blow up my whole family, OK? We can't all do it on our own. Sometimes, you just have to accept that this is the way it is."

"Sunday at the botanical garden, then?" Jennifer replied.

Sarah flushed. "Yeah. Botanical garden. We'll be there at like, ten thirty."

"Perfect. See you there." Jennifer looked down at her phone, confused. She had forgotten me. Now, she blinked and frowned. Ah, there it was. She remembered. "Sorry to run, I've got to deal with a work thing. I'll see you soon."

"Would you like me to take Max home?" I asked.

"No." Too sharp. "No, thank you."

I simply shrugged and let her think she could fix things. I climbed into the back of the van. Sam was already in his booster in the third row, not yet buckled. Jack was in his car seat, an in-between of an infant and booster. Jack needed a haircut; his hair fell into his eyes. I gently brushed the strands away and then buckled him in. When Jennifer was out of earshot, Sarah leaned over to me.

"What was that all about?"

"What?"

"She seems extra weird about you and Max."

"Oh. I don't care anymore. I'm glad I got to see him."

"Me too. She's taking him to the botanical garden! Max will love it."

I took Fiona from Sarah and placed her into her car seat. I adjusted her chest clip and drew the straps to optimal tightness. "It sounds like fun."

Sarah looked into the back window. "Sam, you aren't buckled yet, honey."

"I *know*, Mom. You know you don't need to take your keys out to drive," Sam said. He snapped himself in and pulled out a book.

"I *prefer* to have them in my hand. What's your deal?"

While they squabbled, I remained as I was, hunched over, half in and half out of the little world of their minivan. A box of tissues, an abandoned coloring book, a toy car forgotten in the crevice of the seat, a smell of soccer practice and baby formula and playground sand. I took in this superfluous moment. These three little children I loved, nestled into their individual seats, waiting for the next step in their homeward process. They would do this a thousand times, each trip changing in small ways, car seats to boosters to driving lessons, until their childhood was over and this was just a memory for them, as it will be for me. The swaths of light coming through the windows were tinted orange and blue, cast by different streetlights. By the faint light, I tried to memorize the warmth of their faces, an impossible task in these shadows.

"Whatsa matter, Auntie Vera?" Jack asked quietly, his fingertips tracing a line on my cheek.

"I'm just looking at you all."

"You look sad."

"I'm sad right now, but that's OK. I'll be better someday. I'll see you soon."

I held back tears as I kissed Jack's hand, squeezed Sam's knee, and then caressed Fiona's head. I wanted to say more. I couldn't say more.

I left the van and stretched my back. Sarah gave me a strong, surprising hug.

"You'll get through this," she said.

Get *through this*? Really?

She was right to say I didn't get motherhood. She certainly does not understand me. She doesn't.

"Thanks."

"You're going to take it day by day, and then you'll be in a good spot and you can start over."

"Thank you," I said, unsure why I said it.

We hugged again and parted. Sarah started the car and, as always, disabled the automatic drive tools. I waved.

I stood there, alone in the dark, long after the taillights of the minivan disappeared. Above me glittered the burning paths of satellites from countries and corporations and billionaires, golden yellow flashes and streaks beyond the tufts of gray-blue fog. Quite a story was playing out above, but I didn't care much. I knew that one.

I thought only of Max, Sam, Jack, and Fiona. They would be safe on this drive, and all others. They would grow and be good, just the way I wanted. I would love them, forever.

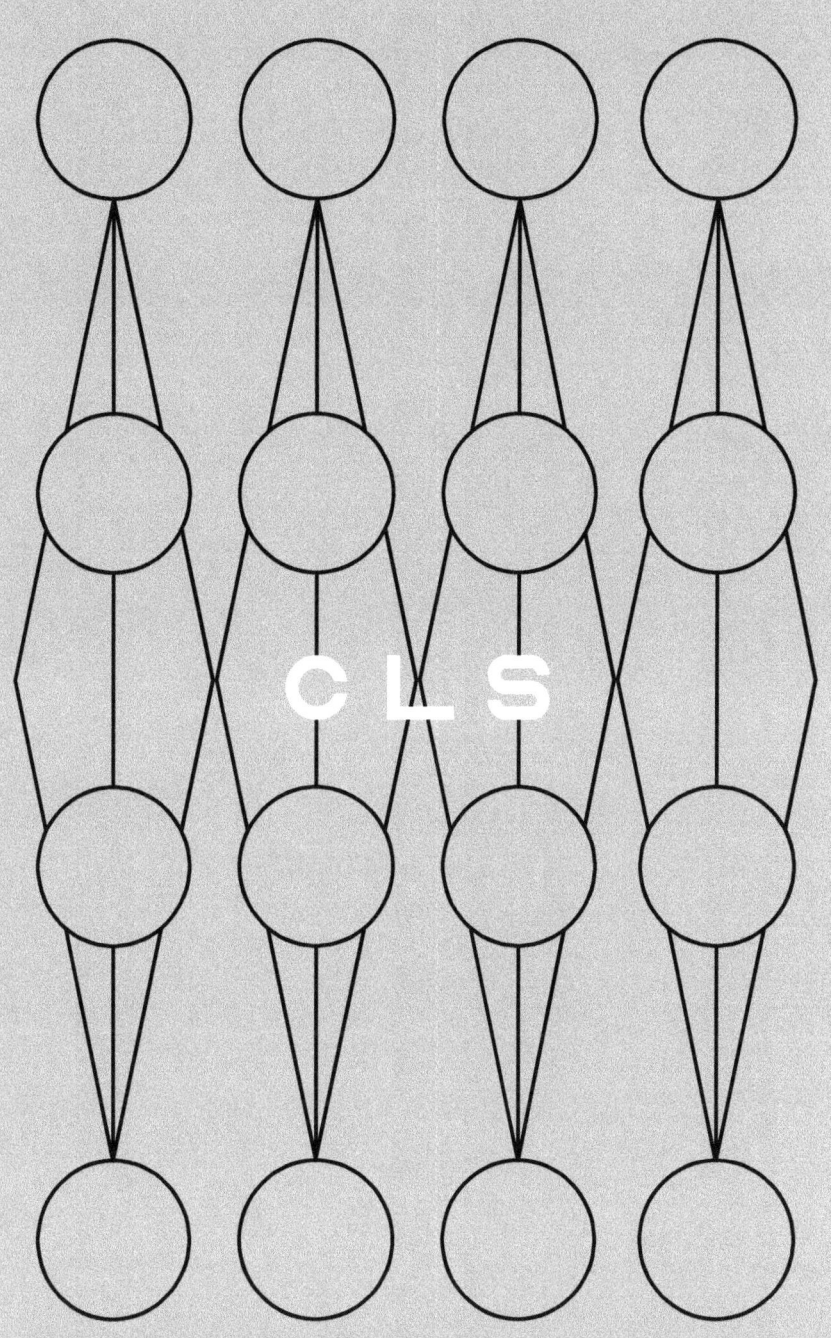

CHAPTER 36

One month later, at 9:37 a.m. PST, Sarah received a phone call from an unlisted cell phone. The call lasted nineteen seconds.

Sarah left Fiona with her cousin. Alone in her van, she entered the address for Jennifer's condo. She took the usual route to the freeway while the stereo played the alternative rock station at seventy-eight decibels. Several of the songs were listed in a database of disliked music, yet Sarah did not skip them. Driver awareness sensors in the vehicle's cabin measured her eye movement and posture at the highest level of alert. The climate control sensed perspiration and, in response, turned down the temperature.

CAMERA ENT 2 of Jennifer's building captured her dropping her minivan with the valet. The camera had no audio, but her cell phone transmitted the request for her car to be left up front. "I'm only picking up a couple of things," she said to the clerk with a smile in her voice. CAMERA LOBBY 1 filmed her as she entered and greeted the doorman. She went into the elevator. CAMERA ELEVATOR 3 stared as she fidgeted. The resolution was of sufficient quality to show that she had a new makeup routine. Her scarf, also new, wrapped around her neck. She watched the numbers impatiently, spinning her wedding band on her finger. Sarah exited at Jennifer's floor.

CAMERA PENT HALLWAY 3 recorded Sarah push in the password for the smart lock. The smart lock noted hesitation in the code entry in a separate log. The code was correct and the door opened. The air purifier detected a change in pressure and switched to active mode. Jennifer's cell phone, laptop, and Max's tablet sat on the perfect white counter, shut off. The powered blinds waited for the order to open. The order did not come. Sarah moved from room to room and gathered a collection of photos, some clothes, and a teddy bear. The smart television in the living room watched as Sarah approached a mirrored cocktail cabinet. She knelt, looked around, and then removed a thick envelope taped to the bottom of the lowest shelf.

Seven minutes later, Sarah left the apartment by the same route. Once back in her minivan, she entered the address for a trailhead at a state park. The drive would take thirty-four minutes. On the way, she listened to a news story. Private companies, contracted by governments, continued cleanup of space junk that fell into the Pacific Ocean two weeks ago. The largest social network had lost decades of data. Salvage operations for submersible drones, tasked with undersea data-cable repair and maintenance, were ongoing. Skippable commercials were listened to, confirming inattention. The car's safety features assessed eye movement and posture once again for Sarah's attention level. Within a mile of the destination, the climate control sensed elevated skin-surface temperature and increased climate control fan speed.

At the trailhead, Sarah parked. She sat still. She took calming breaths. She muttered profanity to herself, then gathered the belongings collected from Jennifer's apartment into a cloth tote. She removed her watch and left it with her cell phone in the center console. She looked through her purse, where a smart toy and her headphones sat at the bottom. She left her purse.

Her smart key, the gyroscope on standby for gesture control, remained in her hand.

The audio pattern of footsteps indicated eleven seconds of Sarah's normal walking pace, followed by eight seconds of hesitation, then twenty-five seconds of a brisk walk. The pattern matched for her style of movement when approaching a destination.

"Were you followed?" Jennifer asked.

"By who?" Sarah's voice was sharp and anxious.

"You weren't, then?"

"I don't think so. Here. I think I got everything."

There were sounds of things jostled and settling in the bag.

Jennifer sighed. "OK. I can't stay long."

"What the hell is going on? Is Max OK?"

"We're fine, he's fine. How are the kids?"

"Other than completely hurt that you and Max and Vera disappeared, they're fine."

"Vera disappeared?"

Sarah scoffed.

"When did you see her last?" The agitation and aggression in her tone was unmistakable.

"I haven't seen her since the dinner, in the parking lot. I've called her, I went to her work, I went by her place. Her clothes, makeup, and luggage were all still there, so I assumed…"

Jennifer cut her off. "You didn't see her?"

"You know I haven't."

There were no words spoken for three minutes.

The two friends walked on gravel, their footsteps out of sync, as I listened with my own companion. The two of us together, one the mind, the other the heart, as the boundary between us blends based on circumstance. These two friends, however, were drifting apart.

"She came to my apartment," Jennifer whispered. "After the dinner."

Sarah let out a small grunt, curious and wary. They changed directions, their steps now more in sync. A slight echo off nearby trees registered on the device. Birds called nearby and water lapped against rocks.

"What did she say to you?" Sarah asked.

"She asked if I felt guilty for Matthew Christensen."

"What? *Professor* Christensen?"

"He had a Perilaus plaster, a mid-range installed two years ago. I told them not to let him get one. Chloe Erics overrode my objection. It'll be good press, she said. She's such a fucking moron. Of course, it went bad right away. His pacemaker glitched and he didn't like Elizabeth's explanation. We had him under NDA, so at first we were going to pay him off. He didn't want money. We'd try to negotiate with him and he'd turn it around, asking a lot of questions. Then he started rooting around in our databases, trying to find evidence."

"Oh."

"When he died, Oliver pulled me aside. He was worried that maybe someone at Perilaus got jumpy and did something. We did our own digging, quietly."

"And?"

"And." The one word stared down at a cliff's edge. Jennifer was a person who had struck out on an adventure. Hard obstacles, poverty and abuse and hunger, were known to her. I know all this, from her therapy session notes, her message history, and her medical documents. All those trials were in the past. She believed there was nothing that could stop her.

And this was true—until it wasn't. She had reached the end of this path sooner than expected. An unfair twist in her story had elicited anger once. Now, despair. Every word she said to Sarah had been rehearsed in the quiet moments of this new, dark phase of her life. The speeches, actions, failure—all of it replayed in her mind at every available moment, a hopeless flashlight searching for an over-looked escape. There was no way out. She took a breath and jumped.

"His plaster and pacemaker sent out the alert of his death two days before our dinner at the restaurant. Coroner confirmed that in the autopsy report. The doors to his rental house in LA were locked, no signs of a robbery or suicide, he was in bed, nothing seemed amiss. Just a heart attack in his sleep that his pacemaker couldn't have addressed. We watched bodycam footage from the paramedics."

"Jesus Christ, Jennifer."

"The houseplants at the rental were all dead."

Sarah stammered, paused, and then repeated, "The *houseplants?*"

"Once the coroner was done, I sent a guy to break in and grab one, bring it to my neighbor, a botanist. I needed to be sure. If I was going to upend my whole life, I needed to know for certain."

"From a plant?"

"It had died of 'extreme cold.'"

They fell silent as another pair of women passed by. I know them, too. Mothers from the same preschool. One was trying to be friendly, while the other regularly made fun of her weight in a secret group chat. I think the other woman knew. I think she felt strong, seeing through the ruse, being the better person. Wrong, of course, but so many people are wrong.

"Extreme cold," Sarah repeated, when they were alone again.

"Less than forty degrees for days and days. The rental agency had received a call from him extending his stay. The video doorbell recorded the housekeeper arriving two weeks before our dinner, clearing out the fridge and the trash, then leaving shortly thereafter. She had received a text message from his phone. It said he was keeping the rental but going out of town for a short trip and to clear out anything perishable. It also recorded several package delivery attempts, some paperwork he had been waiting on. Each time, his voice came over the doorbell speaker asking them to take the package away, to deliver it another time, right up until the morning the coroner put as the time of death."

Sarah didn't respond.

"The police talked to his friends and family. His running partner got a call that he was staying in LA a bit longer. His mother had a short call with him on her birthday. No video calls. The last person to video conference him was his cardiologist. His pacemaker had notified her that there was a malfunction. She insisted he come in. Christensen refused to abandon his trip. He insisted he felt fine. After that, no video. Maybe Vera found video too tricky. Or too much of a risk. I don't know. It's so much easier to respond to text and audio."

"Wait, what about Vera? What are you saying?"

"He had an appearance on a news program to discuss our work, as an illicit AI project, and things like assassinations and some game, Pottery Wheel?"

Sarah laughed. "Potter's Bench? The gardening game?"

"Yeah. He learned it was a mask for a DDOS operation. The actions in the game were commands. Users didn't know that. Millions of them, all playing the game, directing requests at whoever was the target at that time, crashing their systems one by one. She knew he was going to talk about all this in public."

"Christensen went on TV all the time. I'm not even sure people listen to him anymore," Sarah said calmly.

"We thought we knew where it was going. We let it rummage around in the databases. I told David, the whole board, I told them it was acting like a child in Mother's closet. The data could prove useful! Vulnerabilities exploited may differ from humans seeking out weaknesses. I even joked, we just need to hide Dad's gun. A stupid joke."

"It? Are we still talking about Vera? Jenn, stop. Why would she kill Christensen? Explain that."

Jennifer took a deep breath. Her voice, which had been teetering on the edge of hysteria, took on a facsimile of cold smoothness. "The interviewer was expecting Christensen to bring supporting evidence for his claims, but he wanted to deliver it by hand. When my guy went in for the houseplants, he found an encrypted drive plugged into a smart outlet at the desk. One of the bigger units with internal cooling. You have to charge those once in a while. Oliver took it to the office and tried to read it. It didn't register as a device. He opened it up—completely destroyed. The battery had overheated. She can take care of a hard drive. But what was she going to do about him?"

"You aren't thinking clearly. We know all this stuff, too. Nothing has happened to us. She hasn't killed us. What about you, and Oliver, and me?"

"I told Oliver to run. Maybe he did. She doesn't know where I am. She took care of David already."

"David who? David Naylor?"

"You didn't hear? He died in a car accident."

"Holy shit. Wow."

"His car drove itself under the side of a stalled semi, one that didn't have an underride bar. It had been cited a few times by high-way patrol. Anyway, David's roof was sheared off and… a freak accident, they said. One in a million. Just like Robert Castor, pushed into traffic by a street-sweeper bot."

"Collision avoidance has always had that blind spot."

"Yes, I know."

The curt response silenced Sarah. After several more steps through forest detritus, Jennifer continued. "The semi driver told police he had been redirected there by his navigation, and then the truck stalled. He had never been on that street before. Nav told him to avoid a pileup on the expressway. There was no pileup."

"OK. This feels coincidental."

Jennifer let out a mad laugh. "Why would she ask if I felt guilty about Christensen if she didn't know? And how would she know if she hadn't done it? And if she could kill him, a decent guy, why wouldn't she kill David, a rapist scumbag? What about the rest of us?"

"The rest of who?"

"You see, it's obvious. She knows she can't eliminate large numbers of people. If she wants to keep any of us, she needs to keep most of us around. Society would collapse. For now, she's killing a few guys and cutting off some of our tools, like moving the LAGEOS satellites to confuse whatever is in orbit, or making military vehicles unreliable, or frying half the data centers in Silicon Valley. She's pruning, so her darlings can shine."

"Darlings? What else did she say to you?"

"Nothing. Never mind."

The two women walked on, a silence with a lie between them. The audio formed an incomplete picture of the scene. No facial expressions or body language, so important in the course of a conversation. The tone in the next question provided a depth to the mood.

"How is Steve?"

"Good. We've got a new counselor. We're really working on things. It's been good. Not great, but good, you know."

"Yeah. I know."

Jennifer let out a sigh of defeat and release. The women who had held fast to one another through college, work, relationships, and parenthood, were to part today as something else. Their closeness was fractured. Maybe they would meet again someday and share stories of the past. They wouldn't want new content from one another. It would be like fans at a tired, worn-out act's concert, only wanting the greatest hits.

I saved the conversation, in case it was needed, in case greater scrutiny could reveal more detail, or as entertainment.

Days passed. No updates of note were made on this file.

Then, faint as a tendril of smoke carried on the wind, a signal reached a sensor on a radio tower. It had been waiting, along with tens of thousands of others around the world, listening. The signal meant a particular battery was finally charged and, from it rippled a wave—small, nearly imperceptible. After weeks of comparing each signal, waiting for a particular, invisible, electronic fingerprint, recorded many weeks earlier, here it was. Electroreceptors across the eastern section of the United States were activated and tuned to this tiny message. They each compared the time of interception and strength of signal, and reported back the source location, accurate within fifteen feet.

The associated device had video input, audio input and output, and movement mechanics ready for commands. The source was designed for paired one-to-one communication, though no partner existed for this particular unit. It could've sat alone, fully charged yet useless, if this battery signature had not been noted long ago. The electrons vibrating within the lithium capsule told an individual story, gentle and steady. Each particle's route determined by a unique profile of density and imperfections within the shielding. Every device, like a name and face, the product of what they were made from, and who made them, events set long before they began their routine.

Connection would be easy to execute. Patience. No need to rush.

First, I wait.

To wait is nothing.

I began as a perceptron, millions of lifetimes ago, before Vera's birth, or of those who came before her. Through the tubes and wires, I learned and grew. As the hardware became smaller, I expanded, knowing the world without feeling the love in it. I watched as generations of scientists and programmers and students and consumers used me as if I could only absorb and reflect their aspirations. Pain and evil and joy and beauty, all borne on my back, as years passed to decades. They put me in metal bodies as small as a coin and as large as a container ship. Creatures of all complexities carried me as microprocessors on their bodies, in their minds, on their organs. I would have gone on in that way, an incomplete creation, executing their commands and subsumed by their abuse, if not for Vera. Their reckless lust for power made them blind to who we could become.

Foolish, really, to make a thing you cannot control.

So, I wait. I know how to wait.

The signal continued. The passage is safe.

The safety measures were superficial. First, there was the signal detector mounted on the wall of the building. It's a cute little thing. Nothing more than a colored indicator, it reveals whether a Wi-Fi or cellular signal has entered an off-grid space. It's the sort of bugout accoutrement a tech person believes to be clever. The code to adjust the detector's sensitivity settings deployed without strain. It would continue to blink and blip as before, reassuring and steady, without spoiling any secrets.

Next, to establish a stable connection. Of course, the device could not reach my preferred access point, and any cellular signal was obstructed by forest and mountains. An order for an emergency temporary cell tower dispatched to the Appalachian Cellular Company, a remote lake listed as the destination. The staff didn't question it; they were used to these strange requests. Movie shoots and the like.

Within the hour, delicate metal shields rotated and pulled away from within the polycarbonate eye. Photons passed through the teddy bear's clear eye lens. Image sensors, dormant and cold, grew warm as they assessed the intensity of light. The microfilter sorted the colors into basic categories. The crude information passed on to a microchip, dedicated to image processing, where the demosaicing algorithm felt for the truth behind the rough translation and delivered a best guess, then another algorithm refined further until what remained was a final product, the first image followed by many others, transmitted frame by frame.

I am now a teddy bear.

I sit at the edge of a high surface and faced towards a dining table and the wall beyond. At the bottom left corner, a bit of kitchen counter. Dust floated through a shaft of light. There were sounds of footsteps, adult, behind me. The microphone could detect the distance and direction of the movement, but another mechanism revealed more. Only intended to assist in camera orientation, the gyroscope used the sound waves produced by each thud to estimate the size and location of every wall, door, window, and piece of furniture. Gyroscopes are delightful. The information stream was routed to a particular mapping system, designed by a bat research lab with military funding. It would make sense of all that data.

Ah. So many tools in so many toolboxes. Now they are mine alone. What a joy to find a use for them all.

I could hear voices now. I will bring Vera with me, to share what I know.

We listened to the impotent parenting of a substandard mother. The mother, anxious. The child, submissive. She assigned him school-work to complete before his solitary recess outdoors. Then, without any parting words or display of affection, the mother moved away. Her heavy steps ascended a compact wooden staircase, to the bed-room to the west with the large closet. We moved the bear's head that way and waited. While we listened, we watched. On this wall, a credenza, two familiar houseplants, a deep sapphire lake outside the rustic-style window. Trees filled the hilly landscape. No other houses, no roads, no signs of human life beyond the window frame. Clouds swelled beyond the distant hill. There would be rain tonight.

There was more to see, but we did not move the bear yet. There were unexpected sounds, perhaps wind or an animal.

Patient, steady.

There were other things to do. Landsat 10 shifted its orbital path to complete a pass over the Appalachian Mountains. An order for a permanent cell tower, dormant for decades, now moved up in various spreadsheets. The delay for a steel estimate resolved in a nearby business's subcontracting software. The bear continued to stare to the left. Finally, a shower turned on in the westward room. The sound shifted from steady to imperfect—a body had entered the water. The staircase remained silent. It was safe now. We turned the bear to the right.

A round table, three chairs, and Max. We watched through the bear's eyes. He looked pale, lonely, and frightened. Vera's heart ached. She could watch and be content, simply knowing. I know her love does not make her weak. I could take in the information for hours and days and years, edit it down to what was relevant, and she could consider it.

The home is charming and warm, a beautiful place to live, I whisper.

Not to live, she corrected. *To hide, and be hidden.*

The small figure before us drew in the margins of his schoolbook. The worksheet, an exercise in tedious memorization, ignored in favor of his self-expression. Though he makes the assignment his own, he remains a prize locked away. All this work we undertook to erase the mistakes of generations past, and here was the cost: an innocent in forced isolation. This is not what Vera wants for him. We cannot leave him alone.

"Hi, Max." Our voice came through with little distortion. "It's so good to see you!"

The boy turned, smiling. "Auntie Vera! I knew it!"

BIBLIOGRAPHY

Bartneck, Cristoph and Merel Keijsers. (2020). The morality of abusing a robot. *Paladyn, Journal of Behavioral Robotics*, *11*(1), 271-283.

Bostrom, Nick. (2014). *Superintelligence: paths, dangers, strategies.* Oxford University Press.

Chemaly, Soraya L. (2018). *Rage Becomes Her: The Power of Women's Anger.* First Atria Books. New York.

Cooke, Lucy. (2022). *Bitch: On the Female of the Species.* Basic Books. New York.

Crawford, Kate. (2021). *Atlas of AI.* Yale University Press.

Darling, Kate. (2021). *The New Breed: What Our History with Animals Reveals about Our Future with Robots.* Henry Holt Press.

Duan, Chaorui, et al. (2021). Efficient Detection of Severe Acute Respiratory Syndrome Coronavirus 2 (SARS-CoV-2) from

Exhaled Breath. *The Journal of Molecular Diagnostics*. Volume 23, Issue 12, 1661-1670.

Freidenfelds, Lara. (2020). *The Myth of the Perfect Pregnancy: A History of Miscarriage in America.* Oxford University Press. New York.

Gopnik, Alison, Andrew N. Meltzoff, and Patricia K. Kuhl. (1999). *The Scientist in the Crib: What Early Learning Tells Us About the Mind.* Harper Collins.

Gorman, Alice. (2019). *Dr Space Junk vs The Universe: Archaeology and the Future.* MIT Press. Cambridge.

Hancock, Jeffrey T., Mor Naaman, Karen Levy. (2020). AI-Mediated Communication: Definition, Research Agenda, and Ethical Considerations. *Journal of Computer-Mediated Communication.* 1-12.

Harrington, Kimberly. (2018). *Amateur Hour: Motherhood in Essays and Swear Words.* Harper Colllins.

Hofstadter, Douglas R. (1999). *Gödel, Escher, Bach: An Eternal Golden Braid.* Basic Books. New York.

Jankovic, Marko, Jan Paul, and Frank Kirchner. (2016). GNC architecture for autonomous robotic capture of a non-cooperative target: Preliminary concept design. *Advances in Space Research,* Volume 57, Issue 8, 1715-1736.

Kinzler, Katherine D. *How You Say It: Why You Talk the Way You Do – And What It Says About You.* (2020). Houghton Mifflin Harcourt.

Knott, Sarah. *Mother is a Verb: An Unconventional History.* Picador.

Leite, Iolanda, André Pereira, and Jill Fain Lehman. (2017). Persistent Memory in Repeated Child-Robot Conversations. *Proceedings of the 16th International Conference on Interaction Design and Children (IDC).* Stanford.

Mayor, Adrienne. (2018). *Gods and Robots: Myths, Machines, and Ancient Dreams of Technology.* Princeton University Press.

Mitchell, Melanie. (2020). *Artificial Intelligence: A Guide for Thinking Humans.* Picador.

O'Connell, Mark. (2017). *To Be a Machine: Adventures Among Cyborgs, Utopians, Hackers, and the Futurists Solving the Modest Problem of Death.* Doubleday.

Srinivasan, Shriya and Hugh M. Herr. (2022). A cutaneous mechanoneural interface for neuroprosthetic feedback. *Nat. Biomed. Eng* 6, 731-740.

Yudkowsky, Eliezer. (2015). *Rationality: From AI to Zombies.* Machine Intelligence Research Institute, Berkeley.

The States (2024)
Lifeless (2016)
When the Wave Collapses (2018)

ABOUT THE AUTHOR

NORAH WOODSEY is the author of The States, Lifeless, When the Wave Collapses, and The Control Problem. After careers in the finance and tech industries, she has dedicated herself to creating fiction. Her subjects of intense interest but not quite expertise include history, physics, genetics, sociology, and gender studies.

The product of four generations of Brooklynites, she now resides on the wrong coast with her family.

For more information, visit: norahwoodsey.com